"Put dirty jeans and a carpenter's tool belt on Raymond Chandler's private eye Philip Marlowe, stick him on a ranch in Montana's back country around Helena, and you'll get a notion of Neil McMahon's Hugh Davoren. *Lone Creek* is tough, gripping, and true to the convoluted geography and personalities of the new, Old West. It has good girls and bad girls, cowboys and indians, cops and robbers—and a plot that keeps you guessing. A real page-turner written in taut, spare prose that mirrors the rugged landscape—I promise you won't be able to put it down."
                    —Annick Smith, author of *In This We Are Native* and
                                    coeditor of *The Last Best Place Anthology*

"*Lone Creek* is more than a page turner. A vivid sense of place and strong narrative voice make it as big and beautiful as the Montana sky."
                    —James Grippando, author of *Got the Look* and *Last to Die*

"It is a rare day indeed when it doesn't seem either insane or hyperbolic to say that an author has just produced a book that has the authentic sound of that great American original, James Crumley, but *Lone Creek* fits neatly into that exalted place on a pedestal. . . . McMahon has now found his true voice with this splendid and suspenseful novel. . . . What separates this book from other outstanding crime novels is the moral might of the hero. . . . It is the poignant and knowing prose that elevates the novel to literature."
                    —Otto Penzler, *New York Sun*

"McMahon is a writer and a half . . . his words carry for miles."
                    —*New York Times Book Review*

"Besides being one heck of a blood-pumping read, Neil McMahon's *Lone Creek* is a heartfelt meditation on love and memory, and on the powerful forces that shape both our past and our future. If you've ever loved a person or a place, and especially if you've ever lost one or the other, this bittersweet, angry, beautifully written novel will resonate with you."
                    —Jenny Siler, author of *Easy Money* and *Flashback*

"*Lone Creek* is postmodern contemporary western noir. . . . A good, hard ride through real Montana, punctuated by heinous crimes and dry, good humor. Neil McMahon has written a winner."
                    —C. J. Box, author of *In Plain Sight* and *Free Fire*

"*Lone Creek* is an explosive tale of the present-day Wild West, full of action and heartbreak and double-crosses you won't see coming. Neil McMahon writes with eloquence and authority about this haunting landscape and the cowboy heroes who still populate it. Don't miss this gripping saga."
                    —Michele Martinez, author of *Finishing School* and *Cover Up*

"In prose as smooth as worn saddle leather, Neil McMahon's new novel, *Lone Creek*, captures the old Montana verities: the days when a man's word was his bond, the time when neighbors stood together against the forces of weather and outsiders, and when a man was judged by his good work, his bravery, and his moral character. When faced with the lies of the modern world, a man with these qualities doesn't just endure, he triumphs. This is a lovely novel, smart and exciting, set in a landscape that throbs with beauty. I loved it."
                    —James Crumley, author of *The Last Good Kiss* and *The Right Madness*

"Neil McMahon is [a] lifetime expert in the tranquilities and bloody-handed twists and brutalities of working-class life in the northern Rockies. And he's one of our finest fast-action storytellers. *Lone Creek* will keep you up and dodging through the night, and send you to sleep with a sense of relief and pleasure. Sure worked for me."

—William Kittredge, author of *Hole in the Sky* and *The Willow Field*

"*Lone Creek* is a Montana writer's soaring tribute to the people, sorrows, and great beauty of that state. It's also a riveting crime story, an elegy to a passing era, and an exploration of the nature of long friendship. In taut and graceful language, Neil McMahon gives us all that and makes us sorry when it's over. A terrific read."

—Deirdre McNamer, author of *Rima in the Weeds* and *My Russian*

"Neil McMahon's *Lone Creek* runs fast and deep—a classic Montana ranch story with a ripping current of suspense. In Hugh Davoren, McMahon has created flesh and blood, and in *Lone Creek* he has written a smart thriller that turns its own pages."

—Jess Walter, author of *Citizen Vince* and *The Zero*

"Neil McMahon's new novel is rather what I imagine riding a wild horse through the Montana foothills would be like—fast, exhilarating, and dangerous. And when the hero's trusted friend seemingly betrays him, an old nemesis transmutes into his unlikely ally, and his new lover dances him between deliverance and perdition, there's no telling where the hero's ride will end—but the scenery along the way will be stunning."

—Claire Matturro, author of *Wildcat Wine* and *Bone Valley*

"Tight, taut, a place where bad money kills and the dead reach out of their graves to scar the living—McMahon's Montana is a place Ross MacDonald's Lew Archer would have felt right at home in."

—Peter Bowen, author of *Yellowstone Kelly* and *Nails*

"This is the McMahon book I've been waiting for—a tightly paced thriller set on his home turf of Montana. Told with a voice that is both clean and edgy, *Lone Creek* interweaves the stories of an old mystery unfolding in the midst of a new one. Hugh Davoren, a handyman on the ranch he grew up on, finds himself on the run, framed, betrayed, and in danger of falling in love with the ghost of a young girl he once loved. When he elicits the help of his compatriot Madbird, they make for a pair of unlikely heroes who couldn't be more likable, or more human. You won't put this one down."

—Claire Davis, author of *Winter Range* and *Labors of the Heart*

"His finest achievement to date. . . . Beautifully written. . . . A natural storyteller, McMahon is sure to appeal to fans of James Crumley and Jim Harrison."

—*Publishers Weekly* (starred review)

Michael Gallacher

About the Author

NEIL MCMAHON was a Stegner Fellow at Stanford. The author of six novels, he is also a carpenter in Missoula, where his wife runs the Montana Arts Festival.

LONE
CREEK

ALSO BY **NEIL McMAHON**

LONE CREEK

NEIL McMAHON

HARPER

NEW YORK • LONDON • TORONTO • SYDNEY

HARPER

A hardcover edition of this book was published in 2007 by HarperCollins Publishers.

LONE CREEK. Copyright © 2007. by Neil McMahon. All rights reserved. Printed in the United States of America. No part of this book may be used or reproduced in any manner whatsoever without written permission except in the case of brief quotations embodied in critical articles and reviews. For information address HarperCollins Publishers, 10 East 53rd Street, New York, NY 10022.

HarperCollins books may be purchased for educational, business, or sales promotional use. For information please write: Special Markets Department, HarperCollins Publishers, 10 East 53rd Street, New York, NY 10022.

FIRST HARPER PAPERBACK PUBLISHED 2008.

Designed by Joy O'Meara

The Library of Congress has catalogued the hardcover edition as follows:
McMahon, Neil.
　Lone Creek: a novel / Neil McMahon—1st ed.
　　p.　cm
　ISBN: 978-0-06-079221-3
　ISBN-10: 0-06-079221-3
　　1. Ranches—Fiction. 2. Montana—Fiction. I. Title.

PS3568.H545L66　2007　　　　　　　2006046492
813'.54—dc22

ISBN: 978-0-06-079222-0 (pbk.)

08 09 10 11 12　ID/RRD　10 9 8 7 6 5 4 3 2 1

To Kuskay Sakaye, real-life Madbird.
His wife, Susan; and my wife, Kim.
The Atkins and Beer clans of Helena, Montana. Jim Crumley.
And thousands of other great souls of this place and time,
whose lives I have robbed to make this story.

Gonna tell you how it is, cowboy, not how it could be.

—*Brawl-precipitating statement overheard by Eric "the Doctor" Johnson in a roughneck bar near Wolf Point, Montana*

PART
ONE

ONE

I'd only ever seen Laurie Balcomb a few times, usually glimpses while I was working and she was passing by on her way to someplace else. I'd never met her or spoken with her. She and her husband were the new owners of the Pettyjohn Ranch, and they didn't socialize with the help.

But when she came into sight on this afternoon, riding horseback across a hay field, there was no mistaking her even from a quarter mile away. Her hair was auburn shot through with gold, she was wearing a brindle chamois shirt, and the way the sunlight caught her, she looked like a living flame.

I hadn't paid much attention to Laurie before this, other than to notice that she was a nice-looking woman. The sense I'd gotten from her was subdued, distant. Even her hair had seemed darker.

But now, for just a second, something slipped in my head—the kind of jolt you got when you were walking down a staircase in the dark and thought there was one more step at the bottom.

I shook it off and slowed my pickup truck to a stop. This was September, a warm afternoon at the end of a dry Montana summer, and I'd been raising a dust cloud the size of a tornado. I figured I'd let it settle so Laurie wouldn't have to ride through it.

But instead of passing, she rode toward me and reined up. The horse was one of the thoroughbreds she'd brought out here from Virginia, a reddish chestnut gelding that looked like he'd been chosen to fit her color scheme. Like her, he was fine-boned, classy, high-strung. A couple hundred thousand bucks, easy.

"Are you in a fix?" she called. She had just enough accent to add a touch of charm. *In a fix*, I remembered, was Southern for *having trouble*.

I pointed out the window toward the thinning dust storm.

"Trying not to suffocate you," I said.

"Oh. How thoughtful." She seemed surprised, and maybe amused, to hear that from a man in sweaty work clothes, hauling trash in a vehicle older than she was.

She walked the restless horse closer, stroking his neck to soothe him. She handled him well, and she knew it.

"So you men are—what's the term—'gutting' the old house?" she said.

The truck's bed was loaded with bags of lath and plaster, crumbling cedar shakes, century-old plumbing, the skin and bones from the ranch's original Victorian mansion. Nobody had lived there for more than a generation, but the Balcombs had big plans for this place. The mansion was on its way to being restored and turned into a showpiece for the kinds of guests who would buy the kinds of horses that Laurie was riding.

"That's the term," I said.

"You're an unusal-looking group. Not what I would have expected."

"You mean we're not like the guys on *New Yankee Workshop*?"

"Well, there do seem to be a lot of tattoos and missing teeth."

"They're all good at what they do, Mrs. Balcomb."

"I'm sure they are. And don't misunderstand me—I think they're charming."

That opened my eyes. I'd heard my crew called a lot of things, but none of them involved words like *charming*.

"I'll pass that on," I said. "They'll be knocked out."

"So why are you here all alone on a Saturday?"

I shrugged. "Only chance I get to be the boss."

Her smile was a quick bright flash that shone on me like I was the one important thing in the world.

"You look like you could be bossy," she said. Then she caught herself up as if she'd slipped. "I'm sorry, I didn't mean to be impolite."

I was confused, and it must have shown.

"That scar," she said. "It's like on a villain in an old-fashioned movie."

My left hand rose of its own accord and my thumb touched the raised, discolored crescent that topped my cheekbone. It wasn't something I ever thought about any more. The touch broke loose a run of sweat from the hollow under my eye down my nose. It itched like hell, and while I knew that scratching was bad manners, I couldn't help myself. My hand came away smeared with plaster dust and red chalk.

"Just a low-rent injury and a surgeon with a hangover," I said.

She smiled again, but this time she seemed a little disappointed.

"You could come up with a more interesting story," she said. "Think about it." She turned the gelding away and eased him into a trot with her boot heels.

I gave her a hundred yards lead on my dust cloud, then drove on.

"Interesting" wasn't in my job description.

TWO

A mile farther on, the hay fields gave way to timber. I started to glimpse the sparkle of Lone Creek, draining down from the continental divide to the Missouri River. Even in dry years, it always flowed swift and cool. If you followed it upstream, you came to a little waterfall that spilled into a swimming hole. I'd hung out there a lot as a kid, but I hadn't been back since the summer I turned fourteen—almost twenty-five years, now that I thought about it. A quarter of a century, one-third of a good long life, ago.

I'd worked on this ranch that summer, for the first and last time until now. My family weren't the social equals of big landowners like the Pettyjohns—my father was an ironworker, my mother a schoolteacher, and we lived in a modest house in nearby Helena—but my dad had gotten to be pretty good friends with the clan's head, Reuben Pettyjohn, with the common bond that they'd both fought in Korea. We were welcome on the ranch, and I came out here every chance I got, to fish or wander in the woods. The men finally decided that they might as well put me to use.

That same summer, a girl named Celia Thayer had come to live with us. She'd grown up near my family's hardscrabble old homestead near the Tobacco Root range, which my father's brother was still working. She was usually around, hanging out with my cousins, when we went to visit.

Celia was a year and some older than me, just turning sixteen then. Supposedly, her parents decided that she'd benefit from living in Helena—it was the state capital, and with a population of about thirty thousand, one of the few places in Montana that could be called a city. But I eventually figured out that she was already too much to handle for those people from an older world, living in the middle of nowhere. My older sisters were gone, one married and one in college, so we had room. Celia's folks worked out a deal with mine to board her at our house while she finished high school.

She was glad to leave her bleak home behind, except that she was crazy about horses, and already an expert rider. So my dad arranged for her to work on the Pettyjohn Ranch along with me that summer, helping in the stables. She could ride to her heart's content and make some money, too.

I was a typical gawky, terminally shy boy of that age. The issue of girls was just starting to appear as a haze on the horizon of my life, portending the coming storm. Celia fascinated me, but what I felt was more like worship than desire. Even as a little girl, she'd been the bright light in any group, pretty and compelling. At sixteen, she was flowering, with a tough, sultry beauty and a ken that sometimes seemed much older. I was bewildered, humbled, and scared by her.

But what drew me to her most powerfully was my belief that there was a special intimacy between us—that some deep part of her was lonely, wistful, and hurt, and that she showed it only to me. Maybe I only imagined it. I sure learned the hard way that when she did, she could be like a cat offering its belly for petting, then sinking its fangs into your hand when you tried.

While Celia worked with the ranch's horses, I started on the haying crew, two months of killing labor from dawn to dusk. But things relaxed after the first cut was in, and I went to taking care of general chores. Nobody cared if I sneaked away for a swim at the waterfall, so I did it almost every day. Sometimes Celia would come along.

One particular afternoon, I went there alone. I hadn't seen her earlier, and it never occurred to me that she might show up. I was lazing in the stream, not paying attention to anything, and all of a sudden, she came walking into sight. When she was with me I always swam in my jeans, but when she wasn't, I went in bare, and I'd left my clothes on the rocky bank; I hollered at her to turn around until I could get covered.

Instead, she beamed that smile at me and said, "Lighten up, we're practically family." She'd always brought a swimsuit before, but not this time. She peeled off her own clothes and stepped in.

There was no way I could get out of the water after that. I stayed crouched to my chin while she splashed and pranced and tiptoed on the stones like a tightrope walker. She kept talking all along like things were the same as always, just us being kids and goofing around. But I knew that she was doing this on purpose. It was like she was using me as some kind of test, and she was pleased at the result.

I had plenty of other memories of Celia. A lot of them were painful, and I'd done a good job of burying them. But seeing Laurie Balcomb on that horse—if Celia had lived, she'd look just about like Laurie now.

THREE

The Pettyjohn Ranch's dump was a sea of trash the size of a city block fifty feet deep, gouged into a section of prairie toward the northeast corner. It held more than a century's accumulation of old refuse, from kitchen slop to sprung mattresses to entire vehicles. There was also plenty of stuff nobody wanted to talk about—refrigerators, asbestos insulation, tons of toxic sludge from fertilizers and pesticides and lead paint, enough to make a private little superfund out in the middle of God's country.

Officially, it hadn't been used for the past few years—new sanitary codes required that the ranch's refuse was now hauled off to the city landfill. But it saw occasional action on the sly, for things like our construction scrap and items that were inconvenient to get rid of legally.

I had never known that to include carcasses, but I started catching the first hints of the smell before I could even see the dump—the sickly reek of meat gone bad. The closer I got, the more it filled the pickup's cab, lying like a greasy blanket on the warm afternoon air. The dump always smelled some, like any big collection of garbage. But this was special.

About fifty yards out, a bunch of crows and magpies were having a party, hopping, fighting, and tearing with their beaks at something buried. Thumb-size horseflies and yellow jackets swarmed around with a buzz I could feel in my teeth. The old D-8 Cat that was used for maintenance was parked off to the side as usual. It wasn't run often these days, but I could make out fresh ridges from its tracks, leading toward the quarreling scavengers.

The ranch hands must have butchered some cattle, and the remains were ripening in the hazy afternoon heat. It seemed a little strange that they'd take the trouble to bury them—usually they just pitched things over the edge, same as me. But as I drove closer, I could see a hoof sticking up out of the mess.

That was it, then.

There was one good thing—the flies were too busy to bother me. I dropped the truck's tailgate and started tossing out my own load of trash.

The real reason I'd been working alone on Saturdays for the past few months was that I had the job site to myself, without the havoc of a crew around. Every week, I'd try to save a tricky task like cutting stairs or rafters and use Saturday to get through the part that required the most concentration.

Sometimes my buddy Madbird came along, but he liked the peace as much as I did. He'd take off on his own to work on the wiring, and I'd hardly be aware of him except for the occasional crash of a tool or part being thrown and some muttering in Blackfeet that I assumed was cursing.

I'd spend the last hour cleaning up and thinking about what was on the slate for Monday, then make this dump run. I'd come to look forward to it. It was the ritual start of the weekend, full of the anticipation of Saturday night before the crash of Sunday morning. And if you ignored the crater of garbage, you couldn't ask for finer country.

The ranch was about ten miles northwest of Helena, up against the foothills of the Rockies. The view went on forever. This time of year, the larches were turning yellow, big bright splashes on the bottle green slopes. There were no buildings in sight, no sounds in any way human. All in all, it was like the kind of magazine cover that made dentists in Omaha go out and buy a couple thousand dollars' worth of trout fishing gear.

The original owner was Reuben Pettyjohn's grandfather Nathan, who'd fought with renown in the Civil War but had been on the losing side. Like a lot of his comrades, he'd left the South in disgust when the carpetbaggers invaded and had made his way west. He'd had the good luck and sense to acquire this gold mine of property, roughly fifteen thousand acres of well-watered hay fields, pasture, and timber. His descendants had added lease rights to more big chunks of state and Bureau of Land Management grazing land, and parlayed it all into a network of property and other interests that stretched through Montana and beyond.

I, on the other hand, was the kind of guy who'd always bought dear and sold cheap.

I slung the last bag of trash into the pit and gave the truck's bed a quick sweep. Then I paused, realizing that I'd been hurrying, not enjoying this as usual. The reason was that smell. It clung to me like a second skin, putting an unpleasant edginess in my head that was amplified by the buzzing of the insects.

But there was something else bothersome. I'd kept glancing at that hoof as I unloaded, and now I tried to focus on it through the debris and flapping birds. It seemed oddly shaped.

And I almost thought I could make out an arc of extra thickness on it, like an iron shoe.

I told myself I was full of shit, and there was no reason I should care anyway. Even if it was a horse, there was nothing strange about one of those dying on a ranch. There were several working plugs here besides the Balcombs' thoroughbreds, and their passing wouldn't create any stir. I closed the truck's tailgate, got in, and started the engine.

I switched it off again—honest to God, I don't know why. Maybe because of old habits I'd developed during the years that I'd worked on a newspaper in California, maybe just because of a prickly sense that something was really wrong.

I rummaged through the spare clothes I carried and found a hooded sweatshirt to cover my head and neck. I made a mask of my bandanna and pulled on a pair of gloves. Then I started picking my way across the pit. The surface felt queasy underfoot, like I was walking on boards laid over quicksand.

The crows backed up, but not far, and they screamed at me to get off their turf. The flies and hornets stayed, and so did the smell.

The hoof was shod, all right.

The short length of foreleg sticking up had been chewed on, probably pulled free by coyotes. It looked like they'd tried to dig down to the rest of the carcass, layered over by a foot or two of junk, but something had stopped them.

I figured out where the head would be and clawed trash out of the way. A triangular piece of plywood about three feet across was wedged in as a protective covering. Measurements were scrawled on it with a heavy carpenter's pencil.

I recognized them. I'd written them there myself, framing a gable dormer a couple of weeks earlier. I'd carried the scrap here to the dump, too. But I sure hadn't left it anywhere near this spot, and I couldn't believe that the Cat had dragged it here by accident.

My uneasiness climbed a notch. Somebody had taken the trouble not just to bury the horse, but to protect it from predators that might have exposed it.

I got hold of a corner of the plywood and worked it free. Flies settled instantly on the horse's bleared gummy eye. The lips were stretched tight above bared teeth. The dark brown coat was matted and dulled by death. A blue nylon construction tarp was wadded up underneath like a tawdry shroud.

But the real ugliness lay in *how* it had been killed. A chunk of flesh the size of my fist was gouged out of its neck. Bits of spine showed under the raw blood-crusted meat. I'd seen plenty of dead game, including some that had been shot up pretty badly by inexperienced or unlucky hunters. But this was a difference of kind.

My brain didn't want to believe what my eyes told it—that the wounds had been made by a shotgun, at very close range.

Worse still, I glimpsed another, lighter-colored horse under the first one.

I swallowed hard and pulled away more of the junk with one hand, swatting at the bugs with the other. I guess I was hoping I'd find something that would convince me I was mistaken, help me make sense of this. Instead, I saw more big wounds behind the shoulder and on the flank, and enough of the second horse to tell that it was gouged in the same way.

Then I yanked free another good-size scrap of plywood. I just got a glimpse of the gut piles, spilling out of the ripped-open bellies, before the stink exploded in my face.

My own guts heaved up a thin stream of bile. I tore off my bandanna and stumbled away, hacking and spitting out the sour burning taste.

Hunched over, hands on my knees, I could feel the warm still air wrapped around me, hear the insects droning and see the crows flapping. But for a few seconds all that was a screen, and something inhuman and pitiless was on the other side, watching me. I think I yelled, like I was trying to wake up out of a nightmare.

There might have been more I could have seen, but I was done looking. I shoved the scraps of plywood back into place and kicked some trash over them.

As I slogged across the pit to my truck, I thought I could hear a new sound in the distance, like the rippling purr of a small engine.

I twisted the key in the ignition and got the hell out of there.

FOUR

The ranch roads were all rough and this one was worse than most, washboarded and studded with rocks the size of tire rims. There was no speed you could drive at that wouldn't rattle your teeth. Bad as I wanted to be gone, I took it slow.

But within two or three minutes, I saw another dust cloud coming toward me. At its core was a vehicle of a startling arrest-me-red color, doing at least forty. This wasn't the small engine I'd heard. This was an extended three-quarter-ton, four-wheel-drive, diesel-powered Dodge Ram, about the biggest, newest, shiniest pickup truck that money could buy. It belonged to Doug Wills, the ranch foreman.

Stockmen tended to be tough but good-natured and easygoing. But Doug was one of those guys who had to turn everything into a contest and come out the winner. That was probably why he was foreman. I'd heard he'd once been a pretty good bull rider, but he was thirty-five or so now, and like a lot of ex-jocks, he didn't like being over the hill. He didn't like me much, either. That had been simmering since I'd started working here.

Doug drove with that same aggressiveness, so his speed was no surprise. He came charging head-on like we were playing chicken, finally slamming on his brakes and ending up with his bumper barely a foot from mine. He jumped out and stomped toward me, shoving his Resistol cowboy hat back on his head. He was built like a badger, thick and powerful, with a bristling black mustache and a red meaty face.

"You cut that engine and stay put," he half yelled. "Mr. Balcomb wants to talk to you."

I didn't have any clear take on Laurie Balcomb's husband, Wesley. The word was that he'd made a fortune from the stock market in New York, or oil in Texas, or merchandising on the west coast, or a dozen other ways, depending on who you listened to. The one thing that seemed certain was that he didn't know anything about ranching. In spite of that, he was making sweeping changes on the place. By most accounts, he was pleasant and treated his employees well. Not all agreed, or cared for the direction the Pettyjohn Ranch was going in.

Like Laurie until today, he'd never spoken directly to my crew or me. All his instructions about our work got communicated through intermediaries. I didn't exactly fault him for that, but while it was easy to understand how a woman wouldn't feel comfortable coming on friendly to a construction gang, most men would at least say hello to other men working on their property.

The fact that Balcomb suddenly wanted to talk, plus Doug's acting over the top even for him, was a big red flag.

I cut the pickup's engine, thinking that might calm him down some.

"What's this about, Doug?" I said.

"You fucked up, is what." He looked sullenly pleased.

"I did? Balcomb told you that?"

"*Mister* Balcomb."

"Fucked up how?"

"You can ask him."

I almost said, *Let's you and me go take a look at what I just found in that dump.*

But I caught myself. The last few minutes had been time enough for me to go from being shocked to spooked. That smell was still strong in my nostrils, along with the sight of those gaping wounds and ripped-open bellies. I couldn't imagine who had done it or why, but I was damned sure going to be careful about getting on their radar.

I scanned the horizon. I could see at least a mile across the flat hay fields and pastures, but no more dust clouds were disturbing the hazy blue sky. I'd heard that Balcomb had a habit of making people wait for him—a power statement among businessmen, like hesitating before accepting a handshake. I decided it was my out.

"How long's he going to take?" I said.

"As long as he takes."

"Look, I've been busting my ass all week. I'm hot and tired and I want a cold beer. I'm not going to sit here until he decides to sashay on down."

Doug's face took on a knowing look. "He said you'd try to get away. Don't even think about it."

"Get away from what, for Christ's sake? I don't have a clue what I'm supposed to have done."

He snorted. "Nobody's believing *you* anymore."

On top of being scared, I was starting to get seriously pissed.

"Tell him I'll see him Monday," I said. "If he's in a big hurry, I'll be at O'Toole's. I'll even buy him a beer."

"Don't you start your smart-ass shit with me." Doug shoved a pointed forefinger at me through my open truck window.

That jacked up my touchiness level another big notch, partly because my left eyeball was sitting on a piece of plastic.

"You better step back," I said. "Unless you want your foot run over." I reached for the ignition keys to restart the truck.

"You ain't going nowhere, goddamn it!" His hand jumped through the window again, and this time he grabbed my collar.

I jerked up on the door handle and drove the door open with my shoulder, slamming it into him and tearing his grip loose from my shirt. When my feet hit ground, they slipped on the hard pebbly surface and I almost went down. Doug was already coming at me, low and dangerous, like he was going to throw a steer. I had a couple of inches in height on him, but we were about the same weight and he had a formidable compact strength. I knew that if he got hold of me, that was it.

His windmilling right fist caught me just below the heart, close to a spot where a couple of my ribs had once been broken. I felt sparks pop in my head and caught that tongue-touching-a-battery taste in my mouth of being on the edge of knocked out. It hadn't happened for years, but the memory was right there. His left hand came clawing in, trying to grab my shirt again. I blocked it with my forearm and managed to stick a short left onto the point of his nose. It only stung him, but it slowed him down long enough for me to jump back and get some range.

I slammed my left into his nose again, this time with power. It was the kind of shot that could blind a man with pain, and would have taken the fight out of many. Doug's breath exploded in a grunt, but he kept coming, blundering forward with his forearms covering his face.

I spun to his left and looped around with a hook that caught him square on the ear. It knocked him stumbling across the uneven ground.

"That's enough, Doug," I yelled. I was gasping for breath and my legs felt weak. "Back off!"

He glared at me with his teeth clenched, then charged, this time with no show of style or defense—just his hands outstretched to rip me apart.

I speared my left straight at his unprotected face and caught him once more square on the nose. A spray of blood burst out, and he let out a sound that was half bellow and half scream, like a bull calf getting cut. This time I sidestepped to the right, and as he crashed past, I planted my feet and drove my right fist at his jaw with everything I had. I felt the shock run through my shoulder and clear down to my toes. That straight right had always been my best punch.

Doug hit the ground with a thud like a dropped sack of grain. He wasn't out cold, and he kept moving—not trying to get up, I was glad to see, just twitching. His mustache and chin were blood-streaked and his eyes were vague, like he didn't know what had happened. I'd been there. But he looked OK, and I couldn't see that my staying around would make things any better.

When I put my truck in gear, I felt a twinge in my right wrist. It was jammed and starting to swell, but it didn't feel really sprained. I had to drive off the road to get around his Dodge, and jolting over that really rough ground got my ribs reminding me of where he'd tagged me. But I thought I'd dodged another bullet there—I didn't feel that piercing stab like when they'd been busted.

Before I went around a bend a half mile farther on, I caught a glimpse of Doug in my rearview mirror. He'd gotten up and was opening the door of his truck.

I had planned to swing back by the job site on my way out, but I decided just to get on into town. I'd been lucky, and I didn't like to push my luck.

FIVE

By the time I got to the ranch's main road, another mile farther along, I was holding tight to the steering wheel to keep my hands from shaking. I hadn't been in a ring in almost twenty years, and I'd had only a few barroom scuffles since—nothing like a flat-out fight in the sober light of day. The experience hadn't gotten any prettier.

It brought another memory of Celia that wasn't pretty, either.

After she'd teased me at the creek that time, it hadn't taken me long to figure out who she'd been practicing for. Pete Pettyjohn, Reuben's oldest son, was a nineteen-year-old golden boy—good-looking, popular, and the heir apparent to his family's empire. When I was a little kid, I'd had a serious case of hero worship for him.

But as I'd gotten older, I'd come to understand that there was something off about Pete. Usually he was friendly, but then out of nowhere he'd turn stone-cold or even menacing. He'd already started drinking pretty hard. Still, it was obvious that Celia had her sights set on him, and while Pete played it cool, he seemed to be around her a lot. It bothered me for selfish reasons—I was childishly jealous, afraid she'd cut me out.

One afternoon soon after the swimming incident, I wandered down to the stables to visit with her. She was alone in the corral, working with a young mare that she'd been grooming for barrel racing. I was happy just to watch her. I stopped a distance away so I wouldn't interrupt, thinking I'd say hi when she took a break.

But before she did, Pete came driving along in one of the ranch trucks.

As he was passing by, the mare started to buck, tossing up rear hooves and hopping sideways, trying to throw her. It was so unexpected and fast that I stood poleaxed for a couple of seconds. Then I started running for the corral, but Pete was way ahead of me. He vaulted the rail, caught the horse by the bridle, and wrestled it down to where Celia could slide off the saddle. She sagged against him like she was badly shaken. He walked her to the gate with his arm around her waist.

I started to get a glimmer of just how good a rider she was.

They hadn't noticed me yet, and if I'd had any sense, I would have backed quietly away. Instead, I kept trotting toward the corral. I guess I wanted her to know that I'd tried to help.

As they came out the gate, I called out to ask if she was all right. Her head swung toward me and her eyes flared, like she'd been caught doing something wrong. But she bounced back in a heartbeat—gave me her brilliant smile and said, "Little boys ought to know better than to sneak around spying on people."

It cut me to the bone. I stammered a denial and started to leave, but Pete came striding toward me. I figured he was going to show off for her by shoving me around. There wasn't much I could do about it—physically, he was a grown man who outweighed me by fifty pounds.

But when I saw his face close up, I knew he'd taken one of those spooky turns. He looked furious, almost manic. He balled up his fist and hit me in the belly so hard that I doubled over with the wind knocked out of me. He clobbered me again on the side of the head and tripped me as I staggered back. Then he started kicking me while I lay on the ground. Celia came running over, screaming at him and trying to pull him away. He spun around toward her with his fist clenched. I still couldn't breathe, and I watched helplessly, certain he was going to smash her face.

She stopped yelling, but she didn't let go of him or back away an inch—just stared at him. She'd gone from looking upset to excited, and it stuck in my memory that her tongue quickly wet her lips.

Pete lowered his fist, but they kept looking at each other for a few more seconds. Then she let go of him and knelt beside me, petting my forehead and apologizing for what she'd said. Pete helped me to my feet and apologized, too. He was sincere and he looked confused, like he wasn't sure what had happened. I promised them I wouldn't tell anyone. I wouldn't have, anyway.

The beating hurt for days. Celia's treachery hurt far worse. But worst of all was my own weakness—my failure in her eyes. In spite of how she treated me, I wanted desperately for her to think of me as a man she admired instead of a pissant kid.

I made up my mind that I was going to learn to fight. I started taking martial arts lessons, and over the next months, I fantasized a million ways I'd step in and rescue her from harm.

I never got the chance.

SIX

The ranch's original headquarters consisted mainly of a huge old barn that served as the maintenance shop for equipment and also housed the rudimentary office. A few other buildings were scattered around, along with corrals for cattle getting shipped off to feedlots and an acre-size field of rusting equipment that dated back into the 1800s.

There wouldn't be much of anybody around just now, and I figured that whoever was there wouldn't pay any more attention to me than usual as I drove past.

I was wrong. Two of the hands, Steve and Tom Anson, were standing in the road. Obviously, they were there to stop me. Everybody on the place carried walkie-talkies or cell phones these days, and Doug must have called them. It hadn't even occurred to me that things would go this far. I coasted to a stop.

The Anson brothers were both in their twenties, the kind of pleasant, straightforward young guys who tended to gravitate to ranch life. I'd always gotten along fine with them. But they looked tense and distrustful. They tended to operate as a unit, with Steve, the older, doing most of the talking. He walked over to me, while Tom stayed blocking the road.

"Mr. Balcomb wants you to wait for him," Steve said, repeating the start of Doug's litany through a cheek packed with Red Man chew.

"Yeah, I know. You got any idea what this is about?"

"I'm just telling you what I heard."

"What else did you hear? Not to believe anything I say?"

He shrugged uncomfortably and spat a stream of tobacco juice off to the side.

This wasn't helping my temper any.

"I'll talk to Balcomb Monday, Steve, just like I told Doug. Now you guys kindly get out of the way."

Instead, he turned toward a little rise that lay between here and the highway. On top of it was a man sitting astride an ATV. At Steve's signal, he jumped off, unslung a rifle, trotted forward to a good vantage point, and dropped to a prone position. He was clearly aiming at me.

My adrenaline kicked in again, not just because somebody was holding a gun on me, but because of who the somebody was. His name was Kirk Pettyjohn, and in my mind, he was a stick of dynamite with a lit match almost touching the fuse.

Kirk was Pete Pettyjohn's younger brother and the only other child of Reuben and his wife, Beatrice. He was in his early thirties, with the kind of slim build and generic good looks you saw on models in magazines. Wesley Balcomb had kept him on here as an employee, supposedly to help run things. But it was common knowledge that he'd never been worth a damn as a hand, and an open secret that he was pretty heavily into meth. What he seemed to spend most of his time doing was riding that ATV around and snooping. I'd almost gotten used to looking up and seeing him off in the distance, watching my crew through binoculars or a camera.

It struck me that his ATV might have been what I'd heard when I was leaving the dump.

Kirk favored camo fatigues, and he always wore those bug-eyed sunglasses with a neck cord, even indoors. He'd gotten himself an earring shaped like a grinning little skull. His hair was cut in a boot camp bristle, although he'd taken to dyeing it bright punkish blond, presumably to add a touch of glamour.

And he loved guns, especially the one he had trained on me. It was a Ruger Mini-14, a semiautomatic that fired the same high-speed .223 round as an M16, as fast as you could pull the trigger—an excellent rifle for around a ranch, where coyotes and stray dogs might get into the cattle. But Kirk had turned it into a paramilitary weapon, replacing the standard five-round clip with thirty-round clips, and I was almost certain that he'd modified it illegally to full automatic capacity. Every so often while we were working, we'd hear it sound off like a string of firecrackers. I didn't know if he ever shot any stock predators, but he sure made some men nervous.

It all added up to me that Kirk had become the star of a commando movie inside his own head. Maybe that was because he didn't really have much going for him, in spite of the bounty he'd grown up with. My sense was that above all he wanted people to take him seriously, but nobody did, and that was what worried me. Killing somebody would get him the kind of attention he craved, and while I didn't think he'd do it on purpose, there was a lot of room for accidents.

Then there was the long-standing tension between our families—once again, involving Celia.

The office door opened and Hjalmar Stenlund, who everybody called Elmer, came walking out. Elmer was the ranch's stock manager and the model of a sweet old cowboy, gaunt and leathery, close to eighty but with hair still streaked yellow. Like a lot of those men, he'd done his tour in the military—it had been the Pacific for Elmer—and spent the rest of his life on ranches. He'd worked on this place since before I was born, and he moved with a stooped, bowlegged shuffle from a spine and legs rearranged by years in the saddle.

I got out of my truck and went to meet him. He looked puzzled and concerned.

"I'm sorry as hell about this, Hugh," he said. "I wouldn't of stood for it if I could help it."

"I appreciate that, Elmer." I gripped his shoulder and gave it a squeeze. It was bony and still hard with muscle. "I guess I put a hair across Balcomb's ass, but I don't know how."

"Me, neither. Doug got a phone call a little bit ago and blew out of here. I didn't have time to ask him nothing. Then he called a few minutes later and said you was on your way here and we better stop you. I told him I'd talk to you, but what you did was up to you." He glanced sourly at Kirk. "Guess I was wrong."

"You know what a hothead Doug is. Maybe he just popped off and I happened to be in range."

"Maybe," Elmer said. His gaze checked me over. "He sounded kind of rattled. You look it, too. You get into it with him?"

"Nothing serious."

"Huh. Well, Balcomb's supposed to be on his way here."

"I guess that means sometime before midnight."

Elmer smiled. "No, Steve said he's really coming. But he's out riding, so he ain't moving too fast."

In terms of horsemanship, Balcomb was at the opposite end of the spectrum from his wife. But he must have figured he'd have more credibility in the horse raising business if he acquired at least basic riding skills, so he'd brought his own thoroughbred from Virginia, a young bay mare, and spent an hour on her most days.

"Is he getting any better?" I said.

Elmer shrugged. "He's getting more experience. But he won't listen to nobody, and he's ruining that horse."

"Ruining how?"

His face creased in a grimace of groping to explain.

"He wants things his way, so he tries to force her, same as he does everything else. It ain't that he's mean to her—he just can't get it in his head he's got to teach her, steady and patient. He'll get riled up and swat her for no reason, then maybe he'll catch a phone call that makes him feel better and he'll feed her a treat. Poor little thing don't know how she's supposed to behave. She's nervous as a whore in church."

I knew Elmer had been working with Balcomb and the mare, and he'd gone riding with them every day until recently. But that had stopped, and while Elmer wasn't the kind to come out and say so, I had a feeling this explained why—Balcomb couldn't tolerate his disapproval, and so had dismissed him.

Elmer had a deep love and respect for horses, and he was bone honest. I thought hard about confiding in him. Kirk was a long way off and the Anson brothers were out of earshot, too, milling around with occasional nervous glances in my direction. But I decided again to hold off. There was no point in getting him outraged and asking him to keep it secret, and since I was locked into meeting with Balcomb, I might as well find out what he wanted before I stirred things up.

Elmer fished a pack of Camels out of his shirt pocket and offered me one. I didn't usually smoke, but I took it. He hobbled on back to the office. I found a shed wall to lean against and settled in to wait.

Wesley Balcomb's makeover of this place had started when he bought it, about two years ago. The fences had been reinforced everywhere and electrified for roughly a mile around the headquarters. There were several dirt roads running across the property that used to be open for anybody to drive through—you just were expected to close the cattle gates, the old kind that you bear-hugged and slipped a barbed-wire loop over. Now all those roads were sealed off. He'd turned the property's east end into an adjoining compound and built a six-thousand-square-foot house and an ultramodern stable complex there. I'd heard the stables were an equine Ritz, with an enclosed heated arena, forty stalls, and every other kind of luxury. But I'd never been inside the compound—it was off-limits even to the hands, and had a high-security alarm system, ten-foot fences, and a gate with a camera.

While all that progressed, Balcomb had hired and fired a slew of managers, consultants, architects, and other experts. Most of them took themselves very seriously and seemed determined to make that clear. They'd set up a maze of rules and procedures that turned even simple decisions into major productions, and yet they were always screaming demands for better efficiency. They interfered in everything, trying to impose corporate thinking that simply wouldn't fit here. Elmer, who'd forgotten more about livestock than most people would ever know and had run this operation smoothly and profitably for decades, was now overseen by a firm of east coast accountants.

That sort of thing took its toll on the people who were trying to get the hands-on work done. I'd noticed it even during the few months I'd been here. Little irritations kept building up, the kind you didn't pay much attention to, but that started eating at you. It was all amped up by Kirk riding around with his binoculars and rifle. Some of the hands, like Doug, were eager to chop themselves a niche in the hierarchy. Others, like Elmer, looked on with pained weariness.

This ranch had its own persona, an old-fashioned quality that was hard to define. The word *humanity* wasn't quite right, but I couldn't think of a better one. The weather, the land, and the people on it could all be harsh; but fundamentally, they treated each other like human beings. That was true of most such places, and of Montana in general. Beneath the surface beauty lay a less visible and more powerful kind—a quiet understanding that the really important things were to pull your own weight and not fuck other people over. By and large, if you held to those, you could do whatever you wanted.

But now it was changing, not just here, but all around. You could tell from what you heard, saw, read—felt.

It was something else I couldn't fault Balcomb for. He, and others like him, had the right to do as they saw fit with the land they bought. Wanting the old ways to stay was backward, selfish, and above all futile, and nobody gave a damn what I wanted anyway.

SEVEN

Wesley Balcomb came into sight in a few more minutes, riding his pretty mare at a fair clip and bouncing in the saddle in a way that looked very uncomfortable.

He was maybe forty-five, tanned and handsome, with the fit look of someone who played a lot of golf—he'd had an Astroturf driving range and putting green installed behind the compound so he could keep in practice. But he had the stiffness of being uncomfortable doing things that might involve getting dirty. His clothes looked like they'd been picked out by a film fashion consultant—Wrangler jeans, western cut shirt, and off-white Stetson. The rumor was that his outfits were tailored and his boots were handmade Luccheses that went for upwards of fifteen hundred bucks.

Kirk Pettyjohn came down the rise to meet him, carrying himself with importance, apparently thinking the two of them were going to have a confab. Balcomb ignored him completely and rode right on by, straight toward me. Kirk tagged along sheepishly behind. The Anson boys fell in with him, and Elmer came back out of the office. I'd half expected Doug to show up, but there was no sign of him. Maybe he didn't want anybody to see his nose.

Elmer was right about the mare's being skittish, and Balcomb wasn't in good control of her. He didn't rein her up until she was almost close enough to step on my feet, and she stamped and swung her rump around at me, the way horses do when they're ready to kick. I put a hand on her haunch and shoved her away.

Balcomb stared down at me as if it was his wife's ass I'd grabbed. Like Kirk, he hid his eyes with sunglasses—his were aviator-style, giving him the authoritative look of a military officer—and his face was smooth and bland. But I got a quick weird hit that behind his shield, he was nervous.

"You're an enterprising fellow, Mr. Davoren," he said. He spoke louder than he needed to, like he wanted to make sure the other men heard. I was surprised that he knew my name. He even pronounced it right, to almost rhyme with "tavern."

"That's the first time anybody ever told me that," I said.

"Unfortunately, the enterprise isn't an admirable one. It seems you've been helping yourself to ranch property. Lumber, to be precise."

Son of a bitch.

That had crossed my mind a couple of times, but I just couldn't believe it would cause this ruckus.

What had happened was that the plans for the old mansion's remodeling called for tearing out a couple of downstairs walls to open up space. We'd had to redo the second-story floor structure with glu-lam beams to allow longer spans. That had left us with a few dozen of the old joists, full two-inch by twelve-inch clear coast fir, a lot of them twenty feet long and straight as a wedding dick.

Goddamned right I'd been taking them home—a load on my pickup's lumber rack every Saturday for the past three weeks. I'd intended to haul off another one today. Otherwise they'd have been thrown away like all the other scrap. But it was true that I hadn't exactly asked permission. I knew that if I got tangled up in Balcomb's bureaucratic grid, I could kiss the whole thing good-bye. As it was, nobody had cared or even much noticed.

Except for whoever had ratted me off. I glanced over at Kirk. His bug-eyed shades were fixed on me in a biker-style hard stare. But his mouth jerked suddenly in a twitch.

I turned back to Balcomb. It came as a nasty shock, realizing that he had me up against a hard place. I started circling.

"You mean those scabby old floor joists?" I said.

"They're obviously worth stealing, to you."

"That's not stealing, that's recycling."

"It's common theft, in the eyes of the law. Grand larceny."

"For Christ's sake, they'd have ended up in the dump."

"What belongs to this ranch stays on this ranch."

"You're saying you'd rather throw them away than let somebody else use them?"

"I'm saying you owe me for them." Balcomb unsnapped a tooled leather holster on his tooled leather belt and got out one of those Palm Pilots.

"I'll just double-check my figures," he said, punching buttons with a stylus. "You've taken about eight hundred and fifty linear feet, at four dollars and ten cents per. That comes to three thousand four hundred eighty-five dollars—"

"Four dollars a *foot*? That lumber's worthless. It's old and rough cut and full of nails."

"I'm talking about replacement value. Clear fir's very pricey these days."

"All right, I'll bring it back. You want me to take it straight to the dump?"

The bland mask left his face for a second. It wasn't a pleasant look.

"I don't want you on this property again," he said. "You can hire someone to return it. That will take care of restitution. There's still the matter of criminal charges. Oh, yes, and assaulting one of my employees."

I stared at him in disbelief. He turned to the other men, coaxing the mare into sidestepping showily, like he was Roy Rogers or Ronald Reagan. He even put on that same kind of rugged, comradely half smile.

"You see why I warned you against trusting Mr. Davoren," he

said to them. "Considering the position he's in, I don't think he's going to get any more honest. Men like him will say anything, trying to weasel out."

I took a step toward him, my left hand rising to yank him off the horse.

"Hugh!" Elmer said sharply.

Balcomb swiveled, his face turning alarmed. But Elmer was right—busting his head would make a bad situation a hell of a lot worse. I clenched my teeth hard and stopped.

Only then did Kirk, late to the party, throw his rifle to his shoulder and yell at me, "Freeze!"

Elmer walked over to him and pushed the barrel aside, shaking his head in disgust.

"You'd better be very careful, Davoren," Balcomb said, in that same grandstanding voice.

Many times, I'd read the phrase *hands itching to get hold of someone*, but I'd never felt the sensation literally before. It was actually more of a throb.

He watched me, maybe expecting me to humbly agree with him. When I didn't, he waved his hand impatiently at the other men, like he was brushing off a pesky bug.

"We need a word in private," he said. They moved away, Steve Anson stuffing his jaw with another wad of chew, Elmer shaking loose his thirtieth smoke of the day, and Kirk backing up reluctantly with his weapon at port arms.

"Doug Wills told you to stay where you were and wait," Balcomb said to me harshly.

"Doug doesn't *tell* me to do anything."

We both knew that I was really talking about Balcomb.

Flies were zeroing in on the mare, and she snorted suddenly and flicked her tail. Her ass end swung around toward me again. I gave it another shove.

"You seem to feel free to take matters into your own hands," he said. "Even though you're on my property."

"I'm on your property by invitation. Doing the job I was hired to."

I could see a muscle jump in his jaw. "I'm getting very impatient with you."

I waited.

He glanced around, then leaned forward and lowered his voice.

"I was going to give you a chance to make this go away, before anyone else knew about it," he said. "I could still be persuaded to call it a misunderstanding."

"Persuaded how?"

"I want to know if anything—unusual—happened to you this afternoon."

"How would something 'unusual' turn this into a misunderstanding?" I said.

"You let me worry about that."

Any hint of polish was gone from his face now. I could feel the intensity of his gaze burning right through those sunglasses. Out of my side vision, I sensed that Kirk was staring at me just as hard.

That feeling of *wrongness* hit me again. Maybe I was only imagining it. But I was abruptly very glad I hadn't said anything about what I'd found in the dump.

"No, it was pretty much like every other day," I said. "One man starts a fight with me for no reason I can tell, another holds a gun on me, and I get called a thief and a liar over some scrap wood."

Balcomb looked unfazed. If anything, he seemed pleased.

"That's all?" he said.

"It's plenty for me. You want more unusual than that, give me a hint. A guy like me will say anything to weasel out."

He straightened up again, relaxed now, and clucked his tongue like he was chiding a little kid.

"Well, since you haven't done me any good, I don't see why I should do you any. If you'd stayed with Wills, I might feel more charitable. I had to ride another mile and a half to get here."

"Try bag balm," I said. "Best thing for saddle sores."

That venomous look crossed his face again.

"You don't have any idea how far out of your league you are, do you?" he said.

It sounded like a line from a bad movie, but he spoke it with real conviction.

He walked the mare away, pausing to talk to the waiting men. Elmer glanced at me and shook his head again, this time sympathetically. Kirk pulled out his cell phone and punched numbers, looking smugly important.

Wesley Balcomb rode off into the sunset, tall in the saddle after cleaning up Dodge.

Then, from a little copse of aspens down the road, Laurie Balcomb came riding out. There was no telling how long she'd been there—she might just have arrived, or she might have been hidden in the trees and seen the whole show. She glanced coolly toward me with no sign of recognition, then cantered away to catch up with her husband. The two of them continued on side by side, apparently talking. Balcomb pointed back in my direction with his thumb, but didn't turn around.

Oddly, it struck me that she was on a gelding and he was on a mare.

I walked to my pickup. The Anson brothers were waiting there, same as when I'd first driven up.

"I'll get the lumber back here tomorrow," I told Steve.

He spat a stream of tobacco juice. "Doubt it."

I did, too, seeing as how tomorrow was Sunday, and I needed to round up a good-size truck and driver.

"Monday, then." I took hold of the steering wheel, pulled myself in, and reached for the keys. They were gone from the ignition.

I swung back to glare at Steve. "What's *this* bullshit?"

"You're going to jail, Hugh," he said. He spat again nervously, and added, "Nothing personal."

EIGHT

Driving into Helena from the north was usually something I enjoyed. The old part of the city was a pretty sight, built in a pocket at the base of steep forested slopes that rose like waves into the mountains beyond. Downtown was studded with grand old stone buildings. There were quite a few real mansions, and even the modest houses lining the streets conveyed a comfortable old-time feel. The huge dome of the state capitol and the twin spires of St. Helena Cathedral gave a sense of grandeur.

But on this particular trip, two khaki-uniformed sheriff's deputies in a cruiser were right behind me, escorting me to the Lewis and Clark County jail.

By now I'd had long enough to start grasping how slick Balcomb was, how far ahead of me he'd been at every step. All the time I'd worked there, I'd considered Kirk's commando act to be a silly show of "security." Now I realized that he'd really been gathering information, and that had provided Balcomb a ready-made excuse for bracing me. I'd been stupid enough to make it easy, but I was willing to bet that Balcomb had some pretext for getting rid of just about anybody on the place. He'd also had the foresight to impress on the other men that I wasn't to be trusted or believed, before I'd had a glimmer of what was happening.

I stood amazed at the kind of mind that could think like that. I suspected that he'd had a lot of practice.

The jail was in the original county courthouse, in the hills toward the south end of town. Probably its most famous resident had been the Unabomber, when they'd first nailed him a few years ago. I'd spent a night there once myself, the result of a youthful indiscretion involving too much tequila and a barroom brawl that ended with a friend of mine running a bouncer's head through a wall. The bouncer came out of it OK and the only damage was a minor drywall repair, but everybody agreed how lucky it was that he hadn't hit a stud.

When we got there, the deputies put handcuffs on me. The older one was burly and grizzled, with the seen-it-all look of a veteran. He was decent enough to be apologetic about the cuffs, and told me it was a formality for booking prisoners. The other wasn't much more than a teenager, and had a withered arm. Helena was a big enough place so you didn't know everybody, and I didn't know these men, which was just as well—it kept things impersonal. Cops tended to give me a two-edged feeling. On the one hand, they were usually just doing a thankless job. On the other, it was easy to imagine that they liked pushing people around, and the kid with the bad arm sure seemed to.

Inside, they turned me over to the jailers. The place didn't look any more modern than on my last visit, but the drill was different. Back then, they'd just made sure my friend and I didn't have any weapons and thrown us in a tank. Now they took away my clothes and issued me a bright orange jumpsuit, so small that the seam cut into my crotch. They made me take the laces out of my boots, then shuffle in them down a hallway with a few individual holding cells not much bigger than closets. The door to mine, a solid metal slab with a mesh-fortified window about a foot square, locked behind me with a no-bullshit clang.

Late on a Saturday afternoon, it was going to take a while to reach a judge and set my bail. I figured I'd be released on my own recognizance—I was a local, and an upstanding citizen. At least, I had been until an hour ago.

The jail would probably be busy later tonight, but now the other cells were empty, with nothing stirring in the hallway, no windows to the outside world, no diversions except graffiti, scrawled by well-equipped guys eager to meet others like themselves. The bunk was a thinly padded bench too short for me to stretch out on. I sat back with my knees up and my hands behind my head, and tried to make use of my first chance to concentrate.

Maybe Balcomb didn't know anything about those dead horses—would have been appalled to find out, investigated the matter, seen to it that anybody who had it coming got punished. Maybe there'd just been some kind of bizarre accident. Maybe I was overblowing the situation and blaming him out of shock and anger.

But I was more certain now of what I'd suspected right off—that Doug Wills's stopping me didn't really have anything to do with the lumber, and neither did any of what had followed.

I might have saved myself this trip to jail if I'd come clean with the ranch hands or told the deputies when they arrived—cast a cloud on Balcomb and his motives for bracing me. But my credibility was zilch. Nobody wanted to cross a rich landowner, especially the men who worked for him. And given his smoothness, he probably had a way figured out to deflect any blame even if the horses had been uncovered.

But—more important—I was spooked worse than ever. The intensity of his reaction and his warning that I was out of my league had underscored my feeling that something really ugly was at work, and whatever I gained in the short term by exposing it might leave me facing serious trouble.

There were plenty more questions, starting with who had done the killing and why. I had to think it was Balcomb himself. There were other employees at the ranch besides Doug who I didn't much care for, but I couldn't imagine any of them treating an animal that way. Kirk had that twitchy violent edge, and I could easily see him going ballistic and shooting somebody—like me—but I couldn't believe he was capable of that kind of brutality. Balcomb must have figured that the carcasses would stay safely hidden until they decomposed. He'd have been right except for some hungry coyotes and a construction worker dumping trash on a Saturday afternoon. I could only guess that Kirk had spotted me, known that Balcomb didn't want anybody around there, and alerted him. Balcomb had immediately given orders to get me stopped, used the smokescreen of the lumber theft to question me, then fired me to justify it.

I could think of several reasons why he might get rid of a couple of horses—not pretty reasons, but at least they made some sense. The horses might have been old, costing more to care for than they were worth, or carrying a contagious disease, which he'd certainly want to cover up. There were insurance scams, too. A couple of his thoroughbreds, reported stolen, would be worth a sizable chunk of cash. The worst possibility that came to mind was a drunken rage or sheer insane cruelty. There'd been a few of those kinds of incidents around here in the past years. A group of hunters had slaughtered a sitting-duck elk herd, leaving most of them to rot; another time, some out-of-state executive types had chased a penned-up antelope herd in a jeep and run them nearly to death.

But I couldn't imagine anything to explain why the horses had been sliced open. My scalp still bristled every time those images came back to me.

I turned my mind to how I was going to handle this from here. I had an old friend named Tom Dierdorff, a respected lawyer in town and a thoroughly decent guy, who came from a big ranch family that had been here for generations, like the Pettyjohns. Balcomb needed to be accepted by people like that; and with any luck, Tom's influence would get him to drop the criminal charges. I'd get the lumber back to the ranch somehow and be done with this—no worse off except for a couple of hours in jail and the kind of memories that woke you up at three o'clock in the morning.

I hated to be a coward, hated to let something so vile slide. But I couldn't get past that queasy fear, and this wasn't my fight, anyway.

NINE

After maybe forty-five minutes, I heard somebody come walking down the hall and stop outside my cell. I stood up, expecting one of the jailers.

But a glimpse through the mesh window showed me that the man unlocking the door was *the* sheriff of Lewis and Clark County, Gary Varna.

Gary was imposing—at least six-four, broad-shouldered, lanky, about fifty years old, but with no trace of a paunch. His forebears had immigrated from around the Black Sea a couple of generations ago and intermarried with the local Nordic stock. That might have explained his height and his pale blue eyes. But those slanted in a way that harked back to the tribesmen of the steppes, and had a way of fixing on you without ever seeming to blink.

He was also cordial, and as soon as the door swung open, he offered me a handshake.

"Come on out of there and stretch your legs," he said.

I shuffled into the hall in my laceless boots, surprised that he'd even be at the jail on a Saturday evening. I wondered if he'd just happened to stop by for some other reason, or found out I was here and had come on that account. I hadn't seen him for quite a while, but there'd been a time when we'd crossed paths pretty often.

He leaned back against the wall and folded his arms. He wore his uniform only when he had to, and he was dressed now in his signature outfit of sharply creased jeans and a button-down oxford cloth shirt—a sort of spiffed-up cowboy look that helped put people at ease. It was one of the many shrewd facets that made him what he was. He'd been in the sheriff's department close to thirty years, and probably knew more than anybody else about what people in this area were up to. He also excelled at working the political side of the street. He was known for being fair, but in the same way as a hometown referee—if there was a judgment call, you didn't have to wonder which side he'd come down on.

"I hear you hit a rough spot, Hugh," he said.

"I just took home some scrap lumber, Gary. Otherwise it would have gone to waste. I never tried to hide anything—I've been doing it for weeks, broad daylight, right in front of God and everybody."

"That don't sound like much of a start on a criminal career."

"I guess I'm too old to retrain."

He nodded, maybe amused.

"I'll get it back there Monday at the latest," I said. "Honest to Christ, I never dreamed anybody'd give a damn."

Those unblinking eyes stayed on me.

"Something about an assault?" he said.

"Doug Wills, the foreman, came at me out of the blue like he'd gone psycho. Just about head-on'd me with that asshole big rig of his, started yelling orders, then grabbed my shirt like he was going to punch me." I touched the scar on my face. "You know I've got this fucked-up eye. I get hit there hard again, I might lose it."

"Ever have any trouble with him before?"

"We hardly ever even talked to each other. There was sure nothing to set him off like that."

"So this wasn't personal, him trying to settle a score? He was following his employer's orders?"

"Goddammit, Gary, I was just sitting in my truck."

"That's not the point, Hugh. It sounds like he had good reason to make a citizen's arrest. And you resisted."

My eyes widened in disbelief as what he was saying came home to me.

"You're telling me that's how the court's going to see it?"

His shoulders rose in a shrug that meant yes.

"Fuck a wild man," I said, and turned away to stare at the hallway's dead end.

"I'm afraid I don't have any better news. Judge Harris set your bail at twenty-five thousand dollars."

I spun back around. "Twenty-five *thousand*?" The last time I'd been in this place, my pal and I had each paid a two-hundred-dollar fine, plus fixing the drywall.

"It does seem tall, I got to agree," Gary said. "The judge likes his Saturday poker game and Wild Turkey, and he tends to get pissy about being bothered. You can see him Monday, tell him what you just told me, and I'd guess he'll reduce it. With this sort of thing, you're usually talking more like a couple grand."

But that meant staying in here until Monday.

"Everything I own put together isn't worth twenty-five thousand dollars, Gary."

"That's why God invented bail bondsmen."

"I've never done business with one."

"I'm glad to hear that. You know how it works?"

I did. You fronted them ten percent, which they kept as their fee, and they posted your bond to the court. If you skipped out, they had to find you and haul you back in or forfeit the entire amount. They got very serious about looking.

"Yeah," I said sourly. "It costs me twenty-five hundred bucks right off the top."

"Ordinarily. But you might be able to knock that down to a couple hundred."

I perked up. "How so?"

"Well, I'm not supposed to go recommending anybody in particular, but just between you and me, Bill LaTray's been known to cut a deal in a situation like this. You get him the twenty-five hundred, and if the judge does reduce your bail on Monday, Bill will cut his rate to ten percent of the lowered amount and refund you the rest."

Bill LaTray, proprietor of Bill's Bail Bonds, was an extremely tough, heavily pockmarked, mixed-blood Indian who could quiet a rowdy bar with a look. He was built like a bull pine stump, and he favored a fringed, belted, three-quarter-length coat of smooth caramel-colored leather, a cross between native buckskin and something a Jersey mobster might wear. Besides his rep as a bar fighter, it was rumored that he'd done some time for armed robbery and assault when he was younger—sort of an apprenticeship for his later career.

"But I've still got to come up with the twenty-five bills now?" I said.

"That's about the size of it. But you don't stand to gain anything by waiting till Monday. If the judge drops the bail, you'll get the difference back. If he doesn't, you got to come up with the twenty-five hundred anyway. Either that or stay here till your trial, and the way the docket's looking, that ain't going to be for a couple months. So if I was you, I'd pony up and get the hell out of here."

That made perfect sense, except I could no more come up with twenty-five hundred bucks than I could with twenty-five thousand. I didn't have a credit card. My crew got paid every other Friday, and yesterday had been the off one. That left me with about seven hundred in my checking account. I had some folding money stashed at home, that I'd been rat-holing whenever I had a twenty or two that wasn't immediately spoken for. It didn't amount to much over fifteen hundred, if that. My next, and final, paycheck wouldn't come until next Friday.

Then I remembered that Bill LaTray had a sideline as a pawnbroker—his shop was conveniently located close to the jail. I had a couple of guns that I could hock to him to make up the extra few hundred. He probably picked up a lot of business that way.

"I can do it, but I need to get to my place," I said. "If you guys will drive me—"

Gary shook his head. "Sorry, we can't let you out until the bail's posted. I don't make the rules, Hugh. That's just the way it is."

I ran my hand over my hair, trying to see a way through this. My forehead was still caked with dried sweat and grime.

I could have called Madbird to get my guns and the bank money from an ATM, but the cash at my place was hidden, and it would have been damned near impossible to explain where. The only other choice I could see was to borrow it. I hated the thought, but I started going through a list of names in my head.

My parents were passed on, my sisters had long since moved away, and no other family was left around here except a couple of shirttail relatives I hardly knew. Elmer would have helped me and so would some other older family friends and men I'd worked with, but I couldn't bear the thought of asking them. Most of my own friends weren't any better off than me. There were only two people I could think of who probably had that kind of cash available.

Tom Dierdorff was one. But while I didn't mind asking him to talk to Balcomb—that was the kind of favor where it was understood that I'd insist on paying Tom, he'd tell me he'd send me a bill but never do it, and somewhere down the line he'd get me to come to his place and make some minor repair and he'd slip a check into my coat pocket that I'd tear up when I found it—tapping him for a twenty-five-hundred-dollar loan to boot would be pushing the envelope. I might have done it anyway, except he spent most weekends helping out on his family's ranch up near Augusta, about eighty miles away, and I sure wasn't going to ask him to make that drive.

That left one more.

"I guess I'll need a phone call," I said.

"We'll have to make it for you. Those damn rules, you know." Gary waited inquiringly while I ran it through my head once more.

"Sarah Lynn Olsen," I said.

His eyebrows rose just a twitch. Sarah Lynn and I had a lot of history together, and he knew it.

He pushed off the wall and unhooked his keys from his belt.

"I've got to lock you in again," he said. "Sorry, but—"

"Let me guess. Just the rules."

He smiled slightly. "I'll try to get hold of her."

Then he paused and fixed me with that pale steady gaze.

"You sure there's nothing more to this, Hugh?"

It was a perfect opening to blow the whistle about those horses and try to turn this around on Balcomb. I thought highly of Gary and I trusted him a long way. But my unease had kept on deepening. I wouldn't have believed that old Judge Roy Harris would set a twenty-five-thousand-dollar bail even for an ax murderer just because he was annoyed about his poker game being interrupted. It smelled of Balcomb's influence, and there was no telling how far that went.

I decided to wait until I saw the judge on Monday. If it cost me a couple of hundred bucks to get this bullshit over with, I'd take it lying down. If he stood pat, I was going to have to think real hard about whether I was twenty-five hundred dollars worth of scared.

"If there is, Gary, I can't think what," I said.

He nodded and closed the door.

It wasn't the first time I hadn't told Gary Varna everything I knew.

TEN

By the end of the summer that Celia was living here, she'd succeeded in getting Pete Pettyjohn's attention in a big way. Gary Varna had been a young deputy then, and Celia was the reason that he and I first got acquainted. Seeing him always jogged my memory back to those times.

But oddly, the association that tended to hit me first was of an incident from before I'd met him. Some superstitious part of me had come to believe that I'd seen an eerie hint of what was coming—that it was the moment when the wheels had started turning in that direction.

It happened on one of my last afternoons working at the ranch that summer. The older hands were sitting around the shop drinking beer like they always did on Fridays. I'd become sort of a mascot, the tall skinny kid who both exasperated and amused them. But I'd gotten to where I could handle eighty-pound hay bales all day and be reasonably useful doing other chores, and to those men, that kind of help was worth a lot. They pretended not to notice when I sneaked a beer out of their cooler.

I walked off by myself to one of the other buildings, a small house where family members stayed when they came to visit, and sat on the steps. I hung out there quite a bit when the place wasn't being used. The view was long and clear, good for watching what was going on around the ranch, or staring at the mountains beyond.

The only person moving around just then was Reuben Pettyjohn, the ranch's owner, and father of Pete and Kirk. He was doing something I'd seen him do a lot—taking a slow walk that seemed aimless, but really he was checking things out. He'd stroll through the used equipment yard and stop to tap an old engine block with his boot toe, then he'd hook his thumbs in his belt and move on, pausing again to scan some cattle waiting to be shipped off. He was always looking for ways to use or improve things, and probably he was thinking about much more than that.

Reuben was in his mid-forties, bull-shouldered and physically formidable. His beak nose and clipped mustache added to the effect. When I started taking college literature classes years later and saw a photo of William Faulkner, Reuben's face came immediately to my mind. His presence was striking, too, a dense aura that you could feel. He was genial, but tough and shrewd—the epitome of a cowboy businessman, and a state legislator for several terms. You'd see him downtown or at the capitol, carrying a briefcase and wearing a big white Stetson and a western-cut suit with that rolled piping that looked like it was made of Naugahyde. But he was just as likely to be on the ranch, working cattle with the hands.

I sat there on the steps for a few minutes, slipping into daydreams. The afternoon was hot and I was thirsty. I went through my beer pretty fast and started working up my nerve to go score another one.

Then Celia and Pete appeared, walking from the stables toward his pickup truck, probably on their way to town to party. She was striding along playfully, almost skipping, bumping her hip against him. Everybody knew they were an item by now, but they seemed to be having one of those boy-girl wars about public affection. She wanted to advertise it, and she was always trying to hold his hand or drape herself over him. He still tried to act like there wasn't really anything going on, but you'd have had to be blind not to see them up against a fence or shed, groping and dry-humping. I suspected that they'd also been going swimming at the waterfall, and that Pete had gotten treated to repeat performances of the show she'd put on for me. I'd been staying away from there, and from him in general.

Celia looked electric, wearing a halter top and cutoffs, with her auburn hair gleaming and tossing as she danced along. They passed within plain sight of Reuben, but they were too wrapped up in each other to notice him. He watched them go by, with that same thoughtful attention he paid to the other things that caught his eye.

Then behind me, I heard the door of the guesthouse open. I jumped up, trying to hide the beer behind my back.

Reuben's wife, Beatrice, was standing there with her arms folded and her eyes narrowed. Beatrice was another person I tried to avoid, even when I wasn't caught red-handed drinking pilfered beer. It hadn't occurred to me that she'd be inside the house. She must have been cleaning up or getting ready for some visitors, although with her, you never knew. Years later, she would be diagnosed with Alzheimer's, and she was already starting to act in ways that didn't add up.

But back then she was a handsome, accomplished woman who came from another landed family and considered herself aristocracy. By her lights, Pete was destined for much bigger things than poor-girl Celia, and she seemed to blame me for bringing that bad influence into his life. She was also oddly sexless, even prudish—one of the camp who'd have much preferred it if children never found out that roughly half the people on the planet were anatomically different from the other half. I had the feeling that she'd borne her first son out of a sense of duty, and then Kirk because having only one didn't look socially proper. Otherwise, she'd wanted nothing to do with that undignified business. Besides her other quirky behavior, she'd taken on an accusing air, especially toward young people—maybe because she figured, correctly, that they were obsessed with getting their hands on each other.

My worries about the beer vaporized with her first words.

"Don't *you* sit there oogling that little slut, too," she said coldly.

I mumbled, "Sorry, ma'am," and retreated down the porch steps, too skewered by her spear of guilt to defend myself.

Then she spoke again, but this time it was like I wasn't there—she was gazing past me at Celia.

"If you think you're getting into *this* family on your back, you're in for a big surprise." Her tone was calm, definite, not so much challenging as pronouncing judgment.

It turned out to be accurate and swift. Several weeks later, on October 27, Celia was killed on the Pettyjohn Ranch. She'd been alone and tried to ride a young, still half-wild stallion that she'd been warned against. He'd thrown her into the corral fence, and she'd fractured her skull against a post.

The investigation was a rubber-stamp formality, and there was never any autopsy. The sheriff at the time, Burt Simms, was a crony of Reuben's. The Pettyjohn family quietly made their condolences to Celia's parents in the form of a generous check. Officially, that was as far as it went.

Gary Varna was one of the deputies involved in the case, and while he never really questioned me, I could tell he sensed that I knew something I wasn't letting on. After things settled down, I started running into him a lot, just by chance, it seemed. We'd chat and the talk would always get around to Celia. Eventually, I came to realize that he was already on the path to what he would become, and he wanted to know what was under all the rocks—not to make waves, but because that kind of knowledge gave him satisfaction and power.

Gary was a cop right down to his bones, but he treated me well—never forgot that I was a kid who'd lost somebody dear, never tried to bully me, and presented a genuine friendliness. I'd grown to respect him and, moreover, to like him, and I still did. But I never gave up my secret.

What I knew was this: a few weeks before she died, Celia had stayed out late on a Saturday night date with Pete. All the rest of us in the family went to sleep before she got home. She must have come in quietly—nobody else woke up. I did only because she sat down on my bed.

I was half dopey with sleep, but startled. She'd never done anything like that before. The only thing I could think was that she was going to tell me some news that was too exciting to keep till morning.

In a way, she did, and my surprise jumped to amazement. She lay down with her back to me, took my hand, and slid it inside her blouse, pressing it against her bare belly.

There was a slight but definite swell to it that hadn't been there when I'd seen her naked at the creek. Naive as I was, I knew what that meant.

After a minute or so, she got up and left. She hadn't said a word and she never gave any sign afterward that it had even happened.

The reason I'd kept that to myself through the years since then wasn't anything noble like wanting to keep her memory pure. On the contrary, my motives were outright selfish. For that one minute, she had entrusted me with the deepest part of her. It erased all the times and ways she'd hurt me, and still remained the most intense intimacy I'd ever felt.

I was goddamned if I was going to share it with anyone else.

But there were probably others who'd known or suspected that she was pregnant. Her boyfriend, Pete Pettyjohn, for one. The mental unbalance he already had—maybe inherited from his mother—got worse over the next couple of months, and so did his drinking, to the point where his old man started locking the liquor cabinet.

That Christmas eve, Pete broke into it, holed up alone with the bottles he took, and ended up shooting himself in the head.

ELEVEN

Sarah Lynn Olsen and I had been sweethearts in high school and until my last year in college. Since then we'd both been married to, and divorced from, other people. I didn't see her often these days—just when we'd run into each other on the street or in a bar. But she was always warmly friendly, and she was a partner in her family's real estate business, which owned things like shopping malls. I figured those were the best odds I was going to get for a loan, although I wouldn't have blamed her a bit if she'd decided that a phone call from jail didn't fit her Saturday night plans.

But Gary came back to say she was on her way, and he took me out to the visiting room. She must have jumped into her car as soon as they'd finished talking, because she was there within ten minutes.

Sarah Lynn was very attractive, with a sort of earth mother quality—buxom figure, long wheat-colored hair, and a sweetness that sometimes came across as drifty. Old friends called her by her initials, Slo. But right now she looked a little exotic, wearing an expensive black dress that was just short and clingy enough to turn the jailers' heads.

Not surprisingly, she seemed nervous. It didn't help that we were talking on phones with a thick Plexiglas window between us, and everything had the kind of greasy feel you didn't like touching your skin. But I also suspected that I'd interrupted her getting ready to go out, and now she was running late.

"Aw, Huey," she sighed. "Gary didn't tell me anything except you'd asked to see me. What'd you do?"

"Pissed somebody off."

Her eyes widened in fake disbelief. "No!"

"My bail's twenty-five thousand bucks, Slo."

She sat back a little—maybe at the amount, maybe because it suggested a serious crime.

"I need twenty-five hundred, cash, or else I stay here," I said. "I can pay you back most of it as soon as I get out, and the rest within a few days."

"I'm not worried about that, honey. I'm worried about what kind of trouble you're in. Of course I'll help you."

I closed my eyes briefly in relief.

"I'll buy you a drink and tell you all about it," I said.

"Deal."

"You're an angel, Slo. I'm sorry to wreck your Saturday night."

Her mouth twisted in a quick wry smile. "My Saturday night's a bottle of white wine and whatever trash is on TV."

"You look like maybe you had a hot date."

She glanced down at her outfit.

"Oh, that's left over from this afternoon. Once in a while I decide I'm going to go out and do something wild and exciting. I usually end up shopping."

Then she looked at me straight on. Her eyes were a deeper blue than Gary's and usually seemed dreamy, but right now, they were very focused.

"Thanks for noticing," she said.

"It was easy."

She stood up, still holding the phone, and smoothed her skirt with her other hand.

"I'll have to go to the office safe to get the money, so it'll take a few minutes," she said. "What then?"

I told her about Bill LaTray's bargain basement option. She said she'd make sure he agreed to it, and I knew she would. She might have been dreamy in some ways, but she had a good business head, like most people who'd grown up in that world.

She stalked out, looking like a million bucks.

I spent most of another dreary hour back in my cell before a jailer led me to the main desk, where I signed away my immortal soul to Bill's Bail Bonds. Bill was there, with his hit-man leather coat and stony face. He didn't say much, but he didn't have to. We both knew that the last thing in the world I wanted was him on my ass.

The desk sergeant told me to show up first thing on Monday—the judge would see me as soon as he had time. A clerk got my truck keys and my plastic sack of clothes from a storage room.

When I put them on, I imagined I could still smell those horses.

I didn't see Gary Varna again. Sarah Lynn had come in along with Bill LaTray, but she'd disappeared by the time I finished dealing with the paperwork. I thought she'd probably slipped outside for a cigarette.

But when I walked out onto the worn stone steps of the courthouse, she was gone, too.

I sat down and threaded the laces into my boots. The afternoon had turned into a luscious September evening, with the sky a shimmering blue that deepened every minute and the mountainsides going from green to purple. The air was taking on the crisp chill it did that time of year, after the warm days suckered you into thinking it was still summer.

Maybe she'd left to spare me any feeling of obligation. Maybe the tawdriness of this had come home to her, and she'd wanted to distance herself.

Maybe it had to do with a road I didn't care to look back down.

She and I hadn't ever been officially engaged, but it was understood that we'd get married after I finished college. I was the one who'd pulled the pin, for reasons I'd never really been able to explain to her.

On my way out of town, I stopped at Louie's Market for a six-pack of Pabst. They kept their beer ice-cold, and the first one was about as good as anything I'd ever tasted.

Then I headed home, to scrub off that smell, root out my money stash to pay Sarah Lynn, and figure out where I was going to score a truck and driver to haul my ill-gotten lumber back to the ranch.

TWELVE

My father had left me a number of his possessions, most of them well worn, and all grounded in the reality of his world. The pickup truck I was driving was a prime example. He'd bought it new in 1968—a four-by-four GMC, with a lionhearted V-8, spacious toolboxes lining the bed's rails, and a sturdy welded-iron lumber rack. It was already long in the tooth when I'd learned to drive on it, and it probably blue-booked now in the hundreds of dollars. But he'd cared for it religiously, changing the oil every two thousand miles, and I'd done the same. It had paid us back by carrying us almost three hundred thousand miles, through long winters, hunting trips, and construction jobs, with just one short-block rebuild and occasional minor repairs. I'd slept in it, drunk in it, loved in it, and lived out of it to the point where it was more of an old comrade than a vehicle.

But the greatest of my old man's gifts was a chunk of land near the northeast shore of Canyon Ferry Lake—a quarter section of rough hilly timber that he'd bought for a song back when things like that were still possible. Some of my earliest memories were of being there with him. My sisters had lost interest in it after childhood, so he'd willed it to me, compensating them with most of the cash from our slender inheritance. Besides the truck and my tools, it was about all I owned. I'd lived there full-time for almost exactly nine years now. I sometimes wondered if he'd foreseen how critical to me it would be.

The drive from Helena to Canyon Ferry took me about twenty

minutes. Traffic thinned quickly after I left town, and when I got there I had the road to myself. The lake was an impressive sight, a twenty-mile stretch of shimmering blue that stayed hidden until you topped a final rise, then appeared suddenly. It had been created by damming the Missouri in the 1950s, a century and a half after Lewis and Clark had traveled through on their way to finding the river's headwaters. During the summer it was crowded with boats and vacationers, but they dropped off once the weather changed, and not many people lived out there all year round.

I crossed the dam and drove through the tiny village, then turned off the paved road into Stumpleg Gulch, supposedly named for an early trapper who'd lost a limb to one of his own bear traps as a result of an overfondness for whiskey. My place was about two miles up, on a spur that dead-ended in the talus slopes of the Big Belt Mountains. Most of the surrounding land was national forest, buffering it from development. The nearest habitation was well out of sight and sound, and belonged to an elderly Finlander who was a perfect neighbor—glad to help if you needed it but otherwise he didn't care for company, and had been known to emphasize that point to strangers with warning shots. The few other places around were partly hidden little enclaves where families had survived for generations through some combination of raising a few animals, gyppo logging, subsistence mining, and living off the land, which, in practice, included a lot of poaching. The same traditional code that dictated other facets of life figured in there. Residents never noticed jacklights in the woods at night or gunshots out of season. The deer and elk herds stayed plenty strong, and fed people instead of falling to starvation or predators.

My old man had intended our place to be a family hangout during the summer and a base for hunting in fall. He'd built a cabin of lodgepole pine, using a Swede saw, an ax, and other hand tools—I still had them—and later added a good-size shed for storage, dressing game, and emergency vehicle repairs. He'd gotten a well dug and put in a cold water sink, which worked fine in good weather but the pipes would freeze by Thanksgiving if you didn't shut down the system. That was as far as he'd seen fit to take it. Light came from kerosene lanterns and heat from woodstoves. If you stayed up there long enough to want a bath, you filled an old washtub with hot water and hunkered down in it. More organic needs were consigned to an outhouse, with a coffee can full of lime beside the seat.

When I'd moved up there nine years ago, I'd thought at first that my stay was going to be temporary while I figured out what to do next. But eventually I'd realized that I wasn't going anywhere soon, and started making improvements.

The cabin was sound structurally, but drafty and crude—just a wooden box for cooking and sleeping. I'd re-chinked and insulated until it was tight and comfortable, paid Montana Power an arm and leg to bring in electricity, trenched the cold-water intake eight feet deep to protect against freezing, and installed a propane system for hot showers. I'd finally even broken down and gotten a phone.

Everything was dandy now except for the size. The outside walls were barely seven feet high and only a few strides apart. A couple months of winter put teeth in the term *stir crazy*, especially when you felt the need to pace but snow was blowing horizontally outside the windows. I'd been dying to add more space and I'd spent a lot of time sketching plans; but extra money came slow, and more pressing priorities were always cropping up.

When we'd started tearing those fine old floor joists out of the Pettyjohn mansion and I realized they were just going to be tossed away to rot, it was like manna falling from heaven.

That had jump-started me from fantasy to reality. Framing lumber was the big-ticket item that had been holding me back—my cash supply wasn't much, but it would get me a good start on other materials, and there was plenty of lodgepole pine on the land for log walls. The two-by-twelves would carry the floor and make perfect rafters for this country's heavy snow loads, and there'd probably be enough left to mill out for cabinets and trim. I could build the addition high-ceilinged and tie into the existing cabin with a valley roof. After a few years of weathering, the new part would seem like it had always been there. Of course I was looking at a long haul—working mostly alone, on the days I could spare—but I enjoyed that kind of thing, and I wasn't much involved in other forms of recreation.

But now those plans had plummeted back down to fantasy—in fact, quite a ways farther. Easy come, easy go.

I was just finishing my second beer when I reached the spur road to my place. It narrowed to a single lane, through thick forest that darkened the last of the evening to night.

But as soon as I made the turn, I caught a glimpse of something bright up ahead that seemed to be dancing around. The first notion that flashed through my mind was that some bizarre combination of the steep road and windshield refraction was giving me a view of the northern lights. Then the truth followed just as fast.

Flames.

I stomped on the gas pedal and tore the last few hundred yards, jolting and fishtailing. The pipe-metal gate to my property was hanging open. I had never put a lock on it, but I never left it like that. I drove on through and jumped out of the truck with it still rolling.

In those blurry few seconds, I assumed that there must have been a propane leak or electrical short and the cabin was burning. But its silhouette was the same as ever, dark and untouched. Instead, the flames were spouting from thirty yards away.

Right where I'd stacked the lumber that I'd hauled here from the ranch.

I sprinted toward it. The blaze was steady and strong, the heat intense enough to make the air shimmer. I got as close as I could and stared, forcing myself to believe what I saw.

That truckload of clear fir two-by-twelves, thigh high, four feet wide, and twenty feet long, had become a bonfire.

I started running again, making a wide circle through the surrounding forest in case drifting sparks had started other fires. Mercifully, the night was calm, and there didn't seem to be any.

I went on to the pump shed and hooked up another blessing my father had left, an industrial firehose he'd acquired from some job or barter. He'd seen his share of emergencies and was prudent about being ready for them, but he'd never had to use that hose. Neither had I until now.

The blaze sizzled and smoked like a son of a bitch when the water hit, but within a couple of minutes, it died down to flickers. I soaked the nearby area thoroughly, then piled up some rocks and wedged the hose nozzle in them to keep the stream on the fire. I raked the surrounding pine duff and twigs inward to leave a wide circle of bare earth. When the heat was down to where it didn't sear my face, I started chunking at the embers with a shovel. As they broke up and spread out, the water doused the last of the flames. I scraped up loose dirt and threw it on top until nothing was left glowing. For insurance, I left the hose running.

Then I went into the cabin, got my old man's .45 service automatic, and strode back out to go looking for Wesley Balcomb.

My truck door was still hanging open. I tossed the pistol onto the seat and started to climb in. But after a long thirty seconds, I swung the door shut again and sagged against the fender. I was soaked with sweat, coated with ashes on top of the day's other grime, and so pumped up with adrenaline and rage that my teeth were clicking. I had no doubt that I could look Balcomb in the eyes and not hesitate a second to blast him to hell. In fact, it would be a lot easier than taking down an elk or a stately buck deer. Their only sin was that you could eat them.

But that brief moment of satisfaction would destroy my life for keeps.

I walked out into the night-bound woods, trying to calm down. A grumpy yowl and a rustling in the brush told me I had company, a half-feral, torn-eared black tomcat with a kink in the end of his tail, who would come inside only in the coldest weather. I put out food for him every day, and he was always happy to share a beer. But he did a lot of foraging on his own, and he liked to leave me presents of pack rat guts and such to let me know he was on the job. No doubt he was real unhappy about the fire.

A hundred yards farther along, in a brushy little swale, a pair of badgers had denned up and were raising a family. Mom and pop were the size of beagles, fierce and fearless. More than once, I'd encountered one of their white-striped backs stalking down the middle of the road at night, refusing to give ground to my truck. They were known to take on bears. I swung wide of the den as I walked by. They didn't like anybody coming close, and they might also be riled by the fire. But they were good neighbors, quiet, private, and death on varmints.

There was a hoot owl living out here who kept me company late at night when I couldn't sleep. Mule deer were as common as squirrels, and an elk herd that lived in the Belts browsed through often at night, dark silhouettes of huge animals moving quietly as ghosts. Occasionally, I'd glimpse a black bear, and once in a great while, I'd find cougar tracks.

This peaceable little kingdom had its harsh side, for sure. Predators killed prey and the weak died quickly. But it was all within the bounds of what nature ordained. Everybody knew the rules and nobody caused trouble except for the sensible and honest reasons of survival.

Something warm rubbed against my ankle. I caught just a glimpse of the cat's green eyes, flickering in the moonlight, before he disappeared to have it out with a rival or take down a critter.

I started walking back.

I paused at the smoking heap and tried to figure how long ago the fire had been lit. It would have gone up fast—an accelerant had probably been used, and I'd stacked the lumber with the layers separated by one-by-two stickers, so there'd been airflow to create a powerful draw. But it had burned clear to the bottom, toward the center as well as the outsides. The boards had been tight together edgewise, so getting accelerant into the middle would have required something like a spray rig. The odds of an arsonist that sophisticated, around here, were tiny—this was almost certainly the work of an amateur who'd just splashed on gas or kerosene and thrown a match. Balancing all those factors off, I guessed it had been set an hour or more before I'd gotten here.

Balcomb wouldn't have come up here himself. He'd have sent somebody who was familiar with this area, who wouldn't balk at arson—who'd known I was in jail.

The first face that appeared in my mind was Kirk Pettyjohn's.

He knew where this place was, knew its isolation and that he could easily get in and out unnoticed. He was capable of something like this, on every level. And taking a gouge out of me would thrill him.

I wasn't happy about his waving that rifle at me this afternoon, but I'd intended to let it go.

Not this.

But first came the problem that the pile of ashes in front of me literally meant thirty-five hundred bucks up in smoke—on top of the bail money and whatever the hell else might be lurking down the road.

At least I didn't have to worry about finding a truck and driver any more.

With this new wrinkle, my hope that Tom Dierdorff might be able to smooth things over was out the window. Balcomb was twisting the knife as payback for riling him up and smarting off to him.

But there was a much more disturbing message. He had the power to stomp me like a bug. He could easily have had my whole place burned, except he didn't take me that seriously. This was a love tap, a joke. Without doubt, he could arrange to damage me far more in some sneaky way that the cops couldn't protect me from or even punish.

It gave my fears a concrete base. But my anger was still rising, too, and got another charge from the thought that he was probably laughing at me right now.

I dug out my money stash from the loose foundation rock where

I kept it, inside an old metal drill bit box. I was better off than I'd thought, with a little over seventeen hundred. Together with what I had in the bank, that would almost cash out Sarah Lynn.

It would also buy me a disposable camera. The couple of good ones I'd had back in my newspaper days were long gone.

I made a point of locking up the pistol inside the cabin again before I started for town, and promised myself I wasn't going to do anything stupid. But I was getting more in the mood.

PART
TWO

THIRTEEN

Main Street in Helena was also known as Last Chance Gulch, the place where some on-the-ropes miners in the 1860s had discovered the gold that put this place on the map. It was the city's prime downtown business strip, but when I was growing up, it had had several bars where you could get your ass kicked just for walking in. I'd seen that happen more than once, along with men getting thrown out through doors or lying unconscious on the sidewalk in front. Sometimes in the mornings there'd be bloodstains in the snow. Those were people who'd come up in hard times, tough and proud and with a lot of pent-up emotion, including anger. The bar life was one of the few outlets.

Most of those places were gone now. The roughest ones, the Indian bars at the south end, had been torn down to make way for a pedestrian mall. About the closest thing left was O'Toole's— small, dark as a cellar even on bright afternoons, and thick with cigarette smoke that had started building up generations ago. Tonight it was crowded and noisy. When I walked in, I could hear the jukebox playing, but it was impossible to tell what.

I'd hoped that Madbird would be here and he was, standing at the far end of the bar. In a place like O'Toole's, there was always the chance of a fist or bottle coming at you, and it paid to stay on your feet. I made my way over to him, saying hello to a couple of people I knew, trying to act like everything was the same as ever. By the time I got there, he had frosty cans of Pabst and shots of Makers Mark bourbon waiting.

His nostrils widened in a snort as he looked me over.

"You smell like you been rolling around in a ashtray," he said, in a gravelly voice that was like no other I'd ever heard.

I drank down my shot and signaled Denise, the bartender, for refills.

"Deep shit is more like it," I said. "I've got trouble, Madbird."

He lifted his chin in acknowledgment. Deep shit and trouble came as no surprise to him.

He had the kind of harsh powerful face and thick black hair I'd seen in photos of old-time chiefs and braves, and an agile, compactly muscled build like a natural halfback. His grandmother had been born in an Indian camp in Heart Butte, northern Montana, in 1910. His family name was actually Mag-dah-kee, which meant "Bird of Prey." Nobody ever used his first name, Robert. One time when we'd been drinking seriously, he'd let it out that he'd had a favorite step-brother Robert who had died young, and that the name had died with him.

Madbird had grown up near his grandmother's birthplace on what was now the Blackfeet Reservation, legendary for its toughness. I remembered often that when I was eighteen I'd gone away to college in California, but at that same age, he'd been a Marine forward observer in Vietnam.

The two of us had first worked together more than twenty years ago, and steadily for the past nine. He was an ace electrician and carpenter, handling the job in the same cool quick way as everything else. While other guys were standing around talking about what to do, Madbird was getting it done. I'd come to depend on him heavily in a lot of ways. I'd never been quite sure why he liked me, but I had the feeling it was largely because I didn't make any sense to him.

"I was about to go get some pussy, but there ain't any rush," he said. "What's the deal?"

He gazed straight ahead while I gave him a low-voiced, two-minute version of what had happened. When I finished, he shook his head, once.

"I never heard of nothing like with them horses," he said.

"I'm still having a hard time believing it, but I know what I saw."

He didn't move again or change expression for another minute or so, just kept staring at the mirror behind the bar. You couldn't see much of it because of stacked-up liquor bottles, and what you could see was mostly a murky kaleidoscope of talking heads and gesturing hands behind us. But Madbird's face was in the foreground, looking like a chunk of Mount Rushmore.

"You gonna take on Balcomb?" he finally said.

"I'm hoping I can make him back off. I want to go out there and get some photos of those carcasses. But if I get caught on the property, I'm more fucked than ever."

He nodded slowly. "So you could use a ride. Say, in a electrician's van, so you could hide in back if somebody come along."

"I guess that occurred to me."

He raised his beer and drained it. "Funny thing—I just remembered I left my Hole Hawg at the job, and I'm gonna need it tomorrow."

I exhaled with relief. The ranch was probably dead as a tomb right now, but if we did run into somebody, he had an excuse for being there.

Then there was the deeper truth—I wanted him with me, and he knew it.

"You sure?" I said.

"Hell, yeah. My old lady's probably still out with her girlfriends anyway. But you got to buy the beer."

"Denise, how about a sixer to go," I called to her, dropping a ten on the bar.

Madbird scooped up his change and tossed out another ten.

"Make it two," he said. "Why fuck around?"

When we walked to where Madbird was parked, the evening chill was more noticeable, maybe because of the body heat inside the bar. His van was of about the same vintage as my pickup, one of the four-wheel-drive models Ford had made in the early 1970s. It was packed with emergency equipment and supplies, and saturated with the smell that men in this line of work came to savor: oily tools and musty clothes and the building materials that kept this world running. There was even a foam pad—and a couple of sleeping bags on the floor that I could burrow into if I had to take a dive. I wouldn't be proud of it, but I'd rather live with that than add a trespassing bust to the mix.

We drove out of town past Fort Harrison, angling northwest toward the Rockies' foothills. The moon was on the wax, hanging over the high peaks of the divide. This was another drive that I usually really enjoyed.

"That little prick Kirk come on to me in the bar the other night, trying to pal up," Madbird said. "I flicked my finger crost his ear." He snapped his forefinger off his thumb against the metal dash hard enough to make it ring. "That was the end of that shit."

"You better watch it. You can bet he'll be looking for an excuse to take you out, too."

Madbird gave me a fierce grin that I'd come to know well, and that I could never help associating with scalping.

"He don't have to look far. You ain't the only one been helping himself to something that don't exactly belong to him."

I wasn't entirely surprised. "Yeah? What?"

"You know that Tessa?"

"Sure, sort of." Tessa was Doug Wills's wife—a rangy, unhappy-looking bleached blond stuck living in a trailer out in the middle of nowhere, with a couple of young kids. I'd been pulled off our job one time to go there and fix a jammed bathroom door. The floor had seemed carpeted with dirty diapers and *National Enquirer*s.

"Every so often she gets somebody to sit them kids, and I take her for a drive," Madbird said. "She got some rose-colored panties she hangs out in the wash. That's the signal."

I was surprised now. That explained why those sleeping bags were spread out into a bed.

"Christ on a bike," I said. "I've been passing by her trailer every day myself. I've even seen those panties hanging on the line. I didn't know that was any kind of signal."

"That's 'cause *you* ain't a Indian. You don't know how to read the trail."

"I guess I could use some lessons."

"You just got one."

"If you're so fucking smart, how come you're letting yourself get dragged into this?"

"Hey, at least I ain't dumb enough to drag in a drunk Indian."

I took the bait, and said the sort of thing you'd better not say unless you'd spent a few thousand hours sweating together.

"I didn't know there was any other kind."

He rumbled with deep gut laughter and answered me with his hands in sign language, fingers flexing and weaving like snakes. I caught the wheel of the veering van and steered it back onto the road.

"What's that mean?" I said.

"Your squaw give lousy head."

We cracked fresh beers, and I realized I was feeling a little better.

FOURTEEN

Madbird switched off the flashlight beam and we stood there in the dark, up to our ankles in the sea of garbage that was the dump at Pettyjohn Ranch. We'd spent a good ten minutes kicking and pawing through it. We'd found some of the plywood that had come from our job. But there wasn't any doubt. The D-8 Cat had been moved again, and the horses were gone—dug out, with junk then spread around to cover the hole. The only sign that they'd been there was a trace of that rotten smell.

That slick bastard Balcomb had long-cocked me again. Maybe he'd come out here to check and seen that hoof sticking up. Maybe he was just playing it safe.

Maybe I hadn't done such a hot job of convincing him I hadn't seen them.

We walked around for several more minutes trying to figure out where the Cat had taken them. But the ground around the dump was scarred with years of its tracks, and the dirt road was hard as concrete. To the northeast lay a big chunk of grazing land, several thousand acres of scrub timber and prairie where nobody ever set foot. I was willing to bet that those carcasses were out there now, dropped into a ravine or shoved up against a hillside and covered over—this time, thoroughly enough so nothing could get to them.

Madbird stopped, like he was listening. I stopped, too, thinking he was hearing a vehicle. But the night was still quiet. That part, at least, was going well.

"I'm wondering if we ain't looking in the wrong direction," he said. "Forget where they went to—what about where they come from? It don't seem likely they got killed right here. They'd of had to be penned up or tethered. If we find that, it might tell us something."

I rubbed my hair in exasperation. With all the brain racking I'd done, that obvious point had slipped right by me.

"I'd guess he took them out in the woods and tied them to trees," I said.

"Then why didn't he just bury them there? It don't make sense he'd haul them back here." He swung his hand southwestward, toward the ranch proper. "I'd say more likely he was in the hay fields. Then he'd of had to move them someplace he could cover them up, and this is the closest."

We started walking in the direction he'd pointed, making an arc through the meadow that surrounded the pit's rim. Within a minute, his flashlight picked out the Cat's tracks, wide ridged lines crushed into the stubble of second-cut hay.

"Well, will you fucking look at that," he said softly. "You know this place pretty good. What's out there?"

The tracks angled away from the road, straight across the field toward the northernmost border of the ranch. I had to think for a few seconds, but then I remembered.

"An old calving shed," I said. "It's another half mile, give or take."

FIFTEEN

Madbird crouched on his heels, his right hand reading the ground—testing its feel, picking up chunks of dirt, crumbling and smelling them. Every half minute or so he'd edge a couple of feet sideways and do it again. I walked along with him, holding the flashlight so he could see.

The shed was the kind of old structure that every good-size ranch had a few of, made of weathered rough-sawn timber and a corrugated metal roof. This one was a sort of frontier post, used for calving in late winter and early spring. Cows going into labor would sometimes seek out the remotest possible places, and the shed was a sanctuary both for them and for the hands out rounding them up, often in blizzards and subzero temperatures. Four walls and a propane heater could make all the difference. But nobody came here this time of year, and the nearest habitations were the hired hands' trailers, a mile and a half away.

It was a perfect place for dirty work.

The walls were a good ten feet high and the barn doors were wide enough to bring in a midsize truck for equipment and feed. Or a D-8 Cat. It would have been tight, but the dirt floor looked freshly turned, as if the blade had scraped and dragged it over—probably to cover the traces of butchering the horses. What was left was a sour-smelling mash of old hay, manure, and hair, along with some dampness and soil-crusted bits that might have been blood and flesh.

But blood and flesh were what this place was all about. Calf birthings left a lot of organic residue. The lucky ones made it with relative ease, but many came harder, and sometimes there was no other choice than to pull the infant out with a come-along. If one calf lost its mother and another cow her calf, it was common practice to skin the dead calf and drape the hide over the live one, in the hope that the bereft cow would adopt and nurse the orphan that smelled like her own. This earth was soaked with decades of that necessary carnage. Trying to separate out the new from the old would have called for a sophisticated technical analysis, and all it stood to prove was that some horses had somehow gotten into the mix.

Madbird crunched a last fistful of dirt, then tossed it away and stood. I followed him outside and we checked the perimeter, until he stopped at several hay bales lying on the ground.

"What are you doing here?" he said to the bales. It did seem odd. Hay was brought in to feed, but not in this season, and there was no reason to drag it around the building's rear.

He took the flashlight from me and moved the beam slowly across the ground, then crisscrossing up the shed's wall. The siding was pine of random widths, mostly ten or twelve inches, run vertically. The wood had dried and shrunk away from the rusting nails over the years, but the workmanship, although rough, was neat—the product of some long-gone cowboy carpenters who hadn't cared about pretty, just decent.

Except for one piece that didn't look right. It was bowed out at the top, with a few nails missing along its length and a couple more clumsily bent over.

Madbird crouched again, got hold of its bottom, and wrenched. It started coming loose. I got my hands in between it and the pieces to the sides, and we worked it upward, popping it free. The flashlight showed what had bowed it out up top—a nail head sticking out an inch. That was common when old wood was pried loose, especially with soft stuff like pine. The nail would stay lodged in the cross-timber and the board would split or splinter or just disintegrate around it. If you replaced the board, you usually had to get rid of the nail to keep it from pooching out like this one. Whoever had done this either hadn't noticed it or was in too big a hurry to care.

The gap we'd made was about a foot wide. I stayed back and let Madbird peer in, with the flashlight beside his ear. He spent a good long minute there. Then he motioned me over. As the light beam shifted, I caught a glimpse of his eyes. They brought to my mind the old saying, *A good friend and a bad enemy.*

"He probably figured a shotgun was his best bet for knocking them down quick, and the sound don't carry so far," Madbird said. "Muffled it some more, piling up them hay bales and shoving the barrel through. That's what blew this shit loose, him swinging it back and forth." He shone the light on some bits of fresh hay strewn on the floor just inside the wall. "But he couldn't of aimed much—just stood here and kept pulling the trigger."

I was jolted by an electric image of the terrified animals rearing, screaming, crashing against their wood prison in a frenzied attempt to escape the unseen thing that was ripping them apart. Coming across the carcasses had been bad, but this was a whole new level of awfulness. We were looking at an ambush—cold-blooded, premeditated murder, without even the mercy of clean shooting.

I shook my head hard and started walking, not to anywhere, just away.

SIXTEEN

I ended up using all the two dozen frames in the cheap throwaway camera I'd bought, figuring I might as well. But it wasn't much use. The crime scene had been covered carefully—the shed's inside cleaned, the shell casings picked up, even the stack of hay bales knocked down. What was left amounted to zilch and could be explained in other ways. Like a TV cop, I needed a body for real proof.

And I was more confused than ever. I'd assumed that Balcomb could run the D-8 Cat well enough to hide the horses in the dump—that wouldn't have taken much. But whoever had maneuvered it inside the shed was a skilled operator. Either he was better than I'd suspected, or I was guessing wrong about a lot of things.

Madbird and I tacked the piece of siding back into place the same way it had been. Then we started home, driving with headlights out, the van bouncing slowly along the rough road.

When we passed the spur to the old mansion, he turned onto it. I glanced at him, surprised.

"Let's pick up our tools," he said. "You might as well do it while you got the chance, and I ain't working for that motherfucker no more, either."

I felt bad enough already. I hadn't figured on costing him this job, too. It wasn't that either of us was going to end up unemployed. The contractor we worked for, Jack Graves, kept several projects going at any given time. He'd switch us to another and pull men from there to cover here. But we'd both liked this one.

"I'm sorry about all this," I said.

"Hey, I'd rather know about this bullshit than not. I could use a few days off, anyway."

"I'll call Jack tomorrow and tell him Balcomb ran me off. You want me to say anything about you?"

"Jack already knows I got a lot of grandfathers up on the rez, and sometimes one of them dies."

The site of the mansion was the choicest on the property, overlooking Lone Creek and the thick forest rising up into those seemingly endless mountains. Nathan Pettyjohn and his wife once had hosted grand dinners and hunting parties for dignitaries here—governors and senators, European nobility, famous musicians and artists. There was a story that Teddy Roosevelt had stopped by long enough to bag himself a bull moose.

Tonight, the creek's clear rippling water seemed alive with moonlight. It made me think again about Celia. In a roundabout way, she'd been responsible for my starting construction work, like she'd been for so many other things.

After her death, my family's closeness with the Pettyjohns was over, and I didn't go back to do ranch work for them anymore. The next summer, my father got me on as a construction gopher instead. My name was "Hey, kid!" and my job was to run all day, carrying materials, fetching tools for the journeymen, and cleaning up the site. I didn't like it at first, and there were plenty of assholes doing their best to make it tougher. But there were a lot more good men, and as I learned the work, I got caught up in it. It was great training for boxing—every summer I gained more coordination and lean weight. And there was the practical bonus that by the time I finished college, I could build a house from the ground through the roof.

The mansion was coming back to life nicely. One thing I had to give the Balcombs—they wanted top-quality work and weren't pinching pennies to get it. Madbird and I gathered our gear fast, our boot steps echoing in the darkened old building—a dozen kinds of saws and drills, homemade wooden boxes of hand tools, extension cords, leather belts hung with heavy pouches that we wore like pack animals, all beaten into comfortable familiarity and marked with different colors of spray paint to identify the owners.

I'd never been sentimental about walking off a job and I wasn't now, but I felt a tug of loss, mostly because of the crew. Like Laurie Balcomb had pointed out, they weren't a pretty bunch. We had an ex-junkie Mexican plasterer with a full back tattoo of his naked girlfriend, a redneck new age plumber with the insane eyes that came from inhaling too much pipe dope, a finish carpenter who'd once broken his neck getting thrown from a rodeo bucking horse, a laborer who hand-dug like a backhoe and occasionally had to head down to the penitentiary in Deer Lodge for a stint making license plates, and a cast of others like them who came and went with the need. We'd gravitated together over the years because we all carried our weight and stayed off each other's nerves, and we'd all been on many other jobs where that wasn't true. I was the nominal lead man, not because of any enhanced ability, but because as the main structural carpenter, I was in the best position to line out what was coming. They didn't require pushing and wouldn't have tolerated it. Jack Graves took care of the business end of things, paid us well, and left us alone— another rare setup. They were also a hell of a lot of fun. I was going to miss that.

We loaded our tools in the van and started up again. For the next tense mile we stayed quiet, past the ranch hands' trailers and the darkened headquarters. If we were going to get stopped, this was the place. But everything was still quiet, and we made it out as easily as we'd come in.

"So what you gonna do, Huey?" Madbird said.

I pressed the heels of my hands against my eyes. "What would the Blackfeet do?"

He spat out the window. "Hang Balcomb's bloody fucking hair on the lodge."

"I'd love to. But I might as well put a gun to my own head."

"Yeah, you got to be smart about it."

"I'm not feeling too smart right now. It looks like I'm going to lose any way I go. I'm just trying to weigh how much and where."

"That's a real lesson in what it's like being a Indian." His teeth showed in that grin, although this time it looked humorless. "Have another beer. Maybe you'll get a vision."

The beer tasted fine, but I couldn't see much except a few scattered lights in the distance, making this country seem even lonelier than it was.

"I keep thinking about how careful he was, setting that up," I said. "Somehow, that's the worst part of it."

"I been thinking that, too. I don't guess you got a look at a brand."

I shook my head. "They were so torn up and buried in junk, I probably wouldn't have been able to see one anyway. But why would somebody else's horses be in there?"

"I just got this creepy notion. A story I heard about smugglers using dogs as mules. Sewed up dope inside them and run them across the border, then cut them open."

That gave this nightmare a new twist I hadn't imagined.

"Kirk?" I said, thinking of his meth habit. He could sure run that Cat—he'd grown up with it. He could have spotted me at the dump, gotten alarmed, and blown the whistle about the lumber. But I was still convinced that Balcomb was at least in on it—that that was what he'd been driving at when he grilled me—and that Kirk wouldn't kill animals like that.

Madbird had his own reasons for doubting Kirk.

"He ain't got the brains," he said. "Besides, he wouldn't have to pull something like that to run meth. Half the fucking double-wides in this state got labs in them. Heroin or coke would be more likely."

I tried to envision Wesley Balcomb, with his glossy lifestyle and elegant business operations and aristocratic wife, involved in the violent and dangerous world of dealing dope—especially at this level of viciousness. If he was at a complete remove, just putting up money, then maybe—but not hands-on dirty like that.

"Goddammit, it's just too much grunt *work*," I said. "You know what I mean? Up to your elbows in blood and guts and shit, having to lug stuff around and clean up—that's not how guys like him make money."

Madbird grunted assent. "Yeah, I don't buy it either."

We didn't talk much for the rest of the drive. When we got to my truck, Madbird pulled up next to it and we transferred my tools.

When we finished, he said, "I'm nervous about giving advice, 'cause it could backfire. But I guess if it was me, I'd try a bluff. See which way he jumps."

"Bluff how?"

"Tell him you got the pictures of them carcasses. Say you always keep a camera handy from being a news dog, so you had it when you found them. Then you went back later and figured out where they were killed. Show him *those* pictures if he wants proof. With all that together, he might figure it ain't worth fucking with you any more."

I was still standing there as Madbird fired up his van and pulled away. Then he slowed and leaned out the window.

"Hey, Hugh," he called. "*You* better be ready to jump, too."

SEVENTEEN

Indian ways, Irish blood, and alcohol don't necessarily make for a very smart mix. But it can be a potent one.

Back when the job had first started, Jack, my boss, had given me a printout of phone numbers for the architects and managers and ranch offices and everybody's cells. I'd had to contact one or another pretty often, usually to hassle something out, so I kept it in the truck's glove box. It included the Balcombs' home number. I'd never called that one and never dreamed I would.

It was getting toward midnight when I found a quiet phone booth outside an Albertson's grocery store.

A woman answered after four rings.

"Yes?"

I could tell from that one syllable that she was Laurie.

"This is Hugh Davoren, Mrs. Balcomb. I need to talk to your husband."

There was a slight hesitation.

"Do I know you?" she said.

"We spoke, earlier today. You were out riding and I was in a pickup truck."

"Oh, yes, with the faux dueling scar."

"Yeah."

"It's rather late to be calling."

"This is important."

She paused again, as if she was trying to imagine what, in my life, it possibly could be.

But she said, "I'm remembering you more clearly now. Somebody told me something about you."

"Huh. They must have been pretty hard up for gossip."

"You weren't quite honest with me this afternoon. Stanford, is that right?"

I blinked in surprise. I hadn't known what to expect, but it wasn't this.

"I don't recall lying about it," I said.

"Oh, I think the 'aw, shucks, ma'am' routine was a kind of lie."

"I've learned I get along better if I don't answer questions until they're asked."

"All right, I'll ask one," she said. "Why are you making your living out here hauling trash?"

Out of nowhere, I remembered her riding toward me across the meadow, looking for all the world like Celia, by some miracle grown up into her full womanly beauty.

"The guy hauling trash is me, Mrs. Balcomb. The other guy was a suit I tried on that never fit. He's long gone and we're both glad of it. Is your husband around?"

For a few more seconds, again, nothing happened. I was getting the feeling that her hesitations had a meaning beyond anything I could grasp.

It seemed strange that she'd have heard that about me, and stranger still that she'd bring it up.

"I'll get him," she said.

Balcomb took his time coming to the phone—back in his dick-swinging mode of making people wait.

"Mr. Davoren," he said, in his cool, smooth tone. "How interesting to hear from you. This number's supposed to be unlisted. I can see I'll have to change it."

"This is getting out of control, Balcomb. Let's stop it right now."

His sarcasm edged up a notch. "Out of control?"

"Somebody came onto my land and burned that lumber."

"Oh, for God's sake," he said, now with weary patience.

"You don't believe me, come up and take a look."

"I don't believe you about anything, Davoren, and I'm most certainly not going to waste any more time on you. Even if what you claim is true, my first suspicion would be that you burned it yourself."

"*Me*? Why the hell would I do that?"

"Because you thought it might make me feel sorry for you. I advise you to forget about any more such naive little ploys. You committed crimes and you took my property. You're going to pay for that."

"Then it's going to cost you, too," I said.

Balcomb actually sounded amused. "Yes, I thought that would be coming next. When lying and whining don't work, your kind shift to threats."

I was starting to think real hard about driving right through his fucking high-security fence and dragging him out of his house.

"Remember when you asked me if I saw anything unusual?" I said. "I probably should have mentioned—the most unusual thing I didn't see was two shotgunned and gutted horses in the ranch dump."

There came a pause, like with Laurie, but the feel was a whole different order of business. Everything seemed to stop dead.

"I haven't told anybody yet," I said. "But I'm ready to head straight to the *Independent Record* and give them the story. They'll have it all over the wires by morning."

He wasn't shaken for long. He knew the carcasses were safely hidden now. His tone changed to the steely one of a man who had tried to be tolerant but had run out of patience.

"Really, Davoren. This has gone from distasteful to sick. I won't dignify that with a response. But if it was anything but another outrageous lie, you'd have said something earlier."

"I kept my mouth shut so I could find out more without tipping anybody off," I said. "I went back a little while ago and followed the Cat's tracks to the shed where those horses were killed. Oh, sorry—*weren't* killed. Never even existed, right?"

This time he was silent as stone.

"There's a kicker, Balcomb," I said. "Sure, I'm a liar trying to get off the hook, but I'm a liar who happened to be a journalist for seven years. The *Sacramento Guardian*—you can check it out if you want to waste the time. I always keep a camera with my other gear, out of old habit. So I've got a bunch of photos I didn't take. The whole shittarree—the carcasses, the tipped-over hay bales, the loose piece of siding."

I watched a middle-aged couple come out of the store and make their way toward a dusty sedan, pushing a cart filled with plastic sacks—out grocery shopping late on a Saturday night. There was something odd and yet sweetly sensible about it.

"I'm starting to realize that I was wrong about you," Balcomb finally said, with the weariness in his voice again. "Your real problem is not that you're a petty criminal. You're completely unhinged. But I have far too much on my plate to be mired down in something like this. What is it you want?"

See which way he jumps.

"You drop all charges first thing Monday and pay my bail," I said. "We'll call the lumber a wash. Maybe it wasn't mine, but you'd have just thrown it away."

"What guarantee do I have that you won't stir up more trouble?"

"I never stirred up any trouble to start with. And I don't ever want any fucking thing to do with you again. You can believe *that*."

Another blast of that frozen stillness came across the phone, as clear as if it had turned my ear blue.

"Consider it done," he said.

The connection ended.

EIGHTEEN

I got into my truck, shaking like I had after mixing it up with Doug Wills. As I drove, I tried to balance off the plays in this nasty little game. I'd shown my hole card, but so had Balcomb. The fact that he'd given in was as good as an admission. I didn't have the photos I'd claimed, but he hadn't asked to see them—another sign that his denial was a bullshit show. It was going to cost him a couple of thousand dollars, but that was nothing to him. I'd lost the lumber, but it wasn't coming out of my pocket.

I wasn't naive enough to trust Balcomb, like I would have when I was younger. I'd grown up with the dinosaur ethic of somebody's word being everything. It was the way you lived, how you were judged by other people—who you *were*. Eventually, I'd wised up enough to realize how differently a lot of the world saw it. Promises were empty, lures with sucker punches behind them, to be chuckled about later in a boardroom or four-star restaurant. He was powerful, rich, cunning in a way I could never touch. I hadn't forgotten his threat about my being out of my league. And whatever the reasons might have been for that butchery, the chill factor was off the charts.

I just hoped that Madbird's bluff would prove out, and the risk of exposure would spook Balcomb enough, in turn, to get off my case.

I didn't know if Sarah Lynn would still be awake, but I was carrying the wad of cash I'd brought from my place and I wanted to pay her back. She lived not far away, in the hills east of the capital, so I figured

I'd drive by and see. I could have waited for Monday—Bill LaTray would refund her twenty-five hundred after Balcomb paid him. But my sense of honor had taken a serious pounding, and I was going to feel a little better if I made a point of settling the debt right away.

I stopped at an ATM to clean out the seven hundred bucks in my bank account, and learned something I'd never known—I had a daily limit of two hundred, and that was all the son of a bitch would give me. I decided it was the thought that counted, and drove on to Sarah Lynn's.

Her house was modern and expensive, two-level, with a rock facade on the lower one. I knew that she and her ex had owned it together until they'd split the sheets. She'd married the kind of guy she wanted—the son of the local John Deere dealer, who had a cosmetic job working for his father. They had plenty of money and they lived well. But he was a small-town playboy, content to collect his easy checks and spend them on golf, skiing, and other women. Sarah Lynn put up with all that for a long time and probably would have kept on, except that she'd wanted children and they didn't come. Her doctors assured her that she was fine, biologically. She'd pushed her ex to get tested, but after a lot of hedging, he finally flat refused, unwilling to allow the possibility that there might be any trouble with his manhood.

"There were half a dozen problems all the time—like cats in a sack, fighting to get out," she'd told me once. "It took all I had to handle them, but I could. Then that one more came along, and everything blew up."

Now she'd been single for several years—had gone through the shock of divorce, the first acute loneliness, the period of getting used to it, and then the realization that this was how things were likely to stay. There weren't many eligible men around, and she was choosy.

The front picture window was dimly lit. Behind the curtains I could see the flicker of a TV screen. I rang the bell. A few seconds later, she turned on the porch light and opened the door cautiously, just the few inches that the chain allowed.

"Candygram," I said, and held up the sheaf of bills.

She smiled and closed the door to release the chain.

When she opened it again, I could see that she hadn't been kidding about her plans for a big Saturday night. She was wearing a white terry-cloth robe. The TV was showing an old movie, the couch was a nest of pillows and comforters, and a half-full glass of wine was sitting on the coffee table.

"It's a little short of two thousand," I said, handing her the money. "I'll get you the rest Monday."

"I told you not to worry about it."

"I want to keep my credit good, in case I have to hit you up again."

Her gaze sharpened. "I hope that's a joke."

"Me, too."

"You still owe me that story."

"Any time," I said.

There was an awkward little pause.

"I'd ask you in, Huey, but it wouldn't be a good idea," she said.

"I know."

She smiled again, a trace sadly this time, and touched a fingertip to the scar under my eye.

"You ever going to forgive me for this?" she said.

"I never blamed you."

"You did in a way—you just wouldn't admit it. And in a way, it *was* my fault."

"You didn't have anything to do with it, Slo. I dodged left when I should have dodged right. That's all there is to it."

"I was being a selfish little girl."

"That's the best kind of selfish I've ever run across," I said.

For a second, I thought she might change her mind and invite me to stay. Instead, her smile turned wry.

"You've still got the blarney, Davoren," she said, and closed the door, politely but definitely.

The reason I'd come here was to give her the money, and that was the truth. But I admitted that there'd been a fantasy in the depths of my mind that we'd end up in bed. I'd been subsisting for the past years on occasional one-nighters and even rarer connections that lasted a while longer, but never held. That had worn thin to the point where it was almost more trouble than it was worth. Something in me understood that no longer caring about getting laid was a bad sign.

Tonight, with her, it would have been natural and easy—and I knew that was why she hadn't gone for it. It wasn't just that I looked like a goat and smelled worse. She was in the same situation as me, only more vulnerable, and this would have been a dangerous step toward another heartache.

I walked back to my truck, filled with morose admiration for her good sense.

NINETEEN

As I started the pickup's engine, I couldn't help glancing across the seat at a dent in the passenger door panel. It had come into being the same night as my scar, and Sarah Lynn was right—irrational though it was, I couldn't help connecting the two things.

Toward the end of Christmas break my junior year in college, she and I had driven this truck to the town of Rocky Boy, on the Chippewa-Cree reservation up near the Canadian border. They were hosting an AAU boxing tournament and I was on my way to face another light heavyweight, Harold Good Gun.

It was a Saturday afternoon in early January. A chinook had sprung up two days earlier, a freak warm wind that stripped snow from the fields, leaving streaks of dark earth through the cover of winter. The sky was the color of frost, with no visible horizon. From Wolf Creek to Fort Benton, the highway followed the Missouri northeast. We could see it most of the way, winding through the bleak landscape, thawing in stretches that shone metallic gray in the flat afternoon light. Small white crosses marked the roadsides where people had died in car wrecks. Sometimes there'd be several of them in a cluster.

Sarah Lynn was quiet for most of the drive. She'd come along only because we had such a short time together before I went back to Palo Alto, and we wouldn't see each other again until June. This wasn't a part of my life she liked. On the surface, that was because of the brutality, but there was a deeper aspect.

After Pete Pettyjohn had thumped me, I'd stuck with my vow to learn to take care of myself. I took tae kwon do lessons for a while, then segued into boxing because of my admiration for a coach named Jimmy Egan—a tough, salt-of-the-earth mick from the smelter town of Anaconda who taught English at the local Catholic college and shepherded young men into becoming respected and respectful fighters. His view of the sport was parallel to his steadfast religious faith. Dedicated training and clean ring work were along the paths of righteousness. Any kind of moral transgression was punching below the belt.

I trained with Jimmy my last three years in high school, then went on to Stanford. It had long since disbanded its politically incorrect boxing club, but I hooked up with an informal group who worked out and sparred together and sometimes got bouts at a gym in San Jose. I kept on with Jimmy during the summers and took every local bout I could get.

I had no illusions about achieving any major status. There were plenty of amateur light heavies out there who were faster, more experienced, and a lot hungrier. What kept me at it was a passion that had developed over the years. I was still always jumpy when I got into a ring, but fear had become outweighed by the electric charge of the experience. At its best, it thrilled me with a sense of power that nothing else I'd ever done could touch. I had also gotten plenty familiar with the downside—a soundless explosion in my head, then opening my eyes to the sight of another man's ankles, with my face on the canvas and the ref yelling numbers in my ear. But even that had a raw, real edge.

That passion was what troubled Sarah Lynn. She saw it as a threat, almost like another woman. It stood for a side of me that wasn't at all in line with what she wanted, which was to get married and start a family. She'd gone to college the previous year at Montana State, but left after two semesters to work for her father. Now she was just waiting for me to graduate.

I was having my own troubles, but I couldn't grasp why. I only knew that I was more and more restless. That must have been clear to her, and it didn't help any.

We'd brought along a six-pack of beer for the drive home. But as we got close to Rocky Boy, Sarah Lynn surprised me by opening one. She surprised me again by finishing it fast and starting a second. She wasn't much of a drinker. She pulled off her boots and leaned against the far door with her knees drawn up and her feet tucked under my thigh, sipping and watching me. It made me slightly uneasy.

The town of Rocky Boy was several miles east of the highway, a pretty drive along Box Elder Creek. The site was steeply hilly, with a small settlement of houses and a number of reservation agency buildings. The bouts were being held in the school gym, and the parking lot was crowded with pickup trucks and station wagons.

I felt the first real tingle of what was coming, and opened the pickup's door.

"Let's not go in yet," Sarah Lynn said. "Let's drive around."

"Drive? Where?" Havre, the nearest town big enough to have more than a gas station, lay halfway between here and Saskatchewan. There wasn't much else but snowbound prairie for a good fifty miles in every direction.

"We could go to Bear Paw," she said. "Daddy took us skiing there when I was little. I want to see if it looks the same."

Evening had settled in by now. It was around six, the scheduled starting time. But tournaments worked from the lightest weights up, and judging from the number of vehicles, there were going to be a lot of kids tonight. Most weren't big enough to knock each other down, so they usually went the full three rounds. For sure, I wouldn't be coming up for a few hours.

A swirl of the damp chinook breeze slipped across my face and high into my nostrils. I closed the door and started the truck.

I drove a couple of miles along the dead-end road toward the little Bear Paw ski area. The landscape was deserted. Sarah Lynn had gotten animated and was looking intently out the windows, like she was watching for something. Abruptly, she grabbed my arm and pointed at a dirt track leading into the woods.

"Turn in there," she said.

I obeyed, thinking maybe she needed to pee, although I'd have expected her to go into the school. I took it slowly, feeling my way, nervous about getting stuck. But the ground surface was firm and we only had to go a hundred feet before we were shielded by trees. I coasted to a stop and cut the headlights.

But instead of getting out, Sarah Lynn got all over me, her tongue hot and wet in my ear and her fingers tugging at my belt. Startled, I half embraced her and half tried to hold her squirming body still.

"Sarah, baby, we can't," I said. Sex before a contest was an old athlete's taboo, another thing I knew was superstition and yet still had a powerful hold. I caught at her hands, but she was determined, and maybe I didn't fight her all that hard. Then her mouth was on my cock, and I could no more have stopped than I could have walked home with the truck on my back. I pushed down her jeans and panties, with her hips wriggling to help. She straddled me, heaving and then yelping while I heard myself growl, and I came so hard my slamming boot heel pounded that dent into the opposite door.

The noise level in the gym was almost painful, compounded of shouting from spectators, loud conversations of others trying to be heard, and the thudding of blows. I guessed the crowd at about a hundred and fifty, standing around the ring or sitting in the bleachers. Young men and boys were getting their hands wrapped, shadowboxing, snapping punches at coaches who held gloves shoulder-high. Some, their ordeals already over, carried trophies.

Sarah Lynn spotted a couple of other women from Helena in the bleachers, mothers of young contestants, and went to say hi. I stood there a minute longer, watching the eleven- or twelve-year-olds in the ring flail at each other with melon-size gloves strapped to the ends of their skinny arms. It was a little pathetic and really dull. A lot of the parents wore boosters' jackets, made of shiny nylon of various bright colors and emblazoned with the name of their club. The fluorescent overhead lights cast a sheen on those and on human flesh that I'd never seen anywhere but at boxing matches. The yelling faces and the colors seemed magnified in a way that suggested a disturbing dream. Maybe it was because of all the aggression floating around. When I glanced up at Sarah Lynn, I saw that she and the other two women were talking with their heads bowed together. The gym was overheated and stuffy with the smell of sweaty bodies. I decided to take a walk.

As I passed the ticket table inside the door, the hearty black-haired woman in charge gave me a big smile.

"You running away?" she said.

"Damn straight. I'm getting out while I can."

She shook her forefinger at me playfully. "That's what *you* think."

The outside world was deliciously cool and quiet except for the gentle gusting wind. I scanned the license plates in the parking lot. A few were from other states or Canada, but most were from Montana, and most of those from the heartland. You could tell because the plate's first number, one through fifty-six, identified the county. The local boxing club would meet in the back of an Elks lodge or VFW hall in some tiny town like Geraldine that you'd drive through and barely notice. But there'd be a few kids out on those ranches who thirsted for something more, to prove themselves or just to break the monotony, and grabbed at this small glory as a means.

There were scattered lights around the little settlement, but the only place besides the school where anything seemed to be going on was one of the old frame buildings, fifty yards or so up a hill. I could see movement through the windows and I thought I heard a faint sound like singing. I hesitated to intrude, but something about it drew me, so I started over there.

Then I stopped. An eerie sensation was rippling over my skin, like the wind was blowing right through me.

Abruptly, I realized I felt alone in a way I never had before.

I walked on to the building. Three Indian guys about my age were sitting on the steps drinking beer. They stopped talking as I approached. I nodded to them and they nodded back, but none of them looked right at me.

The sound I'd heard was clear now—not singing, but chanting. I went up the steps and along a hall to the room at the end where it was coming from. I stopped at the doorway. Several older people were sitting in a circle on the floor playing a game, casting handfuls of small sticks like dice, while more stood around and watched. Everybody joined in the singsong chanting that would die into laughter or exclamations of disgust as the sticks hit the floor. I was sure they were aware of my presence, but again, nobody really looked at me.

I'd had no idea what I was going to see here, but maybe I'd sensed it somehow and that was what had pulled me—not the game itself, but an extraordinary and powerful force that pervaded the place, the people, the gathering. It was a kind of heart, a center. I'd looked for it in my own world but never found a way to tap in.

But I had no business being there, and I turned to go. Just then, an old man with a headband and a long gray braid raised his face to me—the first direct gaze I'd gotten.

I had noticed him moving his fingers gently over his sticks after he cast them, as if he was reading them. Now I saw that his eyes were clouded with cataracts.

The lighter-weight bouts lasted even longer than I'd expected, and mine didn't start until almost midnight. The wait seemed interminable. I tried to spend it concentrating on what I was there for, but a lot of other things were going on in my head.

I figured out who Harold Good Gun was and watched him warm up, trying not to be obvious about it. He probably did the same with me. He was about my size, six feet one or two and a hundred seventy-plus pounds. It looked like I had a little reach on him but he was thicker through the upper body. I had talked to a couple of people who'd seen him fight, and the consensus was that he tended to come out with a hard flurry, but didn't have much in the way of either stamina or style. My own strongest points were a long fast left jab and a hard straight right. I needed to box him—keep him away at first, then go after him as he tired.

Instead, I let myself get drawn into mixing it up, and just under a minute into the fight, he threw a wild roundhouse right that caught me square in the socket of my left eye. I should have slipped or blocked it easily, and worse, he wasn't even looking at me, just windmilling furiously with his head down. In the upper weight divisions we wore ten-ounce gloves, not much more than ski mitts, and neither of us had on headgear. The impact was something like getting hit by a major league fastball. By the time I came to, sprawled on the canvas, the count was over.

Late the next gray afternoon, while I nursed my world-class shiner and my crushed pride, I felt something pop inside my face. The upper left side filled with fluid so fast it was like it got pumped from a hose. By the time I could get to a mirror, the eye had swelled completely shut. When I pried open the lid and saw just a little crescent of white, I started to realize what had happened. The tissue that supported my eyeball had broken, and it had dropped down into my skull.

Two days later, I got home from St. Peter's Hospital with the eyeball cinched back up in place on a piece of plastic and the bones under it wired together.

Of course Sarah Lynn felt terrible, and I tried to reassure her. I knew she'd been possessive because she was threatened, and seducing me was a naughty way of making me choose her over her rival. The last thing in the world she'd ever have wanted was to see me hurt. That had happened because I'd fought like a rank amateur, and putting any other kind of spin on it was absurd.

Still, she was no doubt right that I harbored subconscious resentment. It was also transparent that she was pleased about my boxing days being over, and that added to the mix. The next summer, we broke up.

By then I was feeling like that punch had smashed right through my face into my brain, jarring me into a new state of clarity. It wasn't especially pleasant. I started seeing a more honest and less pretty picture of myself than the one I had painted in my mind—the kind you might see after you'd been on a three-day runner and ended up alone and wide-awake drunk.

But I also started getting glimpses into my restlessness. It was a longing, an ache that everybody experienced at some point. Boxing, like the religious piety I'd felt as a boy, was a means I'd used to try to cope with it. Its source lay deeper. I realized that the reason I'd been so drawn to the Indians playing the stick game up at Rocky Boy that night was my sense of how close to it they were.

Still, I couldn't identify that hunger, let alone figure out how to satisfy it in a real and long-term fashion. The only thing I could think to do was to keep my options open. I held to the naive conviction that some event of critical importance to my life was out there on the horizon, and if I settled into practicality and security, I might miss it. That was the real reason I'd broken up with Sarah Lynn, who would have given me everything most men would ask.

I got out of Stanford with a degree in history, not good for much except more school, and no particular focus. I decided to try journalism, with a vague notion that wide exposure to new things might help me find the direction I was looking for. I was able to get into a graduate program at USC.

But by then I was seriously involved with one of my former classmates, who had started law school at UC Davis, near Sacramento. The long-distance relationship was a strain, and so was Los Angeles, especially with trying to live there poor. After a year at USC, I left and took a job at the *Sacramento Guardian*. The position and salary were both well below what I'd have made if I'd gotten my master's degree, but I was ready for a change and a steady paycheck. I figured I'd give it a year or two, then go back and finish school.

I never did. Emilie and I got married—Stanford blessed the union between two of its own in traditional fashion, by bold-printing our names in alumni newsletters—and new factors entered the equation. Her father was a wealthy business executive, her mother a socialite. For a wedding gift, they put the down payment on a house, which, privately, made me very uncomfortable. It was no secret that they considered my profession undignified and my earning potential a joke, and they wished I'd grow up and go to law or business school myself. The pressure mounted as time passed, with Emilie joining the chorus.

I didn't have any interest in law or business or anything of the kind, but that wasn't why I dragged my heels. It wasn't out of love for my work, either—I'd lost my illusions early on. Mostly, I covered local-interest topics like Rotary conventions, bureaucratic incompetence, and couples who preserved historic street signs. Occasionally juicier things happened along—an unusual crime, political scandals—but even those always came down to the same sordid underpinnings.

There wasn't any physical punch to shock me into awareness this time—just the growing sense that I'd let myself get put in a box, and even helped to build it. It was a good box, a lot better than most people ever got, but I was having more and more trouble breathing, like the air inside was running out. Almost worse was the crushing sense that the real problem was me—that I didn't belong anywhere and I was blighting everything around me. Discomfort edged into quiet panic. I started drinking too much, jacking the family disapproval level way up.

One night Emilie and I went to bed without touching, as had become common. We didn't talk, either, just lay there side by side awake. I knew she was thinking the same thing I was. Our marriage had been based on our trying to please each other and do what the world expected of us, but now we'd grown, or retreated, into who we really were. Whatever connection there once had been was between two different people.

But I saw another truth alone. I'd allowed myself to believe that with all the external changes, I'd embarked on a new life. In fact, I had only caved in to the very thing I'd avoided with Sarah Lynn. The trappings were different, that was all.

I had just turned thirty then. Not long afterward, I took a solo vacation to Montana, thinking I'd refresh myself for a few days. It was the same time of year as now. The plane arrived just at dusk, coming in from the southwest over a carpet of green mountain wilderness.

Madbird picked me up at the airport and took me out drinking, a great night of cruising the bars and running into old friends. He let me know that he'd started working with a crew he liked a lot, and they could use a framer.

Within another month, my marriage and my journalistic career were both over, and I was back in Montana growing calluses on my hands again. I hadn't left since.

Like memories of Celia, that old restlessness had faded to the point where I'd barely thought about it for years. In a way that was a great relief. But I had never come any closer to resolving it, and in another way, it was like the death of an enemy—you lost a powerful force that had been driving you.

Now I was pushing forty.

TWENTY

I wasn't in any hurry to get home to my dark, empty cabin and burnt lumber, so I took a roundabout way, drifting along the country roads and crossing the Missouri at the York Bridge.

I'd reached the northeast rim of Canyon Ferry Lake when headlights flashed at me out of the darkness ahead—a double flick that was repeated a couple of seconds later. The vehicle was a few hundred yards farther on, down near the shoreline, not moving. Most likely it was a signal for help. That area lay between a couple of campgrounds, a half-mile-plus stretch of brush and gullies that was off-road, but that teenagers often drove into at night. There were little beaches where you could skinny-dip, cliffs you could dive off, plenty of places to drink or steam up your windows. A lot of the ground was sandy and soft, and getting stuck was easy.

It was after one o'clock in the morning now and my mood was far from helpful. But the headlights kept flashing and I decided I'd better at least make sure that whoever was there was OK. I was probably the only person who would come along this way before morning, and the night had gone cold.

I slowed and turned off the highway onto a dirt track that led in there. I knew the landscape well from my own teen years, for the same reasons as the kids nowadays. I was still edgy, and I cut my headlights and stayed in the brush, coming up on top of a little knoll. I got out quietly and walked to where I could get a look.

The other vehicle was maybe sixty yards away now, a little below me on a slope toward the lake. The moon was dropping behind the Rockies, but there was enough light for me to see that it was a dark-colored Jeep, with a man pacing around beside it.

Kirk Pettyjohn drove a black Jeep just like it. And his wiry form and pale hair were unmistakable.

That sure put a new spin on things.

He was staring in my direction, his head swiveling with jerky meth agitation. He'd probably heard my engine and was trying to spot me. Anger and wariness rose up in me together. My first thought was that Balcomb had sent him, maybe to extort the photos I'd claimed to have. He wasn't carrying his rifle, although he could have had it stashed within easy reach or had somebody else hiding.

But it didn't make sense that he'd wait at a place like this and flag me down—taking the chance that I'd just drive on past or even have a gun of my own—instead of nailing me when I wasn't expecting it.

I stood there for most of a minute, trying once again to choose the path of greatest caution.

Then I realized how much I'd been letting fear push me around more in these past several hours. I was sick of it and disgusted with myself, and I was goddamned if I was going to back down from Kirk Pettyjohn.

I drove toward him slowly, watching for nervous glances toward a hidden weapon or accomplice. But his gaze stayed fixed on me, and he raised his hands palms forward in appeasement.

"I come to apologize, Hugh," he called.

That was a possibility I hadn't considered, although "apologizing" no doubt meant trying to lie his way off my shit list.

Visibility was better in the open space of the lakeshore, and for once he wasn't wearing his sunglasses. His eyes were twitching and darting around, and his face was as pale as his hair, and even in the night's chill, beaded with sweat. On top of the meth, he was scared. My anger eased off a little. I hadn't intended to really thump him, anyway—maybe bitch-slap him once or twice. Now I decided just to rattle his cage some more. But as I walked toward him, I didn't have to pretend I was pumped up.

"Now, hang on a minute," he said. His hands rose higher and made pushing motions, like he was trying to keep me away. "I know you're feeling kind of sore."

I kept walking. "You can start your apologizing with that lumber you burned, Kirk. Did Balcomb pay you extra? Or does that kind of thing go with your job?"

"Lumber I burned?" He edged around the Jeep to keep it between us. It was another one of his macho props, called a Rubicon, for Christ's sake.

"If you lie to me, that's just going to piss me off more," I said.

"I'm not lying—I don't know what the hell you're talking about."

"Those old fir planks I took from the ranch. That you ratted me off about and got me sent to jail for this afternoon. Remember?"

His mouth opened in an O. "Somebody burned them? *Whoa* there, goddamn it." He scuttled farther around the Jeep, his words spilling out in a rush.

"Hugh, I swear, this is the first I heard of it. I snitched on you, yeah. That whole deal today, I feel so bad I could walk under a dime with a tall hat on. But I didn't *burn* nothing. Hell, I wouldn't go near your place—I knew you wouldn't like it. I tried calling you, and figured you were in the bars and I'd wait here until you came back."

I stopped. In the quiet, the elephant that was always in the room with Kirk and me—what had happened with Celia and Pete—became an almost tangible presence.

When they'd died, I'd been old enough to understand it at least in an adolescent way, but Kirk was only seven or eight. From the little I'd learned about psychology, I'd gleaned that younger kids in particular were prone to take on irrational guilt for traumas like that—that it was common with divorces, and it certainly seemed likely with the tragic death of an only brother, especially a golden boy like Pete. I'd often wondered if Kirk had subconsciously become a fuckup to punish himself. I knew those sorts of things weren't nearly that simple, that he was probably a fuckup by nature, and that there was the flip side of using the trauma as an excuse. Still, I couldn't help feeling sorry for him. My anger dropped another notch.

Kirk was quick to sense things like that, and he immediately shifted gears into wheedling.

"Look, I want you on my side," he said earnestly. "I got a way to straighten everything out between us. At least listen to me, will you? I been waiting here a good hour."

I didn't care about his apology even if it was genuine, but I'd started to see that I might be able to use this to my advantage—play on his nerves and pump him for information, in case my troubles with Balcomb weren't over after all.

"I've got a real hard time believing you're going to straighten anything up, Kirk," I said. "But go ahead, give it a try."

"This stays just between us, right? Balcomb's got me by the nuts." Kirk shoved his hands into his pockets and stared down at the ground. "I got this little problem. I've been getting into some meth. He found out about it, and now he's holding it over me."

I almost smiled. Madbird was going to love hearing that the shitweasel had been bitten by his own fangs.

"Your secret's safe with me, Kirk," I said. His meth use was about as secret as Clark Kent's other identity.

"I saw you talking to Laurie this afternoon," he said. "Balcomb likes to keep tabs on her, so I follow her around sometimes without her knowing."

I'd already guessed that he was the one who'd spotted me at the dump. But I couldn't see how Laurie figured into this.

"We just passed on the road for a minute or two," I said. "I never met her before and I'm sure I never will again."

His lips peeled back in a grin that, along with his greasy sweat and twitching eyes, was almost a leer.

"She reminds you of somebody, don't she?" he said. "My ma, first time she saw Laurie, thought she *was* Celia."

So—I wasn't the only one, although the validation was undercut somewhat by Beatrice Pettyjohn's dementia.

"Well, what about her?" I said.

"This ain't about her. That's how come I saw you going to the dump."

Anticipation prickled my skin.

"Yeah?" I said, trying to sound impatient. "I've been there a hundred times."

"There was something in it nobody was supposed to see."

"You're going to have to tell me what, Kirk. The place looked the same as ever to me. Come on, quit fucking around. It's cold out here."

He glanced around and lowered his voice conspiratorially, like he was acting in that movie that played in his head.

"Balcomb—night before last, he made me bury a couple horses in there," he said.

Bingo.

"Horses?" I said, shocked. "*Two* of them?"

Kirk nodded emphatically. "He called me up after midnight and told me to get my ass over to the ranch. He never done that before, and when I got there, he was like I never seen him. He can be a scary son of a bitch anyway. Most of the time it's covered over, but when his temper goes off, it's like a hand grenade."

I realized that my gaze was wandering uneasily around the brushy ridges and gullies. Everything was dark and still except for the lake's faintly glimmering surface, rippling in a slow hypnotic rhythm.

"How do two horses die at the same time?" I said.

"He said they were being shipped someplace and he was doing somebody a favor, keeping them overnight—they were supposed to get picked up in the morning. He didn't want them mixing in with the ranch stock, so he put them out in that old shed at the north fence. But a bear or cat must have got in and killed them."

I laid on the skepticism heavily. "Broke *into* that shed and killed them *both*?"

"I thought it sounded pretty weird, but I wasn't about to argue, especially the way he was acting. He didn't want anybody knowing— it'd give the place a bad name. I had to hide them, right now, before daylight. And he didn't come right out and say it, but I got the real strong feeling he'd kill *me* if I breathed a word about it."

Never mind that Kirk was breathing those words right now. And this wasn't part of any apology—he was working his way around to something else.

"I fired up that old D-8 to go get them," he said. "Then when I saw them, I just about shit. It wasn't any critter that got in there. Somebody'd took a shotgun to them."

I stared at him. "That's crazy, Kirk. Are you sure?"

"I know what gunshots look like," he said haughtily.

"You think it was Balcomb?"

"I sure can't believe he went out there at midnight to check on them and just found them that way."

"What in hell would make a man do something like that?"

I imagined that his eyes turned more slippery, if that was possible.

"I don't know and I don't want to," he said.

"Come on, you must have some notion. You know that ranch like your backyard, and you spend all your time snooping around."

He shrugged uneasily. "Sheer meanness, maybe."

It didn't escape me that he hadn't mentioned them being mutilated. There had to be a reason for that, too—maybe that he was more deeply involved than he wanted to admit. I decided to come back around to it.

"So you went ahead and took them to the dump?" I said.

"Yeah. Covered them up and got the hell out of there. I was creeped, I don't mind telling you. I tried not to think about it any more, but then I saw you heading that way and I started getting nervous about how I'd buried them fast and didn't have nothing but a flashlight, and what if I hadn't done too good a job? So I went for a look, and sure as shit, there was a goddamned leg sticking up."

I shook my head. "I never paid any attention, Kirk. I guess I was too busy with my own trash."

"Well, I got worried that maybe you had, and by then you'd took off. So I called Balcomb and told him we better find out."

"And you came up with that bullshit about the lumber."

"I never guessed he'd send you to jail."

"Just brand me a petty crook and fire me?"

"I had to cover my ass, Hugh. If word had got out about them horses because I screwed up, Balcomb would have skinned me alive. He was red-hot pissed as it was."

He flinched as I reached for him, but I only patted him on the shoulder.

"Always glad to do a favor for an old pal," I said. "That's quite a story, Kirk. But I don't get how it's supposed to do me any good."

That earnest look came back to his face.

"I'm thinking you and me could team up, see? Tell Balcomb that now we got something on *him*, and get him off both our backs."

So that was where he'd been going with this. I'd underestimated him. This wasn't just weaseling—it was gainful weaseling.

"Sorry to be a hard-ass, Kirk, but it sounds like you're more interested in helping yourself than me."

"Hugh, I swear to God, the way I got this idea was trying to figure out how I could get right with you. But I got to admit, I don't want to take him on alone. And he's spooked by you. That's why he came down on you so hard."

I was almost amused. "Balcomb, spooked by me? I don't pack any weight."

"That's just it. You pack a kind he ain't used to. He can't figure out how to get his boot on your neck, and he can't stand that."

I supposed I should have been flattered, but it mainly added to my unease.

I tried to make sense of the way the pieces on the board had shifted again. Now I had someone to back up my story, and the chances of getting the sheriffs in action were a thousand percent better. Of course that wasn't what Kirk had in mind—he'd be looking at a meth pop, but that was his problem. My own dilemma was that if Balcomb stuck to our agreement, I didn't need to get him off my back anymore; and if I angered him again, the risks I'd worried about were still in play.

Although the thought of nailing him officially was tasty.

I decided not to decide just then. I'd been running too much stuff around in my head, and I was wearing out. But finding out where those carcasses had ended up would be damned good insurance, and I saw a way to push Kirk in that direction without being too obvious.

"He got his boot on my neck pretty good today," I said. "Well, I'm interested in your idea. But you're going to have to show me those horses."

His eyes got slippery again. "I can't do that."

"Why not? I know he threw me off the place, but we could sneak on."

"He made me go move them again today, soon as it got dark. I hid them good this time."

I hardened my voice a notch. "Then we're going to have to dig them up again. I'm not getting into it with Balcomb unless I know I'm standing on something solid."

"Oh, I can prove what I'm saying. When I went back the second time, I took my camcorder. I got it right here."

I blinked in surprise. I was getting more impressed with Kirk all the time, especially because he'd accomplished what I'd failed to.

I was even going to feel a little bad about taking the camcorder away from him.

He got it from inside the Jeep and gave it to me. His hand was shaking badly and his face was drawn so tight it looked almost skeletal.

The camcorder was a new model Sony, not much bigger than my fist. I flipped open the screen and pressed the start button, bracing myself for the sight of those ripped-up horses.

But sweet Jesus, what appeared was Celia rising up out of Lone Creek, naked and streaming wet and lovely just like in my memory.

I stared, stupefied, as she waded thigh-deep through the pool below the falls. Then it started to dawn on me that this wasn't Celia—it was Laurie Balcomb.

Kirk had been keeping an eye on her, all right.

She was hard to look away from, and maybe I stayed riveted to that screen a couple of seconds longer than I needed to. I barely heard Kirk's feet make a quick shuffling sound behind me.

Something slammed across the back of my head so hard it knocked the camcorder from my hands and buckled my knees. He hit me again as I tried to turn around, and maybe again after that.

TWENTY-ONE

When I started coming to, I seemed to be hanging in space outside my head, and for a few seconds I couldn't get back in. Then I connected, and the harsh ache in my skull brought me awake fast.

I was propped up behind the wheel of my pickup truck. The engine was running and the truck was moving jerkily down the sloping headland toward the lake—which ended in a sheer fifteen-foot drop into the water.

Kirk Pettyjohn was trotting along outside my open window, steering with one gloved hand on the wheel. We had about ten yards to go.

It took me another couple of seconds to start my legs moving. I got my right foot onto the brake and stomped it as hard as I could. The truck lurched to a stop, setting off a clatter of empty beer cans on the floor.

Kirk's hand tore loose of the wheel and he went windmilling onward. The truck bucked a couple of times, still in gear, and then the engine died. As I wrenched the door open, Kirk turned around, but instead of coming toward me he ran past me back uphill.

I knew damned well he'd have a gun in that Jeep.

I stumbled out and went after him, but he had a head start and he was moving faster. The only weapon I had was an old Schrade folding knife that I carried in my back pocket. I managed to claw it out as I ran, but I didn't have time to open it before Kirk reached into the Jeep.

He came out with the cold moonlit glint of metal in his hand—the blued barrel of a pistol. But he hadn't taken off his thick work gloves, and he fumbled, trying to force his finger through the trigger guard. I skidded on my knees, scooped up a handful of loose sandy soil, and flung it at his face.

He spun away, spitting and dragging his sleeve across his eyes, and took off again—but this time he was tugging at his gloves with his teeth. I managed to get my knife open as I chased him.

He stopped suddenly and gave his head a shake like a terrier killing a rat. A glove went flying. He started bringing up the pistol, with his right hand now bare.

I was only a step away by then, the knife clenched in my fist like a chisel, with the edge forward. I drove it at his hands as if I was throwing a right cross, with the last-ditch frantic hope that I could knock the gun aside or land a slash that would shock him into dropping it. But its upswinging barrel caught my wrist and sent the punch glancing off his chin.

I felt the blade drag just slightly, like I'd sliced its tip through an overripe pumpkin.

My momentum carried me a few more steps. I got myself turned around, ready to swing at him again if the boom and slam of a gunshot didn't knock me down first.

But he was stumbling away almost in slow motion, like a toy figure with its battery giving out. His dragging feet seemed to be trying to catch up and get underneath the rest of him. They didn't. His upper body sagged forward farther and farther, and he hit the ground like he was falling onto a soft bed.

I staggered over to him, gasping for breath, and knelt. His eyes were open but empty and his throat was pumping blood.

I fell over on the earth beside him and lay there, staring up into the cold night sky.

I'd only meant to disarm him. But that tiny drag I'd felt from the punch gone wild was the blade's tip catching him just under the jawbone.

My fingers were still clenched around the knife, slick and wet. Twenty-five years of bad blood was on my hands.

I was aware, in a distant way, that I should be panicked with horror at what I'd done. But except for my burning lungs and aching head, I felt like this was happening to somebody else. I got to my feet and limped down to my truck for a flashlight.

The key in the ignition was still in the on position. I switched it off, and noticed that Kirk had put the truck in third gear—the reason it had been moving so jerkily. There were a dozen of the beer cans I'd heard rattling on the floor, along with a nearly empty fifth of Jim Beam. None of them was mine.

And the disposable camera I'd bought, with the film I'd shot of the shed, was gone.

He'd been out to kill me, after all—and while I'd thought I was working him, it was just the other way around. He'd had a much slicker plan than lying in wait and blasting me. He'd probably watched enough true-crime TV to know that that was bound to leave an evidence trail.

So he'd spun his story to get me off guard and, idiot that I was, I'd gone for it. He'd set me up to look at the camcorder, knowing I'd be stunned by the sight of Laurie Balcomb. Then he'd clobbered me and planted the booze containers. I'd have been found in the lake, an angry drunk fired from his job and thrown in jail, who'd been driving wildly or had passed out. My friends might have been suspicious, but I had no family to push for an investigation and no status to warrant that kind of trouble and expense. It never would have gone any further.

I'd underestimated Kirk, all right.

There were more signs that for all his lack of talent at anything else, he'd staged this scene with real cunning. Whatever he'd hit me with was nowhere in sight. He'd probably hidden it or thrown it into the lake. It must have been flexible, a sap or old-fashioned sandbag—my head hurt, but there was no bleeding or damage. He hadn't fastened my seat belt, so if the lumps had been noticed, they'd have been accounted for by the crash. He'd even used a pair of my own goddamn gloves that he'd gotten from my truck, probably so he wouldn't risk losing or leaving traces from his own.

There was no sign of my camera, either. It might have been in the Jeep or one of his pockets, but I was guessing it was also in the lake.

In itself, the film wasn't important, especially now. But the fact that he'd taken it suggested strongly that Balcomb was behind this— that he'd called Kirk after talking to me and sent him to get rid of both me and the photos I'd claimed to have—and Kirk had turned my own lie right around on me, by claiming to have them, too.

The decision I'd put off was made for me now. I didn't have any choice but to take Balcomb to the law.

I didn't want to disturb any evidence, including my truck, so I started walking toward Canyon Ferry village to find a phone.

Then I stopped. A fresh tingle of adrenaline was starting through me, this time for a very different reason.

It was coming to me how this was going to look.

There were no witnesses to the fact that I'd acted in self-defense. On the contrary, the obvious take would be that I'd lured Kirk here to get even.

Investigators would quickly establish that he'd torched my lumber. Plenty of people knew about the long-standing friction that was there between us anyway, and several today had watched his snitching cost me my job and send me to jail, with him holding a rifle on me in the process.

Including, especially, Wesley Balcomb.

By killing Kirk, I'd destroyed my only backup for my story about the horses. I had no idea where they were buried, and the photos I'd seen on that camcorder sure weren't of them.

I had nothing on Balcomb now. But he had plenty of reason—and plenty of means—to railroad me for homicide.

My gaze was pulled to the pistol, lying where Kirk had dropped it, about eighteen inches from his hand—a Smith and Wesson .357 Magnum, with a slug powerful enough to penetrate a car engine. The slightest graze would have sent me reeling, giving him plenty of room to finish the job.

But I had a different worry about it now. Both make and caliber were so common around here that they were generic—you could buy one for a couple hundred bucks in any pawnshop, and cheaper in a parking lot behind a bar. This one was fairly old and a little beat-up. It probably wasn't registered to him—which meant that I could have been the one who'd brought it here—and if it was his, I could have held a gun of my own on him and forced him to give it to me. All the staging he'd done—even using my gloves—could be seen as clumsy attempts on my part to bolster my claim of self-defense.

And without question, the knife that had killed him and the hand that had held it—both were mine.

I'd gotten a real good look at the criminal justice system when I'd worked the crime beat in Sacramento, and as if the vision that Madbird had joked about finally came, I found myself staring into into a tumbling kaleidoscope of probabilities that froze just long enough for me to see to the end with chilling clarity.

I'd be slammed back in jail as soon as the sheriffs arrived, and this time the bail would be astronomical. I'd sit in a cell for months or years while some overworked court-appointed attorney tried to wrangle with the smooth power of Balcomb's wealth and behind-the-scenes influence, and the outrage of Kirk's prominent family. If I was lucky, I might get off with manslaughter, but if suspicion was strong that I'd set this up in advance, then premeditation entered in. I'd trade the county lockup for Deer Lodge, with only the question of how old a man I'd be when—if—I got out.

The invisible grip that had held me all day tightened like a junkyard's car-crushing vise.

Then, through the chaos in my mind, came a thought so clear it almost seemed spoken by a voice.

Nobody knows about this yet.

A weaker voice protested that no, I couldn't, I just wasn't like that. But my body started moving, and gathered speed under the power of a whole new kind of fear.

I spent the next four hours working harder than I'd ever worked in my life.

PART
THREE

TWENTY-TWO

A distant sound jolted me awake, too dazed to grasp where I was.

Then I remembered.

When I'd gotten home, not long before dawn, I'd come in quietly and made sure nobody was around, then gone into the woods to a spot that was well hidden and gave a clear view of my cabin and the road. I'd wrapped myself in a sleeping bag and sat back upright against a little berm, with my old man's pistol in my lap. I wouldn't have believed I could have closed my eyes, let alone slept, but my adrenaline had evaporated and exhaustion slammed down like the lid of a coffin. Now the hazy light of an autumn morning was filtering down through the pine branches around me.

The noise I'd heard was from a vehicle coming up my drive—a sheriff's cruiser.

It pulled up beside my truck. As the driver unfolded his lanky frame out of the car, I saw that it was Gary Varna.

He'd abandoned his usual button-down shirt and jeans and was in full uniform—counting his Smokey Bear hat, six and a half feet of khaki and leather. Ordinarily, you never saw him with a gun—he probably carried a small one concealed, like most off-duty cops—but on formal occasions he strapped on a more traditional Montana sheriff's weapon, a .44 Magnum that looked the size of a jackhammer. He was wearing it now.

I got up fast, shoved my gear into the brush, and hurried to meet him, keeping the cabin between us so it wouldn't look like I'd been so far away. My head, ribs, and wrist all reminded me of details from yesterday.

When I got to Gary, he had my truck's hood up and seemed to be admiring the engine.

"Morning, Hugh," he said. "I haven't seen this much of you in years."

"Sheriff."

"Out for a stroll?"

"Just to take a leak."

"Nice old rig," he said, patting the fender. "What you got in here, a 327?"

I nodded. "My dad had it bored and revalved for the changeover to unleaded, so it's a little bigger now."

"Nice," he said again. He closed the hood with a clang that made me wince.

"Come on in," I said.

His blue-gray eyes took in the cabin's interior without seeming to, in that practiced cop way. There wasn't much to see—the nook I euphemistically called my kitchen, just big enough for an old Monarch wood cookstove and a sink; a bed made of three-quarter-inch plywood with a worn-out mattress on top; a table and some other pieces of furniture; and some bookshelves and prints and such that I'd mounted on the rough log walls.

The clock read 7:39 AM. I hadn't expected this visit so early, or that Gary himself would come. But I'd known that somebody would, and I'd done a little staging of my own, rumpling the bedding and leaving a bottle of Old Taylor and some empty beer cans around.

"Sorry to interrupt you," he said, hooking his thumbs in his gun belt. "You look like you could use some more sleep."

"I got pretty fucked up last night." I didn't have to pretend much about that. I was bleary-eyed, rumpled, and still wearing dirty work clothes—although not the same ones as yesterday.

"The kind of day you had, I can't blame you," he said.

"Thanks. I'll make some coffee."

"Don't worry about it on my account. I already drunk a gallon."

So. He'd been up and on this for a while.

I started filling the kettle, mostly to give my hands something to do.

"You're looking very official," I said.

"Not by choice—just in case something comes up. I got a call about five this morning from Reuben Pettyjohn. *He'd* just got a call from Kirk's girlfriend. I guess she didn't want to talk to our office directly—she's got a couple little drug issues pending. Anyway, seems Kirk never came home last night."

I kept my hands moving and did my best to put on a wry face.

"I don't find that too hard to believe," I said. Kirk had a well-known penchant for sliding around on his live-in squeeze, Josie. Even Helena had its meth whores, and he was popular with them.

"That's what me and Reuben would of figured, and so did Josie, at first," Gary said. "She drove around town a while, checking the bars and other gals' apartments and all that. She kept calling his cell phone and he wouldn't answer, which ain't hard to believe, either.

"But then an hour or two after midnight, her calls started going straight to the phone's answering machine. Now, it's possible he turned it off or it ran out of juice, but she says he was crazy about that phone and he made damn sure to keep it working twenty-four seven, no matter what."

Son of a bitch, his cell phone. He must have had it stashed in the Jeep. I'd rummaged through there quickly, looking for my camera, but I hadn't found that and I'd never even thought about the phone.

"The only other way I know of that can happen," Gary said, "is when they get damaged."

Sitting at the bottom of Canyon Ferry Lake would damage a cell phone, all right.

I glanced at Gary, wrinkling my forehead in concern.

"You think something happened to him?" I said.

"I got two minds about it. I'm still mostly willing to bet he fell in love for the night. Maybe he did turn it off, or dropped it or stepped on it or run over it. But together with him not turning up—that's unsettling. So we're asking around." Gary's gaze stayed on me.

I shrugged. "Last time I saw him was yesterday afternoon at the ranch, right before I came to visit you."

"He was holding a rifle on you, is that right?"

I'd suspected that would get thrown at me sooner or later, too, but it was still the hardest jolt yet.

"Well—yeah," I said.

Then I swung around to face him.

"What are you getting at, Gary? Nothing happened between Kirk and me—we never even talked. He was just there in the background, doing his job."

"That's all I'm doing, too—just my job. This is informal, but if you don't want to talk to me, you don't have to."

It didn't look informal, with that uniform and hogleg.

"Sure I'll talk to you," I said.

He lifted his chin in approval. "Why don't you give me a quick rundown of what you did last night?"

I'd rehearsed this over and over during the drive back here and the hour or so before I'd fallen asleep, but it was still like walking through a minefield. I spoke hesitantly, as if I was trying to remember.

"I got home from jail. I was pissed off and restless. I went down to O'Toole's and had a couple. Then—can we keep this private?"

"For now," Gary said. "Not if it comes to bear legally. So think it over."

"It's nothing that serious. I went out to the ranch and picked up my tools."

"Am I remembering right that Balcomb eighty-sixed you from there?"

"Yeah, but the way he was fucking with me, I was nervous he'd impound them or some goddamn thing and I'd never see them again."

Gary pushed his hat brim back and scratched his forehead.

"I can't say that was a good idea, but I can see it," he said. "Give me a time frame to hang this on."

"I probably left the bar around ten and got back to town around midnight."

"That's a long trip out there and back."

"I took it slow, on the ranch. Kept stopping and listening, in case there was somebody else around."

"All right, you got to town about midnight," he said.

"I stopped by Sarah Lynn's to pay her the money she'd lent me. Then I went home and took that slow, too. I had a lot to think about."

"Anybody see you during all this?"

"Not that I know of. I mean, people might have *seen* me, but there was nobody I talked to."

"What time did you get here?"

"I never looked. It must have been at least two o'clock, maybe three." I hadn't wanted to say that—it was in the time range when Kirk's cell phone would have gone on the blink.

"That puts a little kink in my brain," Gary said. "Your truck engine seemed a touch warm. You'd think on a chilly night like we're getting, it'd go stone cold between then and now."

Son of a bitch again. So that's what he'd been doing with the hood open.

The only answer I could come up with was bone lame.

"I might have driven around longer than I thought."

Gary didn't say anything to that—just took another look around the cabin, then stalked to the door. I followed him.

"OK, Hugh," he said. "That all seems reasonable, even if some of it ain't exactly legal, and we can check it out if we have to. Let's hope we don't."

"Look, you know Kirk and I aren't buddies." I was careful not to use *weren't*. "But we get along. I'd sure never wish him any harm."

"That's good to know. Unfortunately, it don't much matter. What *does* is if something bad happened to him. And with him being

Reuben Pettyjohn's son—" Gary paused, then added, "Make that, 'last surviving son'—it kind of turns up the heat on me, know what I mean?"

I knew, all right. He'd do his damnedest to put somebody away, and he wouldn't bat an eye at bending the rules.

"Anything I can do to help, Gary, just let me know."

"I appreciate your cooperation."

I couldn't tell if he meant what he said any more than I did.

Stepping outside, he raised his head and sniffed the air, then turned his gaze to the heap of charred wood and dirt a hundred feet away.

"I thought I smelled something, coming in," he said. "What you been burning?"

I'd been nursing the faint hope that he'd assume it was slash or other debris and not say anything. Fat chance. I damned well couldn't accuse Kirk—that would give me another motive for revenge, this time in neon lights.

"Balcomb's lumber," I said, shifting my shoulders uncomfortably.

For the first time, Gary showed surprise. "Well, now, how the hell did that happen?"

I looked at the floor. "I pounded down some drinks after I got home from jail, and I just blew up. Next thing I knew, I was scrambling to put the fire out."

"*You* did it?"

"Yeah."

Gary didn't like the sound of this, it was clear.

"How come you didn't tell me?" he said, hard-voiced now.

"I feel like an asshole about it."

"We're not talking about your goddamn feelings, we're talking about withholding information."

"I didn't think it figured in."

"That been happening to you often?" he said. "Blowing up and doing something stupid without even realizing it?"

"Come on, Gary, you know me better than that."

"I used to think so. This worries me, Hugh. Drunk driving, trespassing—hell, those are the kind of things that could happen to anybody. But when a guy goes flat crazy and shoots himself in the dick, that makes an old cop nervous. Anything else you forgot to mention?"

I shook my head, squeezing my closed eyes between my thumb and forefinger.

"It was like you said—I had a world-class bad day. I handled it piss poor, and I'm sorry. Real sorry, because now I owe Balcomb another thirty-five hundred bucks on top of everything else."

"I'm afraid you're going to be more sorry yet," Gary said. "I was just about to tell you your luck was changing. I went out to see Wesley Balcomb first thing after I talked to Reuben, in case Kirk might be around the ranch. He let me know he was dropping all charges against you, including the demand for restitution. Said he only took it so far because you seemed to have an attitude, and he wanted to, quote, 'impress upon you the seriousness of the matter.' Unquote."

I sat down heavily in the doorway. "I think I'm going to cry."

"I don't blame you. I'll leave you to it in peace."

The tires on Gary's cruiser glistened where the black tom had sprayed them, sending a telegram to cats at the next stops along the line. I watched him pull away, with my pulse hammering so hard I could feel it in my head.

All charges dropped. Now I was going to have to wrestle again with whether I'd been wrong about Balcomb, or this was another of his ploys.

But first I had some urgent problems to deal with—starting with hiding a body so it would never be found.

"Had a feeling I better find out how you were doing," a gravelly voice said.

I lurched to my feet, swiveling toward it so fast my neck burned.

Madbird was standing beside the cabin's rear corner, looking like he'd just materialized there.

TWENTY-THREE

"I got another feeling that ain't just coincidence," Madbird said, jerking his head toward the fading dust cloud from Gary's car. He must have hiked in around the back of my property like I'd done last night. In the woods, Madbird was a ghost.

"I didn't tell him anything about you," I said. "But somebody might have seen us leave the bar together."

"I can handle that. Kirk?"

I hesitated. I'd never in my life been so glad to see anybody as Madbird right now. But from this point on, anybody who helped me or even knew about Kirk was on felony turf.

"I've gotten you in too much trouble already," I said.

Madbird acted like he hadn't heard me. He strolled over to the remains of the fire and paced around its perimeter, here and there nudging a clump of wood with his boot toe, each time releasing another cloud of charred dust to crawl up into my nostrils—little reminders that I wasn't the guy who'd started this trouble.

When he came full circle, he looked straight at me and gave me that grin.

"You can't go leaving me half jacked off," he said. "That'd hurt my feelings."

I made the same walk around the fire, kicking at chunks and thinking. Some of the embers were still warm.

"All right, let's take another drive," I said. "Maybe I've got something to show you, but maybe things turn out like last night—it's not there. If you don't see it, you're out of this."

We took his van again We wouldn't be trespassing this time, but my truck was the kind of vehicle that people might remember or even recognize.

Disposing of a corpse wasn't an easy thing to do, I had started to realize. Burying, burning, submerging, every method like that had some weak point that was vulnerable to discovery. Trying to increase the safety net required significant time and preparation. I didn't have a D-8 Cat and several thousand acres of private land handy, and Gary Varna was breathing down my neck.

I'd done my best to cover my tracks last night, starting by transferring the beer cans and pistol to Kirk's Jeep, then driving it half a mile farther along the lakeshore and dumping it over a cliff where the water was twenty feet deep. It made a pretty good splash. Sooner or later it would be found, but time and damage would be on my side.

I'd jogged back, shoveled up all the bloody earth I could find and thrown it in the lake, and scattered loose dirt and brush to make the site look undisturbed. It wouldn't fool search dogs, but unless he'd told someone exactly where he was going, there'd be no reason to look there.

Then I'd turned to Kirk. Especially in my frantic rush, I couldn't come up with anything smart. The single thing I most wanted to avoid was leaving a scent trail to my place that dogs might be able to follow, so I decided to take him in another direction. I had no choice but to carry him in my truck bed, but I wrapped him up good in a nylon tarp, and figured I'd slosh gasoline around the bed when I got home, as if it had spilled. Any scent that came through would be faint, and I could say he'd hopped in for a lift at the ranch a while back. Before I got inside the truck, I changed into spare clothes and boots and stuffed the old ones in a duffel. Later, I scrubbed myself as clean as I could in the shower, and took the final precaution of fishing through my dirty clothes for jeans and a gray T-shirt like the ones

I'd been wearing earlier. I smeared them with ashes from the fire, as substitutes for the ones that were soaked with Kirk's blood.

Those I'd stashed temporarily along with his body, a couple of miles up an abandoned logging road the next gulch over. The area was national forest, empty of habitation and generally deserted. But hunting season would start soon, with sharp-eyed men scanning the brush closely, and there were occasional hikers with dogs. If I left him where he was now, critters would scatter body parts and bones, making discovery likely.

Digging a grave deep enough for security would take several hours; and in this kind of stillness, the sound of metal hitting stone could carry for a mile or more. If someone heard it—say, a forest ranger or game warden—they'd come to find out who was excavating on national forest land. Trying to take him someplace else left all the same problems and added the risks of transportation.

When Madbird and I got to the spot, I was still coming up empty.

We parked the van and I led him into the brush to where I'd carried my burden a few hours earlier. I knelt beside Kirk's head, loosened the tarp's folds, and pulled them out of the way.

Madbird gazed down at the pale face and slashed neck, raggedly streaked with congealed blood. Then he knelt, too, and lightly pushed Kirk's eyelids closed with his fingertips.

"You better understand something, Hugh," he said. "You just walked into a different world. Ain't nothing ever going to be the same again."

TWENTY-FOUR

"How's it looking?" I said.

Madbird leaned back and eyed the cliff face critically. We were dangling ten feet down into a little coulee, roped to a tree, wearing the harnesses we used for bridge work. Kirk was wedged upright into a fissure in front of us, covered with a mixture of sticky foam insulation, dirt, and rocks several inches thick.

"You missed a spot over by his left ear," Madbird said. "The rest ain't bad."

I got another can of foam from the sack hanging off my belt and popped the seal. The gunk came out in a thin rope like toothpaste from a tube and quickly swelled to several times that size, an expansion that was powerful enough to bow window and doorjambs. I filled the divot and packed it with soil to match the surroundings.

He grunted OK. "I'll throw you some brush," he said, and hauled himself up his rope hand over hand.

This time he hadn't just helped me out. He'd flat saved my ass— sized up the situation, muttered that if the old downtown bars were still open we could just set Kirk on a stool and nobody would ever notice, then drove us to town for a quick supply run. When we got back we carried Kirk half a mile farther into the woods, lowered him over the cliff, and started foaming him in.

I took the handfuls of brush and duff that Madbird dropped down to me and created a tangled little deadfall in the narrow cleft above

Kirk's head. Then Madbird trotted around to a vantage point and gave me directions while I dusted the foam once more with scree, trying to make it look like the natural result of years of rain and erosion. Within an hour it would harden like lightweight concrete, and hold its shape after the flesh decomposed. Big animals wouldn't have any perch for digging him out, and varmints or ravens weren't likely to chew their way through several inches of toxic polyurethane embedded with rocks. The foam dried to about the same color as the soil, so any that showed through would barely be noticeable. The rare human who might happen along would see only another debris-choked crevice in a cliff. An earthquake might shake him loose, but this wasn't earthquake country. I was willing to take my chances there.

When we got back to Madbird's van we spent a couple of minutes trying to scrub hardened foam off ourselves, without much luck. You couldn't walk across the street from the stuff without getting it all over you, and although we'd worn rubber gloves and long-sleeved shirts, it had managed to sneak inside them. Gasoline or WD-40 would cut most kinds of gunk pretty well, but it barely touched the top layer of this stuff. The rest came off only with your skin.

But that was only a nuisance. The really bad part had been facing Kirk from only a foot or two away while we'd walled him in. We'd kept him wrapped in the tarp to avoid getting scent on us, but I'd felt him as clearly as if I could see through it. Neither Madbird nor I had suggested turning him around. That would have been like burying somebody facedown in a coffin.

It was starting to come home to me that I had made a living human being dead—someone I'd known all my life. I'd pitied him more than I liked him, but in some strange way, that almost made it worse.

I screwed the top back onto the red plastic gas container and stowed it in the rear of the van.

Then, out of nowhere, I started crying. Blubbering like a little kid.

After a minute or so I was better. I blew some snot onto the ground and got my eyes clear. Madbird was leaning against the van with his arms folded.

"You go a ways up in them mountains, there's a place nobody much knows about," he said. His right hand extended, forefinger pointing northward. Something about the gesture suggested a distance that wasn't measurable on a map. "It ain't exactly what you'd call a burial ground, but people been going there a long time to take care of their dead. My mother and my stepbrother Robert, my first wife and our little girl that got meningitis—their ashes are hanging from a tree in leather bags. We can go there some day if you want."

He spoke casually, still not looking at me. He'd never mentioned this before.

Still shaky, I said, "I'd be honored."

He finally turned to me. I'd never seen his face like that—gentle, patient, with a hint of things he'd been through that I couldn't begin to fathom.

"If you're feeling sorry for him, remember he tried to kill you first," Madbird said. "From behind."

I shook my head. It wasn't just sorrow for Kirk or for myself that I was feeling. It was a much vaster grief, for all of this that was happening and for everything else like it that ever had.

TWENTY-FIVE

We took my bloody clothes from last night to a creek a good mile away, soaked them with gasoline, and burned them to ashes, then dissolved the ashes in the swiftly flowing water. There were a few things left—my knife and belt buckle, some grommets from my boots and the rubbery residue of their soles, and Kirk's camcorder. I'd almost dumped that along with the Jeep, but then realized that experts might be able to recover its images, and there just might be something that would point to me. But I checked it while the clothes were burning, and the only footage was that brief scene of Laurie Balcomb in the creek. I doubted her husband knew that Kirk had done his job of shadowing her so thoroughly.

I pounded the camcorder to small pieces with a hammer and washed them and the other nonflammable stuff clean of blood and fingerprints. Then I took it all down into a thickly brush-choked draw and foamed it into a rockpile like we'd done with Kirk. I kicked a small landslide over the site for good measure, and headed back.

I was sure I'd left loose ends in spite of all my caution, and without doubt the investigation would soon come around to me in a serious way. But this was going to have to do it for now.

Madbird and I drove home.

He followed me through the trees to my cabin, this time carrying the old lever-action 30-30 he kept in his van. I trotted in a crouch to the windows and peered inside. Everything seemed the same as when

I'd left. I turned to him and raised my hand. He saluted, and then he was gone. Neither of us had said much more. It was like we'd been on a fishing trip instead of doing what we'd done. But I knew he was thinking the same thing I was—that it would be best if we didn't hang around together for a while.

It was a little before one o'clock. The afternoon had taken on a hazy warmth. But when I stepped inside the cabin, it felt so cold and lifeless that I stopped in the doorway. I hadn't ever fired up the wood-stove last night, and the log walls held in the chill. I'd never finished making that coffee for Gary Varna, either. The unheated kettle was still sitting by the sink.

I closed the door and walked back out to a big wind-twisted Doug fir that was probably the oldest living thing on the place. The sun was obscured by light clouds that might signal coming rain, but it showed as a ragged yellowish blur behind them. I sat on my heels facing it, with my back up against the fir. I'd started doing this after the end of my marriage and that previous life that had gone along with it. Eventually, I'd realized that it was an unconscious attempt to soak up energy, sandwiching my body between the sun in front and the tree behind, in the hope that this would trickle-charge some internal battery that was drained dry. The warmth always felt good and sometimes it seemed to help in other ways, but not today.

That grief was still with me, but I was starting to wake up to the reality of what Madbird had pointed out. My notion that I might have falsely accused Balcomb had vaporized. I was certain that he'd sent Kirk to kill me. He didn't know what had happened to Kirk, but he'd have realized from talking to Gary Varna early this morning that something had gone wrong. Dropping the charges against me was another of his smoke screens, a way to establish his ignorance of the murder attempt and to keep me off guard.

There were a couple of spin-offs. First, whatever was behind the slaughter of those horses was worth killing for.

Second, Wesley Balcomb was still alive and no doubt still wanted me dead. He would try again. My luck had been twisting and turning, but it had come through for me big-time last night. I couldn't keep counting on it.

I'd be crazy to hang around like a sitting duck. But if I left town, with Gary Varna as suspicious as he was already, it would be taken as an admission of guilt for Kirk's disappearance. The law would damned sure find me, I'd go back to jail, and my little cover-up scheme would be put under the kind of scrutiny that would rip it apart.

I got an armload of split larch and kindling from the woodshed and carried it to the cabin. This time I made it all the way through the door and saw that the phone machine light was blinking.

The voice was Sarah Lynn's, agitated to the point of trembling.

"Hugh, Gary Varna just left here. He said Kirk Pettyjohn's gone missing, and he wanted to know when you were here last night and how you seemed, and all that. What's going *on*? *Call* me."

The little man in the phone machine said the call had come at 8:47 AM. Gary had left here about eight. That meant he'd gone straight to her place.

And *that* meant he was real interested in checking out my story.

I started to punch Sarah Lynn's number, but then hesitated. Rationally, I felt justified about the deceiving I'd done so far, but my gut didn't like it, and lying straight out to her about killing a man we'd both grown up with would be excruciating. I knew I was going to have to do it and keep on doing it, not just with her, but with other people who trusted me. But not just yet.

I made a small fire in the stove to break the chill. My belly was reminding me that I hadn't eaten since lunch yesterday. My mind wasn't interested, but my body demanded food. I dumped a can of corned beef hash into a frying pan and put it on the hot plate, then rummaged for something to go with it. I usually did my laundry and grocery shopping on Sunday mornings, and right now I was out of just about everything. The best I could come up with was a couple of bread heels and half a bag of stale potato chips. I put the bread in the toaster oven and got out cream cheese and Tabasco sauce from the refrigerator. I filled the kettle with fresh water and put it on the hot plate's other burner, ground up some coffee beans, and shook the powder into a filter cone to make myself a good strong cup.

The cabin was warming up, but it felt small and close. When the hash finished browning, I opened the door and ate standing up there, facing the quiet vista of forest and mountains.

The smell of the burned lumber was still hanging in the air, faintly disturbing—and it brought to light another of those slivers festering under the surface of my consciousness.

I'd taken it for granted that Kirk had set the fire and lied to me about it. But it must have started about dusk—right when he said he'd reburied the horses. That would have taken him a while, and the drive from the ranch to my place was close to half an hour. It would have been physically impossible for him to have gotten here that soon. Maybe he'd buried the horses earlier and lied about the timing, too. But I couldn't see any reason for that, and it made sense that he'd have waited till dark. I was concerned because if someone else had burned the wood—like Doug Wills, getting revenge for our fight—Gary Varna might find out I hadn't and I'd be caught in a lie really touchy to explain.

I was just finishing lunch when I heard a car coming up the road. I stayed in the doorway until I could get a glimpse. It was a small, off-white, fairly new sedan, not a sheriff's cruiser and not a vehicle I recognized as belonging to anybody I knew.

TWENTY-SIX

I didn't think someone bent on harm would broadcast his presence like that, but I'd thought the same thing about Kirk, and the car might even be a shill for someone else approaching on foot. I'd brought my father's pistol back into the cabin but it wouldn't do me much good except at close range, and I never wanted another face-to-face confrontation again. I pulled the door most of the way shut and strode to my gun safe. I knew the combination like high school kids knew their lockers', and within thirty seconds, I had my Model 70 elk rifle out.

I stepped to the door again, staying to one side, and jacked a round into the chamber. The car was just pulling up to my gate, about fifty yards away. The driver was a man, alone. I could see him lean forward in the seat, like he was reading the numbers on my mailbox, before he got out.

The rifle's scope gave me a clear look at him. I'd never seen him before any more than I had the car, and he was just as nondescript— my age or a little older, wearing glasses, clean-shaven, and neatly dressed. A bow tie added a prim, even nerdy touch.

Then I saw that he was carrying a nine-by-twelve mailer envelope, like the kind UPS and FedEx used, but colored yellow and green. I recognized it as being from XP-DITE, a local courier, the kind that ferried parcels and car parts around town. He squinted at the cabin like he was trying to decide whether to open the gate and come on up. But then he put the envelope in the mailbox, hung a tag on it, and drove away.

For two or three more minutes I stayed where I was, scanning the woods through the cabin's windows and wondering who in hell would have sent me an express package at all, let alone on a Sunday. Nothing moved that I could see except the tag on the mailbox, fluttering listlessly in the breeze.

I started down there as if I was sneaking up on game, half-crouched, ready to drop prone and shoot. Forty feet short of the gate, I stopped. After another long look around, I picked up a rock and chunked it at the mailbox. I felt like an asshole, but an envelope could hold enough explosives to blow somebody to bits.

I threw like an asshole, too. It took me five tries to connect with a good solid thunk. Nothing happened, not that that was any guarantee. I walked the rest of the way and cautiously pulled the mailbox door open. A few letters from yesterday were still there, a couple of flyers, and some other junk, with the XP-DITE envelope on top. My name and address were typed on a label. There was no return.

I slung the rifle over my shoulder and lifted out the mailer, tingling at the thought of plastic explosives or a cloud of anthrax dust. It was light, with only a slight bulge in the middle. I didn't touch the pull tab. Instead, I carried it back to the cabin and cut off the opposite edge with scissors.

Inside, there was a plain white letter-sized envelope. Inside that were twenty-five hundred-dollar bills.

I sat down in the doorway with the money in my hand, staring out into the forest.

With everything else that had happened, I'd almost forgotten that I'd demanded the bail money from Balcomb. I'd assumed that if he did pay it, he'd deal directly with Bill LaTray. But it made sense that he wouldn't want anyone else to know about it. Gary Varna might believe that he'd dropped the charges out of the goodness of his heart, but his paying my bail on top of that would be a big red flag that there was more to this.

I briefly considered the notion that he was spooked enough by Kirk's disappearance to really back off. But Balcomb keeping his word made me even more nervous than him being straightforwardly out to get me. It underlined the one thing I was sure of—that I couldn't keep on like this much longer, edging around sideways and looking over my shoulder.

The ring of the phone was like an exclamation point to what I'd just been thinking, making my hands jerk so hard I almost dropped the bills. I guessed that this was Sarah Lynn, and tried to phrase an apology.

"*Finally*, you're home," a woman said. "I've been calling you all morning."

It was a different voice from Sarah Lynn's, one I'd only heard a few times, but easy to recognize—refined, musical, softened by the trace of a southern accent.

I couldn't say that Laurie Balcomb was the last person on earth I'd expected to hear from, but that came close.

"My message machine seems to be working," I said.

"I didn't want to leave a message. I didn't know who else might be around. We need to talk, in person."

"Is that a fact?" I was already suspecting another of Balcomb's setups, and the coolness must have come across in my voice.

"I can understand why you don't like me," she said, sounding anxious now. "But I want to help you."

That was just how Kirk had come on. At least he'd had a plausible pitch, but there was no reason I could see why she should be feeling generous toward me.

"Mrs. Balcomb—"

"Laurie, please."

"It's not that I don't like you. To be perfectly truthful, I don't know you well enough to have a take one way or the other. But right off the top, you being your husband's wife doesn't exactly make us buddies."

"When I found out how he treated you, I could have killed him."

She said it very convincingly. My skepticism stayed, but I scaled it back a shade.

"What is it we have to talk about?" I said.

"Will you just please come meet me? I'm in town, at a phone booth. I couldn't get through on my cell phone."

"They don't work up here."

"I should have known," she said impatiently. "That somebody like you would be living in the dark ages. Pick a place; you know the area. Not a restaurant or anything like that—I can't be seen."

I weighed it for a few seconds longer. In town, in broad daylight, I'd be less at risk than here. Whatever her pretext, I might learn something useful.

And I had the time. It wasn't like I had to get ready for work in the morning.

TWENTY-SEVEN

Saint Helena Cathedral was a lovely Gothic structure built in the early 1900s, designed by an Austrian architect and modeled after a church in Vienna. A pair of Irishmen had been the driving force behind it, one a bishop and the other an immigrant who'd struck gold. My own paternal grandfather had grown up in a stone hovel near the north bank of the Shannon, four miles from the nearest little village, and no one in the family even had a bicycle. He'd spent his life working in the mines instead of owning one. The name had been O'Davoren originally, but he'd dropped the "O" at Ellis Island. That was in the days when there was a lot of "No Irish Need Apply" sentiment around, especially back east, so he'd kept moving on until he ended up here.

I'd suggested the cathedral to Laurie as a meeting place because I wasn't sure how well she knew her way around, and you could see its twin spires from miles away. I told her to park nearby and I'd find her. The neighborhood was residential and quiet, so she wouldn't have to worry about being seen.

And it was as unlikely a spot for an ambush as I could think of.

But I recognized something else at work in my mind. The cathedral carried a strong association with Celia. Except for my own brief boyhood fling with piety, my family had pretty much been the Catholic equivalent of jack Mormons—sincere enough, but playing fast and loose with the rules. Still, we rarely missed Sunday Mass.

Celia would go with us, always wearing a pretty dress and behaving like she was at first communion, although by the end of that summer her confessions must have burned the priests' ears.

She'd just gotten her driver's license then, and in the afternoons after church, my folks would let her take our old Ford Falcon for a couple of hours and I'd tag along. Our usual routine involved a stop at Gertie's Drive-In for whatever fast food we could afford, then just cruising. She liked to drive the steep hilly streets on the west side, checking out the majestic old houses that had been built when Helena was awash with mining money. It was the kind of wistful daydreaming that all kids did, but hers had a practical and determined edge. She'd guess at their values, and if one was for sale, she'd look it up in the paper and find out. She'd even describe the kind of furniture she'd buy for the place if it was hers.

For a hardscrabble ranch girl like her, there was only one way that was ever likely to happen—hooking up with a rich guy like Pete Pettyjohn. And oddly enough, we started running into him more and more often. Soon it became clear that on those Sunday excursions that had started with just Celia and me, there was no more room for a fourteen-year-old little-brother type.

I cleared my head of the past when I got to the cathedral, and started looking for the vehicle that Laurie Balcomb had told me she'd be driving, a new silver Mercedes SUV. It wasn't the kind of rig you'd want to take hunting, but no doubt it was fine for the highway and around town, if a little over the top. I circled the block in my pickup until I spotted it.

She was waiting in the driver's seat, wearing huge sunglasses, a wide-brimmed hat, and a scarf covering her hair and tied under her chin. It wasn't a bad look—the sort of thing you saw on tabloid covers in grocery store checkout racks, of celebrities trying to dodge paparazzi—although around here, it was likely to draw more attention than it deflected. But it was true that she was hard to recognize.

I pulled up next to her and leaned across the seat to open my passenger door. She stared like she couldn't believe I was driving this old crate that she'd seen hauling trash yesterday—and that I expected her to get into it. But she did, with her nostrils twitching. I had quickly showered and changed again, but that hadn't done anything for the truck.

She gave me a nervous smile and pressed my hand with her own. The warmth of the gesture took me aback. She was wearing the same kind of tight jeans I'd seen her in yesterday and a soft eggshell turtleneck, an outfit that showed off her figure. I couldn't help remembering that image of her on Kirk's video, rising bare-skinned out of the stream.

Couldn't help remembering what had happened to me next.

"I appreciate your thinking of me," I said. "Sorry if I was bristly on the phone."

"I understand completely. You've had a terrible time." Then she bit her lower lip, like a little girl. "But I'm not sure you'll still thank me after what I have to tell you."

"I'd rather know it than not," I said.

Her grip tightened on my hand. "Will you promise to keep it just between us?"

It was another echo of Kirk.

"Sure," I said.

She let go and settled back. I started driving, keeping an eye on the rearview mirror for anyone following.

"My husband was very upset after you called last night," she said. "What did you say to him? He didn't tell me."

"That somebody came to my place while I was gone and burned the lumber I took from the ranch," I said.

I couldn't see Laurie's eyes behind those sunglasses, but her mouth opened in dismay.

"And that I figured he was behind it," I went on. "That I was going to call the sheriffs and start an investigation, and it was going to mean a whole lot of trouble and bad publicity for him and his business. But if he dropped the charges against me, I'd call it even."

"No wonder he was so enraged," she murmured. "Wesley does *not* like it when someone puts his back against a wall."

I wasn't heading anywhere in particular, just letting the pickup find its way. We'd been going south on Rodney Street toward the city's outskirts, but I turned right on Broadway, looping back downtown.

"Let's get back to your bad news," I said.

"The sheriff came by and talked to Wesley, early this morning. Kirk's gone missing. Did you hear?"

I nodded.

"When Wes came back inside, he went ballistic—even worse than last night. He told me not to breathe a word to anybody that there was any kind of trouble. The way he looked was frightening. And— he can be dangerous. I thought you should know that."

Leaving aside that this wasn't exactly news, it was very interesting that she was both warning me and betraying him.

"Has he ever hurt you?" I said.

Her face turned away. "Not directly. He has other ways of handling things."

"That doesn't sound like a very cordial arrangement."

"Maybe I'll tell you a story some day," she said, with her face still averted.

In a perverse way, that made me feel better—her fear helped explain why she was siding against him.

"Why not now?" I said.

But she backtracked. "I don't mean he's a bad man. He's charming, and most of the time he treats me well. But he's such a control freak. The truth is he's very insecure. He grew up dirt-poor."

That didn't buy him much sympathy from me. I knew a lot of people who'd been in that boat—Madbird had flat gone hungry sometimes as a kid—and my own family had never been more than a paycheck or two away from disaster.

"I think that's the real reason he wanted to raise thoroughbreds," she said. "They're beautiful, graceful, well bred—everything he feels he's not. The irony is, he doesn't like horses."

The parallel between the thoroughbreds and Laurie herself was clear, and she must have realized it. Maybe it was another part of the reason she was doing this.

There was no telling how genuine her concern for me was, and I didn't want to come right out and suggest that Balcomb and Kirk might have been involved in something illicit. I decided to try sneaking up to it.

"So when Balc—your husband—blew up this morning, it was about Kirk?" I said.

"I don't know what it was about." Her curtness dead-ended the probe. "Are you friends with him?"

"We've known each other a long time. I wouldn't call us friends."

"Of course I hope nothing bad happened to him, but he creeps me out," she said. "I started to get the feeling he was almost stalking me."

She'd have been a lot more than creeped out if she'd suspected how close to the truth she was.

We coasted down the Sixth Avenue hill and crossed Last Chance Gulch. Downtown was as quiet as an old photograph, with nothing open but the bars and nobody moving on the streets. The truck, of its own accord, climbed the next hill toward the west side and the grand old houses that Celia had loved.

"Well, thanks for the heads-up," I said. "I admit I don't know what to do about it."

"You're not going to leave here?"

"I would, but I can't."

"Funny," she said quietly. "It's the same with me."

"You mean leaving your husband?"

She nodded.

"Can't or won't?" I said.

She held up her hand palm first to silence any more questions. I realized I was crossing a line.

"I'll try to help," she said. "I'll watch him like a hawk. If I think he's up to something I'll call you. So answer your damned phone, OK?"

"Yes, ma'am."

"Where were you all morning?"

I was startled at her sudden, out-of-the-blue left turn—and I imagined a hint of jealousy in her tone.

"Sweating out a hangover," I said. "Cutting firewood."

She sniffed. "How manly." Then her voice took on the teasing tone she'd left me with yesterday. "By the way, I haven't forgiven you for not being honest with me."

"Who told you about my old life?" I said.

"I have my sources."

I pulled the truck over to the curb and swung around to face her.

"More to the point, why'd you ask?" I said. "Why are you bothering with me?"

Maybe I spoke more strongly than I meant to. Her coquettish look vanished, and she pressed back against the door, turning her face aside again.

"I feel drawn to you," she said. "You seem so at home here, in a way. But really, you're not at home anywhere."

"I guess I don't see the draw in that," I said.

"Maybe I should have put it differently. A kinship." Her left hand fidgeted to the gearshift, fingers brushing it lightly, then dropped away and returned to clasp her right.

She said, "I'd better go."

I started driving again, this time back toward her car.

"These old houses are so beautiful up here," she murmured. "Don't you wish you lived in one?"

It was the kind of thing anybody would have thought.

TWENTY-EIGHT

Laurie hadn't told me much that I didn't already know. I was still skeptical about her motives, and I had a strong sense that she'd evaded my question about what had set Balcomb off this morning. But she'd convinced me that I'd damned well better keep him on my radar until I was sure he was really done with me. Then there was Gary Varna nosing around.

All together, it got me thinking that as long as I had time on my hands, I'd be wise to find out as much as I could about what was going on behind the scenes. Information might be my best defense, and possibly my only one.

I decided to start with somebody who'd be easy to approach— Elmer Stenlund, the ranking cowboy at Pettyjohn Ranch, who'd been present yesterday at my confrontation with Balcomb. Elmer was an old friend, rock solid in all ways, and I was sure he was sympathetic to my situation. He'd lived on the ranch most of his life until it was sold; then he'd bought a little house near Scratchgravel Hills. The new place was closer to town and easy to maintain, and with his kids gone and his wife having died a few years back, he was glad for neighbors. But I knew that the real reason he'd moved was that he didn't like Balcomb any more than I did.

Still, I was a shade uneasy. Elmer had been Reuben Pettyjohn's right-hand man since before I was born, with a connection and loyalty that went so deep they were impossible to fathom. For sure, he'd know by now that Kirk had disappeared. If he'd also heard that there was a shadow over me, that might change things. But if so, he'd be straight about it; and as stock manager, he was my best bet for finding out where those slaughtered horses had come from.

I found a phone booth on Euclid, the long commercial strip that became the highway west to Missoula. As I got out of my truck, I realized I'd subconsciously picked a place that was clear across town from the phone where I'd called Balcomb. It was silly, but that was the way I was starting to think.

"Elmer, it's Hugh," I said when he picked up. "How's it going?"

"*I'm* OK. How about you?"

"I've been better. Things were settling down. But now there's trouble over Kirk."

"Yeah, I talked to Reuben a couple times. I'd of figured he was out chasing tail, but I guess he still ain't turned up."

"I've got a feeling I'm a suspect, Elmer. Gary Varna came to my place and grilled me pretty good."

His pause was so shocked I could almost hear it. It came as a relief.

"The hell," he said. "Where's he getting that?"

"Because of the flap yesterday, mainly. Kirk standing guard on me with that rifle."

"Aw, for Christ's sake. Nobody'd take him that serious—it's just Kirk."

My relief deepened.

"There's some other strange stuff going on I'd like to run by you," I said. "OK if I swing out there for a few minutes?"

"Sure, I ain't doing nothing. Watching one of them ball games where nobody ever gets a hit. Pitchers' duel, I guess they call them."

"Well, if you're feeling restless, how about I buy you a drink?"

"You know, that don't sound too bad," he said. "I got a few things I could stand to take care of in town anyway."

"When's good?"

"Oh—why don't you give me an hour, maybe a little more."

"Red Meadow?" I said, naming his favorite watering hole.

"That'll do 'er. See you there."

It was just three o'clock. I wouldn't have time to check out other possibilities, and I was too owly to do anything practical like buying groceries. I was tempted to go straight to the Red Meadow and get a head start, but that was a bad idea.

I got back in my truck and drove on west to where the town pretty much ended and the Rockies started. Then I turned off to the veterans' cemetery at Fort Harrison.

Laurie's words about not feeling at home anywhere kept resonating in my head. Until yesterday, I'd considered myself about as well off as a man could be—broke, maybe, but free in all the ways that counted, at least to me. I had good health, a marketable skill, a place to live that was all my own, and, above all, I wasn't beholden to anyone.

But while she couldn't have realized it, she'd stabbed her finger right into that old wound. What I'd scarred it over with was really a patch rather than true healing—an illusion of freedom. It was the crutch I needed to get by, and it worked pretty well. I didn't often have to face a reminder that, at heart, I'd given up.

And with Celia on my mind anyway, it had triggered more thoughts of her. I knew she'd felt that same thing. We'd never talked about it, but it had been the basis of the bond between us. Her fantasies of a storybook life as Mrs. Pete Pettyjohn were her own crutch.

Maybe Pete had sensed this, and he hadn't been able to handle knowing that he wasn't enough for her, and that even if he bucked his mother's opposition and married Celia, the marriage would inevitably come crashing down. I'd come to wonder if in his black drunken depressions he'd seized on a way of sheltering them both in the only way he could see.

It was easy to imagine that death would be the cure.

The afternoon was clouding over with dark blue-gray strata, driven by an agitating breeze. At this hour the cemetery was deserted. A lot of people came out to pay their respects after church, but the rush was over. The headstones were mostly small and uniform, laid out in rows with military precision, an exactness found after life ended but rarely available during it. Many were decorated with flowers or wreaths, and some had carefully tended plants growing from the earth.

My father's had none of those things, and I felt a pang of shame. I hadn't been here for a while—more than a year, and now that I thought about it, closer to two. It wasn't a ritual that I observed on any particular dates. Sometimes it felt right, and at other times necessary. I stood there for a minute or so, then walked out into the bleak rolling prairie.

The old man had been like many others of his time and place, genial but distant. He'd grown up on a ranch, and in a way, he'd raised his family like we were stock. As long as things operated smoothly, he let us run, and he busted his ass to make sure we got all of what we needed and some of what we wanted. But like most of those men, he also had an iron-hard edge that you didn't want to cross. By and large, things operated smoothly.

Far and away the most serious time I ever saw that dangerous side of him was a couple of weeks after Celia died. I hadn't been sleeping well. Late on a Saturday night, I heard the house's front door close, the way it had the time she'd come home from her date and lain beside me. Half in a dream, I tiptoed down the hall to the top of the stairs.

My father was just about to walk out the door. He had his service pistol in his hand and was shoving it into his coat pocket.

He turned to look up at me. I'd seen him angry plenty of times, but this was beyond anger. There was a coldness in his eyes that froze me motionless.

Then his face softened—not with love, but with the wry understanding that he'd been caught. He put down the pistol, sat on the couch, and started taking off his boots. I went back to bed, scared and heartbroken. I didn't comprehend what I'd seen, but somehow it brought home the reality that she wasn't coming back.

As I'd gotten older, I had fit the incident into the overall scenario

I constructed. It started with Celia informing Pete that she was pregnant. He knew his mother was dead set against marriage. That left him trapped between the two women in a vise of stress he couldn't handle. I could easily envision Celia taunting him as he waffled, and him losing his head like he had when he'd beaten me at her slight goading—except that this time, he took his rage out on her.

Then his wealthy, powerful family had stepped in to protect the son who carried their lineage and their hopes, quashing an autopsy because it would have shown her pregnancy and injuries not consistent with the supposed cause of death. Their consolation gift to her parents was really a buy-off.

My father had been gone from home all evening before I saw him with the gun—probably drinking. I had come to believe that he'd suspected the cover-up, and had decided to call on Pete or Reuben and find out the truth. But he'd seen me crouched on the stairs and turned back—not from fear of prison or even of getting killed, but from realizing that he still had his family to care for.

He didn't take well to being helpless, and he was stonewalled by powers that he couldn't counter without damaging our lives. The fight seemed to slip out of him after that, and more and more, it was like he was going through the motions. When he learned that he had terminal pancreatic cancer, he seemed almost relieved.

I had to admit that my scenario was pure speculation. I'd never found any tangible reason to believe anything other than that Celia had been thrown by a horse. And while Pete had sentenced himself and carried out the sentence, some part of me wished I'd never awakened that night and stopped my father from whatever truth he might have uncovered.

TWENTY-NINE

The Red Meadow was a no-frills blue-collar bar near the Labor Temple, with a clientele mostly of older men whose hairlines were compressed from wearing cowboy hats or hard hats or military helmets all their lives. It usually got busy at quitting time on weekdays, but right now there were maybe half a dozen regulars talking quietly at tables, holding off the drag of a Sunday afternoon. I liked the Red Meadow fine, but I tended toward places like O'Toole's that had more exotic aspects, such as women, and I came in here only once in a while after work.

Elmer hadn't yet arrived. The bartender, a spry gent of about sixty with a ducktail haircut and a neatly folded apron, greeted me with the old-time saloon keeper's question:

"What's yours, pard?"

It almost made me smile. I told him, laying down one of Balcomb's hundred-dollar bills. I'd brought along several of them, thinking I might have a chance to finish settling up with Sarah Lynn. I didn't want his money in spite of the bullshit he'd put me through, and I'd already decided that if the judge did drop my bail, I was going to send back whatever was left over. But he could damned well buy Elmer and me a few drinks, and I was going to set aside a few more for Slo and for Madbird.

The bartender got out a frosty can of Pabst, poured a generous shot of Makers Mark to go with it, and was just setting down my change when he looked sharply toward the door. His face was not happy. The rest of the room went quiet. I swiveled around.

Bill LaTray, my bail bondsman, was standing there with his granite stare fixed on me.

My feet just about left the floor, from the shock of seeing him, confusion about how the fuck he'd known where I was, and worry over what he wanted.

He didn't come inside and he didn't pay attention to anybody else—just jerked his head in summons and stalked out again.

The bartender's gaze swung back to me. It hadn't gotten any happier, and I realized he figured I was one of Bill's clients. I wanted to say, *Wait, it's not what you think*.

But it was.

I pushed a couple of dollar bills toward him for a tip.

"I'll be right back," I said. I hoped to Christ that was true.

Bill was standing on the sidewalk when I stepped out, wearing his trademark caramel-colored leather coat. He looked like if you hit him with a baseball bat, it would break. His face was an exploded minefield of pockmarks and scars; his eyes were the color of mud. He had on some kind of cologne that got my own eyes watering from five feet away, which was where I stopped.

He cupped a match and lit a rum-soaked crook cigar, inhaling a drag that burned half an inch of it, then crushed the still flaring match between his blunt fingers.

"You blow town, it's gonna cost me twenty-five thousand bucks," he said. "You know what that means?"

"I'm not going anywhere. The charges are being dropped."

"That ain't official till tomorrow. And I hear you got something else on the burner, a lot bigger. So let's get this straight—you're there at the courthouse first thing in the morning."

I'd calmed myself a little by realizing that *how* he'd found me wasn't so mysterious. I'd driven past his pawnshop, only a few blocks away. That was one disadvantage of having a highly visible vehicle like mine. He must have seen it, jumped in his own rig, and caught up with me here.

But the *why* of it was a lot less soothing. If his contacts in the sheriffs' department had told him I was a flight risk, and he was nervous enough about it to chase me down, it suggested that I was still very much on the radar in Kirk's disappearance—that if anything, the heat was rising. They might even have come up with new reasons for suspicion since this morning.

"What did you hear?" I said.

The lit end of the cigar pointed at my face. "Don't bullshit me. You know what I'm saying."

"I'm not bullshitting you. Gary Varna talked to me about Kirk, yeah, but everything seemed OK."

"That's between Gary and you. What I'm telling you is if you don't show, you don't know what trouble is."

That might not have been entirely accurate, but it was true that he made the law look benign.

"I'll be there," I said. "Trust me."

He blew out a contemptuous snort of smoke.

"Let me give you a little advice. Don't never say that to a bondsman."

"Sorry," I said. "It just sort of slipped out."

His stare bludgeoned me a few seconds longer, but then he gave a nod that seemed grudgingly satisfied.

I wanted to find out what he knew, but it was clear he hadn't come here to share information, and I'd heard stories of him punctuating these kinds of warnings with a couple of thumps that would leave a man pissing blood. I started edging toward the door of the bar.

But Bill seemed to relax, his tone turning almost friendly.

"If things go your way tomorrow, your girlfriend got some money coming back," he said. "She can come by the shop and pick it up."

"Thanks, I'll pass that on," I said, remembering unhappily that I'd never returned Sarah Lynn's call.

"Or you could leave it on retainer. Let's say the pop's a hunnert next time."

"What? A hundred *thousand*?"

"Right. That's ten grand up front for me, so we're talking another seven and a half," he said, with an air of cheerful companionship. "Now, if a guy's got trouble coming up with that kind of cash, I'm willing to work with him, but I'd need some collateral. You got a place up Stumpleg Gulch, right?"

"Jesus Christ," I said. "Are you telling me this is about to happen?"

"You never know. I'm just saying you got backup, that's all." He stepped forward abruptly and gave my deltoid muscle a viselike squeeze between his thumb and forefinger. No doubt it was intended as encouraging, but it made me feel like a chicken being sized up for the pot.

My new best friend lumbered away. I walked back into the bar, lightheaded, like I'd just gotten up from a knockout punch and wasn't quite in touch with where I was. I told myself that he didn't really know anything solid. It was perfectly reasonable that he wanted his hat in the ring if a lucrative bond came around. He was just a businessman trying to drum up a little trade.

The bartender hadn't dumped my drinks and eighty-sixed me, thank God. He still seemed wary, but I'd kept my trouble outside, which was the cardinal rule, and the hundred-dollar bill had probably helped.

I downed the shot and chugged half the beer, and bought another of both.

THIRTY

Elmer came in a few minutes later, wearing the pearl gray Stetson he saved for town. He was well known at the Red Meadow—all the men greeted him, and when he came to stand next to me, I could feel my status rise. The bartender brought his drink, a brandy sage, without his having to ask. I'd never known anyone to drink sages and presses—short for Presbyterians—except these kinds of aging westerners. Probably not many bartenders knew how to make them anymore.

When Elmer reached for his wallet, I stopped him, and we went through the little hand-wrestling match that men did in situations like that.

"This is on me," I said. "Least I can do for you taking the time."

"Hell, I was glad for the excuse. Besides, you ain't even got a job anymore."

"Yeah, but I just came into a little windfall."

He put his wallet away, gruffly pleased. I wished I could have told him where the windfall was from—that would have tickled him more still.

The bartender retired to the well to wash glasses, leaving Elmer and me in private.

"I know I'm putting you in an awkward spot," I said quietly.

"Don't you worry about it. If Kirk got in trouble, I'll give you ninety-nine to one there ain't nobody to blame but Kirk. I don't know what all he was up to, but I know some of it wasn't much good. So does Reuben, and probably so do the sheriffs."

"I sure hope so."

He cocked his head to the side and eyed me. "From what you told me, it sounds like you got a notion."

"There's something ugly rustling around out in the bushes, Elmer. That's about all I know at this point, and I've got to be real careful what I say."

"Never mind about that, neither," he said. "You get to be my age, there's more and more you'd as soon not know. Ask what you want and I'll tell you what I can, and that'll be the end of it."

We touched glasses and drank.

"I'm interested in a pair of horses that showed up at the ranch a couple days ago," I said. "Thursday, near as I can tell."

The creases in his forehead deepened. "I didn't hear nothing about it. Thoroughbreds?"

"I don't know, but they didn't go to the new stables. They got put in that calving shed at the north end, and they were gone next morning."

He pushed his hat back with his knuckles. "Well, I promised I wouldn't get nosy, so I won't ask how the hell you know that. But I don't see how it could of got by me."

"Maybe it was set up that way," I said.

I could see that he wasn't just puzzled now—he was real unhappy that something like that had happened on his turf.

"Anybody moving stock on or off the ranch is supposed to come to the office and file a record," he said. "It goes into a computer now, but I don't get along too good with that, so I get a paper copy, too. I look them over every day before I leave, same as I always done. And I'm damn sure there ain't been nothing about horses."

So—it sounded like they'd been sneaked in, probably at night. I doubted Balcomb had brought them himself. Unloading horses from a trailer was no job for somebody who didn't handle them well. It might have been Kirk, or another accomplice, or just a delivery driver who wouldn't have had any reason to suspect anything was out of the ordinary.

But there was still no hint about where they'd been brought from, or why.

"Anything else that's gone on around the ranch that seems, you know, not right?" I said.

" 'Not right,' " he said musingly. "Well, nothing flat-out wrong, at least that I know of. There's plenty that don't make sense to me."

"Such as?"

"Their thoroughbred operation, for one thing. It don't much exist."

I'd been aware of personal tensions on the ranch, but this was the first I'd heard that things weren't going well inside the inner sanctum of the Balcombs' compound. Elmer was the only person I knew who had access to it, and I'd never talked to him about it before.

"I thought that was the whole point of them buying the place," I said.

"That's what they told everybody, all right. Big-time breeding, and selling all over the world. But there ain't any *horses* there, to speak of—just their own two, and a couple it seems like they keep more for show than anything else. Not a one bought or sold yet, or bred, neither. Stands to reason they'd take a while to get started, but it's getting on two years now."

It seemed clear that Balcomb didn't care for horses, and the reason Laurie had given for his wanting to raise them seemed supplied. Still, it was hard to understand why a shrewd businessman would sink a ton of money into a setup and then sit on it. There was plenty of expert help available, and the word was that Laurie's family connections would provide a springboard to the high end of the market. A top thoroughbred could sell for millions of dollars. A stud fee could go well into six figures.

"I guess they must have enough of their own money," I said.

"I guess. The cattle operation pays for itself and then some, but it sure ain't paying for all that new building. Well, I'll double-check about them two horses, Hugh. Balcomb probably just didn't bother to tell me. Seems like the only reason he even keeps me around is so when he gets visitors, he can trot me out like I'm Buffalo Bill or some goddamned thing."

"I can see where that wouldn't sit too well," I said.

He shrugged. "At first I kept thinking I didn't mind too much, but then I started minding *thinking* that, if you know what I mean. Anyway, it just don't feel right any more. I'm about ready to get out—probably should have when it sold. Reuben treated me real good, so I'll get a couple thousand a month as long as I live, plus Social Security and the VA. It's just—"

He lifted his Stetson with his right hand, smoothed back his hair with his left, and replaced the hat, a gesture as unconscious and automatic as breathing. His face looked weary and disturbed.

"That's been my life, pretty much," he said. He raised his glass and drained it, the ice cubes gently rattling. I signaled the bartender for refills.

There went another piece of the real old west.

THIRTY-ONE

I got back to my place about five o'clock, parking down the road in the trees and looping around the back on foot like Madbird and I had done earlier. Everything was quiet and seemed untouched. I was starting to feel the strain from nerves and lack of sleep, and the temptation to crash came down hard on me. But—especially if I was going to end up back in jail soon—I had more ground to cover.

I wanted another look at the calving shed where the horses had been killed, this time with good visibility. And as long as I was at the ranch, I might as well try making a peace offering to Doug Wills, the man I'd fought with yesterday, and take a shot at picking his sullen brain. If I'd had my preference, I'd never have laid eyes on him again. But he was the foreman—out and around the place all the time, handling stock and privy to business dealings—and the other person besides Elmer most likely to know something about those horses.

If I hustled, I could make it to the shed before dusk, but there was still the problem of getting caught. Besides the Balcombs, only a few hired hands lived on the ranch, and none of them would be working now. But somebody might be driving to town or out on another errand.

I'd been thinking hard, and I'd come up with a possible answer— to go around the ranch instead of on it. The shed was just inside the north border. Beyond that lay a couple of miles of empty grazing land, with no roads or people. I knew where I could cut off the highway and cross it—except that darkness would fall long before I could make the hike, and even a four-wheel-drive pickup would be stopped by deadfalls and rock slides. But a motorcycle would be just the ticket.

I went out to the garage my father had built. Occasionally I still worked on the truck or dressed game in there, but mainly I used it for storing stuff like tools and camping gear. It also housed a 1966 BSA Victor that I'd bought in high school for a hundred and fifty bucks. The previous owner had stripped it down into a bastardized dirt bike, a beefy, dinosaur four-banger that couldn't begin to maneuver with the newer two-stroke MX models. But I loved its deep rumble and solid feel, and I'd gotten to where I could horse it around pretty well up hills and over trails. Riding with my friends I was usually last in the pack, but for a couple of summers, I'd had a hell of a good time on it. When I'd gone to college I let it fall into neglect. Then, during my first solitary summer back in Montana, I'd refurbished it, spending weekends learning about the marvels of British engineering and finally turning it over to a pro for fine-tuning. It had been another part of that illusion of freedom, but a good one. For a while I'd ridden a lot, mostly in the back country nearby, where I could cruise for hours on the network of trails and disused roads without seeing a soul. That had fallen off again, but there were a couple of days every summer and fall when taking it out for a spin was the only right thing to do.

This was one of those times, although not for the same reasons.

I topped off the tank and stomped on the kick-starter. I'd taken it out not long ago, and it lit right up. I didn't have license plates for it, which didn't particularly worry me; but I didn't have lights either, which did. Getting that far meant riding on highways, and I'd be coming back after dark. I got my best flashlight, a big bright mag that I carried in the pickup, and duct-taped it onto the handlebars. It wouldn't help much in terms of my seeing the road, but at least oncoming drivers would see me. I stuffed some extra batteries into a rucksack, then added an unopened fifth of Knob Creek bourbon that my crew had given me last Christmas, and that I'd been saving for a special occasion. I hated the thought of wasting it on Doug Wills, but it was the best overture I could think of.

I put on a hooded sweatshirt and a fleece-lined thigh-length brown duck jacket, good protection against wind and rain, and boots with a waterproof Gore-Tex lining. I added a pair of old ski gloves. Anybody who'd ever spent much time on a bike knew that your knuckles would freeze even in comparatively mild weather.

Finally, I rooted around the cabin until I found an old baggie of crosstops, stuffed in a drawer with some other things, like my wedding ring, that I didn't really want to keep but hadn't been able to make myself get rid of. I hadn't touched them in years and you didn't see them around any more, but in the past a lot of working guys had used them—small tabs of clean mild speed, nothing like meth, just enough for a smooth energy charge to get you through a wearying afternoon and a long drive home. I took two and shoved the bag into my pocket.

Heading down Stumpleg Gulch, I got another little glimmer about the way I was starting to think. I'd never been a high-powered investigative reporter, and I hadn't done anything of that kind since I'd left journalism. But I'd spent plenty of time in those days trying to get information from people who didn't want to give it or, if they did, were determined to shade the truth. I'd learned to size up the situation pretty fast when I started an interview, and to tailor my own approach accordingly. It was something I hadn't been comfortable with, like lying to my friends.

But the stakes were way different now, and I was slipping back into it like putting on a well-worn favorite shirt.

THIRTY-TWO

I stashed the Victor in a stand of quaking aspen a quarter mile short of the shed and walked from there. The ride had gone about like I'd expected, starting out in prairie and sparse timber and then getting into rougher country, including one narrow rocky defile that almost turned me back. But the bike had run like a champ, and the reason I'd stopped short wasn't a physical obstacle or worry about somebody hearing me.

The storm-thick sky had brought a premature twilight bearing down on the land, a restless tapestry of shifting clouds, driven by a wind that grabbed at my hair and clothes. Maybe it was only because the lift I'd wanted from the crosstops had kicked in by now, heightening my senses and probably also my imagination. But moving through that kind of weather in that kind of country at dusk was like being in a thrilling dream that hovered on the edge of turning frightening at any second. I had become aware of that feeling early in childhood and had felt it on a thousand occasions since, and I'd never gotten over its message—that extremely powerful forces were aware of my being on their turf, and while they might tolerate me, they didn't like it and they were capable of changing their minds completely at any second.

The instinct that had arisen in me was to pay the toll with respect. That was why I'd decided to hike the last stretch. There was something arrogant about speeding through on a noisy machine. Going on foot was humbler and gave me a deeper appreciation, even awe, of my surroundings. It was a small gesture—I could only hope the thought counted. In general, I spent a fair amount of energy in my daily life trying to find little ways to propitiate those powers in advance for times like this, when I had to cut corners.

The ranch's electric fencing didn't extend this far into the hinterlands—there was just old-fashioned barbed wire strung on posts of lodgepole pine. I climbed over it, waded Lone Creek without taking off my boots, and stopped inside the edge of the sheltering line of trees along the stream.

The shed was about a hundred yards away, a dark bleak mar against the horizon, underscoring the solitude in the way that abandoned signs of human presence sometimes could. Nothing moved in the surrounding stubbly hay fields except some scatterings of alfalfa and timothy that the swather had missed, their fronds dipping and tossing in a submissive little dance to the wind.

When I got there everything looked the same as when Madbird and I had left last night, with the hay bales still at the ambush site. I opened the barn doors to let in light and started prowling. I didn't have any specific ideas of what to look for—only the faint hope of turning up something we'd missed.

He was right about there being shotgun pellets in the walls—I found a few right off. But like the organic residue, they were worthless as evidence—a ranch hand could have been hunting rats or just expressing himself after downing a six-pack or two. It didn't offer any hints about what was behind this, either. I kept looking, but I didn't see anything else that seemed out of place.

I'd been there about ten minutes when I thought I heard a faraway sound deeper than the wind. I strode to the doors. I couldn't see anything new moving out there.

But my eye was caught by a strip of bright blue embedded in the ground a few yards in front of the shed. I'd missed it on my way in—it was tiny and hidden, from most angles, by a ridge of dirt.

A ridge, I realized, that had been made by the Cat's blade.

I knelt beside the blue strip and pulled it free. It was a shred from a nylon tarp—like the one that had been wadded up with the carcasses in the dump.

Then I heard the noise again, a low rumble like an engine's. It might have been a passing plane or even thunder, but I couldn't take the chance. I slammed the shed doors shut and ran in a crouch for the trees. My wet boots were heavy to pick up and slogged down with ankle-turning clumsiness, and the distance seemed a lot longer than a hundred yards. I got behind a good-size bull pine and leaned against it, breathing hard. The sound was clear now, even over the pounding of my pulse. I edged my face out for a look.

Sure as hell, a pickup truck was approaching on the dirt road. It looked like one of the several almost identical gray Fords that belonged to the ranch.

I sagged back against the tree. I couldn't believe that anybody had seen or heard me coming here—the country I'd crossed was as deserted as the dark side of the moon. But it was almost as hard to believe that somebody would happen along, in this blowy Sunday twilight, for any other reason. Maybe I'd tripped some kind of security device I didn't know about. I faded another twenty yards into thicker cover. But I couldn't resist getting a look at who was in that truck.

The driver was just stepping out—a fit-looking man wearing jeans and a cowboy hat pulled low. But I didn't recognize him as any of the hands, and he seemed to walk a little awkwardly, like he wasn't used to his boots.

It was Wesley Balcomb himself.

Ordinarily, he drove a sunburst orange Humvee. I'd never seen him in one of the ranch rigs. The Humvee was a glossy, pristinely kept showpiece—maybe he hadn't wanted to take it over rough dusty roads. But my stronger guess was that he didn't want to be recognized by anybody who might glimpse it.

Instead of going to the shed, he walked away from it until he had a clear view in all directions. Then he turned slowly in a full circle, taking in the wide horizon of what he owned. There was no way in hell he could have seen me, crouched in the timber almost two hundred yards away. But I'd have sworn that his gaze paused for a couple of seconds just after it passed.

I didn't move again until he'd driven away.

THIRTY-THREE

The hired hands' trailers lay deeper into ranch property, but I was able to ride most of the way there still staying outside the boundary. I stopped just short of where the electric fence started. This time when I cut the engine I spent a good long minute listening. The trailer settlement was the one place on the spread where people would definitely be around right now, and the coincidence of running into Balcomb, if that was what it was, had me feeling extra edgy.

No man-made sounds broke the evening stillness. Everybody was probably inside. I climbed the barbed wire again and quietly walked the half mile to the trailers' lights. There were half a dozen double-wides, set far enough apart and shielded by trees to give reasonable privacy. It looked like Doug Wills was home—his big red pickup was parked outside.

I spent another minute thinking about what-ifs. It was all too likely that he'd take one look at me and call the sheriffs to bust me for trespassing, or even try to regain some of the macho turf he'd lost yesterday. I was banking on the good Knob Creek bourbon I'd brought to soften him up. But I was ready to bail out fast, too.

I hyperventilated a few times, then climbed the few steps and tapped on the trailer's flimsy aluminum door.

Doug answered the knock himself. His badly swollen nose stood out like a hazard light, and he had deep purple bruises under both eyes. I swallowed hard and held up the bottle in offering.

"Look, I know you're really pissed at me, and I know I'm not supposed to be here," I said. "I came to apologize." I'd taken that cue from Kirk. Even though I hadn't believed him, it had lulled me into dropping my guard.

Doug glared at me, then at the whiskey, then at me, then at the whiskey again. Finally he took the bottle in his fist and stepped back, leaving the door open.

"All right, I ain't holding any grudges," he said gruffly.

I exhaled quietly in relief, but I stayed wary as I followed him inside. It felt too easy—I'd expected at least a show of teeth. But the fight seemed to be out of him. No doubt the broken nose figured in—that would leave a man sore all over and laboring to breathe for some time to come. And yet, he looked puzzled, distracted, rather than whipped. Maybe it was because in his own mind he'd been the kingpin of his little world, and that idea had been shaken enough for something else to start working its way in.

The trailer's inside was cramped and noisy, with a huge satellite TV screen blaring a reality cop show and kids running around hollering. I knew there were only three, but the place seemed to be full of them. The diaper smell and clutter were the same as I remembered from the time I'd come in to unjam the cheap pocket door to the bathroom.

The living room and kitchen were separated only by a counter, where Tessa—Doug's wife and occasional horizontal passenger in Madbird's van—was chopping vegetables for dinner. She gave me a brief cool stare, but if she recognized me, it didn't show. She was tall and angular, with wide flat hips and a blond shag hairdo bleached almost stiff. Her mouth had a tough set to it and her face would have been prettier with a few corners knocked off. But that made it more attractive in an odd way—for sure, more interesting, with a hint of wildness. I didn't have any trouble seeing why she appealed to Madbird.

Doug walked on to the kitchen, automatically stepping over children and piles of stuff. I stayed just inside the doorway, still nervous that he might pick up a phone or gun. Instead, he got a couple of tumblers from a cupboard and filled them with bourbon. Tessa ignored him completely.

He handed me one of the brimming glasses and went to his chair, gesturing me to another one. But even though things might be OK with Doug, I didn't want to be trapped inside if somebody like one of the Anson brothers showed up, who knew I was trespassing and wasn't inclined to shrug it off.

"Thanks, I'd just as soon stand," I said, and pressed my hand under my heart. "If it makes you feel any better, you damn near broke a couple of my ribs. I don't think anybody ever hit me that hard." That wasn't true, but I could tell it smoothed things over a little more.

"I know you were some kind of boxer," he said. "I never done any of that, but you try riding a two-thousand-pound bull some time."

"I agree absolutely. No comparison."

We both drank. I took a sip, but he knocked back a quarter of his glassful.

"I'd apologize to Mr. Balcomb, too, if I could," I said, careful to refer to him respectfully this time. "I'd like to get my job back. Why was he so mad at me? You know as well as I do he doesn't give a rat's ass about that lumber."

"I don't know. When he called me and told me to stop you, he made it sound like you were running off with the company safe. Then after all that bullshit, I found out it was some old wood—it don't make sense."

He took another long drink. No doubt this figured into his air of puzzlement—realizing that the employer he'd been sucking up to had paid him back by making a fool of him.

"Why, then?" I said. "I never even talked to him before. My crew's been doing fine—no complaints except from those pissant consultants once in a while, and they whine about everything."

"You got that right." Doug set down the glass with a thunk and wiped his mouth with his wrist. "Them fucking accountants back east telling *me* how to run the ranch."

That was the best stroke yet, and I wasn't about to point out that being foreman wasn't exactly running the ranch.

"I'm wondering if Kirk poisoned the well somehow," I said. "Wanted to get rid of me, and got Balcomb—Mr. Balcomb—worked up about that lumber."

"Why would Kirk want to get rid of you?"

"Well, he doesn't like me much, but that's always been true. I don't know—I got this notion that he's up to something and he was nervous I'd stumble onto it." I waited, watching him closely.

Doug shook his head. "Nothing more than usual, least that I know of. I guess he's took off."

"Yeah, I heard."

"Nobody'd pay it any mind, except he's Reuben's kid. Same as here. Everybody else busting their ass from dawn to dark, and all he ever did was fiddle-fuck around."

He drained his glass and stomped to the kitchen. While he refilled it, I noticed Tessa glance at me. This time her gaze seemed more interested. She walked past Doug, ignoring him again, and disappeared into a bedroom. I spent a little quality time with the TV, watching steroid cops busting hookers who were wretched enough to finance their junk habits by blowing guys in cars.

When Doug came back to his chair, he brought the bottle along. It was close to half empty now.

"This ain't bad stuff," he said, and made a halfhearted gesture of offering it to me.

I declined with a wave at my own glass, still almost full.

"Thanks, I'm easing off a hangover. This is plenty."

He sat down heavily, with the contented look of a man who knew he had a pleasant few hours ahead, all the sweeter because he hadn't expected or paid for them.

"You're not the only one who thought that about Kirk," I lied. "I've heard other guys talk about how he had an inside track with Balcomb. It almost seems like they're in on some secret together."

Doug frowned in concentration. "Balcomb don't know his way

around here," he said. "Kirk does. Plus he's a good whipping boy, and Balcomb needs that, too."

It was a sharper insight than I'd expected, but it still didn't do me any good. I tried to phrase another question, but Doug wasn't finished.

"I been watching how it works," he said. "I grew up stupid about that kind of shit, but I'm getting smarter." His head made a disgusted circle that took in the trailer and a whole lot more. "Look at this, and then look at what people like *them* got."

I couldn't fault him for thinking like that. Most people sold out in some way—I'd done it many times. The only question was price. But while he might get smarter, he was never going to develop the natural cunning of someone like Kirk or Balcomb. I was sure he hadn't been hedging his answers to me, and that he didn't have anything to do with the lumber being burned—I hadn't even seen a hint that he knew it had happened.

Just then the biggest of the kids, a grinning gap-toothed four-year-old berserker, lunged across the room and threw himself gleefully against his father's legs. He'd been playing a game that seemed to involve tackling whatever caught his fancy—he'd already taken out his wailing little brother and a laundry basket full of clothes and made impressive assaults on the furniture, all without parental rebuke. Now I braced myself for some yelling and maybe a slap.

But Doug only reached a hand down to catch and steady him as he careened away, paying no more attention than if it had been a newborn calf stumbling around. The gesture was so carelessly gentle and sheltering that it almost stunned me—swept away everything else I'd ever thought about him and left me confused. It was a kind of love, a generosity of spirit even if only toward his own flesh and blood, that was foreign to me.

The mellowing shift of gears didn't last long.

I heard a door open and glanced over toward the sound. Tessa stepped out of the bedroom, wrapped in nothing but a towel. Her legs were very long. I turned away hastily.

"Lord, woman, what the hell you doing, walking around like that?" Doug said, startled harshly out of his comfortable bubble.

"Taking a shower, what's it look like?"

"A shower? At dinnertime?"

Her voice took on an edge that pressed me back against my chair.

"I spend half my *life* trying to keep this place clean. But it's goddamn impossible and I always feel grubby, especially with all the shit *you* track in."

She walked on to the bathroom. Doug, glowering, knocked back another big drink of whiskey. Things probably would have been OK if they'd stayed there.

But Tessa said, archly, "In case you don't know, that's the man who fixed this door, so we could have some privacy."

I swear I wouldn't have looked at her again, but I realized that she was talking about me, and the response was automatic. She smiled over her shoulder, then tugged at the door to close it, but somehow her towel got caught in it and fell to the floor, and she had to kick it free before the panel slid home behind her. Her ass was a little on the generous side, but firm and quite attractive.

Doug saw me see it, and his eyes lit on fire.

"So you could have some *privacy*?" he barked at me.

"No, Doug, so *you* could—your family."

But he was heaving himself up from his chair. I backed ungracefully out onto the trailer's steps. On top of his busted nose and hammered ego and Christ knew how many other hard-ons, plus a bellyful of whiskey to amp them all up, he probably suspected Tessa'd been jumping somebody, and she'd just made me the odds-on candidate.

"Goddammit, it's not what you think," I said, but he kept stomping toward me the way he'd done yesterday, seeming to inflate like an old-time cartoon villain, while I felt myself shrinking like one of those mice. I hopped down the stairs and took off. I was in trouble enough for what I *had* done, and I wasn't about to get my ass kicked for what I hadn't.

As I trotted away, I caught a glimpse of the clothesline. There was just enough light around for me to recognize that rose-colored thong flying in the breeze like the defiant flag of a small republic, declaring its independence.

I was going to have to tell Madbird that while he might be done with the construction project, his services were still in demand out here.

THIRTY-FOUR

As I rode to Helena I started getting into a drizzle that turned the pavement slick and the visibility poor. With just the flashlight duct-taped to the handlebars, I stayed on back roads and streets, making my way toward the area around the county courthouse. It seemed I'd been spending a lot of time there lately. The neighborhood was old and largely working class, although some younger professionals involved in the Montana version of gentrification were moving in. There was also a substantial element of small-time criminals, conveniently residing close to the jail. It couldn't have been much more different from the pristine country where Kirk had grown up, but it was where his girlfriend Josie lived, and he'd moved in with her when the ranch was sold.

I hardly knew her, mainly just to nod and say hi when I'd seen her out with Kirk. She hadn't grown up around here—I had it in my head that she was from the coast, Seattle or Portland. She was about twenty-five, with shoulder-length brown hair and a small slim build, quite pretty in an anorexic way—the kind of girl you'd see sitting at a bar on a summer afternoon, wearing cutoff jeans and a tank top with a little bow, and she'd seem fresh and appealing and amusingly smart-mouthed. But in time you'd notice the dark circles under her eyes as her makeup wore thin, and how she started seeming a lot older than her years, and that the tantalizing patter was never going to go anywhere except toward what was in this for her. When I was younger, I'd been quite good at not catching on to that sort of thing. It had taken me on some rides, but I couldn't recall one that hadn't turned out sour or outright troublesome.

The only time I'd exchanged more than a casual hello with Josie had been on a night several months back, when she'd come up to me in O'Toole's and asked if I'd seen Kirk. He must have been off on one of his runners. When I told her no, she said he was supposed to pick her up hours ago, and she was tired and wanted to crash, and would I drive her home? As soon as we'd gotten into my truck, she'd started asking me to make other stops—first at a convenience store for cigarettes, then at somebody's house where she probably scored some dope, and then she'd wanted to go to another bar. Instead, I'd driven straight to her and Kirk's place and stayed behind the wheel while she pouted her way inside. Back at O'Toole's, it wasn't long before I saw her come in again. But that time, she looked right through me as she walked past. I hadn't run into her since.

There was no reason to expect that she'd be happy to see me. I was starting to realize that a lot of people weren't. But she was bound to know some things about Kirk's drug dealings, and I'd been thinking more and more about Madbird's guess that that might have been how the horses were used. If the shred of nylon I'd found at the shed had come from the tarp wadded up with their carcasses, it suggested that the Cat had picked it up and carried it to the dump along with them. I was wondering if Balcomb had put the tarp down to keep from losing any cargo in the swamp that their blood and entrails would have made on the shed's dirt floor.

Josie's apartment was on the second story of a run-down frame house on Ewing Street. I pulled the Victor up to the curb, shut it down, and sat for a minute, absorbing the neighborhood's own peculiar kind of desolation. It was closed in by steep hills, with the buildings packed tightly together, giving it the secretive feel of an older time and place. The lights of the tree-lined streets were dim and the windows heavily curtained, with no signs of activity and no sounds but the faint patter of rain and the rumble of a car with a shot muffler passing a few blocks away. I knew there were plenty of people and plenty going on around me, but everything was hidden inside the walls, working by its own rules, apart from the rest of the world and wanting to keep it like that. The sense was similar in a way to what I'd felt approaching the ranch—that I was an intruder being watched, but not by any*body*. The difference was that out in that wild country, it had been exhilarating. This was a lot less pleasant.

The building's outside entrance was unlocked. It gave into a little hallway with a mailbox and a shadowy staircase leading up to the door of the apartment. I hadn't been able to tell if Josie was home— her windows, like most of the others around, were covered and barely lit. But she must have either been watching outside or heard me on the stairs, because the door opened against its chain before I raised my fist to knock.

Her face appeared in the gap. She looked wary, like she didn't remember me, which was entirely possible. Then again, maybe it was because she did—or because she'd learned that I was under suspicion in Kirk's disappearance.

I said, "Hi, Josie."

"Kirk's gone."

"I know. That's why I came by."

"Did you hear something?" she said sharply.

"Nothing besides that. I need to talk to you. It won't take long."

Her eyes narrowed. "What about?"

"I had a run-in with Wesley Balcomb. I need help figuring some things out."

"So this isn't because you're worried about Kirk, right?" she said, with chilling precision and speed.

"Hell, yes, of course I'm worried about him. If I do any good, it could—you know—" I floundered, and finished up, "Help him, too."

Her face relaxed into a calculated look. It was oddly more natural.

"Come on in," she said.

She didn't look so pretty tonight. She was wearing a University of Montana Grizzlies football sweatshirt so big and baggy that she seemed lost inside it like a little kid, and skinnier than ever. The sleeves came down to her fingertips—she kept fidgeting, pushing them up to her wrists, but they'd flop loose again immediately. I suspected they were hiding track marks. Her face was tense and twitchy, and her nostrils had a raw peeled look.

The apartment was a train wreck, but not a comfortable kind of organic mess like at Doug's trailer. The pastel blue paint on the walls had peeled in patches to reveal a mosaic of previous colors, and the carpet, a green-orange shag that screamed remnant sale, was stained and cigarette-burned and trodden down to a dismal mat. The room reeked of smoke, with an undercurrent of decay from the kitchen or the plumbing or God knew what else.

But that all went with the turf. The jarring element lay in the newer things. For openers, Josie was sporting a diamond engagement ring like you'd see on rich widows in Miami, with one stone the size of a chickpea surrounded by several smaller ones. I was no judge of that kind of thing, but they gave off the kind of sparkle that I didn't think came from paste.

There was a full-blown home entertainment center with a TV even bigger than Doug's, plus a DVD and a VCR and a stereo and all the other bells and whistles, encased in a slick cabinet set. A new leather couch that they must have had a hell of a time getting up those stairs took up most of one wall. A couple of large western-theme paintings were hung above and around it, the kind of imitation Charlie Russells that were one step this side of black velvet, but that sold for ungodly prices in rustic art galleries.

And clothes. The front closet was so packed with coats and boots that the door wouldn't close. Jeans and tops trailed off the furniture onto the floor and formed a path to the bedroom. Pretty much everything, to be blunt, looked slutty. But most of it was new, too—some of the items still had tags.

The strong implication was that she'd been living low to the ground, then suddenly had come into a chunk of cash and tried to buy some class. But she didn't know how, so she'd retreated to filling up the place with the familiar security of clothes.

The psychology involved didn't particularly interest me. What did was the more tangible matter of where that money had come from—not just for all this, but for Kirk's new Jeep and guns and other pseudo-military toys. I was sure that Josie didn't have a job, and there was no way Kirk's salary went that far. Maybe it had come from his family, although he'd done plenty of barroom pissing and moaning about his father's stinginess. Maybe they'd bought it all on credit.

Maybe.

Josie turned to me with her arms folded and a no-bullshit stare. Her mouth was a tight line turned down at the corners.

"Look, I don't know where Kirk is or what's going on," she said. "I'll talk to you, but you got to do something for me, too. He didn't leave me any money, man. There's no food here, I'm starving."

It looked like coyness wasn't going to figure into this, which was good. I opened my wallet, thinking I'd give her a twenty. But I'd had only a few bucks of my own to start with, and out of the hundred-dollar bill I'd put down at the Red Meadow, only some singles, a couple of fives, and a fifty were left. Elmer and I hadn't drunk much, but I'd been careful to take care of the bartender—who in return had topped our glasses to the brim and bought us a round, the way it ought to be—and a shot of good bourbon wasn't cheap these days even at a place like that.

I wanted Josie in a cooperative mood, and it was Balcomb's cash anyway, so I set the fifty on top of a clothes pile, making sure she saw the denomination. Instead of being impressed, she looked at it like a waitress in a classy restaurant would look at a two-bit tip. I shouldn't have been surprised. I'd seen it often enough, people who'd never had to earn money thinking that people who did should throw bushels of it at them.

"What do you want to know?" she said. Now she seemed impatient.

"What did Kirk—" I caught myself, and coughed into my hand to cover. "What does Kirk have to say about Wesley Balcomb?" I breathed a silent thanks that I'd screwed up with her and not someone who might have noticed. I was going to have to watch it.

"Not much," Josie said. "Back when he first started that job, I asked him about it a couple of times, and he told me to shut up. So I stopped."

"Why won't he talk about his job? Most guys do."

"Maybe he just doesn't want to, OK? Maybe Mr. Balcomb told him not to."

"Did Kirk tell you that?"

"I said maybe." Her impatience was getting clearer.

"Did you ever get the feeling that Kirk and Balcomb were into something together?" I said.

"Like what?"

"Like dope, big-time?"

Her eyes widened in disbelief. Then she snorted with what seemed to be genuine amusement.

"You gotta be kidding." But it wasn't so much a denial as, *You think I'd tell you?*

"Everybody knows he's into crank, Josie," I said. "And all this expensive stuff here—a guy's got to wonder. If I was a cop, I sure would."

A trace of alarm softened her tough look.

"What the fuck's it to you?" she said.

"Let me worry about that. We made a deal."

"I didn't make any deal to get set up, man."

"I've got nothing to gain by setting you up, for Christ's sake. I'm trying to help myself."

"Kirk never sells dope," she said emphatically.

"Yeah? But he must buy it. Enough for two people, huh."

She shrugged, her face hardening again. *Read the mail, asshole.*

"So where's all that money coming from?" I said.

"Hey, I don't have time for this bullshit," she said, and stepped forward, reaching for the fifty.

I grabbed it first. "All right, you can tell the sheriffs instead," I said. "If Kirk doesn't show up quick, you better believe they're going to have your little tits in the wringer."

She caught my arm before I got to the door, with a pleading expression that I translated as *God, I'm sorry, I'm so fucked up I can't think.*

"I'm really scared," she whispered. "I think he's gone for good."

I put one arm around her and let her sob a few times against my shoulder. I didn't doubt that she genuinely cared for Kirk, or that she *was* scared for all kinds of reasons, including her future. Going back home probably wasn't an option. Kirk's family wasn't going to help her out, and her friends were all like her.

But right this minute, I was pretty sure that she was mostly scared I was going to walk out the door with that fifty-dollar bill.

"Let me tell you again, Josie, I'm not out to take anybody down," I said. "Just to stay above water myself."

She nodded and pulled away, wiping her eyes with her sleeves.

"Will you still leave me that money?" she sniffled.

"Yeah. Now let's go back to where Kirk's been getting his."

The way she hesitated seemed a touch dramatic.

"Panning gold," she said.

"*What?*" The thought of Kirk Pettyjohn panning gold was arguably the most preposterous thing I'd ever heard. There was nothing he'd hated more than physical work.

Her mouth took a sulky twist, like she knew how it sounded, but her eyes were stubborn.

"It's a major secret, OK?" she said. "That's why I didn't want to tell you. If it gets out, people will move in on him."

"I'll keep it quiet. Just give me a general idea of what he does."

"He goes someplace for a couple of days and gets the gold, then sells it and comes home with money."

Sure. Nothing to it. That was why there were so many small-time miners all over the state driving around in Rolls-Royces. There was also the fact that liquidating mineral ore tended to be a lot more complicated than walking in someplace with a sackful of it and walking back out with cash.

"Who's he sell it to?" I said.

"He never told me."

"How often does he go?"

"Every couple of months. Except, you know, like January and February."

"When did he start this?"

"I don't know exactly. After he moved in here."

"Do you ever go with him?"

She shook her head, managing to toss her hair at the same time.

"I don't even know where it is, man."

I might have been able to push her farther, but she was getting that fuck-you edge again. It was like one of those old inflatable Joe Palooka dolls that kids used to pound on—it would keep springing back up many more times than I could knock it down. And it added to the distaste that I felt anyway.

Then, abruptly, I glimpsed the subconscious reason that I'd judged her harshly. I didn't so much dislike her—I resented her, and I had since the first time I'd seen her with Kirk.

Reuben Pettyjohn was in his seventies now. Kirk had been the only surviving heir. When Reuben died, the purse strings that he kept such a tight hold on would finally come open. And if Kirk had married Josie, or if they'd had a child, a big piece of that fortune would have fallen to her.

But deep in my mind, absurd but unshakable, lay the conviction that it rightfully should have gone to Celia. Every time I'd ever looked at Josie and known that she was likely to get it instead, I'd felt a little stab in my guts. Seeing her in action tonight sure hadn't added any new respect.

I decided I'd process her information and come back if it seemed worth pushing farther.

"One more question," I said. "When was the last time Kirk made one of those runs?"

"Three, maybe four weeks."

"OK," I said, and held the fifty toward her. "You keep quiet about this, too, huh?"

She pulled it from my hand with a roll of her eyes that said, *finally*.

I'd gotten about halfway down the stairs when I heard her call, "Hey."

I paused and looked back up. She was standing in the apartment doorway with her hands on her hips.

"My tits aren't that little," she snapped. "They look that way when I'm dressed, 'cause I have a very slender rib cage. My doctor says it's 'exquisite.'"

She disappeared behind the door and slammed it, returning the stairwell to shadows.

THIRTY-FIVE

When the south end of Last Chance Gulch had been turned into a mall, some of the grand old commercial buildings had been torn down and others had been revamped for purposes like legislative and law offices. But a few still stood pretty much untouched.

Reuben Pettyjohn owned one of those.

I was thinking more and more that Kirk had been handling drugs in some big-time way. At a stretch, I could see Balcomb involved financially. It was even conceivable that on Kirk's supposed gold-panning runs, he really picked up a pair of dope-loaded horses each time and brought them back to the ranch. But he hadn't left town for the past few weeks, unless Josie was lying, and I was sure she didn't know or care enough about this to go to the trouble. I couldn't believe, either, that horses had been getting slaughtered routinely on the ranch without somebody catching on.

I wanted to see Reuben even less than I'd wanted to see Josie or Doug. Although he and I were on cordial terms, there was plenty of strain between us because of Celia and there'd be more now. And of all the deceiving I'd done, lying face-on to the father of the man I'd killed would be the worst.

Then there was the fact that it was really tough to put anything past Reuben. If he was willing to talk to me, I'd probably give away more than I got. But he knew more about that ranch than everybody else put together, and he was far too shrewd not to be aware that Kirk had been living beyond his means.

It was worth a try.

Reuben's building, at six stories, was the tallest among its neighbors and gave an unimpeded view in all directions, with the town spread out at its feet. He'd always kept offices there, and he had often worked late hours, what with the terms he'd served in the state legislature and his many business interests, so he'd had the top floor turned into an apartment—not a luxury penthouse, just a sensible convenience. But it also had been handy for entertaining his drinking and gambling pals, and, according to rumor, occasional lady visitors.

After Pete's death, Reuben had gotten out of politics and become less active in business, but when he sold the ranch, he'd moved to the apartment full time. I probably wouldn't have known this except that Elmer had mentioned it, bemused by Reuben's choice. City people moving out to the country might want rustic, but when those old cowboys finally came in from the cold, they tended to go for modern suburban-style houses that didn't have many stairs to climb, were easy to maintain, and had lots of gas heat and electric lights and all the other fingertip conveniences they'd spent their lives without.

My own guess was that Reuben wanted to live there because it was the last place left where he could gaze down and be reminded of the empire he'd once had. That was pretty much history now, except for numbers in bank accounts and some scattered properties. It must have been hard to take, and harder still that he himself was approaching past tense. A new generation of politicians and movers and shakers had come along, and while men like him might be remembered the way kids admired a baseball legend like Babe Ruth, more and more they were old and in the way.

Downtown was dead on this drizzly Sunday evening. The neon signs in the windows of O'Toole's and the Rialto offered the reality of liquor and the mirage of a safe haven, and there'd be a few people inside taking in both. But the rain-slick sidewalks, glistening with reflected light from the streetlamps, were empty.

It looked like Reuben was home—there were lights on behind the top-story windows. But I hadn't thought through the elementary problem of getting inside. The lobby that gave access to the ground-floor shops and the elevator was locked. I couldn't very well stand on the street and throw pebbles. I started walking to the Rialto, the closest pay phone I could think of. I didn't have his number and I wasn't sure he'd be listed, but I didn't see any other possibilities. At least it would warm me up for a minute.

Then I remembered something from my early teen days, a sort of small-town urban legend—that when Reuben had built the apartment, he'd had a buzzer put in around the building's rear so his girlfriends could come and go without being seen. As kids, we'd been fascinated by this concept we understood nothing about except that it involved the looming lure of sex. We'd checked and confirmed that the buzzer existed, although nobody I knew ever had the balls to push it. You didn't play those kinds of tricks on Reuben Pettyjohn.

It was still there, inside the alcove of the service entrance—one of those old intercom systems with a doorbell-type button and a little round grille to talk into. It looked like it hadn't been used since I'd last seen it at age eleven or twelve.

Without any faith, I pressed the button. I waited half a minute, pressed it again, waited a few seconds longer, and was just stepping out of the alcove when a raspy, static-edged growl made me jump.

"Am I hearing things, or is somebody there?"

Even with the crackling, it was easy to recognize the voice.

I leaned down to talk close into the chest-high grille.

"It's Hugh Davoren, Reuben. I wondered if you could spare a minute."

There was a brief pause. I didn't think he was ever taken by surprise, but this probably came close.

"Well, hello, Hugh. I'll be glad to visit with you, but goddamn, I don't believe I've used this thing in twenty years. Let me try buzzing you in. If it don't work, ring again and I'll come down."

The buzzer jumped to life with a sort of snapping sound, like it was startled to be roused out of its own long sleep. The service door opened at my push.

I walked through a back storage room and then the main hallway. The interior of this place hadn't been fancified or restored—the woodwork was scarred; the plaster was chipped; and the marble floor, while clean and polished, was badly worn. The elevator creaked like something in a spooky old movie, and by the time it came down from his apartment, picked me up, and got back again, I could have climbed the stairs faster. Reuben certainly had the money to upgrade, and he would have drawn higher prices for the spaces he rented out. But maybe the antiquated feel was part of what he was hanging on to.

The top-floor hallway was like a smaller version of the lobby below. Reuben hadn't converted it—just built his digs around the perimeter. It was lined with paneled, transomed doors that once would have served individual offices. All were long disused except for one toward the east end that was open, revealing a parallelogram of dim light from inside.

When I got there, I could see right off that this was the room Reuben mainly lived in. A comfortable blaze of split larch was burning in a stone fireplace. An antique rifle and a pair of crossed sabers, probably dating back to his grandfather's Civil War days, were on display above the mantel. The walls were hung with several paintings, and these were the real thing—fine old oils, a couple of them looking like they might have been genuine Charlie Russells or Frederic Remingtons. A rich antique Persian rug covered most of the hardwood floor.

Reuben was sitting in a worn old recliner, tilted back with his feet propped up, facing the panorama of the lighted city and the dark countryside beyond. He was grizzled now, his beaky face lined and worn, but he still possessed the power that wasn't so much dynamic as a kind of gravity. A line from *Julius Caesar* used to come into my head when I thought of him: "Why, man, he doth bestride the narrow world like a Colossus."

Nobody had ever questioned Reuben's fairness or integrity, but nobody had ever accused him of being a particularly nice guy, either.

He drove a hard bargain, and he had no objection to walking over people if that was what it took. He rewarded loyal service like Elmer's, but he demanded a lot in return. The vast majority of the time, he got what he wanted.

He had been a tough act for his sons to follow, and he hadn't been easy on them when they didn't measure up. He hadn't been easy on his wife, Beatrice, either, and there were people who thought that had hastened the onset of her Alzheimer's disease. Eventually, she'd gotten to where she had to be watched every minute—she'd do things like run away on foot in her nightgown, in winter, and everybody would have to go out searching for her, fearful that she'd freeze to death. When Reuben sold the ranch to the Balcombs, he'd finally put her in a home.

He raised a hand in greeting as I stepped into the room. I'd expected a combative edge, but his look seemed oddly gentle. He was wearing a maroon robe with velvet lapels, and slippers. His knotty calves were mottled with blue veins.

"I apologize for intruding on you, Reuben," I said.

"If I didn't want you here, I'd have told you. Get yourself a drink."

One wall of the room was taken up by a handsome old bar that must have been salvaged from a saloon and reassembled up here. The back bar was ornate hand-carved cherrywood, stocked with every kind of liquor, but a dark green bottle of Lagavulin scotch was set out in front. He was rolling an old-fashioned glass of it slowly between his hands. That appeared to be his only other company. Reuben wasn't the kind of man to want people caring for him when he was wounded. He'd run them off and hole up alone until he got through it.

I took another old-fashioned glass from a shelf and poured a splash of the scotch. It tasted like bottled smoke, and burned from my insides out, right through the evening's cold and wet.

Although he'd hardly ever known me as anything but a kid and we hadn't run into each other for a couple of years, Reuben started right off like we were old friends continuing a personal conversation.

"I'm confused, Hugh. I don't like admitting that."

I took another, bigger, swallow of scotch.

"When you're young, you sketch a picture of who you figure you're going to be," he said. "You color it in as you go along, and of course, it don't turn out like you thought. You look back and see a lot of things you could have done better, and some you wish like hell you hadn't done at all. But I always had the notion that a man was entitled to that, if he put himself out hard enough in other ways."

I caught only a glimmer of his meaning. Clearly, he'd given it a lot of thought.

"I'm afraid that's beyond my grasp," I said.

"Mine, too, I guess. Maybe that's what I'm supposed to learn—I never ought to let myself think like that in the first place."

I groped for another response that wouldn't sound entirely stupid, but came up empty. Reuben kept rolling his scotch glass between his hands. He didn't seem to be drinking so much as using it as a crystal ball.

"All right, you didn't come here to listen to an old man drool in his whiskey," he said. "I assume it's about Kirk."

"This is touchy, Reuben."

"I've got a pretty good layer of callus, son."

"I stopped by to see Josie," I said. "She said Kirk's been making all his money by panning gold."

Reuben's face swung toward me. His expression was probably just about the same as mine had been when I'd heard that from her.

"And she believes it?" he said.

"She seems to. I don't think she's, you know, overly critical."

His lips twisted sardonically and his head sank back against the chair.

"She didn't know where he was going to do the panning, or at least she wouldn't tell me," I said. "I wondered if you had any idea."

Reuben stayed quiet for a good long minute—eyes open and seemingly gazing out the window, but he was obviously weighing this further. He was too realistic not to have accepted by now that

Kirk had met with either an accident or violence. My coming here and asking about this was a red flag on top of the suspicion already hanging over me. And he no doubt saw already that I hoped to divert that suspicion by coming up with other reasons why Kirk might have gotten in trouble—by linking him to something illegal, which would harm him if he was still alive and reflect badly on the Pettyjohn family in any event.

"Well, maybe that explains something," Reuben finally said.

He spoke on at some length—measuring his sentences carefully but without any gamesmanship, and answering my occasional questions without reluctance. I'd been pleasantly surprised that he hadn't dismissed me outright, and I was almost startled at his being so forthcoming.

But what really threw me was that right up to the last, I was braced for him to demand whether I knew anything about Kirk, or at least why I was asking what I asked.

All he said as I was leaving was, "Stop by again, Hugh."

THIRTY-SIX

When I got down to the empty wet street, my crosstop high was fading and I was starting to drag. I entertained a brief notion of going to Sarah Lynn's, giving her the rest of her money, and apologizing for not calling her. It was strange—of all the things I felt bad about, that was the one that kept coming up in my mind. And in there, too, of course, was the thought that maybe this time she'd take me in. But pushing it would be a mistake. I decided I'd do it tomorrow, instead—go see her at work, with a dozen roses and a dinner invitation.

I started the bike and headed homeward into thin night rain that stung my face, thinking over what Reuben had told me.

Back during the days when oil was first being recognized as black gold, a fair amount of drilling had started in the northern part of the state. Reuben's father had taken a stab at getting in on the action and had acquired a few bits of land. Nothing much had come of it—most of the operations had decayed to rusting skeletal derricks out in desolate fields, now worth only the scrub grass they might grow to graze a few head of cattle. Reuben leased out the rights for a pittance and otherwise paid no attention to them.

But soon after he'd sold the ranch to Balcomb, Kirk had approached him respectfully and asked for ownership of a particular one, in an area called the Sweet Grass Hills. It was a pretty spot beside a creek, with a shack on it. He claimed that he'd gotten interested in prospecting and wanted to fix the place up and nose around.

"I didn't much buy it," Reuben had said. "There used to be some gold mining up around there but it got picked clean years ago, and he knew it. He never gave a hoot in hell about anything like that, anyway. I figured more likely he was hoping to convince me he was finally amounting to something, so I'd start cutting him some cash."

Still, Reuben had signed the place over to him, and arranged to cover building materials and other expenses. He hadn't tried to explain why to me, but I understood. With all the anger, guilt, and grief that had pervaded that family, with Pete's suicide and Kirk's worthlessness, it was Reuben's last-ditch attempt to salvage Kirk as his son and himself as Kirk's father.

We hadn't talked about the obvious implications, either. The place was only a few miles south of the Canadian border, deep in a region that was barely populated and virtually roadless. The official crossing points were at least fifty miles apart, with no settlements in between. Border agents didn't have nearly enough manpower to patrol it all effectively, and the only barrier across the vast empty fields was a standard barbed-wire fence. It was so vulnerable there had even been a public-service TV commercial urging ranchers to keep a watch for terrorists, who, as a friend of mine had put it, could skip across in their jockstraps.

You couldn't ask for a better setup to run contraband.

The Victor didn't have a rearview mirror, but I was careful to keep tabs on what was behind me with quick, frequent glances over my shoulder. Traffic was light tonight, and nobody tried to pass me until I got a few miles east of town, out beyond the reservoir. Then I realized that a vehicle was gaining on me fast.

My first thought was that I'd been spotted by a cop. But it didn't turn on flashers, and as it got closer, I was able to see that the headlights were high and far apart, like on the oversize pickups called duallies. With somebody driving that kind of rig in a hurry and me without even a taillight, I was asking for it. As soon as I spotted a place to turn out, I hit my brakes and skidded into it.

The other vehicle roared past a few seconds later—a tow truck, probably driven by a guy who'd had to handle a wet Sunday evening emergency, was grumpy about it, and wanted to get back to his nice warm house.

The road was mostly straight for the next couple of miles, and while the tow truck gained a comfortable lead on me, its taillights stayed in sight. I didn't pay much more attention to it at first—just assumed that it would turn off. But it kept on going toward Canyon Ferry. I started to get puzzled. I hadn't gotten a good look at its logo, but I was pretty sure there was nobody living out this way who ran a tow operation. Maybe there'd been a freak wreck. Maybe the driver had a girlfriend out here.

Maybe Kirk's Jeep had been found.

That thought hit a lot harder than the worry about a cop. But it was next to impossible. The water was deep enough at that spot so you couldn't see the bottom even in clear daylight. In this weather the surface was choppy and murky, and the Jeep was black besides. There were hardly any people around at all, and for sure no swimmers. Searchers could have found it by dragging, but there was no reason to look there.

The last stretch of road before the lake came into sight was hilly and twisty. In spite of my rationales, I braced myself for coming over the final rise and seeing a cluster of flashing lights on the far shore.

Everything was dark over there. I exhaled with relief.

But the tow truck was still moving in that direction, approaching the bridge. Queasiness rose in my guts again—the fear that something else had turned up to arouse the suspicion of the authorities. I couldn't imagine how a tow would figure in, but this was too unsettling to just brush off.

The curves were slowing the big truck down. I knew that road almost literally well enough to drive it blindfolded, and the rain had pretty well let up by now. I switched off my jerry-rigged headlight and sped up. The truck came in and out of sight through the tight curves beyond the village. Without hesitating, it passed the place where Kirk and I had fought, and, a half mile farther, the submerged Jeep. Relief washed over me again. The driver was probably headed to Townsend or White Sulfur Springs or some other place east of here.

But when the rig got to Stumpleg Gulch the taillights brightened suddenly—braking. The bright amber cab-top flashers went on and it turned up the road toward my cabin.

This time I got a jolt of flat-out alarm. None of my few neighbors would ever call for a tow—they had their own heavy equipment and mechanical skills. There hadn't been a wreck up there throughout my entire lifetime.

I followed at a careful distance. As I got close to my place, I started to see more lights pulsing faintly in the night sky. It was eerie, like an alien spacecraft had landed in there.

The new lights were red and blue.

A sheriff's cruiser was parked at my gate facing the road, in position to intercept anyone who came along. I could see at least one more flasher through the trees, near my cabin.

I pulled the bike off the road and cut the engine.

The deputy at the gate got out and walked to the tow truck. In the headlights, I recognized the tall lanky shape of Gary Varna. He talked to the driver for half a minute, then stepped back from the window. The truck drove on toward my cabin. Gary got back in his cruiser, made a one-eighty, and followed.

I stayed where I was, poleaxed by the realization of what was happening.

They were impounding my pickup truck.

The implications came fast and hard. Along with the fact that Gary himself was here, it meant that they'd come up with a serious cause, and it had to have just happened. But what in hell could have triggered it at nine o'clock on a rainy Sunday night? All I could think was that they'd received new information—say, from somebody I'd talked to, who'd told them I'd been nosing around about Kirk. Not Elmer or Reuben, for sure. Doug, maybe, but I doubted it—besides, he hadn't even seemed to know I was under the gun.

That left Josie. Lights in my head started blinking on. Gary Varna had mentioned that she had a couple of drug charges pending. I could just see her picking up the phone as soon as I'd left her place and calling the sheriffs to cut a deal—ratting me off in return for special consideration with her own problems.

And then she'd probably stuffed my fifty bucks into her supposedly not-so-little bra and burned ass out the door to buy some crank.

A rush of anger at her and shame at my own stupidity heated my face. I squeezed my eyes shut and clamped my teeth together, trying to throw it off. What mattered right this minute was what the fuck I was going to do right this minute. This new turn of events was a different order of business. I'd known in an abstract way that it was on the horizon, but I hadn't let myself believe it could happen so soon.

I had to think that if Gary was going this far, he was planning to arrest me, too—have his deputies keep checking the place tonight, or leave a man here. The straight-up thing to do would be to ride on through the gate and cooperate respectfully with the powers that rode herd on human life. Maybe I was wrong and he'd leave me free, and I could keep on bluffing. There was still a chance I could dig up enough information to bolster my claim of self-defense or at least mitigate my sentence. But if not, my bail—if there even was one—would be astronomical, like Bill LaTray had said. With that and legal fees, I could kiss everything I owned good-bye, including my place, and I was back to the scenario of being up against Balcomb's lawyers.

Or I could become an official fugitive—go someplace far away and take on a new identity. But I'd been hopeless enough at that years ago, when I'd been younger, more malleable, and not wanted by the law. At this point in my life, I just couldn't see myself inventing a radically new Hugh.

There was a third course. I could sneak away and stay free till morning—pretend I hadn't known they were looking for me and I'd spent the night someplace else. It was silly, like a kid trying to dodge an inevitable disciplining. But I couldn't see that I had anything to lose, and it would give me a few more precious hours of freedom.

Only minutes ago, I'd been anxious to get someplace warm and dry. Now I wished I could wander through the rainy night woods forever.

THIRTY-SEVEN

After Gary's cruiser and the tow truck disappeared into the woods toward my cabin, I swung the Victor around and started pushing it back downhill through the trees. They were probably out of hearing range by now, but the bike made a pretty good growl starting up, and Gary might even have a lookout posted. The grade steepened in another fifty yards—I could hop on and coast, then kick it into gear when I was ready and let gravity turn the engine over quietly.

But just as I was about to jump on, I heard the drone of another motor behind me.

The bare-wire nerves I'd been running on took over. I shoved the bike a few steps into some brush, laid it down, and dropped flat beside it. Even as I hit the ground, I realized that trying to hide was idiotic. The sheriffs had spotted me, and this was one more nail in the lockbox of guilt that was forming around me, a nail I'd driven myself.

But no lights showed—no flasher, no searchlight, not even headlights. Still, the engine's sound got louder.

I sighted the vehicle a few seconds later—an unlit silvery shape on the road, at first barely visible in the darkness, then coming more into focus as it neared. Confusion overlaid my panic. It wasn't a sheriff's car or anything else that registered with me. As it passed, I made it out as some kind of SUV, a fairly new model. I started thinking it must belong to an off-duty deputy or maybe a volunteer.

But the pale blur of the driver's face seemed to be fixed straight ahead, not scanning to the sides. And something—not details I could see clearly, but the posture and the way the hands gripped the wheel at ten and three—gave me the strong sense of a woman.

A connection clicked in my mind, one that was so absurd I dismissed it as fast as it appeared. But as I stared after the fading silvery shape, it came back and stayed.

Laurie Balcomb in her new Mercedes toy.

I heaved the bike upright and stomped on the kick-starter—the hell with caution, although part of my brain screamed that there was no way it could be Laurie, it was a sheriff, and not only was I about to throw myself in jail, I was going batshit.

The SUV was creeping along with an occasional brief flash of brake lights, feeling the way down the tricky, night-bound gravel road. I came in behind it close and fast, hunched low over the handlebars, hoping I could identify the make without being seen. If it wasn't a Mercedes, I'd fade again. I had to wait for the brakes to give the taillights their next red glow before I could get a glimpse.

Sure as hell, the emblem on the rear door was that trisected circle. I'd never seen another vehicle like that around here. Certainly no cop could afford one.

What with the darkness and the high seat headrests, I couldn't get a good look inside. But I couldn't let it go. I swung around to the left, goosed the bike's throttle, and pulled up beside the driver's window.

For just a second, like when I'd seen Laurie on horseback yesterday, I got that prickly sense that I was looking at Celia.

Laurie swiveled toward me, her mouth opening. She looked scared to death—I must have seemed like a disembodied head appearing out of nowhere.

I called out, "Pull over." But the window was closed and she didn't seem to hear me—just kept staring.

"*Stop*, goddammit, you're going to crash," I yelled, and thumped the window with the heel of my hand. She jerked away as if that snapped her out of her daze, and she braked so hard I had to drag my left foot to stop along with her.

Her window slid down. If she recognized me, it hadn't calmed her any. Her eyes were huge, and she seemed to be trying to say something that wouldn't get past her lips.

"Take it easy, it's Hugh," I said. "What the hell are you—"

I shut up. She wasn't just stuttering, she was mouthing a word. Like, maybe, *run.*

The edge of my vision caught a movement on the backseat floor, like a restless black dog squirming around.

I thought it was just a shadow until a man came lunging up out of there. He jammed a rifle barrel through the window behind Laurie's head, pointed at my face.

I stared into it, with my body and brain both locked.

Then Laurie screamed, a sound so piercing and charged with rage that it was like a spike through my ears. The other man flinched, and he raised his right fist like he was going to club her. But before he could, she ripped the key out of the ignition, whirled around in her seat, and stabbed it at his eyes, a movement as quick and vicious as a viper's strike. He reared back away, dropping the rifle and clapping his hands to his face.

Laurie seemed frozen, like she couldn't believe what she'd done. But her scream started my blood moving again. I yanked open the SUV's door and managed to get hold of her arm and drag her toward me, shouting at her to climb on. There came a few wild seconds of thrashing around while she squeezed outside and onto the bike behind me, and I fought to keep the son of a bitch from dumping and make sure she was still hanging on.

The opening door had tripped on an interior light. This time it was easy to see the man in the backseat, swinging the rifle toward us again. I popped the clutch so hard the front wheel came off the ground, and cut the handlebars hard to the right, passing in front of the SUV so the gun's muzzle couldn't follow us. We jumped over the road-edge hump into the woods.

I yelled at Laurie over my shoulder, "Hide your face!" She pressed hard against my back with her arms wrapped around me like I was a spar in a shipwreck. I ducked my head low and powered on through the trees, whipped by low-hanging branches and raked by stumps.

I couldn't even guess how any of this had happened and I didn't give a rat's ass. The only thought in my head was to get out of there as fast and far as I could.

PART
FOUR

THIRTY-EIGHT

After Laurie and I had gone about a mile, it started to sink in that we were intact and not being followed. My panic eased off some, and I slowed the bike along with it. I knew where we were, not far north of the lake. I kept on going until we came to the top of a ridge that gave a view of that long stretch of water and the highway that skirted it. Everything out there looked as dark and still as when I'd followed the tow truck in.

By the clock, that had been several minutes ago. In my head, it was a lifetime.

I stopped and cut the engine, thinking that Laurie would let go of me. She didn't, and now I could feel that she was shivering hard. That was no wonder after what had happened. But when I unlocked her fingers from around my waist and eased us both off the bike, I realized that she was wearing the same light turtleneck she'd had on earlier today, with just a shawl over it. The rain had thinned to a mist up in the woods, but the night was still chilly and damp. Along with shock and fear, she must have been freezing. I was just the opposite by now, heated up and sweating from wrestling the bike around. When I pulled off my coat and wrapped her in it, the cool air was welcome.

"What the hell is going on?" I said.

Her hands clenched my shirt again, her face pressed tight against my chest now.

"That man's a killer, a torturer," she said through chattering teeth. "He's here to kill *you*."

I stared at her, trying to get my mind around that. Something else was starting to sink in—the sense that I'd seen his face before.

"How do you know that?" I said.

"I recognized him—from before."

"From before?"

She kept gasping out words, the bits of information coming in like punches, wild but fast and hard enough to stagger me.

"No, I don't mean I know him. I only ever saw him once. I don't even know his name—I call him John Doe. But I saw him with Wesley today, and Wesley gave him that rifle. I followed him to your house. He hid there and waited. But then the sheriffs came, and I guess he was running away, and he found me."

"What were you doing there?"

Her forehead butted against me in a way that was still agitated but oddly shy.

"I was hiding, too," she whispered. "I had to tell you, and there wasn't any other way."

I stroked her hair, trying to calm myself as much as her. This woman who barely knew me had come up into the cold dark woods, knowing that a hired killer was nearby, in order to save my life.

Then it came to me where I'd seen him. He was the man who'd delivered Balcomb's twenty-five hundred dollars this afternoon. I remembered him hesitating at my gate like he was thinking about coming up to the cabin. He must have decided to play it safe—just check the place out and come back after dark. But his disguise would have taken me in. If he'd approached politely, he could have shot me dead before I raised my rifle.

"I guess the sheriffs found out about him," she said, her words still muffled against my chest. "I don't know how. *I* didn't call them."

"They're not looking for him. They're after me. I'm a suspect for killing Kirk."

Her face lifted swiftly, eyes wide with alarm. I put my finger to her lips. This wasn't the time to trade stories.

"Let me think a minute," I said.

She nodded, although doubtfully, like she didn't have much faith in my abilities along those lines.

Neither did I. The rug had been jerked out from under me all over again, and I was more brain-fried than ever. But a few things stood out clearly—first and foremost, that I didn't have to wonder anymore whether Balcomb would keep his promise to back off.

With a professional after me, I was as good as dead. Laurie was at risk, too, as an eyewitness who could identify him. And a man like that who'd been stabbed in the eye by a woman with a car key was going to have a serious personal ax to grind.

Now there was no choice but to turn myself in.

In a way, it was a perverse stroke of luck. The other information I'd gathered was sketchy and circumstantial, but Laurie's testimony would be rock solid, and would powerfully reinforce my claim that Balcomb had sent Kirk after me first, and I'd acted in self-defense. It was still a risk, and I'd be likely to do some time anyway for my cover-up—but this nightmare would be over.

"Let's head for town," I said. I'd have gone straight to Gary Varna, but I didn't want to chance running into John Doe on the way.

"Do you have a place to stay there?"

"Yeah, the county jail."

Her eyes went wide again. "No! We can't."

"Don't worry, not you—they'll put you in a motel or something until things settle down."

She shook her head violently. My confusion deepened. I'd expected that would be what she wanted. Then I reminded myself that while she might not be fond of her husband, I was asking her to send him to prison.

"We have to," I said. "Otherwise, John Doe's going to come after you."

"He'll come after me if I do tell the police—him or somebody else." Her eyes stayed big but her voice was sharper. "You still don't get it? After what just happened? If something threatens Wesley, that something disappears."

"You're his wife, for Christ's sake."

"You don't know him," she said, almost with contempt.

I was getting to.

"I thought he treated you well," I said.

"Except for once. I tried to leave him. That's how I know what I'm saying."

"What if we played it like this never happened?" I said. "You go back to him now, tonight, and swear you'll never breathe a word?"

"He'd say yes. But the truth is I've crossed him, and he'll never forgive it. Someday soon, I'd have an accident. And John Doe would still come after you."

I stepped away and pressed my hands against my temples, trying to squeeze intelligence out of the brain between them. The situation kept getting worse by leaps and bounds—and yet simpler. All other bets were off. Now we were down to saving our skins.

When I turned back and saw her huddled inside my coat, it struck me that not only did she not have extra clothes or a car, she didn't even have her purse—no money, no credit cards, no identification, nothing.

"Is there somebody you trust that you can call to come get you?" I said.

"Come get me? Here?" She looked startled.

"In town. I can drop you at a motel and give you a couple hundred bucks, but I just can't do anything more, Laurie. You saved me. I'll always owe you. But the sheriffs are on my ass. I can't go back to my place—they're even taking my truck. You better look out for yourself."

"What are you going to do?"

Try to buy some time was all I could think. I needed rest and a clear head. But I couldn't jeopardize people I knew by asking them to take me in. Staying in the area would be risky, anyway—if the sheriffs didn't already have an alert out on me, they would soon. That knocked the pins out from under a plane or bus or rental car, and I wasn't going to get far on a dirt bike with no plates or lights.

"I'll figure out something," I said.

She took hold of my shirt and butted her head into my chest again.

"Forget about running from Wesley," she said quietly. "He'll never give up looking for both of us, not as long as he's alive. Don't leave me alone, OK?"

THIRTY-NINE

I warned Laurie to be ready to scramble—if we saw headlights, we'd either try to hide or run for it. The shortest way out was the riskiest, with first the bridge and then a narrow stretch bound by the lake on the left and cliffs on the right. But the alternatives were a lot slower and just as likely to have deputies on the lookout, so I went for it, riding fast and without the light. We cut south and made it to Highway 12 without trouble. The paved road ended there, but I went straight on across and turned west on the Montana Rail Link tracks. It was rough, bouncing along on the ties, but we only had a couple of miles to go and nobody would see us.

Madbird's place was up the McClellan Creek drainage, another isolated gravel road through thick woods. I started smelling the pine smoke from his stove as we got close. Unlike me, he had a real house, high-ceilinged and cedar-paneled, that he'd been smart enough to build with a VA loan when he came back from Vietnam. The windows glowed pleasantly, although as you came into their light you'd start to see the animal skulls mounted in the surrounding trees. There was a lot more that you didn't see but you had to be pretty dense not to feel. Strangers rarely got close.

I was sure that by now, Laurie was wishing with all her soul that she'd never heard of me. But she hadn't made a sound of complaint or even asked where we were going. She still didn't when I stopped the bike, but she stumbled a little getting off, staring nervously at the centerpiece of the fence gate—the bleached skull of a squirrel with its teeth still clamped in the piece of twelve-two electrical cable that was the last thing it had ever tasted. That one was kind of a joke.

All through the ride, I'd thought about how to handle this. I hated like hell to hit on Madbird again. But I knew he was willing, and he knew that if I got busted, I'd keep him out of it. The real problem was bringing Laurie in. There was no telling how things were finally going to shake down, or if she and I would even still be around. But if she did end up dealing with the authorities, I couldn't expect her to commit perjury to protect him. Any help he gave me would be abetting, and might also start them digging deeper into his other involvement. I'd thought about leaving her someplace while I talked to him, but that wouldn't be much of a hedge. I needed a vehicle, and if she described it to the cops, they'd quickly put together where it had come from.

I'd ended up deciding to go for the flip side—to keep her with me and cue Madbird. He'd pick up on it instantly and run with it. That way, she'd be a witness to his innocence. If she made him too uncomfortable, he'd let me know it and we'd move on. I wouldn't blame him a bit.

I took hold of Laurie's wrist and brought her around to face me.

"We can't put my friend at risk, so we've got to lie to him. And I've got to trust you."

She nodded, slowly but decisively. "Just tell me the lie."

"Not a word about John Doe or the cops or any of the rest of it. We got caught in an awkward situation and we need to get away for a day or two, where nobody will look for us."

Her head tipped a little to the side and her eyebrows rose.

"Caught in an awkward situation, like, by my husband?"

"That's what my friend will think, but he won't ask. OK?"

"OK," she said. Her tone was cooler, but that was understandable.

I kept hold of her wrist and led her toward the house. Without doubt, Madbird had heard the bike and was watching. By now, he'd have recognized me, and probably Laurie, too. He was going to be real interested in what this was about.

His two dogs were waiting inside the fence—half-feral Blue Heeler crosses, lying silent and flat to the ground. You wouldn't have guessed they were there if you didn't know. These weren't dogs that barked if another creature violated their space. They ripped its throat out. They were extremely smart and well behaved, they obeyed Madbird absolutely, and they tolerated other people as long as they sensed his approval. I'd gotten to be pretty good pals with them, and they usually came to greet me as soon as they caught my scent or the sound of my voice. But coming in at night, particularly with someone else they didn't know, might spook them.

I held my hands to the gate, palms first, beside my thighs.

"Soup. Ajax," I said. "How you guys doing?"

Soup, female, older, and the boss, rose cautiously and came over. I kept talking while Ajax did the same. After a little sniffing, they started wagging their stumpy tails.

Then an invisible Madbird said, "Looks like you check out OK with the bouncers."

Laurie's wrist jerked in my hand like she was going to break free and run. That was understandable, too—with that voice of his, he sounded like the captain of the guard on Judgment Day. The dogs lay back down.

"I'm sorry to bust in on you, Madbird," I said. "Laurie and me, uh, kind of had to go for a ride in a hurry, and we've got to keep going. I was wondering if you could lend us a rig."

I couldn't see his eyes, but I knew he was watching her, and I was sure that she knew it, too.

He stepped into sight from the house's shadowed doorway and walked forward to meet us. She tugged at me again. He was wearing jeans and an old vest made from an elk hide. Besides the Marine tattoos on his arms, he had a wine-colored birthmark across his bare chest the size and shape of a splayed hand, as if it had been burned there by fiery fingers reaching for his heart. His hair was a black mane and his face looked like a cliff side.

It was very clear that this was the force behind those skulls.

"Come on into my house," he said.

That invitation was a huge thing, and I hoped to Christ we wouldn't end up violating it.

The dogs fell in behind Laurie as soon as we got through the gate and followed at her heels, noses busy. They were too polite to be crotch sniffers, but they had a job to do. By the time we'd walked the twenty feet to the door, she was fixed forever in their memory banks.

As we stepped inside, I caught Madbird's eye and brushed my thumb across my lips. He lifted his chin an inch.

The walls were hung with tribal masks, some Native and some from Africa, where he'd traveled after the service. The coffee table was a vintage surfboard from the 1950s, handmade of wood and fiberglass. There was a rack of rifles and shotguns, and a pistol and a couple of hunting knives hanging from pegs. But potted plants spilling greenery suggested a feminine hand, and the furniture had enough hair on it to make it clear that he wasn't as tough on the dogs as he pretended to be. My earlier rush of sweat had long since chilled away, and the heat from the big iron stove felt fine.

"We ain't ever been introduced, but I seen you before," he said to Laurie. Then he nodded toward his girlfriend, who was sitting, relaxed but attentive, on the couch. "That's Hannah."

Hannah was also Blackfeet, and a thoroughgoing piece of work. You couldn't call her pretty, but she had a trim little figure and a tough sultriness that was magnetic. She was fiercely Indian—her teal-colored sweatshirt had a logo of four braves in full war regalia, and the caption HOMELAND SECURITY: FIGHTING TERRORISTS SINCE 1492—but she worked in management for the Forest Service and she knew her way around the white man's world real well. Maybe the most impressive thing about her was that she held her own with Madbird.

I could see that she was checking out Laurie like he'd done, although probably not entirely for the same reasons.

"This is all my fault," Laurie said abruptly. She put her face in her hands and shuddered, as if the reality was just hitting her. Maybe it was. I tensed, thinking she was going to start babbling, and then we'd have no choice but to leave.

"I wasn't careful," she said, still into her hands. "My husband followed me, without me knowing. It'll be OK, but I've got to let him cool down."

I exhaled quietly in relief.

Hannah hadn't yet moved or spoken. But now she stood, went to Laurie, and touched her auburn hair, feeling its texture between her fingers. Laurie raised her face, looking pale and scared. Whatever passed between the Virginia heiress and the smoky reservation girl in the next few seconds stayed silent.

"You're going to need some things," Hannah said. She turned away and left the room.

Madbird picked up a bottle of Napoleon brandy off the surfboard coffee table, twisted the cork out, and handed it to Laurie.

"Lighten up a little," he said. "This'll make your husband appreciate you more, trust me. It's kind of like your pony ain't worth much unless another Indian tries to steal it."

A ghost of a smile crossed her face. She tipped the bottle up to her lips and drank.

I took it from her and did the same, then handed the bottle to Madbird. He swigged and started to set it down, but Laurie caught his arm.

"Can I have one more taste?" she said.

His eyes widened. "Hell, yeah, you can have all you want."

We both watched her drink, a lingering, greedy pull.

"I'm sure we lost Balcomb, but we better not stick around," I said. "He's got long arms."

"You got a place in mind?"

"I was thinking maybe where we saw those wolverines that time."

Laurie's mouth opened a little.

"Yeah, that'd be good," Madbird said. "Won't nobody find you there. Take the van, you can sleep in it." He peeled a key from his key ring and handed it to me. "Grab whatever gear you need. I'll get you some food."

He strode into the kitchen and started pulling cans from the cupboards, giving me a quizzical glance on the way. I turned Laurie toward the front door and nudged her to start walking. Then I made a quick gesture of writing on the palm of my left hand. His chin lifted again.

The van was in the big adjoining shop-garage I'd helped him build several years ago. I opened the passenger door for her, but she hesitated.

"Wolverines?" she said doubtfully.

"Laurie, anything with four legs is the least of our worries. Go on, hop in. I've got to load some stuff."

I trotted back outside and wheeled the Victor into the shop, leaning it against a wall and throwing a tarp over it—just in case the sheriffs decided to come calling on my friends. Then I started choosing camping gear from shelves and packing it into the rear of the van—a couple of down sleeping bags, a cooking kit, and the sorts of necessities you never thought about until you couldn't run down to the store for them. Every time I loaded something, I took out some of his tools to make room—including his work belt, which contained pencils and his tape measure. That had a sticker plastered onto it, a kind that was sold at building supply stores—the size of a beer can top, with a surface that worked like a blackboard. You could write down several measurements, take them to where your saw was set up and cut the materials, then wipe it clean and use it again.

I printed on it while I shifted stuff around, making sure Laurie didn't see me: *Watch it. B hired pro killer. Still after us, cops too.* Then I sneaked it back into its pouch and put the belt on a workbench.

As I was finishing loading the gear, Madbird walked in carrying a bulging paper grocery sack

"I took out most of your tools," I said, stepping over to the workbench and tapping my finger on the tape. "Figured you might need them."

"Yeah, you know, I try to stay out of work, but it just don't seem to happen that way."

The door opened again and Hannah came in, followed by the adoring dogs. She was carrying a nylon-shelled goose-down jacket and a lady's traveling bag, the kind that looked like an oversize purse, made of woven wool with a pair of leather handles. She gave the jacket to Laurie through the window of the van.

"It's not pretty but it'll keep you warm," Hannah said.

Laurie pressed her hand earnestly. "God, I don't care about pretty. Thanks so much."

While that was going on, Madbird stepped to the bag and parted its handles, peering inside.

"You stay out of there," Hannah said sharply, and slapped his hands. He dodged, pretending to cringe—although more than once I'd seen him come to work with a bruised cheek or raked skin, and it wasn't any man who'd done it to him.

"Hey, I'm just trying to make sure you ain't lending her something dainty that he shouldn't see." He jerked his thumb toward me.

Hannah made a scornful sort of "puh" sound. "Look who's talking about dainty," she said to Laurie. "I've never seen *him* once"—she gave Madbird a shove—"without dirt under his fingernails."

He drew back in mock outrage. "You ever had better dirt?"

"You think I'd tell you?" She shoved him again and handed the bag to Laurie. "You take care, hon," Hannah said. "When this is over, come on by and we'll talk about men. Maybe you know a couple."

She tossed her hair and stalked out of the room.

For the next thirty seconds or so, Madbird and I carefully didn't look at each other.

Then he leaned against the van with his forearms on Laurie's windowsill. It was like a scene out of one of those teen movies, with a dangerous cool guy from the wrong side of the tracks and a shy but fascinated rich girl.

"Now, I got to ask you something," he said to her, in a growling theatrical whisper. He nodded toward the doorway where Hannah had left—and where she was probably still standing inside, listening. "She beats me up, like you just seen. I wake up in the middle of the night, she's kneeing me in the ass, and other things I ain't gonna tell you. What you think I ought to do?"

I couldn't see Laurie's face well and I was looking at Madbird's back, but it felt like another of those moments when something silent transpired.

"I think you'd better buy her something dainty and watch her try it on," Laurie said. "If you can't take it from there, then she and I are going to have a lot to talk about."

He turned to me and nodded approvingly. "I'm thinking maybe she got some Indian blood in her."

I climbed into the van and started it. "I'll get this stuff back to you soon," I told him.

"No hurry. I got some shopping to do." He pressed a button on the wall to open the garage door. It rolled up with a metallic clanking that made me think of the iron grates that locked the hallways of Deer Lodge prison. I remembered them well from times I'd gone down there to box.

We backed out. The garage door started rolling shut again.

I just got a glimpse of Madbird stepping to the workbench and picking up the tape measure.

"I don't know exactly how to put this," Laurie said. "I didn't know there *were* people like that."

"There aren't many."

"Did I do OK?"

"You did great."

She had passed all the tests with straight A's. Or at least that was how it seemed.

FORTY

We drove to the town of Lincoln, about an hour away, then went several miles farther north into the Scapegoat Wilderness. By the time we got where I wanted to go, the dirt road had petered out to almost nothing. I drove the van another couple of hundred yards through the trees to a little clearing beside a creek, a place that Madbird and I had found when we were fishing a few years ago. It was about as isolated as you could get and still have access to a vehicle. Hunting season hadn't yet opened and we were far from the horse trails that outfitters used to set up their camps. The chance that anybody would just happen by was next to nil.

I built a fire and broke into the grocery stash. Tonight's entrée was Dinty Moore Beef Stew. It seemed like most of what I'd eaten the last couple of days had come from cans. Still, filet mignon wouldn't have tasted better to me. Laurie looked skeptical while it was heating, but she took to it fast, finally abandoning her spoon to sop up the gravy with slices of bread, then licking her fingers clean.

And Madbird, God bless him, had stuck that brandy bottle into the sack. That, she was very happy to see.

Now the fire was burning down to embers and so was I. Adrenaline and the speed had both worn off, and I felt like my veins were full of lead. I still had another dozen or so of the crosstops, but I'd reached the point where nothing could take the place of sleep. I got to my feet and trudged down to the creek to wash the dishes.

Weather-wise, we'd gotten a break. The elevation here was a good six thousand feet, and I'd feared that the rain might turn to snow. Instead, it had lessened as we'd gone deeper into the mountains, and this area was still dry. But the clouds blowing in from the west gave only occasional glimpses of stars, and the moon was a barely visible blur. The storm might move right on through, or settle in and get serious. The air was thin and sharp and clean with the scent of the forest. Even this early in the fall, the night wind carried the news of winter.

I scrubbed the kettle and utensils with a Brillo pad, and the stew cans, too. There were a lot of bears in the Scapegoat, including a fair number of grizzlies. They weren't any more likely than people to be around this particular spot, but it didn't pay to advertise. I brushed my teeth with a new toothbrush from Hannah's bag. She was on my God bless list, too. I carried everything back to the van, stashed it in the front seat, then got a shovel and went to put out the fire.

Laurie was sitting huddled on the other side, watching it in that kind of hypnotized glaze that was easy to fall into, especially with fatigue and alcohol.

"Time to crash," I said.

She looked at me swiftly. "What?" Her face had a peculiar expression—confused, alarmed, even a little wild-eyed. Her trance must have been deep.

"We've got to sleep."

She shook her head, maybe to clear it or maybe in disagreement.

"Well, *I've* got to sleep," I said. "Stay up if you want. Just make sure you put this out when you're done. Bust up the embers and cover everything with dirt."

Her face and voice both turned suddenly sharp.

"I know how to deal with fire."

She stood up huffily, plucked a Kleenex out of Hannah's bag, and stalked out to the far edge of the circle of firelight. I hadn't intended to insult her wilderness skills, but I was feeling touchy about fire just now. I leaned the shovel against a tree and headed in the other direction, to give her some privacy.

The forest was a lot like around my own place except that everything was magnified. The trees seemed ancient and gigantic, swaying and moaning as if the creature the Indians called the Wendigo was up there running across their tops. The wilderness wrapped around me with such intensity that after twenty yards, I felt like I might never see another light.

I picked my way along a little farther and came to a treeless rocky slope that gave me a window of open sky. I took a piss, apologizing half-unconsciously to anything I might offend, and started to turn back. But I kept standing there instead, with the wind crawling inside my shirt and lifting my hair.

Wesley Balcomb wanted me dead, badly. If Laurie was right, not distance or police or even prison—for either him or me—would stop him.

And now I wasn't just on the run. I was on the run with his wife, who had betrayed him.

On the drive here, she'd told me how she'd come to be waiting for me. She had kept her promise to keep tabs on Balcomb, even watching him with binoculars when he left the house. Late this afternoon, she'd seen him drive to the fence around their compound and toss a black plastic garbage bag over it into the weeds. He'd seemed furtive, although it was Sunday and the place was deserted. Then he'd driven on into the ranch.

That would have been just about the time I'd seen him at the shed.

He clearly hadn't thrown the bag at that particular place by accident. It was a dead end, one of the dirt roads that had been blocked off by the fence, with nothing around and no outlet. But it was a good drop spot. A vehicle could turn off the highway and drive in a quarter mile to the fence's other side, hidden by trees and without having to go on the property.

A few minutes later, a nondescript modern sedan, like a rental, did just that. It sounded like the same vehicle John Doe had been driving when he'd delivered the money to my place. I'd realized by now why Laurie called him that. He was the most ordinary-appearing man I'd ever seen, the kind you looked right through and wouldn't remember thirty seconds later. No doubt that was part of why he was good at his job.

He got out of the car and picked up the plastic bag that Balcomb had thrown. When Laurie recognized him, her fear jumped to outright terror.

"What happened to make you so afraid of him?" I'd asked her.

She'd shivered and said, "That's the story I said I'd tell you. But I don't even want to think about it now."

John Doe opened the bag to check its contents, and she caught a glimpse of a rifle inside. She'd already guessed that he was here to kill somebody, and the most likely candidate was me. She didn't dare call the sheriffs for fear of her husband's wrath. She tried to call me, but I wasn't there to answer. So she ran to her SUV and drove to my place as fast as she could, hoping I'd have come home by the time she got there.

But my cabin was dark and empty. She couldn't chance waiting there—if John Doe showed up, that would just have gotten her killed, too. She started to take off, thinking she could find a hiding place along the highway and flag me down. But she feared that John Doe was close behind her, and Stumpleg Gulch Road was barely wide enough for two vehicles to pass each other. If she met him, he'd certainly recognize her. She pulled her SUV into the trees, intending to wait until he drove by and then sneak on.

Her instinct was a good one. His car soon came into sight. But instead of driving farther, he stopped short of her and hid his own vehicle in the trees. She knew he'd hear her engine if she started it. So she sat there for close to two hours, shivering with cold, fear, and a dread of watching helplessly while I drove into a spray of gunfire.

But when headlights did appear, they belonged to a pair of sheriffs' cruisers.

Laurie almost wept with relief. She didn't know what was going on, but John Doe wasn't going to be shooting anybody with sheriffs around. After they passed, she started her SUV and eased her way through the trees toward the road, thinking that with the distance and the sound of their own engines, they wouldn't notice her.

But John Doe did. He appeared out of nowhere, smashed the passenger window with his rifle butt, and had the muzzle to her head before she had time to comprehend it. He got in the seat behind her and told her to keep driving.

He had probably assumed the same thing she had—that he'd been made somehow and the deputies were looking for him. He didn't take his own car for fear it had been identified, so he'd started to escape on foot. Then he'd heard the SUV or seen its silvery shape moving through the trees.

I had to hand it to Balcomb again. I'd gotten a good enough look at the rifle to be sure it was Kirk's Mini-14—he stored it inside the ranch office when he left the property because his Jeep was vulnerable to theft. Balcomb had given it to John Doe so the slugs found in my body would identify it as the murder weapon. Kirk's disappearance would remain a mystery, but the sheriffs would assume it had to do with the grudge between us—that he'd settled it and then vanished again. Balcomb didn't know for sure that he was dead, but even if he'd turned up, there'd have been a cloud of confusion to cover Balcomb—and Kirk would have been the one who'd have had to explain his way out of it.

I walked on back to the fire. Laurie had gotten into the van and made a nest of the sleeping bags where Madbird had sported with Tessa Wills and no telling who else. She was lying there curled up on her side. I sat down inside the open doors, next to her feet.

I owed a lot of people now in ways I'd never imagined—Madbird, Hannah, Sarah Lynn. But I owed Laurie my life. This afternoon while we'd driven around town, she had talked about feeling kinship. But it was hard to fathom her risking her own life for that.

"I can understand why you warned me today," I said. "Why you kept watch on your husband, why you tried to call me when you saw John Doe. But driving to my place with him right behind you—I mean, you hardly know me."

"What would you have done? Stood by and let somebody die?"

I shook my head. I had no idea what I would have done.

"I've started to say thanks a hundred times," I said. "But it sounds so feeble."

She patted my hand. "It sounds very sweet."

I knew she meant that, but somehow it underlined the fact that all the words in the universe were worthless. The only thanks that would count would be getting her out of this mess.

"We'll start making sense of things tomorrow," I said. "You better put your shoes inside your sleeping bag, otherwise they'll freeze." The bags were good ones, heavy goose down that would keep you warm even below zero, but footwear or damp clothing left outside would be stiff as a board by morning.

Among the gear I'd thrown into the van were a couple of foam pads, the kind you rolled up to carry backpacking. They weren't great for comfort but they helped keep the chill of the earth from creeping into you. I tucked them under my arm and started gathering up the empty sleeping bag beside her.

"Where are you going?" she said anxiously.

"Just outside."

"To *sleep*?"

"Well, yeah. I want you to have your space."

She sat up and grabbed my sleeve. "What about the wolverines?"

I wouldn't have believed that I ever could have laughed again. But Laurie was not amused.

"Why is that funny?" she said coolly.

"They're tough little bastards, but even they can't chew their way in here."

"I'm not worried about in here. I'm worried about out there."

"I'll leave the keys in the ignition. If there's nothing left of me in the morning but bloody bones—"

"Asshole," she snapped. "I need a lot more from you than the fucking keys, and you better be here for me." She let go of me and thumped herself down again, this time with her back turned.

I rubbed my hand over my hair, feeling like I'd been punched. I'd been trying to lighten things up. But after watching her stab John Doe, I should have known she was volatile.

"Sorry," I said. "I wasn't thinking."

"I don't even know what they are, really," she said, still facing away.

"What what are?"

"Wolverines."

"Kind of a skunk on steroids, with an attitude like a pit bull," I said. "But they don't usually come near humans."

"Then why did they come near you?"

"They were hungry."

"See?" She sat up again triumphantly.

"No, not hungry for us—"

"Who was us?"

"Madbird and me."

"And?" She folded her hands in her lap and looked at me solemnly. My clouded brain grasped that she had changed, within a few seconds, from a fiercely demanding woman to a child expecting a bedtime story. Auburnlocks and the Three Wolverines. And yet, I still felt like she was the grown-up and I was the kid.

I sat back down and told her.

A couple of years earlier, Madbird and I had been looking for a new place to fish—driving back roads, drinking beer, mostly just enjoying a fine Saturday in May. Neither of us had tried this spot before, and we stopped to check it out. The stream was too fast and clear to look really promising, but there were pools, and the place was as pretty as they got.

"What kind of flies were you using?" Laurie said. It had the feel of a question she'd learned to ask to sound knowledgeable.

"The kind called worms."

"Oh." She looked taken aback. "I thought that was—well, bad form."

"So do the trout." To a hungry rainbow or brookie, a fat squirming nightcrawler was a Big Mac with fries.

We'd judged the stream correctly—after a couple of hours we'd caught four or five and kept just two, barely pan-size. We were reaching the point of having to decide whether we were really fishing—in which case we knew a spot on the Little Blackfoot, on the way home, where we could pull out a half dozen pretty good ones in short order—or just fucking around, and we'd hang there a while longer and drink another beer and save ourselves a bunch of fish cleaning. Things were definitely leaning toward the second choice.

Then I heard Madbird say, "We ain't got much, but you're welcome to it."

He was a little way upstream, his voice loud enough to carry over the rushing water. For a second I assumed he was talking to me, but his words didn't make any sense, and he was looking straight ahead. I followed his gaze.

A wolverine was standing across the creek in the forest maybe a hundred feet away, watching us. I'd never seen one before, and my immediate hit was of a bear cub. But then I registered the white markings and the low, built-for-assault body shape. Something behind it was rustling around in the brush. After a few seconds I glimpsed a kit, then a second one. There might have been more.

At this elevation, spring came late. There was still a lot of snow around and not much food. Wolverines were voracious, and a single mom with a family to feed would be hard-pressed—hungry and aggressive. They were lightning-fast, vicious, and fearless, capable of chewing their way out of a cage of eight-inch logs in a matter of hours, known to attack grizzlies, and rumored to have killed humans. I didn't know if that was true, but she sure wasn't backing away.

Like a lot of animals, wolverines had figured out that people were likely to have food around—they were notorious for raiding unoccupied cabins and camps. She might have smelled our fish or even known that men doing what we were doing sometimes caught fish. She wanted to bully us out of there and have lunch.

That was fine with me.

But Madbird, moving slowly, set down his fishing rod, crouched at the water's edge, and pulled out the net bag with our pair of keepers. He tossed one toward her onto the rocks of the opposite bank. The wolverine shifted in agitation, a quick sinuous movement that brought her a few feet closer, and had me ready to run for it. But she didn't charge us. The trout was still alive enough to flop feebly. Mom lifted her nose, sniffing hard.

Madbird tossed the second trout. "Stick around, I'll try and get you something better," he called to her.

He backed away and, with that same almost lazy lack of haste, reeled in his fishing line and picked up his other gear. I did the same. Mom watched us until we'd retreated twenty or thirty yards. But then she started warily toward the fish, with the kits running around her like berserk little satellites.

When we got to the van, Madbird pulled out his 30-30.

"I'm gonna see if I can bag them a chuck or something," he said. "I won't be long."

I stowed the fishing gear, then opened a cold beer and walked back down to where I could see the lunch party. It was long since over—it had probably lasted about ten seconds—but they were still there, with mom watchful again. Her head moved constantly, taking in everything that was happening around her. But her gaze kept coming back our way and lingering. I was sure she wasn't seeing me. I got the damnedest feeling that she was counting on Madbird to deliver.

She didn't have to wait long. Within a few minutes I heard the rifle's crack, maybe a hundred yards away. The 30-30 was not an ideal varmint rifle, but Madbird had been hunting since he was old enough to point a gun, and had been a rifle range instructor at Pendleton. He knew where the critters hung out and how to get close to them, and when he shot at something, he generally hit it. I figured he'd be back in another minute carrying a woodchuck or hare by the tail.

Instead, he whistled, a quick piercing sound that meant, *Get your ass over here.*

When I found him, he was kneeling beside a little spike mule deer buck with spring velvet on its antlers. Its blood was pooled on the ground below its neatly slit throat, and he was just finishing cutting through its sternum. Now he was moving very fast.

My mouth went dry. I had no problem with jacking an occasional deer, and I believed in my heart that Indians should have special rights that way, and an Indian doing it to feed wolverines was so twisty it made me want to vanish.

But the Fish and Game Department didn't see it like that. May was about as far as you could get from the end of the last hunting season and the start of the next one. You usually tried to poach where you had a good security buffer, like on private land, and not in broad daylight. The sound of a 30-30 wouldn't carry all that far, but rangers and game wardens had sharp ears, and even a hiker or fisherman might come to check it out and report us.

Then there were grizzlies, also very hungry in the spring, and some hunters had found out the hard way that bears were learning to associate the sound of a gunshot with a fresh kill. That was no rumor.

"We'll leave them the guts," Madbird said, not looking up. "That'll make mama happy."

"We're taking the meat?"

He looked at me like I was an eighteen-year-old who'd asked how babies were made.

"What the fuck you think this is, *Dances with Wolves*? Start cutting, we ain't got all day."

I pulled out my knife and went for the scent glands in the rear hocks.

Mom probably would have smelled the gut pile, but Madbird wanted to make sure. He draped the carcass over my shoulders to take back to the van while he dragged the intestines to the creek. She'd start there and follow the scent trail to the rest. It seemed to me that it took him longer than it should have. Maybe they were conversing some more, or maybe I was just nervous about getting caught. But we made it home fine, and for the first time in my life, I grilled fresh venison steaks for Memorial Day.

Laurie had relaxed in stages while I'd talked, first back against the van's front seat, then on one elbow, then down to horizontal again. Her eyes were still open, but she looked like she'd fallen back into that same kind of trance as beside the fire. I'd always had a talent for edge-of-the-seat storytelling.

I gathered up my sleeping gear and eased away.

"Do you know any poetry?" she murmured.

"Not much. Why?"

"There's this line that's been coming into my mind. 'Build a thousand bridges.'"

I stopped, almost choking.

"Where'd you hear that?" I said.

"I don't know. It's like it's from a poem I read a long time ago and can't remember. It sounds so exotic. Do you recognize it?"

"No." I started to close the van's doors.

"Leave them open—please?" she said. "And don't go far?"

I broke up the last of the embers with the shovel and smothered them with dirt. I found a reasonably flat spot without too many rocks and spread out my bedding, then wrapped up my boots in my jacket and put them under the bag's head flap. It made a decent pillow, and would keep them warm enough. Stretching out on the cold hard ground felt so good I almost groaned. I could have slept on a bed of nails—except that now I had yet another something on my mind.

I recognized that line, all right. You could call it exotic if you wanted, but it didn't come from any poem. It was an old construction workers' riff, tossed around with grim humor when competent men busting their asses on tough jobs under bad conditions got hassled by bean counters who rode around in heated pickup trucks wearing clean white hard hats.

"Build a thousand bridges, they'll never call you an engineer," was how it went. "Suck one cock, they'll call you a cocksucker for the rest of your life." The sentiment probably dated back to the Stone Age. Laurie must have picked it up somewhere, without any notion of the tag line or meaning.

But what shook me was that it had been Celia's favorite bad-girl taunt.

Growing up like she had on ranches and around workingmen, she'd learned that kind of stuff early, and by the time she'd come to live with us, she had it honed into a multipurpose weapon. Most often, she'd used it when somebody took her to task for a chore she'd done poorly or not at all. She'd roll her eyes, sigh, and say those first few words, "Build a thousand bridges." Men, in particular, would tend to stop cold and back off in confusion. Then she'd go right on doing as she pleased.

I couldn't for the life of me come up with a reason why that would appear in Laurie Balcomb's mind right now.

As I drifted off, the movie screen behind my closed eyes started playing an image of Laurie or Celia or the two of them together inside one bare shining skin, rising up out of Lone Creek with a million crystal shards of water exploding into my face.

FORTY-ONE

I awoke to the sound of a woman weeping. That had happened a number of times before in my life, almost always because she was wishing that one of us was someplace, or somebody, else.

Lord knew that Laurie Balcomb had plenty of cause for that.

It was still night. I couldn't tell how late. I knew I'd slept a while, and I sure could have kept on going. But her muffled sobs pierced me like little stabs. Whatever bond of kinship she might have felt had been safely abstract, but now it was shattered by the waffle-head hammer of reality. She was in a hell of a spot, and all because of me.

I crawled out of my sleeping bag into the near-freezing chill, hobbled to the van, and sat beside her feet again, trying to drag up words of reassurance that I didn't feel.

"I know you're scared," I started, but she cut me off.

"Of course I'm scared." She was curled up like a child, her face hidden by her hair. "Not of Wesley. I mean, I am, but that's not it." She shook her head. "I don't know how to explain. There's something happening to me. It's almost like a voice in my mind. Maybe I'm going crazy. But it seems so *right*."

I was still groggy, and this bewildered me. It wasn't at all what I'd expected.

"What does this voice say?" I said.

"That I'm not really who I always thought I was. Like I've been living in a dream that's pretty, but all for show, and I'm starting to wake up."

She pushed her hair aside and looked at me. Her face was a shadow, but her legs, pressed against me now, were warm.

"That you and I go way far back," she said.

"How do you mean?"

She turned away again. "Now *you'll* think I'm crazy. I started feeling it when I first saw you, months ago. It wouldn't leave me alone."

"Months ago? I thought you didn't know who I was until yesterday."

"I had to pretend. I couldn't just come out and tell you," she said impatiently.

"No, I guess I can see that."

"So I arranged for us to accidentally meet."

"You arranged it?"

"I knew your routine, knew you'd go get rid of that trash at the end of the day. So I went riding out there. I'd finally decided—this isn't a nice thing to say, but I thought if I got to know you a little, I'd see how silly it was."

"That would have worked pretty quick, all right. It's just your bad luck that all this other stuff happened instead."

But she shook her head again. "It's here right now, stronger than ever," she said quietly. "Not an 'it'—a 'she.'"

My scalp started to bristle.

Laurie rose up on one elbow and put her other hand on my arm. Her shoulders were bare.

"Do you know at all what I'm talking about?" she said, with a hint of pleading. "Or is it just me?"

I stared at her hidden eyes.

"What do you know about her?" I said.

"That she died young. That you were in love with her."

My rational mind told me this was insane, some kind of folie à deux. But that came about when two people developed it together— it didn't arise in them independently.

Then there was the fact that my whole world had gone insane.

"It's not just you," I said.

She sank down again, exhaling like she was letting out a breath that she'd held to the lung-bursting point.

"That's why I'm afraid," she whispered. "That I'm going to lose this as soon as I found it."

Her hand slipped down my arm into mine.

"She loved you, too, but she couldn't show it," Laurie said. "She wants to, now."

No doubt it was wrong, too, in all kinds of ways, but what the hell did right and wrong have to do with anything anymore?

The rest of Laurie was bare, too. I shut down my thoughts and let my hands dare to warm themselves on her silky skin.

FORTY-TWO

When dawn broke a couple of hours later, Laurie had fallen asleep, but I could tell I wasn't going to. I gathered my clothes quietly and dressed outside. My boots had gone cold and stiff, but I hardly felt them as I pulled them on. I walked into the trees to hunt for firewood, finally starting to think about what to do next.

The bit of sleep I'd gotten and the bracing morning air both helped to get my brain working again. But Laurie's warmth had been a far more potent reviver. Although our troubles hadn't lessened in any tangible way, I was gliding in an almost goofy rapture, an invisible shield that allowed me to see the situation without its choking me, and which pushed back the fatalism that had gripped me last night. Formidable as Balcomb was, he wasn't all-powerful. There still might be a way to take him down.

By the time I had a little blaze going, I'd formed a plan of sorts. It might not have been smart, but I didn't really care. There was a lot to be said for cheerfully accepting that you'd lost your mind.

I filled Madbird's camp kettle with clear water from the stream and put it on the fire. I was reluctant to wake Laurie, but I was feeling restless. I waited until the water boiled, then made a cup of instant coffee and took it to her. She looked tousled and pleasantly dazed, like she'd spent the night doing just what she had.

"I'd like to hit the road before too long," I said.

She stretched luxuriously, then lifted the sleeping bag's cover enough to give me an alluring glimpse inside.

"Sure you don't want to come back in?" she said.

"Soon, don't worry. I need a break. I'm out of shape for that kind of thing."

"Me, too," she said, a little shyly.

She'd seemed as hungry as me, that was for sure, and it pleased me to know that I wasn't sharing her with Balcomb.

She took the coffee mug, sipped, and grimaced.

"*That* woke me up," she said.

"There's sugar if you want it, and that nondairy creamer stuff."

"This is fine. Where are we going?"

"The Hi-Line. Up near the Canadian border."

Her face turned puzzled. "What's up there?"

"Kirk had a place in the Sweet Grass Hills. I want to look around it."

"Kirk? What's he got to do with this?"

"I'll tell you on the way." I started toward the fire to make a cup of coffee for myself.

"So you really did kill him," she said.

I managed not to turn around too fast. She smiled, like she was teasing me. I hoped so. The way she seemed to know things I couldn't explain was very unsettling.

"Where'd you come up with that?" I said.

She shrugged. "Just a feeling. You want to go there to make peace with him somehow."

Going to Kirk's didn't have anything to do with that—I would have sworn it on a stack of Bibles. But I felt that prickling in my scalp again.

"Sure, I killed him," I said. "That's the real reason I wanted to go to the sheriffs last night. Tell them all about it and get myself thrown in prison."

"All right, that was dumb. I just don't want you fooling around with any other ghosts. *Laying* them is what they say, you know."

"We're not at all sure Kirk *is* a ghost, and he's not my type, anyway." I leaned inside the van and kissed her. "Besides, the one I've got's already more than I can handle."

She bit my ear, not too hard, but not too soft, either.

"You do possess a certain rough-hewn charm," she murmured. "Where can a girl get a bath around here?"

I held Hannah's down coat for her while she slipped demurely into it, then led her to the creek. The water was icy and this wasn't a sunny afternoon when you could jump in for a pleasant shock and then lazily warm yourself, so I showed her how to take a cowboy bath, crouching on the bank with a bar of soap and splashing face, armpits, and crotch, without getting in and freezing completely.

It was still very cold. She watched me skeptically, staying huddled up in the coat. I toweled off with a denim jacket of Madbird's I'd found in the van, then reversed it and gave it to her. The inside was flannel and a lot softer, although it smelled about the same. She took it gingerly, like she'd decided that being a little gamy wasn't so bad after all. But while I got dressed, she started rummaging through Hannah's magic satchel. She took out a little makeup kit and then a new packet of panties. They didn't look dainty, more like the everyday white cotton variety, and she examined them critically.

"Looks like Hannah got you covered for every contingency," I said.

"Well, these aren't the kinds of things *I'd* pick. But they'll do until I can get my own."

"Hey, no problem. There's a Bloomingdale's just down the road."

She gave me a contrite glance. "I didn't mean to sound rude. It's very sweet of her."

Probably no woman, in her heart, ever really approved of any other woman's taste. I walked to the campsite to clean up.

Apparently she found her nerve—when she came back she looked cold and damp, but fresh. She got into the van to dress. I heard the sound of plastic tearing, then the snap of elastic.

"Hannah and I *are* about the same size," she said. A minute later she got out, walked around to the van's side mirror, and started putting on lip gloss.

I was stowing the last of the gear when I heard a little clatter. I glanced at her and realized that she'd dropped the makeup kit. But instead of bending to pick it up, she was staring into the woods.

A man was walking out of the trees toward us. He was dressed in outdoors clothing that looked like it had just come off the shelf at Cabela's, and otherwise was completely ordinary-looking.

Except that he was carrying a leveled rifle.

As John Doe advanced, staring back at Laurie, his forefinger rose to tap menacingly beneath his right eye. It stood out like a stoplight, bloodred around the pupil.

Her knees gave a little kick like they were going to buckle. I stood stunned, with a single realization burning through my numbness— there was only one conceivable way he could have found us.

Madbird.

My great old friend had contacted Wesley Balcomb and turned Laurie and me into cash.

FORTY-THREE

John Doe took hold of Laurie's hair and pressed the gun's muzzle into the small of her back—not roughly, but with the air of a man who knew he was absolutely in control. This was the first real look I'd gotten at his face. Behind the blandness was something that suggested the kind of kid who enjoyed pulling the legs off bugs.

"Get down on your knees," he told me. His voice was an accentless monotone. "Then walk me through these last two days. Everything you saw, everybody you talked to, everything you said."

I didn't have any grandstand play of bravery in me. If I'd been alone, I might have gone for him out of sheer desperation. But he kept Laurie carefully between us, and if I did, she'd drop to the ground with her spine snapped in two. I didn't kneel, either. I would have, or flopped on my belly or back or done anything else in the world if I thought it would keep him from pulling the trigger. But he was going to anyway. I knew I'd end up screaming and groveling, but I'd go out feeling like less of an asshole if I did it after he shot me instead of before.

His mouth tightened. "All right, let's start with her," he said.

The rifle's muzzle slid down the back of her right leg to the pocket behind her knee. She was wild-eyed and panting, but this time there was nothing like a car key at hand.

I dropped to my knees.

He shifted the gun barrel to beside her waist, so it was pointed toward my belly. I sucked in my breath, staring at that quarter-inch circle inside a ring of blued steel that could hurl out a slug the size of a baby's fingertip with enough speed and force to turn a human being into an agonized lump of flesh.

A *boom* and a shriek ripped into my ears, so close together they were almost the same sound. My body convulsed, braced for the terrible surge of pain that would come in an instant.

But it didn't, and I started to grasp that the scream hadn't been mine.

John Doe was reeling backward, his arms flying upward like he'd just stepped barefoot on a hot wire. Blood was spilling out of his right upper arm. Laurie was stumbling away from him, moving like she was running underwater. The rifle was lying on the ground.

I scrambled to my feet, lunged forward, and full-faced John Doe with my right fist, catching him on the side of his mouth. The sound was like an ax splitting a chunk of wet larch. He screeched again and went spinning away.

I was starting after him to rip him several new assholes when a familiar gravelly voice spoke out.

"Sorry that took so long. I was trying to line up a better shot. Finally couldn't wait no more."

Madbird came walking into the clearing, holstering his long-barreled .41 Magnum pistol. He pulled a thick wad of bills out of his pocket and handed it to me.

"Here's your half," he said.

FORTY-FOUR

We found Laurie a hiding place up in a rock pile with a good view of the terrain, just in case Balcomb knew where we were or someone had heard the pistol shot. We made her comfortable with sleeping bags, food, and water. Then Madbird and I took John Doe for a hike deep into the back country, shoving him stumbling along with his elbows duct-taped tight together behind him and more wraps of it as blindfold and gag. Madbird had done this before. He stayed quiet and so did I. I wasn't about to intrude on what he might be remembering.

The way he'd engineered this left me helpless with admiration. Like I thought, he'd called Balcomb and offered us up for ten thousand dollars.

"Hot enough to fuck twice," was how he described Balcomb on the phone.

But Madbird had refused to identify himself, or give up our location, or meet face-to-face. Instead, he'd insisted that John Doe drop the money where the dirt road to here turned off the highway, and wait a few hundred yards away. Madbird then had appeared out of the woods, riding my Victor for maneuverability, scooped up the cash, and led John Doe to this spot. He'd marked it by throwing a towel on the roadside, then hauled ass. John Doe couldn't kill him before that, not knowing where the place was, or catch him afterward. A half mile farther, Madbird had dumped the bike and run back through the woods. John Doe had been wary, probably on the lookout for exactly that. Before he'd moved in on us, he'd hidden and waited ten minutes. With only the pistol, Madbird hadn't been able to get close enough for a decent shot until John Doe decided he was safe and got busy with us.

Five thousand bucks was a lot of money for me, especially if I figured it by the hour. Better still, another hired gun disappearing was going to drive Balcomb nuts. The more frustrated and desperate he got, the more likely he was to make a mistake.

After we'd marched John Doe four or five miles, we came to a rock shelf above a steep, deadfall-choked ravine.

Madbird gave me a nod and said, "This'll work. Tape his wrists."

He sliced John Doe's elbows free, at the same time torquing his wounded arm up into a hammerlock. John Doe thrashed and snarled into his gag. The round hadn't lodged in his triceps, just torn a gouge, and the bleeding had pretty much stopped. But it must have hurt like a bitch. Madbird shoved him face-first against a thick Doug fir. We forced his wrists around it so he was hugging it and I taped them together good and tight.

I'd been following Madbird's lead, assuming half-consciously that John Doe wouldn't be coming back with us, but not thinking about specifics. Now that the moment was here, my heart was starting to pound again. I tried to slow my breathing, reminding myself of what he'd been about to do to Laurie and me.

Then it occurred to me that you didn't need to bind somebody to a tree to shoot him.

John Doe seemed to be realizing the same thing. He craned his head around at us, cheeks puffing in and out like gills as he tried to mouth threats or pleas through the tape.

Madbird unsheathed his knife again—a scalpel-sharp, crescent-bladed Puma game skinner.

"Time you learned how to do this," he said to me. "I'll get you started, then you take over."

Learn how to do what? I tried to say. But my breath stuck in my lungs. Madbird put his left hand on top of John Doe's head like he was palming a basketball and slammed a hip into his back, pinning him against the tree.

"You grab hold here," Madbird said. He closed his fist and jerked the head back by the hair.

Then he pressed the knife blade just under the far left edge of the hairline.

"And slice toward you, nice and careful."

John Doe squealed, an impressively loud sound considering the duct tape.

My stopped-up breath exploded out of my mouth.

"Jesus, Madbird! Wait!"

He glanced over his shoulder at me, annoyed.

"You ain't got to yell, I'm standing right here."

I floundered to explain. "Shouldn't we at least kill him first?"

"What's the point of that?"

"Well—it just seems like, you know, common courtesy."

He lowered the knife and stepped away, shaking his head.

"Fucking white people. You already tell us how we're supposed to do everything else, and now this?"

John Doe was trying to hop around the tree, or maybe climb it. A thread-thin red streak a couple of inches long had appeared on his forehead where the blade touched and blossomed into a dribbling stream of blood. Madbird thunked the knife into the bark beside his face, raising another squeal.

"Your call," he said to me. "But if you don't mind a little advice, you're gonna have a problem. His hair got some kind of greasy shit on it." He sniffed his left palm and wiped it disgustedly on John Doe's back. "You got to reef on it pretty good to tear it loose, 'cause of all them roots going down. So I brung some dikes. It's kind of cheating, but *I* ain't gonna tell." He felt around in his pockets and pulled out an old pair of lineman's pliers, their scarred plastic grips wrapped with electrician's tape, and slapped them into my hand.

I walked to the bull pine and wrenched the knife free. By now John Doe was slamming his head against the tree, blowing snot like a mule and maybe trying to howl. I slammed my hip against his back like I'd seen Madbird do, clamped a hank of his greasy hair with the pliers, and twisted up hard. He bucked and gurgled, cheeks bulging. I raised the knife with my other hand and pressed its edge against his hairline.

Then I let go of him, and stepped around to the other side of the tree, and cut the tape on his wrists.

FORTY-FIVE

We sat John Doe on the ground, pulled off his stiff new hiking boots, sliced them to pieces, and threw those into the brush. Then Madbird crouched beside him with the knife point to his cheek and spoke close to his ear.

"Now, you go telling anybody what really happened here, it sure ain't gonna make you look good. If I was you, I'd disappear and let Balcomb worry. And you ever come near any of us again, you best believe I'll find you. I used to make my own living killing people. 'Cept it was hunting other soldiers in the jungle—not gunning down unarmed civilians."

John Doe had been clasping his wounded arm with his other hand, but now he raised it shakily to start tugging at the tape across his eyes. Madbird pressed the knife to his cheek again, a little harder this time, just enough to draw blood.

"I didn't say nothing about that," Madbird said. "Leave it on."

He jerked John Doe to his feet and gave him a shove toward the ravine. We watched him start picking his way down into it, mincing and stumbling in his socks.

"I wouldn't go yelling," Madbird called after him. "Lot of griz around. They hear you, they'll come check it out, and soon as they smell blood—like hot sauce on a taco."

"Rattlesnakes are what I'd worry about," I said. "They're going to be sunning on the rocks, and it's breeding season. They get real aggressive."

"You ain't lying. One of them motherfuckers bit me on the thumb one time. Arm swole up twice its size, doctors thought they were gonna have to cut it off."

In fact, the odds were next to nil of a bear taking enough interest in him to attack, and there were few, if any, snakes at this elevation. But it would give him something to keep his mind off his other problems.

Much more quietly, Madbird said, "I never scalped nobody, are you kidding? Never tortured, never raped. Never killed unless I had to." He paused and reconsidered. "Well—maybe if they really needed killing."

I'd picked up fast that the scalping was bogus—a harsh scare to pay back John Doe for his own cruelty. I'd realized, too, that Madbird was leaving his fate up to me.

I hadn't been sure until the last second whether or not I was going to cut his throat.

I wasn't sure why I'd backed off, either. It wasn't from fear of consequences or any other solid reason, like there'd been with Kirk. This terrain was so far from any beaten track, so rough and thickly wooded, that I was near to being lost myself. If we'd thrown him down into the ravine there'd soon have been nothing left but scattered bones, and even if somebody ever did chance across those, identifying him and linking him to me was a possibility as remote as this spot itself. Most likely my reluctance had stemmed from a deeply embedded knee-jerk concept of who I was. Killing Kirk in a frenzy of violence had been bad enough. Cold-blooded execution was unimaginable.

But now I started thinking it was really cowardice—that I'd shirked a grim but necessary duty, and excused myself by calling it mercy.

If ever I'd run into someone who needed killing, it was John Doe.

He was still practically crawling, easily within range of the long-barreled .41 Magnum. It was a very powerful pistol and, especially if you lay prone or braced yourself against a tree, quite accurate. All he'd feel would be an instant of impact to the back of his head, over with too quickly even to cause pain. Christ only knew how much more pain *he* was going to cause to how many people, maybe including us.

"You think I should do it?" I said to Madbird.

He rubbed the back of his hand against his jaw.

"Whichever way you go, you'll spend the rest of your life being glad of it and wishing you'd gone the other, both. Hard to tell which'll weigh heaviest."

"What about gunning down an unarmed civilian?"

"That ain't a unarmed civilian. That's something dressed up human."

I ran it through my mind again, this time with more focus, and finally got a glimmer of what was really holding me back.

"It's like I'm being offered some kind of free chance in a game," I said. "If I use it to take him out, that's one worry out of the way. But then I've spent it, and I might need it a whole lot more somewhere down the line."

Madbird nodded. "The way things been going, I'd say that's a real good bet."

We stayed and watched John Doe crash around in the brush until he finally disappeared. His odds of making it were pretty good. The Scapegoat was big and wild, but lost people usually survived in these kinds of woods, even for several days under far worse weather conditions. Especially in this climate, his wound wasn't life-threatening. Eventually he'd run into a marked trail, or he could follow a stream downhill if he had enough sense.

Although if he was both stupid and unlucky and kept going north into the Bob Marshall, he was in for a long walk.

FORTY-SIX

Laurie and I split off from Madbird, with him and me agreeing that I'd
contact him in a day or two. He drove his van home with the Victor in
the rear. We took the vehicle that John Doe had used. He'd switched
from his rental car to one of the Pettyjohn Ranch pickup trucks, a
four-wheel-drive king cab Ford that Balcomb must have given him
to navigate the Scapegoat's rough terrain. It was good cover—those
kinds of rigs were as common as rocks around here, and I was sure
that Balcomb wouldn't get the cops looking for it for fear that might
somehow connect him with John Doe.

The drive to the Hi-Line took several hours, and dusk was settling
in as we got there. We kept on going toward the Canadian border,
following the directions that Reuben had given me to Kirk's patch
of land. The highway was narrow and deserted, and the last of the
pavement gave out not long after we left the town of Sunburst, which
consisted largely of a café and a feed store with a few gas pumps.
From there, the roads were all dirt for more than a hundred square
miles.

Laurie had been silent for a long time. This country would do that
to you. We'd already been in the middle of nowhere, but this was a
different kind of nowhere—prairie that stretched almost unbroken
for a hundred miles south and west, several hundred miles east, and
north to the Arctic Circle. A friend of mine who'd been stationed at
Air Force missile silos around here claimed that if you stared long

enough into the vista, you could literally see the curvature of the earth.

The wind was ceaseless, rippling across the fields and whipping the yellow thistles that lined the road. Flocks of little swallows skimmed along in front of the truck, and everywhere, we heard the liquid warble of meadowlarks closing down the day. Oil derricks in the fields bobbed patiently up and down like giant insects from a sci-fi movie drinking the earth's blood. We saw some cattle, a couple of pronghorns, and one hawk. But there were no people or vehicles and hardly any signs of human presence except for an occasional ranch mailbox or a distant building. The deepening twilight underscored it all, bringing the uneasy sense of choking off the last connection to the world we'd always known.

That left just her and me alone together, with everything that had happened and everything that might. It filled the cab like the engine's drone.

"I tried to find out more about you," she said suddenly. "But I didn't want anybody to know I was interested, so I didn't get far."

Her voice came as a pleasant little shock. Staying quiet had suited me—I had plenty to think about. But having her back was nice.

"Find out more what?" I said.

"The usual things women want to know. Like how many ex-wives."

I glanced over at her. She looked alert and inquisitive, out of her withdrawal. The West Butte of the Sweet Grass Hills was coming into sight, a craggy upthrust of almost seven thousand feet that relieved the somber bleakness. And maybe it had occurred to her that the farther we went, the farther we left behind John Doe and Balcomb and all the rest of that. Still, it was another measure of her sand that she could start up a conversation like we were on a first date.

"Just one," I said.

"Kids?"

"Nope."

"Previous work experience?"

I smiled. "I spent some time as a journalist."

"Really? Was that the 'other guy' you talked about? Or should I say, didn't talk about?"

"That was what he did for a living."

"What else did he do?"

"Failed, mostly," I said. "I'd just as soon keep not talking about him."

"Painful to remember?"

Both more and less than that, I thought.

"It's kind of like what you told me about another ghost," I said. "I want you all to myself."

Her eyes changed slightly, enough to show that she was pleased.

I'd been driving slowly, partly because of the rough road and partly waiting for full night. Most likely we'd go unnoticed. But particularly when we got to Kirk's, I wanted to be extra careful. His place was surrounded by private ranch land that I was going to have to cross. I was sure the rancher had been contacted about his disappearance by now, and would probably be keeping an eye out in case he showed up.

"How we doing for time?" I asked Laurie.

I rarely wore a watch. Hers, a slender gold Bulgari that was probably worth more than the truck we were driving, had caused a minor panic earlier today—as we'd been leaving the campsite, she thought she'd lost it. We'd hunted around a couple of minutes with no luck and left without it, but then she'd realized it had probably slipped off while she and I were thrashing around last night. We were still on the dirt road in the Scapegoat with Madbird right behind us in the van, so she'd jumped out of the pickup and gotten in with him to look for it. When we stopped at the highway a few minutes later and she came hurrying back to the truck, I'd seen with relief that she was wearing it.

She told me it was a quarter to seven. We were within a few miles of Kirk's now and darkness was settling fast. I started refocusing on why we'd come here.

"Now let me ask you some things," I said. "What made you and your husband decide to buy the Pettyjohn Ranch?"

"Wesley wanted it."

"You didn't?"

"I thought it was insane from the first. But I went along, like always."

"So tell me why a city businessman who doesn't know anything about horses or even like them decides to move to Montana and start raising them? I mean, I can buy it up to a point that he's trying to compensate for his feelings of inadequacy or whatever. But that's a hell of a lot of compensation."

"There was also a much more practical reason. He needed money. Like always."

"I don't get that, either. From what I've heard, he's not making any or really even trying to."

"That's not what I mean. It was a way of getting his hands on more of mine."

I shook my head, confused still further. My sense of finances didn't extend much beyond going to work and bringing home a paycheck, and the more macro the economics got, the more micro my grasp was. The concept of trickle-down threw me completely.

"My inheritance is controlled by trustees," she explained patiently. "They let Wesley invest out of it at first, but he went through several million and ended up with nothing but debt. My family got furious and had us cut off. We got an allowance, but no capital."

Life's hard lessons, I thought. The "allowance" probably would have financed a third world nation.

"Then Wes came up with the ranch scheme, and he made me go to the trustees and convince them it was for me," she said. "I'd fallen in love with the west, it would be my lifelong dream, all that. They finally agreed to give him the down payment, but that was the end."

"But he didn't gain any cash, right?" I said. "Just the opposite—he took on a huge mortgage to pay off." I had only a rough idea of what a place like that was worth, but for sure it was more than twenty million and maybe closer to twice that. "He must have known there wouldn't be any short-term profit. How'd he figure to make money? How *is* he making it?"

"Is this why you wanted me all to yourself?" she said, with sudden sharpness. "To interrogate me about my husband's business?" She swung away to gaze out her window, crossing her arms.

I exhaled. "Laurie, I've hardly been able to think about anything but you and last night. But I need to make sense of all this. It's the only chance I can see for us getting out of it." I reached over and touched her knee. "I intend to give you my full attention real soon, believe me."

She squeezed my hand forgivingly but didn't turn to look at me.

"Wesley found a new investor," she said. "A man named DeBruyne. The kind you never hear about, but very rich and powerful. I think he's Belgian originally, but he has homes all over the world."

I blinked. That was news.

"How did Balcomb 'find' this guy?"

She shrugged. "Business contacts, I suppose. I really don't know."

"And he just started writing checks? Let's face it, Laurie, your husband doesn't have the kind of track record that would draw most smart investors."

"Monsieur DeBruyne literally has more money than he knows what to do with. What matters to him is the huge cachet—a ranch in Montana and fine thoroughbred horses."

"Has he ever been here?"

"No. Wesley wants their partnership kept secret. I'm not even supposed to mention his name."

"I'd say all those kinds of bets are off now."

For a couple of seconds, I thought she hadn't heard me. Then she turned and gave me a smile, warm and steady.

"Of course they are," she said. "It just hasn't sunk in yet."

FORTY-SEVEN

The ranch that surrounded Kirk's place was owned by a family named Jenner. We drove past the headquarters, a distant cluster of lights inside their main gate, then another couple of miles to the back road Reuben had described. I didn't want to risk driving on their land, but Kirk's was only about a mile and a half in. I figured I could make it there on foot, take a quick look around, and be back within an hour. There was no good place to hide the truck—not a tree in sight, and the landscape was flat as a lake—but we still hadn't seen anybody, and the odds were slim that we would. I found a roadside patch of tall weeds, gave Laurie the rest of the brandy, and told her if somebody did come by to spin a story about a spat and a boyfriend out taking an attitude adjustment walk.

The autumn chill had a real bite up here, borne on that wind that never stopped. It gave me extra incentive to travel fast and I made good time, with enough moonlight for fair visibility filtering down through the hazy clouds.

The site was easy to recognize from Reuben's description. The flat terrain dropped abruptly into a shallow coulee, sheltered and pretty, with timbered slopes and a little creek running through. The road was carved to the bottom in a few long switchbacks. Near where they ended, I could just make out the small dark shape of the shack. I walked on down there, moving quietly now on the tiny chance that someone might be keeping watch for Kirk. But it seemed as deserted as any place could ever be.

I wasn't surprised to see that his building repairs hadn't gone any farther than hauling in some materials and dumping them haphazardly outside. The lumber was warped from long exposure to the sun and the insulation had the dead soggy look of many soakings. I turned on my flashlight and stepped inside. Even calling it a shack was saying too much. It was a box hardly bigger than a pickup truck, with a sagging tin roof, rotting floor, and gaps in the barn-wood walls. Broken glass panes in the couple of windows were stuffed with rags. The furniture consisted of a bunk like a workbench, a rickety table, and a pair of chairs. The bedding, dishes, and a few cans of food were all layered with dust.

So was the mining equipment—picks and shovels, a couple of gold pans, a chemical kit, and a collection of smaller items like hammers and a compass. There were also half a dozen books on the subject. Most of the stuff was brand-new, as if he'd gotten a list somewhere, walked into a store, and bought everything on it. There was an element both laughable and pathetic about it, like with a kid who decides he's going to take up a hobby and acquires all the gear, then quickly loses interest.

But it strengthened my guess as to the actual reason Kirk had wanted this place. He'd never intended to prospect or even spend any time here to speak of. The mining tools and building materials were for show—an excuse to come here and a red herring for the ranch hands. They probably shook their heads at his ignorant belief that he was going to find gold—but never suspected what he was really up to. The Canadian border was within another two miles—just a waist-high barbed-wire fence across those empty fields. The contraband could easily have been brought here or even thrown over the fence for him to pick up.

I also didn't have much doubt by now that I'd been wrong in thinking Wesley Balcomb wouldn't be involved in something so crude. His horse-raising business was just as much of a sham as the gold panning.

The pieces were fitting together better by the hour.

When I'd talked to Reuben last night—Christ, was it only last night?—he'd told me the story behind the sale. Balcomb had already looked at several other pieces of property around the state, without making any offers. But he'd quickly gotten serious with Reuben and agreed to the asking price.

Reuben was dubious. As a matter of course, he'd checked Balcomb's financial history and learned that it was shaky. Because of that and Balcomb's inexperience, Reuben figured the venture was doomed to foreclosure. But Balcomb came up with a down payment of more than three million dollars, which must have been the last of the money he'd been able to squeeze out of Laurie's trust, plus financing for the remainder. Reuben was surprised that any bank would give him that kind of loan—and more surprised when Balcomb not only kept up with the payments, but started throwing a ton more money into building projects.

"Everybody but the government understands that if you're already up to your ass in debt and you keep spending way more than you bring in, you're bound to crash," was how Reuben had put it.

He did some more clandestine checking through his banking connections, but all he could find out was that Balcomb's money was coming from numbered offshore accounts. His puzzlement turned to suspicion about the legitimacy of the income's source. But Balcomb had cashed him out and now owned the ranch, so at least officially, Reuben no longer had any dog in the fight. He let the matter go.

But now I knew that the money was coming from an ultrarich Belgian "investor"—a connection that Balcomb wanted kept secret.

For a man like DeBruyne to acquire, say, heroin in Pakistan or Afghanistan and transport it across Russia would be easy. Alaska was a short hop from Siberia, and its northern regions and the Canadian Arctic were so wild they made this area look like Disneyland. The tricky part would be getting the stuff into the continental United States. For the kind of money we were talking about, the quantities would have to be fairly large and the runs frequent. Strangers around here often would quickly attract attention, and would also face the vulnerability and complications of transporting the stuff a long way to its final destination. Kirk had a legitimate ticket to travel in and out of this area and an influential family name as an added buffer. He could get the contraband to the ranch quickly and safely, and Balcomb could put it on a private jet.

That was why he'd agreed so readily to Reuben's terms. The Pettyjohn place was a perfect glossy cover—nobody would dream that a wealthy, upper-crust gentleman rancher might be involved in such a thing—and Kirk was the perfect mule, already dabbling in crime and easily persuaded to go deeper.

The timing bolstered my guesswork. Soon after Balcomb's arrival on the scene, Kirk's supposed interest in gold panning here had flared up. Soon after that, he'd gotten flush. And Balcomb's much bigger money train had come rolling in, with the bonus of stroking his ego through living on a grand estate like a feudal lord ruling over his serfs.

There were plenty of gaps in the framework, but the only piece that really didn't fit was those murdered horses. What Madbird had suggested was still the only thing that made sense. But with Kirk's smooth setup in place, why the need for it? I had to think they'd been brought across the border under the eyes of the authorities—otherwise, using them for concealment wouldn't have made sense—and that meant extra risk and expense, plus the trouble of getting the contraband into them.

Not to mention the horror of getting it back out.

I spent a few more minutes poking around through Kirk's stuff. There wasn't much to see—nothing to suggest that he'd done more than occasionally pass through. The dates on the food cans were all about two years old. Then I noticed a folded sheet of paper sticking out slightly from one of the books. I was surprised that he'd ever opened them. It was a paperback titled *Consumer Guide to Precious Metals And Gems*. The sheet had numbers scrawled on it. I slipped the book inside my shirt. I doubted that people who might check on Kirk would notice that it was gone, and if they did, all they'd know was that somebody else had been here.

I hiked back up to the rim of the coulee, out of its shelter and into the cold raw wind, and stood there for half a minute, looking down at this little pocket of land that embodied Kirk's easy-money, wise-guy dream.

My hand had killed him, but that dream had pushed my hand.

FORTY-EIGHT

When I got into the pickup truck, Laurie gave me a kiss that was generous and sweet with brandy.

"Let's get away from here," I said. "Then we'll find a place to spend the night."

"You promised me your full attention, remember?"

"I remember, believe me." I started the engine and pulled out of the weeds onto the road. For another half minute, I hesitated, reluctant to trespass on her affectionate mood. But this was too important to put off.

"Laurie, did you ever think your husband might be involved in some kind of illegal operation?" I said.

I could feel her shrug, nestled against me.

"He's committed crimes. But you don't need me to tell you that."

"I mean smuggling."

That brought her sitting up straight. "Smuggling?"

"Yeah. Using Kirk's place to run dope across the border."

"That's just crazy." She looked at me in some combination of amusement and outrage, then moved away and rolled her window down a few inches. A breeze swept into the cab, ruffling her fine hair.

"What about that guy DeBruyne?" I said. "Could he be in the heroin business?"

"Why would a man that rich deal heroin?"

"Maybe that's how he got that rich."

The breeze was chilly. She rolled the window back up.

"I told you, I don't know much about him," she said.

"You know his first name?"

"Guy something—one of those hyphenated French first names. Guy-Luc, I think."

"Did you ever meet him?"

"No. Look. Forget about your theories. Wesley is determined to have us both killed. What does it take to get that through your skull?"

"Like I've been saying, the only thing that might help—"

"None of this is going to help! It's just you jerking off."

I'd already had glimpses of the edge she could get, but this time she flared up white-hot, scorching me with her glare and voice.

"I've sat around and waited for you hour after hour, slept in a greasy toolbox, peed on the ground, and now you drag me to this asshole of the earth. I want a hot bath and a bed. I want decent clothes."

She twisted around and grabbed something out of the cab's rear seat, then yanked open her door and flung it out onto the roadside. The truck's interior light flicked on, and I just had time to see that the something was Hannah's bag.

I hit the brakes hard, got out, found the bag, and brushed it off carefully.

When I got back to the truck, Laurie was hunched over with her face in her hands.

"I can't believe I did that," she whispered. "It was terrible. But there's so much going on inside me, I feel like I'm going to explode."

I set the bag on the rear seat and started driving again.

"I don't blame you for being pissed at me," I said. "But that's an insult to my friends. Who were incredibly good to you."

She inhaled slowly and deeply, like she was trying to calm herself.

"I told you I tried to leave Wesley once before," she said. "That's why I recognized John Doe. I know he's gone but—" She shook her head, still in her hands. "It keeps coming back in my mind."

It cooled me down some to remember her terror of John Doe. I stroked her hair until she raised her face to me.

"Will you tell me about it now?" I said.

She nodded, then took a drink from the brandy bottle and passed it to me. There wasn't a whole lot left.

"It started the way a lot of sad things do," she said. "Naive young woman in love with an older man. Sinclair Teague, a local polo star." She shook her head ruefully. "But he'd screw anything that would stay still long enough, and one night I went to his house and found him with some slut. I screamed and broke things. He threw me out. I drove to our country club to drown my silly sorrows.

"Wesley was there. I hardly knew him. He'd sort of drifted into our social circle, nobody seemed quite sure how. He didn't come from our kind of people, and there were rumors that he had shady dealings. But he was smart and charming, and he saw how upset I was, and he bought me drinks and let me cry on his shoulder."

I'd encountered that story, too, back when I'd been working on the newspaper—have-nots and poseurs who circled the rich like sharks, striking when they smelled blood. Most of the time the motive was money, but often enough there was a craving for power, the satisfaction of dominating social superiors. That could make things particularly vicious.

"I went home, alone," Laurie said. "Then later that night—someone set fire to Sinclair's stables."

"Jesus," I said. That was a variation I hadn't heard before. "Were there horses inside?"

"Whoever did it let them out first, thank God. It was still horrible." She breathed in deeply again. "There were people who thought it was me."

I listened, numb with astonishment, as she talked on. Her enraged lover, Teague, had gone to the police with the story of their fight.

Laurie was known to be hot-tempered, and he suggested that she had set the fire to get back at him for cheating. It didn't help that she'd been drinking and that no one had seen her after she left the bar. But that was all there was, a vague cloud of suspicion. It was essentially unthinkable that a young gentlewoman in a wealthy Virginia enclave could do something like that, and family and friends were supportive.

So was Wesley Balcomb. He came to see her immediately after news of the fire broke and checked on her every few days, making it clear that his shoulder was available to lean on again—and even hinting that he had connections who could work behind the scenes if she ran into trouble.

That trouble wasn't long in coming. About two weeks later, the woman Teague had been dallying with, a barroom pickup from a nearby town, called Laurie. She'd worked up her nerve enough in the interim to threaten blackmail. She claimed that when Teague had gone running to fight the fire, she'd looked out a window and seen Laurie driving away. Her price for silence was a hundred thousand dollars.

Laurie was distraught. She had no way to prove her innocence. At the very least, her reputation would be tarnished forever. She had no one to turn to, either—her lover was an enemy now and she couldn't bear dragging her family into a nightmare of police, lawyers, and media.

She was putting together the money when Balcomb stopped by—a sympathetic, powerful figure who knew how to handle situations like this. She confided in him. He assured her that he would take care of it. She agreed, insisting that she didn't want anyone hurt, just scared into backing off.

Laurie never heard from the woman again. It seemed that she left the area abruptly.

Now Laurie both owed Balcomb and had reason to fear him. He traded on that to insinuate himself firmly into her life, and soon started talking marriage.

"I guess I'd known he must want something in return, but I never dreamed it would be that," she said. "I put him off as long as I could. But he's very good at playing on people's weaknesses, and I was a mess."

All had gone smoothly enough at first. Balcomb's charm burgeoned with his newfound stature, along with the family purse strings being cut loose. Their lavish lifestyle stood in for love. But now she started to learn that her husband was a lousy businessman. He ignored sound advice, made disastrous decisions, and refused to back down. The worse things got, the more stubborn and arrogant he became, until her angry family and trustees cut him off. He treated Laurie more and more coldly, almost to the point of menace.

Then the real ugliness started. The remains of a woman were discovered in a nearby river and identified as those of the would-be blackmailer. The police learned that just before her disappearance, she had done some barroom boasting about getting a large chunk of cash just for making a phone call.

The raw truth hit Laurie fast. Balcomb had set the whole thing up in order to gain control over her and her fortune. He'd seen his chance when he'd found her drinking that night, gotten someone to light the fire, bribed the woman to make the threat—and then removed it.

"I thought my heart was going to stop," Laurie said. Her voice had dropped to where I was having trouble hearing her over the engine's noise. "All I could think was, he'd promised he wouldn't hurt her but then he'd had her killed. Except really, it was me that had her killed."

She'd been alone in their house when she realized this. She'd thrown some things into a suitcase and left, to try to cope with these new demons. The only thing she was sure of was that she was done with him. At first she drove aimlessly, but then she turned west toward Kentucky and a place called Avondale Farm, a renowned thoroughbred center where she'd gone to riding camp as a girl—following an instinct to go where she'd once been safe and happy.

She got a room at a nearby bed-and-breakfast and spent the next day wandering around Avondale, trying to lose herself in the beauty of the place and its graceful animals.

But she had thoughtlessly paid for her lodging and meals with credit cards.

Late that afternoon, while she was walking in a secluded area of the grounds, she heard a rustling behind her. Before she could turn, a stunning blow between her shoulder blades sent her stumbling through a gap in a hedge. A second blow knocked her flat on her face. The force felt electric rather than just blunt, maybe coming from a Taser. A knee pressed into her back, a forearm clamped around her throat, and she felt a sting in her arm. After a few seconds she couldn't move, although she stayed dimly conscious and she could still feel. She had probably been injected with something like Valium or Versed. A man carried her to the trunk of a car. He was wearing a golf shirt and pleated slacks, like he'd just come off the links. His face was as bland and ordinary as a concrete sidewalk.

John Doe.

He drove for a length of time she couldn't estimate, then opened the trunk again. The surroundings were silent and she could see treetops overhead. He pushed up her blouse, took out a small vial of clear liquid, and spilled a few drops onto her right breast. They burned like red-hot iron. He watched for a couple of minutes while she silently screamed and struggled feebly to move. Then he did the same to her other breast.

After that he set the vial in front of her face and left her alone for some time. She waited in terror, certain that he'd continue the torture and leave her dead in this forsaken spot.

But he closed the trunk's lid, drove back to where he'd found her, and left her lying hidden behind the hedge. Before much longer, she was able to move again. She managed to get to her inn. Next morning she went back to the husband who'd had this done to her and swore she'd never leave him again.

Laurie uncapped the brandy bottle and tipped it high, draining it. The glisten in her eyes spilled out onto her cheeks. I pulled off the road into one of the bleak fields and held her, wishing to Christ I'd known that story earlier today when Madbird and I had taken John Doe into the woods.

FORTY-NINE

We drove on south to Great Falls, stopping at a big Safeway emporium to buy a gourmet picnic of fresh sourdough bread, pâté, cheeses, and wine; and then at a liquor store where I replaced the bottle of Knob Creek bourbon I'd given Doug Wills. My pocket was fat with the roll of hundred-dollar bills that Madbird had given me, and I didn't see any reason to save for the future.

Then we went looking for a room. Great Falls was a fair-size place, with more than twice the population of Helena and plenty of motels. I didn't want to risk using my ID, but I was sure that a woman like Laurie, flashing fifty thousand dollars worth of jewelry, could float a story about losing her purse but having enough cash to pay for the night. The first place she tried, a new-looking Best Western on the Tenth Avenue strip, was happy to oblige. She registered under a phony name and let me in through a back entrance.

She ran a bath while I poured drinks, sauvignon blanc for her, whiskey on the rocks for me. When I took the wine to her, she was just stepping into the steaming tub. She knelt slowly, holding the sides, then sat back and slid forward up to her neck, with a little "oof." She accepted the glass with a radiant smile. I lingered for another moment. There was something very special about watching a lovely woman luxuriate in a bathtub. I hadn't done it in a long time. It was worth the wait.

After she was done we got into the smorgasbord. We'd eaten

sandwiches from a convenience store earlier in the day, but we were plenty hungry again, the food was delicious, and we pretty well demolished it. Then I took a shower and shaved, savoring yet another pleasure of hot water and feeling clean.

When I came out, she was sitting up in bed, looking solemn.

"She loved horses, too," Laurie said.

Her eerie revelation about Celia last night had been swirling around in my head with all the other craziness. The only explanation I could come up with was that my overheated brain had given Laurie's words a meaning that wasn't really there.

But goddammit, she was starting again.

"A lot of people do," I said.

"I mean in a special way. She could feel them—their pain."

"I'm not sure what you mean. No horse she was around ever got mistreated."

"Maybe not outright. But we geld the males, force the females to breed with strangers, take away their children."

I'd never thought of it like that.

"They loved her back," Laurie said. "They wouldn't have hurt her."

I blinked. This was getting less imaginary.

"How do you know she got hurt?" I said.

"I just do."

"Do you know how?"

Hesitantly, she said, "There was a stallion."

That flat startled me. It was a stallion that supposedly had thrown and killed Celia.

"You said a horse wouldn't have hurt her."

Laurie shook her head, confused now. "It's gone from my mind. It was there for just a second, and it seemed right. No to a horse, yes to a stallion."

I sat on the bed beside her. I still couldn't believe this was anything but crazy, but I couldn't stop a tickle of wondering if I'd been maligning Pete Pettyjohn all these years.

Her face softened and she relaxed against the pillows, turning on her side toward me.

"Do you want her again?" she said.

"I want *you*," I said, but in truth, I was talking to her and Celia both.

FIFTY

I was falling into the sleep that my whole being craved, soothed by the good bed and the comfort of the woman beside me. Her fingernails stroked my chest, sending me into near rapture. But then they started digging in, harder and harder until I opened my eyes.

"We can't rest yet," she said. She was propped up on an elbow, watching me.

"We can't?" I said groggily.

"I've been hopeless for so long, Hugh. But I feel like you've given me a new chance."

That was sweet to hear, but I couldn't see that I'd done much to earn it. When she'd yelled at me about jerking off, she was right. My scenario might have enough meat by now to get the cops interested, but the danger from Balcomb hadn't changed. He was probably already working on a replacement for John Doe. I'd been clinging to this dream time with her, holding off the snarling black dog of reality. But she was right about that, too—we couldn't just hide out and wish it away.

But all I could see was the same wearying labyrinth of dead ends.

"I was hoping I'd have something smart by now, but I don't," I admitted.

Her fingers returned to their light delicious teasing.

"You know there's only one real answer," she murmured.

I did—killing Wesley Balcomb.

The thought came instantly and naturally, without any element of shock. I realized that Laurie was only voicing aloud what had been growing in my mind all along.

But while I'd turned over many plans during the day's driving, I hadn't come up with any that weren't risky as hell. Right off came the problem of getting physically close without alerting him. Then there was the near certainty of getting caught. Rationally, I knew that spending my life in prison was preferable to both her and me being dead, but I still couldn't bring myself to accept it.

"I'd do it," I said. "I just can't see a good way."

"Maybe I can help."

I waited, not expecting much. Suggestions were cheap.

"That rifle is Kirk's, right?" she said.

"Yeah?"

"But nobody knows you have it. I mean, the police would never find out."

I ticked off the chain of ownership in my head. Balcomb had given the rifle secretly to John Doe, to plant the suspicion that Kirk had murdered me. For either of them to admit that would incriminate them. Laurie, Madbird, and I were the only others who knew what had happened to it.

"Probably not," I said.

"Wesley's a night owl. He's in and out of his office all the time, checking business on his computer. There are windows around the desk."

That got my full attention. I sat up.

"You drop the rifle like you panicked, and you hurry back here," she said. "The drive's not long, is it?"

"An hour and change."

"So it'll still be night. Nobody will see you. And I'll swear you were with me the whole time." Her fingers kept moving, making slow circles on my chest. "They'll find Kirk's rifle and think it was him. You'll have an airtight alibi. I'll have money again, so if there's any trouble, we'll hire the best lawyers in the country."

I had no trouble understanding her wanting Balcomb dead. Still, I was impressed at how much thought she'd given it.

"You think he'll be checking his computer, with everything else that's going on?" I said.

"He's compulsive about it. He'd do it if there was a mushroom cloud on the horizon."

"How would I get inside that fence?"

"I don't think you'd have to. It's not that far from the house."

I'd never been inside the compound, so I didn't know the layout.

"Show me," I said. I got up, walked to the window, and pulled aside the curtain. The vehicles in the parking lot glinted with unnatural colors under the sodium vapor lights. She came to stand beside me, scanned the area for a few seconds, then pointed at the logo above the entrance to the motel.

"That sign."

The distance was about sixty yards. The Mini-14 was very accurate at that range, and would fire thirty rounds as fast as you could touch them off. A backlit, stationary man framed in a window would be a prime target—a variation on what cops called a vertical coffin.

I closed the curtain and we got back into bed. She settled in snugly beside me, her breasts teasing my skin.

"You know it's not just us," Laurie whispered. "It's *her,* too. She's afraid she'll be hurt again. And this time, gone forever."

I gazed at this woman who I barely knew, and realized that she'd again touched something hidden in my thoughts. It didn't make any more sense than the rest of this. But it didn't have to.

She had already given me the gift of fulfilling a dream in a way that few people ever did. Now fate was offering me a second gift: redemption. As a boy, I had appointed myself Celia's protector, and I'd failed her.

If I could keep Laurie safe, I'd allow myself to believe I was also saving the mysterious presence of Celia that seemed to be touching her.

I found the bag of crosstops, swallowed four, and pulled on my clothes.

FIFTY-ONE

I left Great Falls in a state of cold euphoria, with my path lit by the dark inner lamp that Laurie had kindled. It was about one-thirty in the morning. The roads were almost deserted. I stayed just under the speed limits and casually shielded my face when another vehicle did come close.

Laurie had sketched a rough map of the compound while I dressed. Knowing that Balcomb would be in that room was the key. The rest fell readily into place. I'd leave the truck at the dead end of the same dirt road where Balcomb had tossed Kirk's rifle for John Doe to pick up. From there it was a few hundred yards on foot, skirting the fence, to the stakeout point. There was no one else staying there now, and the closest residences were the ranch hands' trailers, a good mile away. If anybody heard the shots, I'd be gone before they could get there. Most likely he wouldn't be discovered until somebody missed him and went looking for him.

The logistics of covering my tracks were trickier. The mistakes I'd made with Kirk still scared the shit out of me. The upside was that I'd given a lot of thought to what I would have done differently, and that kicked in. The downside was that my margin was a lot narrower this time. For openers, the sheriffs weren't going to have any trouble finding the crime scene. I could only try to minimize the risks.

First came the rifle. I had barely touched it—just picked it up by the stock to put it in the truck, back at the campsite—and I'd

carefully wiped it clean since then. But I couldn't count on doing that
again effectively, in haste and in the dark. I didn't have gloves, and I
didn't want to chance buying anything that a clerk might remember.
Wrapping it would be easiest, but that might leave fabric traces,
even microscopic, that were identifiable—any clothing or gear that
belonged to Laurie or Madbird or me could link it to us. I didn't want
to use anything from around Great Falls, either—the fact that I'd
been staying there would be known, and material from there turning
up at the scene would be a highly suspicious coincidence.

The safest course I could see was to go scavenging when I got to
Helena. I could filch a garbage bag out of a dumpster for wrapping
the rifle. The thin plastic wouldn't impair my shooting, it would
keep my clothes and skin free of residue, and I could shove it inside
my shirt when I dropped the weapon and burn it on the way home.
I'd obscure my boot prints by lashing a couple of small green pine
branches to the soles like miniature snowshoes. There were plenty of
haystacks along the way where I could cut baling twine.

The best thing about this, giving me a grim and maybe ugly
satisfaction, was that it would point strongly to Kirk's settling a score
with Balcomb—exactly the setup that Balcomb had intended for me.
Besides obvious evidence like the rifle itself, there were some extra
factors that stood to work for me more subtly, such as that Kirk had
almost certainly loaded the clip. I hadn't touched it and I didn't see
any reason why Balcomb or John Doe would have, so Kirk's prints
would be on the shell casings. Wiping down the rest of the rifle but
forgetting the bullets was just the kind of fuckup that everybody
knew he was airhead enough to pull.

The aftermath was likely to be the most treacherous part, but
that was falling into place, too. Laurie would maintain that she'd
sensed her husband's long-standing menace toward her jumping
to an almost psychotic level over the past days. When he'd left the
house Sunday afternoon, she'd discovered that he'd taken her purse,
including the keys to her SUV—leading her to think that he intended
her harm. There were a few ranch vehicles around, and she knew that

the keys were usually left in them. That was how she'd gotten this pickup truck.

She'd fled in panic, coming to me because I was also on Balcomb's wrong side, I knew my way around this area, and she felt an affinity for me. She'd insisted that we not call the sheriffs, fearing that they'd inform Balcomb and he'd find her. We'd driven around until we were too worn out to go any farther, then checked into the motel. The following day—the day that stretched ahead now—we'd learned the shocking news about her husband.

What would happen next with her and me, we hadn't talked about. But we both knew what had started.

The future hinged on getting clear. There'd be suspicious investigators—Gary Varna, for damned sure—and it was all too possible that I'd get tripped up by my own bungling or some forensic detail I'd never imagined. But I'd have a powerful ace in the hole— precisely the kind of slick lawyers that I'd feared, but on my side. All I had to do was stay within the limits of reasonable doubt.

That, and kill Wesley Balcomb.

FIFTY-TWO

But by the time I got to the red rock canyons of Wolf Creek, I'd become aware of a disturbing undercurrent that I couldn't get hold of. It wasn't any hesitation about whether I could pull the trigger. It wasn't fear, either. I'd been getting more scared as the reality neared, true, but also more exhilarated. It was something like getting into the ring, although with infinitely higher stakes.

I turned off the freeway at the exit to Lincoln, the shortest route to the Pettyjohn Ranch. But then I pulled over and waited by the roadside a minute.

I hadn't planned on seeing Madbird—I figured I'd bring him up-to-date as soon as I got the chance. But now I decided it would be best to warn him—even Madbird might slip up if he got blindsided. I'd made good time getting here and it wouldn't take much longer.

At least that's what I started off telling myself. But really, it was about that different world that I'd blundered into, where nothing would ever be the same again. Madbird had opened his great fierce heart to me, been my guide and protector, taken huge risks, for no reasons that logic could touch—just his odd liking for me and the joy of being a guerrilla Indian.

I was a child there. I needed him again, this time not for tangible help, but for some form of blessing. Maybe that would quell the uneasiness that was crawling around under my skin.

I got to his place, pulled the pickup into his drive, and waited beside it. He'd hear it and come out, although he wasn't going to be real happy to see me in the middle of the night.

The door opened a minute later. He walked out wearing jeans and a sweatshirt that looked hastily pulled on.

"What's the problem, you run out of beer?" he said.

"Sorry to wake you."

He grunted, his gaze checking out the truck.

"Where's your pal?" he said.

"Great Falls."

"Lucky girl. So what's going on?"

I had a hard time speaking the words. They felt like bluster.

"I'm going to take out Balcomb," I said. "I thought I'd better tell you."

Madbird folded his arms and cocked his head to the side.

"Well, I ain't saying that's a bad idea," he said. "I hope you got it figured real careful. You know the cops are going to come down hard on you."

"The best I could. Whatever happens, I'll keep you out of the loop."

"Laurie OK with this?"

"She told me how to set it up."

"No shit?"

"He'll be in his office," I said. "Lit windows, easy shot."

"What about after?"

"She'll back me up with money and lawyers."

"No shit," Madbird said again.

Then he stepped forward, a movement so swift and abrupt it was almost a lunge, and clenched my shirtfront in his fist.

"Let me tell you something, white boy." His voice was harsh and his eyes were hard. I stared into them with disbelief. Madbird had never treated me like that.

"You remember when she said she lost her watch? That was bullshit. I seen her pull it out of her pocket. She wanted a excuse to ride with me. Soon as she got in, she was all over me—tongue in my ear and her hand like this." He slapped his inner thigh.

My jaw sagged open. I couldn't speak. I felt like I was floating, with no power of control.

"She wanted me to ditch you," he said. "Said she knew I was the warrior that got sent to save her. I told her, go home with the one that brung you."

He shoved me ungently against the truck and stalked back to lean in the doorway.

"You got to kill that motherfucker, go kill him," Madbird said. "But don't do it for her."

With the blinders ripped off my eyes, I saw with sudden vicious clarity the imp that had been tormenting my subconscious, hidden under the intensity of the long day past.

When Laurie had come racing to my cabin to warn me about John Doe, how the hell had she known how to get there? Finding a place like mine took work. Even with directions, maps, a GPS system, somebody who didn't know the area wasn't about to home straight in on it, let alone when she was driving in panicked flight from a hired killer.

She had been there before. She had pointedly avoided telling me so. She had to have a reason for both those things.

The jolts kept rocking me hard and fast.

I know how to deal with fire.

There were people who thought it was me.

I finally got my voice back.

"My lumber," I said. "She's the one who torched it. That was her."

When I got back to Great Falls, she was gone.

PART
FIVE

FIFTY-THREE

I kept on driving after that, like a ghost haunting this land where I'd once lived—like I'd felt on the night of my last ring fight up at Rocky Boy all those years ago, sensing that I was unreal to the Indians. Except now it seemed turned around, with Madbird my only point of contact.

Little memory bytes kept coming all along the way, combining into an ongoing ache. When the first hints of dawn thinned the darkness, I was getting toward Lewistown, where my carpenter buddy Emil had grown up. Several summers ago, he'd gotten us a job framing a house in the nearby hills, a nice little gig except that you had to shit out in the brush and there were a lot of rattlesnakes living in that. It was funny, sort of.

I cut south through Judith Gap to Harlowton, then west again, following the Musselshell and the abandoned Milwaukee Road tracks. Twodot was the next town along the way, a place that lived up to its name. There wasn't much there but the Twodot Bar, where my boxing partner Charlie and I had stopped for a beer one time on our way home from Billings. He and a rancher's daughter fell in love, and I'd ended up hanging around drinking and playing pool for two days before they fell out again.

A few miles ahead, the other side of Deep Creek Canyon, I could see the peaks of Mounts Edith and Baldy. I'd taken Sarah Lynn camping up there early on in our courtship, a long hike to a pristine, deserted little lake. There we had shyly and clumsily lost our virginity to each other.

I'd sure been a sweetheart to her through all this.

The small road I was on dead-ended in a tee intersection with Highway 89. I put on my right turn signal, stopped at the stop sign, and carefully looked both ways. The vista was empty—no vehicles, no people, nothing moving but some cattle in a distant meadow.

But when I let out the clutch, my hands didn't turn the steering wheel. I just drove straight across the highway, through the dead end and into the grassy field beyond, until the truck's front wheels dropped into the roadside ditch and it lurched to a stop.

I had to put it into four-wheel drive to get out of there, but I managed to do it before anybody came along and saw me. I backtracked a mile or so along the Musselshell and found a dirt spur road that led down to an old railroad trestle.

Then I pulled the truck behind its shelter and crashed in a sleep of exhaustion and defeat.

FIFTY-FOUR

I waited until dusk to go to Madbird's place, figuring that if the sheriffs came around to talk to him, they'd most likely do it during the day. As it turned out, they hadn't yet, and that made me nervous. He was due.

"Keep a eye open for Bill LaTray, too," Madbird said. "He called today, asking if I seen you. I didn't tell him nothing. Most Indians I could talk to and get things straight, but he ain't one of them."

Hannah looked tough and foxy and gave me a big warm hug. I returned her bag, with deepened shame at how Laurie had treated it and how I'd been too besotted to heed that warning. I couldn't bring myself to mention it.

"This was great," I said. "Like one of those fairy tales where every time you reach in, you pull out just the right thing."

"I figured that with her, you were going to need all the help you could get," Hannah said.

That took me aback. I'd thought Laurie had passed muster fine.

"What made you think that?" I said.

"I just didn't have a good feeling."

Madbird cut in. "She put it a little different, soon's you two drove away. How'd that go again, baby?"

"You shut up," Hannah said fiercely.

"'She already got his pecker on a string, he better watch out she don't hang him by it'—something like that," he stage-whispered to me.

I couldn't help smiling, although pathetically. I went outside to stash Balcomb's truck in the woods.

I'd slept only a couple of hours when I'd bombed out earlier today, but I'd slept hard, and it had helped a lot to clear my mind. I'd spent most of the time between then and now parked up a secluded Forest Service road in Deep Creek Canyon, pacing around through the trees and trying to put things together.

Laurie had recognized a special connection between her and me, all right—that I was fuckhead enough to rid her of the husband she hated and feared, and put her in control of her money again. The way she'd set it up was worthy of Balcomb himself. Clearly, she'd learned a lot from him.

She also clearly knew quite a bit about Celia, and not from any ethereal wavelength. I remembered something Kirk had said when we were out by the lake, which hadn't meant anything to me at the time—Beatrice, his mother, had mistaken Laurie for a grown-up Celia the first time they met.

My guess was that Laurie had been curious about that, asked around, and learned the story. Someone must have mentioned that I figured into it and I was now back working at the ranch. The information had germinated in her mind and sprouted into an idea. She'd cultivated that into a plan.

It had run into trouble as soon as she made her move, with me getting fired and thrown off the ranch, ending her pretexts for "accidentally" running into me and furthering our acquaintance. But she'd seen a way to turn that around—to keep the drama going, send my rage at Balcomb into orbit, and insinuate herself as my ally, all in one brilliant stroke. She knew that I was going to jail and that she'd have time to find my place.

And to set that lumber on fire.

But she hadn't known about what was going on behind the scenes—how desperate Balcomb was and how dangerous things would get. Once that came home to her, she'd realized, correctly, that Madbird was a much better bet for protection than me, and she'd made a grab for him. Probably she'd figured that she could convince him of the need to kill Balcomb, and he'd be a lot more skillful at that, too. But she'd ended up stuck with me, and Madbird had added insult to injury by turning down her advances—the underlying reason for the fury that led her to pitch Hannah's bag out the window.

She'd rebounded fast again and gotten the train back on track, sending me chugging along to what looked like a sure thing after all. Then she'd left me to twist in the wind. I'd discovered today that she'd peeled several hundred dollars off my roll of bills while I was in the shower or asleep, like a hooker rolling a drunk. She could have gone to another motel or another city. There was no knowing what kind of story she planned to tell the authorities; but for sure, Madbird was right—I'd have been on the wrong side of those lawyers once more, this time with cold, and highly visible, blood on my hands.

The Celia angle was another brilliant stroke, and she'd played it beautifully, starting slow, gauging my reactions, and jacking it up a little at a time. She'd picked up specifics somehow, like the bits of information and mannerisms she'd dropped. I guessed that her being on horseback when she'd first come on to me was no accident. She'd obviously known that Celia had done a lot of riding on the ranch, and probably intended for me to subconsciously make that association. I even suspected that she'd gotten a photo or detailed description of Celia, and had dyed her hair to heighten the resemblance—I remembered thinking that on the previous glimpses I'd gotten of Laurie, the color had seemed a subdued brown, but when I'd first seen her coming across the meadow, it had struck me as that same flaming auburn as Celia's.

I didn't think that without that aspect, I'd have let her lead me so far. But Lord, the way I'd bought it made me want to weep.

Most of my anger was for myself. I'd not only let myself get drawn into the fantasy—absurd, adolescent, and self-serving—I'd largely created it.

As for Laurie, with everything she'd done for me and to me, everything that had happened and everything that still might, she had, without question, blessed me with a precious gift.

An education that took her kind of woman to teach and my kind of fool to learn.

FIFTY-FIVE

When I got back to Madbird's house, he made it clear that I was welcome to stay as long as I liked, and showed me how to slip into a closed-off part of the attic in case the sheriffs came—a sort of priest hole, like Catholics had used to hide their clergy during the English Reformation. I tried to take some comfort in the thought that the worst I was looking at was nothing compared with back then. Getting caught usually had meant the rack—the Jesuit Edmund Campion had been stretched four inches—followed by castration, disembowelment, and other niceties in the name of God.

But staying here still would be an extra risk to them, and it wasn't going to solve anything for me.

Madbird broke out some of his homemade venison sausage and started making spaghetti sauce. I sat at the kitchen table and gave him and Hannah a quick rundown of what had happened. Usually he really got into cooking, but as he listened, he seemed to be just pushing the sausage around the pan. He didn't comment, and his silence told me he had things figured pretty much the same grim way I did and didn't want to say so.

Hannah was in the next room unpacking her bag. In the silence after I shut up, she spoke in her lilting accent.

"Is this a present for me?"

She held up the book I'd lifted from Kirk's cabin, *Consumer Guide to Precious Metals and Gems*. I'd brought it into the motel room last night, thinking I might get a chance to look through it. But I didn't, and when I'd gone back this morning and realized that Laurie had disappeared, I'd crammed it into Hannah's bag along with our other stuff. Then I'd forgotten about it.

"It's Kirk's," I said. "I took it because there's some writing inside, but I'm sure it's nothing."

She brought it to the table and we all spent a couple of minutes trying to make sense of the scrawled entries on the folded sheet of paper.

> 2—6612 least—10716 most
> 1700
> 1000
> ?
> 13416 maybe more
>
> ½—1138   1857
> 650
> 380
> FUCK
>
> 2887 X 4 = 11548
> 24964 MAYBE MORE

The writing started out relatively neat but he'd gotten sloppier as he went down the page, finally scrawling FUCK in frustration. School hadn't been his strong suit. He'd probably had a calculator for the simple math—at a glance, that looked correct, and there were no signs of figuring. At the very bottom, it looked like he might have tried a more complex calculation, but that was scribbled over with the pen point dug into the page.

"Heroin?" I said. "Trying to figure the value? Say the first number's the weight, the next ones are money, and the difference is whether it gets sold as a chunk or dealt in packets."

"If them weights are ounces, it ain't much dope, and if they're pounds or kilos, it ain't much money," Madbird said.

"Maybe it's just his cut. Say that's how he was getting paid."

He flicked a fingertip at the line that read *13416 maybe more*.

"So if this is what two of them's worth, whatever the fuck they are," he said, and moved down the page to *2887 x 4 = 11548*, "and this is four times a half, how come it's less? Dope don't get cheaper when they sell it in smaller amounts. The other way around."

I shook my head. It was a feeble premise anyway. The thought of gold crossed my mind, but the entries didn't make sense that way, either. Besides, I was still sure that Kirk hadn't found any gold or even looked. I flipped through the book. There was no other writing and nothing that struck me as related to the numbers. I closed it again.

I wanted to do one more thing before I left.

FIFTY-SIX

I hadn't used my journalism training to speak of in almost a decade, and Hannah had to spend a couple of minutes showing me around her computer. But things came back fast, and the task wasn't complicated.

A quick search for Laurie Balcomb gave me her maiden name, Lennox, and the location of her family's estate in Virginia. There were plenty of news archives available—it looked like genealogies were a big thing in that part of the country. I went to the nearest newspaper, the *Charlottesville Daily Progress*. It mentioned her a few times as a debutante and equestrienne.

And then as an arsonist.

The few brief items on the stable fire she'd told me about matched her account pretty well—except that by all indications, she had, in fact, set it. There was no suggestion of a delayed attempt at blackmail. She'd been caught red-handed, with the eyewitness reporting her to firefighters as soon as they arrived on the scene.

The story disappeared from the news, as such stories usually did. I doubted that she'd gone to jail or even to trial. An influential family in a place like that would most likely be able to settle the matter quietly. Or maybe Wesley Balcomb really had played a role somewhat like she'd claimed—scared the eyewitness into backing off, or even silenced her for good. I couldn't find any more mention of her in the *Daily Progress*. If she had, in fact, been killed, it was possible that her body had been discovered in a different area, and the two events were never connected.

The one thing I was sure of was that the scars on Laurie's breasts were real. She might have lied about how they'd been caused, although I was quite sure that her terror of John Doe was real, too.

As to what would happen to her now—whether her husband really would have her murdered—that was out of my hands.

It was time for me to finally decide what was going to happen with me.

I sat in Hannah's office a few minutes longer, weighing the factors once more. As near as I could tell, I had three options. The first, keeping on running, didn't look any better than it did to start with. The second, turning myself in, looked more disastrous than ever. Things had gotten so much more complicated that I'd trip all over myself if I tried to spin a tailored story. My only course would be to stonewall completely, but that was practically an admission of guilt, and would leave me helpless to defend myself against a case built against me.

Both choices carried the added problem that Laurie might decide that the best way to save herself would be to cooperate with authorities. If they leaned on her hard enough, she might let it slip that I'd set out to kill Balcomb, adding another major felony to my list. She might also drag Madbird in, and now we weren't talking just about abetting a fugitive. Conning Balcomb out of that money and working outside the law would have both those parties furious. No doubt Madbird would be charged with felonies there, too. Especially with him being an Indian, he'd land in Deer Lodge along with me for sure.

My third option was a final hike in the woods with my old man's pistol—with a stop at Balcomb's first to carry out last night's aborted mission. I could leave a written confession—admitting that I'd killed him and Kirk and giving the location of Kirk's body—but leaving out everything else. The cops would run a routine investigation, but there'd be no point in pushing it, and nobody involved had anything to gain by talking, including Laurie—with her husband dead, she'd have gotten what she wanted. I'd have the satisfaction of protecting my friend, avenging myself, and ridding the world of a scumbag.

My rational mind still rejected the idea, but some deeper part was starting to think about choosing a place to draw my last breath.

When I went back out to the kitchen, Hannah was sitting at the table with Kirk's book open in front of her again.

"I'm just thinking," she said, ignoring the dogs trying to wrestle their way into her lap. "Whenever I see Josie in the bars, she's always flashing that ring around?" She twisted her right fingertips around her left third finger to indicate where a woman wore an engagement ring.

I couldn't see how Kirk's girlfriend might figure into this, but I said, "What about it?"

"My friend Carol, she makes jewelry? She says the big diamond's, like, two carats, and it might cost ten thousand dollars or even more. The smaller ones, maybe they're like a half carat each."

"She's lucky somebody ain't cut off her finger for it," Madbird muttered.

"Jewels aren't like drugs," Hannah said patiently. "The bigger they are, the more they're worth, on a sliding scale."

Madbird's hand stopped. He strode to the table and crouched over to stare at the page with the scrawled numbers. I stepped beside him.

Hannah's forefinger pointed at the top entry.

2—6612 least—10716 most
　　　　　　1700
　　　　　　1000
　　　　　　?
　　　　13416 maybe more

Her finger moved down to the next entry.

½—1138　　　*1857*
　　　　　　650
　　　　　　380
　　　　　　FUCK

2887 X 4 = 11548

"Now look at this," she said, and pointed to the page the book was opened to. It was a chart of diamond values, correlating several factors like shape, weight, color, and clarity. One of the low-end values listed for a two-carat stone was $6,612. The figure 10,716 appeared toward the higher end. All the variable factors made the figuring very complex, but it seemed that enhanced qualities like better clarity or cut could raise the value by several hundred dollars or more.

Madbird slowly straightened up and raised his face toward heaven.

"Fuck, oh dear," he said. He swung around toward me. "You got any idea how much we're gonna owe her for this?"

Hannah smiled shyly.

I stood there bewildered. He took hold of my shirt like he had last night, but this time the grip was a good one.

"I'm sorry I called you white boy," he said. "You sure ain't as white as you used to be. I watched you when we first started working. Heard you were going to college and knew all kinds of smart shit, kept expecting you to deal down to the rest of us. But you never did."

He let me go and opened the refrigerator door, came out with three cans of Pabst, shoved one at me, and took another over to Hannah.

"Then I started seeing you got something fucked up in you. But the same kind of fucked up as her and me—" his hand moved to caress her hair, rough and gentle at the same time—"and the other fucked-up people we hang with, 'cause they're *our* fucked-up people."

I still couldn't grasp what was happening. Madbird exhaled in exasperation.

"Look, I respect you for all that schooling, but you got a way of not seeing what's right in front of you. Hannah just told you it ain't dope them horses were carrying. It was diamonds."

FIFTY-SEVEN

A little before ten o'clock that night, I did something I never thought I'd do again—pressed the old doorbell around the back of Reuben Pettyjohn's building in downtown Helena.

Twenty seconds later, his voice rasped through the grille.

"There's only one person I know of who remembers this thing. Playing hooky from the sheriffs, aren't you, Hugh?"

"Say the word, Reuben, I'll keep right on moving. But I've got something important I'd like to tell you."

"Well, that's intriguing, and I don't figure I owe Gary Varna nothing. Come on up."

The buzzer crackled and the door opened at my push. I walked through the ghostly quiet of the hallway and waited for the creaky elevator to crawl down from the top floor. I had Kirk's *Consumer Guide* and the paper with the numbers, plus some information I'd picked up during another hour on Hannah's computer.

The diamond industry had more than its share of unsavory aspects, especially the legacy of slavery in the mines. But the grimmest reality nowadays seemed to be blood diamonds—so called because they financed terrorist groups, including Al Qaeda and several factions of African rebels, like the Janjaweed, who made their own lands into living hells for millions of people.

Blood diamonds were impossible to distinguish from any others—there were no reliable methods to identify the stones' origins without damaging them—and often of high or even superior quality. They got smuggled out of the Congo, Angola, Sierra Leone, and other African nations, following complex routes to major world markets, blending with the flow of legitimate trade. They represented an estimated twenty to forty percent of the overall—conservatively, billions of dollars per year. Along the way, they'd usually get cut in clandestine factories—China, Pakistan, and Armenia all had burgeoning industries—and also inscribed with phony laser marks to imitate known brands. These marks were microscopic—only experts using highly sophisticated equipment could tell the fakes from genuine ones; and if the marks were well done, even that was difficult.

They sold initially for next to nothing, as little as a dollar per carat. By the time they got to retail, even those of modest size and quality could go for several thousand times that. There were five carats in a gram. If you figured an average of only one thousand dollars per carat, that came to five million bucks per kilogram, a little over two pounds.

There was no way to guess the quantities Kirk had been muling, but he could have carried a lot more than that at a time, and he'd been making a run every couple of months.

Heroin, my aching ass. That was chump change. No wonder Balcomb was willing to kill.

Of course the profit wouldn't all be his. Everybody handling the jewels along the way would take a cut, and especially as contraband, they wouldn't hit full value until they went to retail. But the markup was still astronomical and tax-free, probably pumped clandestinely into his numbered offshore bank accounts and then laundered through his other financial shell games. And while handling dope didn't seem his style, pimping diamonds fit him to a tee.

I'd spent a few more minutes running another search, on the mystery investor who'd started pumping money into Balcomb's nonexistent horse business. I'd half expected that he was another of Laurie's fictions. But the name Guy-Luc Marie DeBruyne popped up right away in dozens of listings. Most were brief mentions in foreign-language newspapers and business journals; some were in tabloids. The several that I checked added up to a cohesive picture without much in the way of specifics—he was fiftyish, Belgian in origin but an international player, and a sort of éminence grise, with considerable wealth and power but staying behind the scenes. No clear alliance was mentioned with any particular religious or political cause. On the contrary, the sense was that he was a wily mercenary who did business with any faction that could pay the price. He was fond of women and gambling and enjoyed plenty of both, keeping a villa at Cap d'Antibes for convenient access to Monte Carlo. It was taking jaunts like those, usually with a beauty on his arm, that landed him in the focus of the paparazzi.

Finally, I seemed to be uncovering some solid information. The question was what to do with it. I wasn't sure what had made me think of Reuben—maybe that this turned Josie's ring into a tangible, personal connection with Kirk, like an evil talisman that Balcomb had used to lure him in. It was also hard evidence of Balcomb's crimes that had set this ugly chain of events in motion.

I still wasn't sure what I was going to do, either. That was going to hinge on what happened here. I'd decided to give Reuben an edited version of the story, telling him pretty much everything but leaving out all mention of Madbird and Laurie.

At the least, I'd feel the relief of confessing to him personally about Kirk. Reuben might pick up a phone and call the sheriffs, but I doubted that. More likely, he'd just order me to leave. But I admitted having a hope that he'd offer his support, and that with a man so powerful on my side, we could turn this around on Balcomb.

When I'd run the idea by Madbird, he'd spent some time thinking about it.

"I don't know Reuben much," he finally said. "I used to go drink at the VFW once in a while, and I'd run into him. He was always friendly. But you and him got that other thing going, right? That girl getting killed, way back when?"

"Yeah."

"I can't call this one, Hugh. But if anybody got the juice, it's him. And let's face it, you ain't got much to lose."

Reuben's apartment door was open, but this time when I stepped inside, he wasn't there. A minute later he walked in from a back room, wearing boots and jeans and buttoning up a faded old plaid flannel shirt. He probably hadn't wanted me to catch him in his robe and slippers again. He waved his hand toward the bottle of fine scotch on the bar. It looked like the same one as last time, but I suspected it wasn't. I poured myself a short drink. Why the hell not?

"Let's not run around the bush, Hugh," he said. "What's on your mind?"

I handed him the book and paper.

He settled into his chair, this time staying sitting up instead of tipping it back, and examined them, turning them in his thick hands and flipping through the pages. Then he looked at me inquiringly.

"I took them from Kirk's shack," I said.

"You went there, huh?"

"Last night. We were right, the gold panning was bullshit." I pointed at the numbers on the paper. "I think he was trying to figure out the value of those diamonds in Josie's ring."

Reuben frowned. "Come again?"

"The weights are probably rounded off, but the big one's about two carats and the others are a half carat each," I said. "These columns are prices he got from the book, with markups for better quality. He didn't know how to judge that—he was just ballparking high and low end."

"If he bought them for her, how could he not know what they cost?" Reuben's gaze sharpened. "You telling me he stole them?"

"No. I think he got them from Balcomb."

The grooves in Reuben's forehead deepened.

"I knew Kirk was coming up with money some way I couldn't explain," he said. "But why the hell would Balcomb give him diamonds?"

"Payment, Reuben. Kirk was muling them across the border. That's why he wanted that place."

Reuben settled back then, dropping the book on the floor and reaching for his glass.

"Say Balcomb gave him the jewels and told him they were worth twenty grand or whatever," I said. "Kirk wanted to make sure he wasn't getting screwed, but he couldn't get them appraised right away. He'd bought this book for his gold panning act, and he gave it a shot himself."

He gazed past me out the windows, his lower teeth gnawing at his mustache. I knew I'd just made things a lot more complicated for him. If Kirk was still alive, he was facing serious prison time, and even if he was dead, it was a stain on the family. Bringing Reuben down like that didn't make me feel any better, but I had no choice.

"Any way to prove this?" he said.

"I've got a place to start. If I'm right, the diamonds will have phony laser stamps. We'd have to get the ring from Josie and take it to a lab. Maybe they could do it at Montana Tech."

He nodded, looking bemused now.

"You know where he is, Hugh?" he said.

His tone was so casual, the question so out of the blue, that the dread I'd awaited this moment with took a second to hit me.

Everything, everything, hung on what would happen if I told this man not only that his son was dead, but by my hand. I gave one last thought to hedging. But there was an insistence in my head that I owed him the truth.

"I do, Reuben." I swallowed, trying to ease the dryness in my mouth. "Balcomb sent him to kill me, late Saturday night. He damned near did. Knocked me silly and started to dump me in the lake."

I waited. Reuben only took a slow sip of scotch, gazing straight ahead.

"I know how this sounds, but honest to Christ, I was just trying to protect myself," I said. "He had a .357. His glove jammed in the trigger guard. I slashed at his hands with my pocketknife to try to get him to drop it. He jerked away and the knife caught his throat. If it helps any, it happened so fast, he barely knew it."

Reuben's head moved slightly. It might have been a nod of acknowledgment or a tremor.

"Then I got scared," I said. "I'd had that run-in with Balcomb earlier. Kirk was in on it—he'd held a gun on me, a lot of people saw that, and we weren't exactly pals anyway. All I could think was, it was going to look like I'd lured him out there to get even, and I was going to be up against Balcomb and you and your lawyers. So I hid him."

I shut up then and stood there with the sound of my pulse throbbing in my ears. Reuben deliberated for another long minute.

"When you say 'hid him,'" he said. "You think he's—comfortable— where he is?"

"Well—I guess *I* would be," I said.

"He's not, you know, just shoved under something?"

"No, no, it's real decent. Dignified, even. I'll show you, if you want."

"Maybe someday." He finished the scotch in his glass and handed it to me to refill. His sharp eyes looked softened, almost glazed.

"I've been carrying a weight of my own a long time, a right heavy one," Reuben said. "Never unloaded it because it might have got used against me. But if there's anybody who ought to know, it's you."

My hands, opening the scotch bottle, stopped.

"I've got a feeling I already do know," I said.

"I figured you'd think that. Go on, tell me."

This was almost harder than confessing about Kirk. I poured a fresh couple of inches into Reuben's glass and gave it back to him.

"Pete got Celia pregnant," I said. "Beatrice wouldn't let him marry her. He got in a rage, maybe from Celia taunting him, and got too rough with her. You covered it up."

Reuben nodded heavily. "That's pretty close to the money, except for one thing. It wasn't just her picking at him that set him off. She told him who that baby's real father was."

An image clicked like a slide in my mind, giving me a glimpse back to that day when I'd seen Pete and Celia walk past Reuben without even noticing him, but he had stopped what he was doing and watched them attentively. Then Beatrice's sudden harsh words: *Don't you sit there oogling that little slut, too.*

I sat down hard on a bar stool. Then I groped for the scotch to pour myself another drink, not because I wanted it, but because I couldn't think of anything else to do.

"I decided to show her who was boss, was how it started," Reuben said. "Saw how she had Pete so poleaxed. Arrogant bastard I was, I didn't think there was any woman I couldn't handle, let alone a girl. But pretty quick, she had me damn near as bad as him. She'd laugh in my face, then whisper in my ear, and next thing you knew, we'd be—" He exhaled. "I knew there was bound to be trouble, and I should have got her out of there. But I couldn't get enough of her."

It hit me with painful keenness—a powerful man in his prime with a cold wife, suddenly beset by beautiful, sultry, sassy Celia. And I had no doubt that she'd done more than her share to kindle the flame.

"I can see how she'd have been hard to resist," I said.

"There's a couple things I want you to understand. Pete never meant to hurt her, any more than you did Kirk. He blew up like you said. They were out in the shop. He gave her a shove, she tripped and fell against a workbench and hit her head on a vise—that knob where the handle attaches. It cracked her temple like somebody swung a hammer."

Reuben wiped his eyes with his thumb and forefinger.

"He came and got me," he said. "Lord, the look on his face. Going in and finding her laying there. Then two months later, finding *him* dead. And it was all my doing. That's the other thing I want you to know, Hugh. Nobody to blame but me."

Emotions, memories, connections that suddenly snapped into place were rushing through me.

Reuben had been carrying a weight, all right.

I stepped to him and put my hand on his shoulder.

"I wouldn't call it that way, Reuben. If I'd been in your place, I'd have done the same. Probably most men would have."

His eyes changed, to a look that was surprised and maybe grateful.

"I loved Celia and I admired Pete," I said. "But she knew damn well what she was doing, and a lot of it wasn't good. Pete always took it for granted he'd get everything his way—he never bothered much about anybody else. And there was some pure bad luck."

Reuben patted my hand brusquely. I sat at the bar again. We both knocked back an inch of scotch.

"'Course, there were other people who suspected," he said. "Your father. Gary. They had their reasons for keeping it to themselves. But how come you never said anything?"

In that moment, I realized that in spite of what had happened with Laurie and how idiotic I felt about it, I still couldn't let go of the special intimacy with Celia that my imagination had constructed. I gave an answer that was as true as it needed to be.

"I don't know, exactly," I said. "I was fourteen—it wasn't like I thought it through. I guess I figured we'd all lost enough already."

His eyes widened a little.

"That's a damn fair way to put it, Hugh. All right, I've said my piece. Now tell me the rest of what you know about my son."

It wasn't easy concentrating after the way I'd just been slammed. I kept it terse, and he seemed satisfied—at least he didn't ask any questions, just kept gazing out the window and rolling his glass between his hands.

"Suppose I was to suggest we ought to pay a call on Wesley Balcomb," he finally said. "You got any ideas how we might arrange it?"

In one way, that was the last thing in the world I'd ever have expected. In another, I wasn't even surprised.

"I do, Reuben," I said. "I've been thinking a lot about paying him a call myself. Assuming we're talking about the same kind."

He heaved himself to his feet and stalked into the back rooms of the apartment. When he came out, he was carrying a twelve-gauge Remington Model 870 shotgun. He didn't look like an old man now.

"We're talking about this kind," he said.

I stepped to a phone, punched Madbird's number, and waited for his gravelly "Hello."

"That project we've been talking about," I said. "I've got an idea I'd like to run by you. Now would be a real good time."

FIFTY-EIGHT

It was getting toward midnight when the lights in Wesley Balcomb's office went on. Madbird and I were waiting outside the compound's security fence, in the spot where I had earlier planned to shoot from. He had a powerful flashlight. I was lying prone a few yards away with Kirk's rifle, just in case.

When Balcomb walked into the room and sat at his desk, Madbird started shining the flashlight in quick bursts. Balcomb's head swung toward it in alarm. He jumped up and lunged for the light switch. The windows went dark.

Then we heard the sound of one of them cautiously being opened.

"Identify yourself," Balcomb said harshly. "I'm warning you, I've got a gun."

"I'm the one called you last night about them people you were looking for," Madbird said.

Balcomb's voice turned furious. "Who the hell are you? What are you—"

Madbird cut him off. "I found them again. Get your rig and follow me, I'm parked up at the highway. You ain't there in two minutes, I'm leaving." He turned and started loping in that direction.

"You'd better have my ten thousand dollars, goddammit!"

"Gonna cost you ten more," Madbird yelled over his shoulder, and kept running.

I took off running for the road, too. This was the best plan I'd been able to think of for luring him out of there without leaving a phone record. I wasn't at all sure he'd go for it. He always operated at a remove, and he'd be real unhappy about dealing with Madbird. But he had to be going crazy by now, with no idea what was happening and two of his hired guns vanished—primed to grab at any chance.

Within another minute, a vehicle engine started inside the compound. Headlights appeared, with the hulking shape of Balcomb's Humvee behind them.

The security gate opened in front of him and closed after he drove through. He advanced slowly until Madbird turned on the flashlight again, flagging him to stop.

Balcomb's window rolled down. I could see the glint of metal in his hand.

"Go ahead and shoot me," Madbird said. "We ought to get to hell just about the same time."

Reuben stepped out of the shadows with his shotgun leveled.

"I'd let go of that gun if I was you, Wesley," he said. "You know what kind of a mess one of these can make."

I stepped to the window and put the rifle's muzzle against the back of Balcomb's neck.

He let the pistol fall to the ground. It looked like a Smith & Wesson Airweight with a shrouded hammer. They were easy to conceal, very reliable, and very effective point-blank—probably what he'd intended for Madbird. I scooped it up and shoved it in my pocket.

"We're going to take a drive," Reuben said. "Hear what you got to say about dead horses and diamonds."

FIFTY-NINE

We made sure Balcomb wasn't carrying any other weapons, then put him in the front seat of the ranch pickup truck that I'd driven here. Madbird took the rifle and he and Reuben sat behind us.

Balcomb kept his cool and put on quite a show.

"Hugh, I'm really sorry about what happened," he said. "I'm sure we can get past it."

So we were finally on a first-name basis. I didn't answer.

He made a play for Reuben's sympathy next, not realizing how misguided it was.

"Any news of Kirk?" he said. "I'm worried sick about him."

None of us spoke. He tried again.

"Reuben, I can't think of anything I've done to get on *your* bad side. Will you at least tell me that?"

"We'll get around to it, Wesley. Now, you got a chance to negotiate here. But I'm starting to get impatient."

I could almost hear the gears whirring in Balcomb's head for the next thirty seconds.

"You want diamonds?" he said. "All right, I'll get you diamonds. You're going to have to let me go for a few minutes."

"Wesley, I don't believe I've ever seen a man as sick as you," Reuben said, in a voice that could have broken stone. "You're one red hair short of dead, with your goddamned guts all over that dashboard in front of you."

The gears whirred again—not as long this time.

"Take that road," Balcomb said, indicating the gravel track that circled the outside of the compound's perimeter. I started the truck and turned onto it, headlights out.

Balcomb kept talking in his smooth, persuasive way. Some unfortunate things had happened, but they were over. He congratulated us on our shrewdness, laughed ruefully at himself for getting conned by Madbird, and intimated that he was taking us into his confidence—was prepared to pay us handsomely and even cut us in on a very lucrative setup. The unsubtle message was that we were all men of the world, conducting business—the catchall word to justify a million ways of fucking people over—and that we'd be fools not to join him.

The road continued on past the compound through the woods another quarter mile, then opened into a wide level stretch of ground. Light from the moon and stars filtered through the hazy clouds to create a sort of luminescent dome, enough to see that the terrain looked like grass, except there was something slick and unnatural about it. Off to one side lay a whitish depression about twenty yards across. I hadn't been in this area for many years, but I realized this must be his Astroturf golf range, and the white spot was a sand trap.

"Over there," Balcomb said, pointing at a small shed. When we got closer, I made it out as one of those cute prefabs you saw advertised at the big building supply stores—shaped like a miniature barn, with a gambrel roof and a big white X on the door. It had probably been brought here on a flatbed boom truck and set in place entire.

A few bags of golf clubs and other paraphernalia lined the walls inside, but most of the space was taken up by a fancy motorized cart. That seemed strange—there was no actual course here. I supposed he used it to run back and forth collecting the balls he hit on the driving range.

I held the flashlight, keeping a close watch on Balcomb's hands as he got into the cart and started it up. He backed it out and parked it, then crouched down inside the building and pried up a half-sheet of plywood flooring that the cart had been covering.

So that was its real purpose—disguise.

The nail heads had been left in so the plywood looked permanently attached, but the shanks were clipped flush on the bottom. The joist backs had been chiseled down a quarter inch or so, with Velcro strips glued onto them and matching ones on the plywood, so if someone did walk on it, it wouldn't squeak or seem loose.

The two-by-eight floor joists were set on flat concrete pads, giving a couple of inches of space between them and the Astroturf underneath. Balcomb pulled loose a three-foot square section of that and slid it aside, revealing a round metal hatch with a recessed handle, like a giant pot lid. He slid that aside, too. Below it was a cylindrical cavity about two feet deep, formed by a section of corrugated iron culvert like the kind used for road drains, but set vertically. A heavy-duty safe lay inside it, faceup. Its back edges had been spot-welded to the culvert's metal bottom.

We all stared. It was a pretty goddamned slick hiding place. I could see why'd he'd wanted it outside his house or the other main buildings. Installing a vault in those would take skilled construction, and even well concealed, it would be vulnerable to discovery by searching, checking blueprints, and questioning the men who'd done the work. But all this had taken was a shovel and some basic tools. Nobody would ever think to look here, and he could come and go without attracting attention. There was nobody and nothing anywhere near, just a rich man's little golf playground.

Balcomb glanced at Reuben.

"Kirk can be very industrious when he has the proper incentive," he said.

There was just enough light for me to see Reuben's jaw tighten.

I kept the flashlight carefully on Balcomb's hands again while he worked the dial, in case he had a gun inside. But there was only a flat box of aluminum or stainless steel, about the size of a laptop computer. He took it out, set it on the floor, and opened it. It was lined with plum-colored velvet.

And studded with dozens of diamonds, a couple as broad as a man's little fingernail. If Josie's was two carats, these must have been five. Most were in the range of hers—still good-size stones. All of them shone with a luster that was almost breathtaking. I felt that if I'd turned off the flashlight, they'd have kept on glowing like stars. There had to be close to a million bucks in that box.

Balcomb rocked back on his heels and looked up at us, with a hint of a Cheshire cat smile.

"I've saved some of the finest ones as they passed through," he said. "Go ahead, each of you take a couple. We'll call it a goodwill gesture—a down payment on what's to come."

That was another wrong thing to say to Reuben—reminding him that Balcomb had offered the same lure to Kirk.

"That's a good start, Wesley," Reuben said. "Now tell us about those horses."

A hint of nervousness started creeping into Balcomb's voice, and there was a clear sense that he was shading the story to justify himself. The horses had been used for the most recent run of diamonds, he said, because the human mule on the Canadian side of the border had gotten arrested. The charge wasn't related to the smuggling—like most of his colleagues, the mule had an extensive criminal career—but it raised the fear that he'd roll, and the police would stake out the area where he and Kirk had been crossing. There was no time to scout a new route and no way to delay the shipment.

"Believe me, gentlemen, the people at the top of that operation do not accept excuses," Balcomb said. "If the diamonds don't arrive on schedule, they collect body parts instead."

So the Canadian operatives had enlisted a veterinarian to implant the cargo into the horses—roughly half a kilogram in each, pumped in a slurry into their stomachs through a tube. They'd been taken quickly across the border, along with a shipment of others, by a professional stock transporting company that made routine crossings and got rubber-stamp inspections. The truck driver, unaware of the implants, had then delivered them to the ranch.

Balcomb claimed that the first thing he'd known about it was a phone call telling him the horses were on their way. He'd protested but had no choice, and once they arrived, he'd had only a few hours before a courier was due to pick up the diamonds. There was another wrinkle besides. Not surprisingly, the vet who'd done the tubing was at the low end of the scale in terms of competence—Balcomb had gleaned that he was a drug addict—and had admitted that he might have mistakenly passed some of the stones into their lungs instead, which apparently wasn't uncommon when administering medicine by that method. With no veterinary skills of his own, Balcomb hadn't been able to tranquilize them—he hadn't even trusted his ability to handle them. Desperate, he'd resorted to slaughter, and had to thoroughly eviscerate them in order to make sure he recovered all the stones. He was very convincing about how gruesome the experience had been, although it leaked through that his outrage was more for himself than for them.

"Kirk did all your other shit work," I said. "Why not that?"

His eyes shifted evasively. "I couldn't get hold of him until late that night. He was off on a tear and wouldn't answer his phone."

I was sure that Reuben and Madbird picked up the same thing I did—the truth was that Balcomb had been enraged at the position he'd been put in, and had taken it out on the horses.

Reuben lowered his shotgun barrel and gave the lid of the diamond box a tap, knocking it shut.

"Being as how this is the U. S. of A., you're entitled to a trial by jury," he said. "Let's go, they're waiting."

SIXTY

I drove with headlights out again to the shed where Balcomb had shot and butchered the horses. His cool started to evaporate as he realized where we were going. As it came into sight, a dense dark rectangle against the night sky, he swiveled around in his seat toward Reuben.

"Look, this has gone far enough. You've made your point. You want *all* the diamonds? Take them. What else?"

I stopped and cut the truck's engine. We hadn't rehearsed or even talked about what came next. It just happened.

"Kirk wasn't a particularly good kid," Reuben said. "But he wasn't a bad one, either. Kind of weak, kind of dumb, but he was muddling through all right. Then some snake like you comes along."

"Now, Reuben, all I did was offer him—"

Madbird leaned forward and gripped Balcomb's larynx between his thumb and forefinger.

"Lot of things we never could figure out about white people," he said. "Why you want to shit in the lodge, or carry your snot around in little rags. It don't *bother* us any—it's just weird."

He tightened his hand grip. Balcomb made a choking sound and clutched at Madbird's wrist.

"But killing a animal the way you did them horses, scaring them half crazy and tearing them all up," Madbird said. "That pisses us off."

He released his grip contemptuously. Balcomb glared, massaging his throat, but didn't speak this time.

It was my turn. I understood real well my personal anger at him. But the feeling cut much deeper, and all through the past days, an undercurrent had been running through my mind as to why. There were millions of facets, but they came down to one.

"The reason people like you get ahead, Balcomb, is because you don't carry the same loads the rest of us do—no fairness, no generosity, no sense of obligation. Maybe you've got superior genes for survival. I don't care. It makes me sick knowing you're on this planet."

We all got out. I opened up the doors of the shed. Reuben gave Balcomb a shove with the shotgun barrel toward the interior. He must have believed that we were just out to scare him—we were two-bit rednecks who wouldn't dare to really harm him, and his revenge would start as soon as he was safe again. He stalked forward, shaking his head in scorn.

But when he got to the doors, he hesitated. He took a step in, but immediately backed up. He stayed there maybe fifteen seconds, staring into the darkness inside.

"This has gone far enough," he said again, but this time he muttered it.

He turned around, looking distracted and furtive. Then he made an abrupt lunge, trying to scurry past Reuben.

Reuben brought the shotgun barrel up sharply and clipped him across the head.

Balcomb reeled away into the shed, spinning and clutching at air. Reuben followed and belted him again, this time with a full home run swing. I'd never heard anything quite like the sound it made.

In the stark silence that followed, Reuben said, "Got into some hand-to-hand on the Yalu. Too thick for a bayonet to do much good. Best deal was to take your rifle like that and swing it."

Balcomb was sprawled on the ground, where he'd come to rest after crashing against a stall. Reuben dragged him by the shirt to a scattering of dung that the Cat's blade had pushed against a wall. He turned Balcomb facedown into it, then put a boot on the back of his head and gave it his weight.

I'd once read a rumor about Cardinal Mazarin, Richelieu's successor, whose arrogance and harsh treatment of the common people had greatly stoked the fire that would become the French Revolution. In his last years, he'd suffered increasingly from an unknown disease, possibly syphilis. The hapless pseudo physicians of the day tried every remedy in their repertoire, to no avail. As he lay dying in agony, an old peasant woman appeared at his palace with a wondrous poultice, which she claimed would save him if it was applied inside his throat. Never mind that this smacked of witchcraft, and Mazarin had enthusiastically condoned the torture and burning alive of women accused of it—in desperation, he agreed. The old crone faded quietly away and was never seen again.

The poultice turned out to be manure mashed up with cheap white wine. Thus, with his mouth packed full of horseshit, the world's most powerful man went to meet the God he had professed to serve.

Wesley Balcomb, the poor boy who had craved to be among the elite, had achieved a bond with one of the biggest names in history.

SIXTY-ONE

Reuben and I caused quite a stir when we showed up at the courthouse a little after eight o'clock the next morning. Handcuffs practically flew onto my wrists. Besides the trouble I was in, the deputies didn't like what they saw. We both looked like shit anyway, and we'd gargled scotch and knuckled our eyes red to fake hangovers. Reuben added to the effect by lumbering around like a wounded bison, glaring and just itching for somebody to get in his way. Nobody did.

Gary Varna came out of his office right away and took us back in with him. He sat us down, unlocked my cuffs, then eyed us.

"If you think we were out having fun, think again," Reuben said belligerently.

"'Fun' ain't a word that comes to mind, Reuben. I'm just trying to get used to this. It's—unexpected, to say the least."

The room had a cell-like feel, with just one small window, and it was neat to the point of severity. Photos of Gary's family were the only personal touch—his pretty wife who was a nurse, his son who'd played football for Montana State, a daughter in pharmacy school, and another with two cute kids of her own. It gave me a twinge, a little stab that in his life, he'd done right all the things that I'd done wrong.

Reuben came out of his corner swinging. Some of it was a smoke screen, but not all. He'd made the point that if we wanted something from Gary, we'd better give him something, too.

"We've been figuring Wesley Balcomb and Kirk were in on something together," he said. "They were both coming up with money there was no accounting for."

Gary's slate blue eyes focused a click.

"Something like what?" he said.

"That we don't know. But we're thinking they crossed somebody and Kirk went on the run." Reuben paused, his gaze wavering, as if he recognized the other possibility but refused to allow it. "I want you to take a hard look at Balcomb, Gary. I've got some financial information I can give you, and Hugh found out some things."

"Well, now, ain't that interesting." Gary leaned forward and clasped his hands on his desk. "We just got a call from your ranch— excuse me, ex-ranch. Seems Balcomb's gone missing, too."

We did our best to look blearily shocked.

"He didn't show up for an appointment this morning," Gary said. "The video camera on his security gate shows him driving out about one AM. But he left his vehicle there, and nobody knows where he went."

Reuben slapped his palm down emphatically on the desk.

"You can't tell me that's just coincidence," he said. "Both of them taking off for no reason, in the middle of the night. I'd say that gives our notion some pretty good clout."

Gary glanced at me. "I guess if it was true, you'd be off the hook."

I wasn't sure how barbed that was—somewhat, without doubt. I kept my mouth shut.

He settled back again, gazing past us, tapping one forefinger on the arm of his chair. Then he checked his watch.

"I'll be glad for whatever information you fellas have, and believe me, I'll start digging," he said. "Right now, it's going to look bad if I don't put in a personal appearance at the ranch for an eminent citizen like Mr. Balcomb. Hugh, I need to know where you've been. We can talk quick and informal, same as last time. You can wait for a lawyer if you'd rather."

I could wait for a lawyer, sure—in a little cell down at the end of that long jailhouse hallway.

My much better bet was that one of the most influential men in the state was sitting beside me, in my support, which in itself made clear his belief that I didn't have anything to do with his son's disappearance. He was also vouching for my whereabouts when Balcomb went missing. I'd spent the last hours preparing my story according to his advice—including not to say one more word than necessary, and to let him handle the rest.

"I stopped by Reuben's yesterday evening," I told Gary. "I wanted to tell him in person I didn't know anything about Kirk, but I'd found out some stuff that might interest him. He had a bottle of good scotch going and invited me into it. We started talking and putting things together. Then it was dawn."

Reuben nodded gruffly in affirmation. Barring disaster, that much was solid. It would take a hell of a lot to start anybody doubting Reuben Pettyjohn.

"All right," Gary said. He picked up a sheaf of notes off his desk and paged through them. "The last we know of you before that was, let's see, just about forty-eight hours earlier. We got a call from Josie Young, saying you'd been to her place."

So it *was* that little bitch who'd ratted me out.

"After you came to see me, I knew I was under the gun, so I tried to play detective," I said sheepishly.

"You ever do it for a living, that'll cure you." He kept watching me expectantly.

This part of the story was going to be a lot tougher to float than the last one. "Try to make it just unlikely enough so he might believe it," Reuben had said. Oddly enough, I'd remembered something Laurie had told me that seemed to fit—that when her fear of her husband had erupted and she'd tried to flee, she'd gone to a place where she'd felt safe as a child.

"I kind of went on a retreat, Gary," I said. "You know, like in grade school?"

His head tilted skeptically to the side. But then he gave me a cautious nod. Gary was a steady Catholic, and I was doing my shameless best to play on that.

"I seem to remember you were maybe going to be a priest," he said.

"I was maybe going to be a lot of things, and I fucked them up." I spoke too sharply, and I saw that both men were taken aback. I hunched over and rubbed my eyes with the heels of my hands.

"Sorry," I said. "I'm wrapped tight as hell and wiped out, both. And I've got something that's hard to admit. I saw you at my place Sunday night."

Gary's eyebrows rose.

"I was on my motorcycle," I said. "I rode it to sneak onto the ranch and talk to Doug, the foreman. Then I went to Josie's. On my way home, a tow truck passed me. I followed it to my place. You were waiting there." I paused and exhaled. "I freaked out. All I could think was that Balcomb had found some new way to hammer me, and it was really serious this time."

There was a longish silence. Reuben cleared his throat. Gary's finger started tapping again.

"So you took off on a retreat," he said. "A church here in town?"

"I dumped the bike and hiked on up into the Belts. That's what I used to do when I was a kid and I got bummed. I had this whole deal laid out—tree stumps that were stations of the cross, a nook in the rocks that was a confessional. Like that."

"Huh. Well, I wouldn't want to go violating a sacrament, but can you give me a hint what you confessed to?"

"Stealing that lumber—although I still have a mental reservation that I salvaged it, and Balcomb was just being a prick," I said. "Acting like a pissed-off kid and burning it, there's no excuse for that. Running from you instead of facing up. Some other things like that."

He shook his head ruefully. "I wish my conscience was that light. Hell, if I was on the other side of the screen, I'd let you off with an Our Father and a couple Hail Marys."

"There's more, but it's hard to explain," I said. "My life's been crashing, getting out of control. I was trying to figure out how it happened and what to do about it." I shrugged. "I didn't, but I came away feeling a little better."

"Well, I wouldn't call that exactly an ironclad alibi," Gary said. "You were up there the whole two days, huh?"

"I came back next afternoon."

"How'd you manage? You know, eating and sleeping."

"I keep my camping gear in that garage back of my cabin. I sneaked in and threw some stuff in a pack while you guys were busy with my truck."

He grimaced. "My boys ain't going to be happy to hear that."

"If it helps any, tell them it was because they scared the shit out of me."

"I don't suppose anybody else saw you."

"I didn't want anybody to see me. That was kind of the point. I know that country pretty good, and there's hardly anybody around there anyway."

"That might not have been real smart," he said.

"I wasn't trying to be smart. Not like that, anyway."

Reuben had stayed silent, and seemed not to be paying attention. But he broke in suddenly.

"Now, Gary, how important is this?" he said. "Nothing happened during that time. Kirk was gone already and Balcomb not yet."

"That's true, Reuben. But they still are missing, and Hugh's right in the middle of the squall."

I'd seen many confrontations between men, sometimes open and even violent, more often couched in the underhanded courtesy of the professional world. This was a silent showdown between two aging bulls who'd known each other all their lives, weighing the many factors that hovered between them—power, indebtedness, loyalty, and that unwritten code they'd grown up with.

Gary couldn't control the investigation completely, but he could do a lot to steer it. This was potentially big, and his reputation was on the line. His safest course would be to keep the pressure on me. But Reuben was ready to fight.

Maybe Gary guessed that the reason had something to do with Celia.

He looked at his watch again and stood up.

"OK, Hugh," he said. "I ain't saying this is over, but I don't see enough reason to hold you now."

I sagged and mumbled thanks. Reuben gave me a curt, congratulatory backslap.

"I'll talk to Judge Harris and get him to drop everything," Gary said. "I found out why he set your bail so high, by the way. Balcomb told him you'd been screwing one of the ranch wives, and that was the real reason he wanted to give you a hard time."

I shook my head in disbelief at Balcomb's bottomless bag of tricks. He must have known that the judge was an old-school gentleman who enjoyed his liquor and gambling, but was notoriously straitlaced about sex.

"That's the first goddamn thing I've been accused of I wish was true," I said. Reuben grunted appreciatively and Gary's lips curved in a slight smile.

But then the irony hit me, verging on the eerie, that I had been dallying with one of the ranch wives. Balcomb's.

"Stop at the desk and sign for the stuff we took from your place," Gary said. "Everything checked out clean. I'll get your truck brought around."

I caught myself just before I closed my eyes in relief.

Reuben and I followed Gary out to the main office, where he issued brief instructions and got my paperwork started.

"I'm going to mosey on home and get some sleep," Reuben said quietly. "Keep in mind what the man said—it's a long ways from over."

I knew he wasn't just talking about the investigation, but about what we'd revealed to each other last night. From then until now, we'd been carried by adrenaline, common interest, and his shrewd toughness. But that was going to give way to the ugly truths we'd both learned, and rationality and emotion would go to war. Whatever truce we might end up with would be uneasy at best.

We had evened out our long-standing grievance, but it was a devil's bargain.

I thanked him for his support, assuring him I'd stay in touch. We shook hands, and he left.

I signed the release papers for my possessions—besides the truck, a plastic bag with a computer-labeled tag containing the dirty clothes and spare boots I'd planted, which the sheriffs had also taken and checked out.

I stepped through the courthouse doors into the outside world, carrying the bag over my shoulder like a homeless man—but free once again to legally walk the streets. The deputy with the withered arm who'd first brought me in was standing in the background, watching. He didn't look happy to see me go.

SIXTY-TWO

I spent a couple of minutes waiting out front for my pickup truck to come back from wherever they had it impounded. The morning was clear and crisp, the weather getting into that glorious Indian summer that was the best part of the year around here.

My liberty might not last long, but Lord, did it feel fine.

Like Reuben had said, a minefield of worries still lay ahead. With someone of Balcomb's stature, a host of authorities would step in, probably including the FBI. I could count on being grilled again, and it was all too possible that I'd slip up or that some damning piece of evidence would come to light. John Doe might come back for revenge, or Balcomb's smuggling partners might decide to get even with whoever had disrupted their operation. If none of those exploded under me, there was still Kirk's Jeep, which would almost certainly be found next summer. With any luck, the sheriffs would decide that he'd been in it when it crashed—had gotten thrown out of the open top and carried away by underwater currents. But the fact that it had just happened to end up in my neighborhood was going to raise Gary's hackles.

In my favor, there was good reason to think that Kirk and Balcomb had been involved with high-level criminals, which was true. No doubt Balcomb had plenty of other enemies to cloud things further. Only a few people knew what really had happened, and all of them had good reasons to stay silent. Madbird. Reuben. John Doe, if he was still alive. Laurie might or might not ever turn up again—with her money, she could stay vanished forever. But if she did get questioned, there was still no reason for her to do anything but feign ignorance. And she sure knew how to spin a story.

As for Balcomb, we had disposed of him, on Reuben's suggestion, at an old homesteader's cabin about two miles back into the mountains. There was nothing left of the structure except a rock-and-mortar foundation. But there also was a crumbling cistern dug into a hillside, which collected from a spring. I'd known the place was there, but not about the cistern—probably the only other living person besides Reuben who did know was Elmer. It was covered by brush and partly filled by erosion, but about two feet of murky scum-covered water remained on the bottom, fed by the still trickling spring. We'd weighted Balcomb down with rocks, kicked dirt in from the hillside to fill the cistern the rest of the way, and rearranged the brush for cover. It was almost as secure an entombment as Kirk's.

Then we'd gone back to the golf driving range to tidy up there.

"I know there's blood on these diamonds," Reuben had said, picking up the box, "but I guess I'm too much of a hard-ass old prick to think letting them stay buried here would wash it off. I'll liquidate them quietly and put the money where it'll do some good, if you boys are amenable." Madbird and I were. We covered up the safe, drove the cart back in over it, and went home.

And right now, all I cared about was the sight of my pickup truck, turning the corner and coming my way.

When it pulled up to the curb, I was taken aback to see that Gary himself was driving, with his elbow perched jauntily on the windowsill. He patted the dash, apparently admiring the truck again.

"This is some rig," he said. "Runs smooth and handles real tight."

"I had the steering gear replaced not long ago."

"I miss those old days. You had a ride like this, a girl, and a six-pack, that was as close to heaven as it got."

"I still can't think of much better," I said.

He shifted position experimentally, like he was getting used to the seat. He didn't seem in any hurry to climb out.

"You know, I'm kind of sticking my neck out, doing this," he said.

"I do know that, Gary. I can't tell you how much I appreciate it."

"Well, if you'd answer just one question, it might clear up something that's been bothering me a long time."

Everything in me stopped.

"It don't have anything to do with this, directly, anyway," he said. "I guarantee I won't hold it against you or breathe a word about it."

That didn't reassure me much.

"I'll try," I said.

"Did Pete kill her?"

I shoved my hands into my pockets and took a couple of steps, gazing up at the mountains.

If we want something from Gary, we better give him something, too.

I turned back to him. "Yeah."

That might have helped satisfy his curiosity, but it sure didn't please him.

"I didn't lie to you back then, Gary," I said quickly, trying to head off his wrath. "I didn't know."

"So how is it you know now?"

"You said just one question."

His eyes went hard as stone and his forefinger rose to point at my chest.

"I'm the goddamn sheriff of Lewis and Clark County, son, and I'll ask as many goddamn questions as I want."

I waited, braced for an ass-chewing that would take me out at the knees.

But then he lowered his hand and sat back again, his expression turning wry.

"All right, a deal's a deal," he said. "I can pretty well fill in the blanks from there, anyway."

We were both quiet for another half minute. He still didn't get out of the truck.

"When's the last time you went to confession, really?" he said. "You know, in a church?"

My unease swept back in. I didn't think I was imagining an element of sarcasm about my story of a cathedral in the woods.

"Not for years," I said. "Mass, either."

"I go every Sunday. But the difference between that and what I see every day—" His mouth twisted in the same grimacing way it had earlier. "It's kind of like this situation. On the one hand, I'm all for letting people solve their problems on their own, especially if they do it clean and decent, and double especially if it's no bother to me. On the other hand, that ain't necessarily how the law's supposed to work."

"I'm not sure I follow you," I said, although I did, all too well.

"Reuben's bullshitting. You and me both know it, and so does he. If Kirk and Balcomb were dealing with somebody that serious, Kirk's dead. Maybe Balcomb was slick enough to get out. Maybe not."

He swung his head toward me and skewered me with those slaty eyes.

"Maybe it was something else entirely," he said.

I kept my mouth shut once more.

"There ain't many bodies buried around here that I don't know where," Gary said. "It's something I kind of pride myself on. What do you suppose the odds are I'll run across another one someday?"

"I wouldn't want to bet against you on much of anything, Gary."

"You better give Bill LaTray a call. He's got a way of dislocating a skip's shoulder before they start chatting."

He finally opened the truck's door, got out, and handed me the keys.

"Be seeing you, Hugh," he said.

SIXTY-THREE

Sitting behind the wheel of my good old pickup again was a pure joy. I started home. But I hadn't gone more than a few goddamned blocks when I heard a *pop* outside the window, then felt the drag in the right rear that meant a blown tire.

"Son of a bitch," I said. I had a good spare and jack—I just couldn't believe I was going to have to fuck around with something like that right now.

I was on Ewing, a narrow street with cars parked almost solid, and of course there was somebody right on my ass. I turned down the next side street, found a place to ease over to the curb, and got out to take a look at the damage.

The vehicle behind me also turned—a big four-door Chevy pickup truck of a generic white color, so new it didn't yet have license plates, just a temporary tag. As it pulled up beside me, I got a glimpse of a logo that read *Grenfell Chevrolet, Great Falls, Montana.* The windows were smoked so I couldn't see in, until the rear one closest to me rolled down. There were two men, one driving and the other in back. I assumed they were going to offer me a ride to a gas station, and I started to say thanks, but I had it covered.

Then I realized that the man in back was resting a pistol barrel on the windowsill. It ended in a vented cylinder the size of a roll of quarters—a sound suppressor.

"Get in, please," he said. The words were clear but had a crisp accent. He pushed open the door and slid back across the seat, with the gun still pointed at my chest.

Balcomb had been quick about hiring new killers, all right. He must have set this up before we'd gotten to him last night.

There wasn't another human being anywhere in view. My body felt completely drained of power, like a bag of hair. With the sick hopeless certainty that this was it, I got in.

The interior's pleasant new-vehicle smell was almost overcome by cologne that reminded me of a bad air freshener, with a heavy admixture of garlic. The man in the back with me had a wiry athletic build and a handsome, sharp-featured face. Together with his accent, his looks suggested northern Europe. The driver was older, heavier-set and darker-complexioned, with black hair and a thick mustache—maybe Latino or Mediterranean. By and large, they were almost as ordinary-looking as John Doe.

Except that both were decked out in full cowboy regalia, from Stetsons and shirts with mother-of-pearl snaps down to pointy-toed boots, all as new as the truck. It would have been laughable, except that there was nothing funny about these two. John Doe had only been scary. They were at ease.

"Wesley Balcomb's gone," I said, in the feeble hope of canceling their mission. "He disappeared last night. Maybe hiding out. Maybe dead."

The man in back with me nodded calmly.

"Yes, we know," he said.

They must have been paid in advance.

I couldn't imagine how the hell they'd found out about Balcomb so fast, or how they'd located me—a police scanner, maybe, or something far more sophisticated. I wasn't about to ask. In a way, the worst thing about it was knowing that the last laugh was going to be Balcomb's after all.

But then—late, as usual—the obvious occurred to me. If he had known they were after me, he would have used that as a bargaining chip last night.

That didn't make me feel any better, just more confused.

The man in the backseat watched me comfortably. His gaze never left me, and the gun barrel never wavered. They obviously had familiarized themselves with the area—the driver tooled along like he'd lived here all his life, taking us smoothly and unhesitatingly up Davis Gulch, a narrow dirt road that climbed into the forested mountains south of town. When I was a kid it had been deserted—we used to ride our dirt bikes and sight in rifles up there. Now there was a little development, but it was still pretty much no-man's-land, with all kinds of places where a body could simply be tossed out of a truck and not noticed for a good long while.

After a couple of miles we came to a clear-cut plateau that they must have found out had good cell phone reception. The man in the back with me took out his phone and spoke into it tersely. The language seemed familiar but I couldn't identify it. It resembled German, but I was sure it wasn't, nor Scandinavian—it didn't have those inflections. Dutch was the closest I could guess. He listened, spoke again, then handed me the phone.

"Hello, Mr. Davoren," a male voice said. It had just a trace of the same accent, but overlaid by the kind of precise British pronunciation that foreigners learned at Oxford.

"I'm sorry, I don't know who I'm talking to," I said.

"I'm afraid that's precisely the problem. You do. The charming Laurie Balcomb informed you that I was in business with her husband."

For a few seconds, my confusion deepened. The only one of Balcomb's associates that I could remember Laurie talking about was John Doe, and for certain, this wasn't him.

Then the answer came to the surface, along with the realization that the language the men were speaking must have been Flemish.

All I could think of to say was, "Oh."

I'd worry later about how Laurie had managed to hook up with Guy-Luc Marie DeBruyne.

"I gather that you set out to dispose of her husband," he said.

"No, I backed off, I can prove it. I started thinking about—"

"Your reasons don't concern me, Mr. Davoren. Neither does losing the enterprise, really. It was lucrative, but I have many others. To be truthful, I wouldn't have entered into it except that Wesley Balcomb introduced me to Laurie, and arranged for the two of us to spend some delightful time together. She was very persuasive on his behalf."

Did you ever meet him?

No.

"Anyway, what good is it to wail when the horse is out of the barn?" he said.

I winced.

"Look—sir," I said. "I didn't mean to interfere with you. I was just trying to save my skin."

"Oh, I don't bear you any ill will. My worry is strictly professional—that you may have talked about my connection to her husband. Especially since you've just had an interview with the police. It would draw undesirable attention, and that, I can't allow."

Business.

"No way I'd do that," I said.

"Oddly enough, I was sure that was what you would tell me."

"It's true, I swear," I lied, working to keep desperation out of my voice. "I'm suspected of murder, and I'm sweating blood trying to get the cops off my back. If I breathed a word about you, they'd be all over me. I didn't even tell them I ever saw Laurie. I never heard your name. We're not having this talk."

We rounded a curve and I caught a glimpse of the city spread out like a carpet of buildings below, a long ways away and getting farther every second.

"What did happen to Balcomb, do you think?" he said.

"My best guess is it was the mule, Kirk. He disappeared, too. He's the one I'm being blamed for. Probably he had some kind of grudge and came back to settle it."

"Do you know where we could find him?"

"I don't know anything about *any* of this. A few days ago I went to throw away a load of trash and next thing I knew, I was up to my neck in shit. Wait, sorry, I didn't mean to be offensive."

"*Bouf.* I spend a great deal of time in France, and there is no word more common than *merde.* Let me talk to Patrice again."

I handed the phone to the gunman. He spoke, listened, and said something to the driver. The truck pulled off the road. Outside my door, the ground sloped steeply down into a brushy ravine.

My mind pointed out, with idiotic pedantry, another little irony. I had managed to barely evade disaster all along, mostly through luck. But I'd ignored one of the basic rules—to be careful what I wished for. I had conjured up imaginary heavies to mislead Gary Varna, and now they'd sprung to life and turned on me.

The gunman, Patrice, handed me back the phone.

"Well, Mr. Davoren, it's been a pleasure talking with you," DeBruyne said. "I'll be saying good-bye now. But hold just a moment, you might want to thank Laurie. She assured me—again, very persuasively—that you can be trusted."

The driver eased the truck through a cautious three-point turn and headed back toward town. Patrice lowered the pistol into his lap.

"I hope she's correct," DeBruyne said. "From what she tells me, you sound quite entertaining. I'd like to have a drink with you one day. Rather than to your memory."

The phone felt like it had the weight of an anvil.

"Are you there?" Laurie said.

The sound of her voice burned right through me.

"Yeah," I said.

"I'm sorry I ran. I lost my nerve, alone in that motel. I called Guy-Luc. He sent a plane for me. I didn't know those men would be on it."

"It's OK," I said. I'd decided already that we were even, and maybe that I even owed her, for the persuading she'd done. "If you get questioned, you and I never saw each other. Your husband was acting scary, you took off, and that's all you know."

I listened to her breathing for a few more seconds.

"I really do care for you, Hugh," she said. "I meant what I said about our kinship."

The connection ended.

Goddamn me, I almost could have believed her.

The truck pulled up beside mine, right where they'd picked me up. I started to open the door, but the driver turned to look straight at me for the first time and, with one hand gesturing eloquently, growled a sentence. I could tell this was French, but it was too fast for me to catch. Along with his words came a blast of garlic I could almost taste. I stared back helplessly, wondering what final trap they were springing.

"He ask your pardon that we break your tire and not help to repair it," Patrice translated. "*Mais faut qu'on parte*—we must go. You understand?"

I started nodding and kept on. "Yeah, sure. Don't worry, I've done it a million times. Thanks, though."

He tipped his hat, Old West style. The window rolled up. They drove away.

The bullet hole that had caused the flat was neatly centered in the treads—not surprisingly, a very professional job. I got the spare on in record time, in spite of my hands shaking and my head swiveling like a Ping-Pong ball in play. I just knew that the next thing coming down the pike would be Bill LaTray, leaping out of his rig and piling into me like a freight train.

When I finally drove through the gate to my cabin, the first thing that hit me was the lingering smell of the lumber that Laurie had burned.

SIXTY-FOUR

I called Bill's Bail Bonds first thing, apologized to Bill for the trouble I'd caused him, and informed him that Gary Varna had cut me loose. He didn't seem angry—considering what he dealt with routinely, this was no doubt a mosquito bite—and he told me I could come by any time to pick up my refund. I offered to pay a late fee, but he said forget it, and that he'd be glad to buy me a drink.

I took that to mean that I was still a potentially valuable client.

There were a few phone messages on my machine, and I started to check them, then stopped. I didn't want any kind of news just now, good or bad—only to bask in the rapture of being back in my own place, with nobody trying to kill me. I was fried with fatigue but too wired to sleep. I started puttering around and trying to think about banal necessities like groceries, laundry, and a new used tire.

But I was uneasy, and after a few minutes, I couldn't ignore that a bad switch had flipped in my head. The privacy I'd always loved up here felt like emptiness, and the solitude, a loneliness that almost amounted to dread.

It wasn't because nobody else was around.

I knew it was temporary, just a function of the last couple of days' madness. But I couldn't get past the restlessness. I decided to take a shot at tying up one more loose end—following up my guess that Laurie had gotten her information about Celia from Beatrice Pettyjohn, Reuben's wife. I drove back to town.

Reuben had moved Beatrice to the Pineview Assisted Living Facility after her Alzheimer's disease got to be too much for him to handle. It was a nice new place out by the golf course. The woman at the admitting desk told me I was welcome to see Beatrice, but warned me that she got combative when something touched her off, and that this wasn't uncommon. I asked if she had many visitors. Yes, the desk lady said, obviously proud of this connection to ranching royalty. Reuben stopped by often, other old friends came occasionally, and a new friend had come by several times over the past couple of months—Mrs. Wesley Balcomb.

A young woman attendant went with me to Beatrice's private room. She was propped up in bed watching the Weather Channel on TV. Her formidable bearing had lessened—she'd become pale and thin. But she still had a sharpness in her eyes.

I hadn't been at all sure that she'd recognize me, or understand who I was if she did. But the instant she saw me, it was clear that she knew at least one thing—she didn't like me any better now than before. I'd thought I might have to coax her into conversation, but she took the bit and ran with it.

"Oh, the way you looked at her," she said witheringly. "You were the worst of them all."

The attendant gave me a glance that was wary but maybe also interested.

Clearly, there was no point in formalities here, or in trying to persuade Beatrice contrary to what was set in her mind.

"What did you think when she first came back, Beatrice?" I said.

"I told her she didn't have any more business here now than she ever did, and she could just turn around and leave again. That's what."

"But she didn't. She started coming to see you here, right? What did you talk about—the old days at the ranch?"

Beatrice's eyes took on a crafty look. "She asked about *you* plenty. So you're finally getting what you wanted, is that it?"

"No," I said, but it was futile—I had set her off. Her look changed again, this time to anger, and she struggled to get up out of bed, clenching one gnarled blue-veined hand into a fist and punching at me.

"Time for you to go—oh," the attendant said, in a playful singsong tone.

I backed away with a hasty apology, and left the building. I got into my truck, but then just sat there, watching the few golfers still strolling the links.

I could see why Beatrice would have grabbed at the connection with Celia the first time she'd seen Laurie, like she'd done with me just now. If there was one thing that would stick in her addled mind, it would be the obsession about what had destroyed her family.

That mistaken identity must have triggered the first part of Laurie's scheme. She'd then managed to pump Beatrice for information, maybe by overcoming the hostility and making friends, maybe by playing on fear—pretending that she'd come back from the dead to settle matters.

It didn't make me feel any better to think I might have fallen for the same trick as a delusional elderly woman.

I knew that being objective about Beatrice was impossible for me. Even before Celia's death, I hadn't liked her any better than she'd liked me. I knew that was uncharitable, what with her illness. I knew, too, that she'd had good reason for disapproving of Celia's attempt to work her way toward the Pettyjohn fortune in a time-honored, but not exactly honorable, fashion.

Still, to my mind, nothing justified the haughtiness that Beatrice had shown. In holding that Celia wasn't good enough for Pete, she'd really meant not good enough for herself. That and her coldness toward her husband had added a lot of fuel to the engine of the disaster. A less arrogant and more generous woman would have accepted her son's wishes in spite of her own feelings, or at least found a way to handle the situation without causing such grief.

In any event, learning about Laurie's visits here pretty well satisfied me as the solution to the mystery of how she'd gotten her information—except for one thread still hanging that I couldn't quite clip.

In the motel room, there'd been a few seconds when Laurie had seemed genuinely confused, and she'd said the words, "No to a horse, yes to a stallion." At the time, I could only think she was suggesting that Celia really had been thrown and killed like the Pettyjohns had claimed.

But now I knew for a fact that Pete had done it, and I'd started to wonder if Laurie could have meant stallion in the sense of stud, and she'd been referring to Reuben—the dominant male—as the baby's real father.

In all probability, she hadn't meant anything at all—those were just words that had slipped out during her prattle to con me. If she *had* known, she must have learned it from Beatrice—although I wasn't sure whether Beatrice had been aware of Reuben's affair with Celia, or even that Celia was pregnant. That was the main thing I'd hoped to pry out of her, but I never would.

It was a quarter after three in the afternoon. I decided that as long as I was in town, I might as well pay one more call. I started the truck and headed for a flower shop.

SIXTY-FIVE

I walked into Sarah Lynn's office at twenty minutes to four, carrying a dozen long-stemmed roses wrapped in green paper, along with an envelope containing the rest of the cash I still owed her. The place was quite a contrast to Gary Varna's spartan digs—a corner room with big windows that let in a flood of light, walls of a delicate eggshell white that accentuated it, and a thick ecru carpet. The paintings and furnishings were very tasteful and very expensive.

She was sitting at her desk, wearing a deep blue dress that lit up her mane of tawny hair. She glanced at me, then turned right back to her computer screen, her fingers barely pausing at the keyboard.

"OK," I said. "I just want to leave these, tell you I'm sorry, and I want to take you to dinner if you'll ever talk to me again."

She kept typing for a few more seconds, but then sighed and held out her hand to take the flowers.

"They're beautiful, Huey," she said, and raised them to her face and inhaled. "So what is this? Payoff? Buyout? Drag bet?"

"I don't know what. But none of those."

Her voice turned angry, and her eyes, hurt. "Where've you been? Why didn't you call me, dammit?" My raw sense of unworthiness dug at me like a hair shirt around my heart.

"Things went from bad to worse," I said.

Her eyes turned concerned. That was even harder to take.

"Are you still in trouble?" she said.

"A better class of trouble. I'm straightened out with Gary, at least for now."

Sarah Lynn inhaled the flowers' scent again, watching me over their blossoms like a geisha with a fan.

"I'd love to have dinner with you," she said. "But I'm not going to be your fallback squeeze."

"That's not what I'm trying to do, Slo. It's—" I groped for words.

Then, abruptly, I was slammed by the exhaustion that had been hovering over me. I started to sag, and I had to physically brace myself back up. I felt like I could have collapsed into a puddle on the floor.

"It's not like that," I finished lamely. "I'm wiped out. I've got to go. I'll call you. I will."

"You better," she said, but she smiled. She lowered the flowers, inviting a quick kiss. I gave it to her, torn between shame and happiness. Then I stumbled out.

Helena's little rush hour was gathering steam, and I forced myself to concentrate on the traffic. But as it thinned, my feelings began to surface as fatigue-dulled thoughts, centering on whether Sarah Lynn and I might have another chance.

She was everything that Laurie wasn't. I still loved her in some way—not with the consuming passion of our youth, but with a deep, comfortable affection—and I was sure she felt the same. I wouldn't be much of a catch for her, but I was warm and breathing, and I wouldn't beat her up or steal her money and head to the casinos. She could probably even dress me up and take me out once in a while. From my side, I'd never come close to another woman who was simply so good, or to the satisfying life she had to offer. We had our differences, but they were far from insurmountable. And that young man who'd walked away from her was long gone.

Yet just in these past few days, something fundamental had changed for me and my life. I couldn't get hold of it, but I was already pretty sure that no amount of effort or good sense was going to turn me back toward being the kind of man that she needed and deserved.

When I got home, I fired up the woodstove and dug my last can of corned beef hash out of the cupboard. While it fried, I drank a beer and a couple of splashes of Old Taylor bourbon. I sat on the steps to eat, and drank another couple of shots as the day faded toward dusk.

Then, at last, I slept a real sleep.

SIXTY-SIX

The next day was another of those autumn beauties, with the air clear and crisp and the sky almost shockingly blue. There wouldn't be many more of them this year. In the afternoon, after making sure nobody was keeping tabs on me, I fired up the Victor and rode into the Belts behind my place.

I had slept in a near coma from yesterday evening until this morning, getting up once to stumble outside and take a leak, then collapsing again. For the first few hours after waking, I'd wandered around in a stupor. But finally my mind had cleared and I'd started thinking about practicalities, like the scrutiny I'd soon be facing. Top priority was to make sure that Kirk's interment was as hidden as I thought. Hunting season would be starting soon, and somebody just might go wandering by there.

The place where Madbird and I had stashed him was about three miles away as the crow flew, and a shorter trip overland than going down to the highway and looping up again. I took the familiar back trails through the woods and rock formations of my childhood sanctuary. That part of what I'd told Gary Varna was true. I left the bike at the logging road and hiked the last stretch through the brush.

The news was fine about the job we'd done. The site appeared perfectly natural—a passerby would never give it a second glance.

But I could almost imagine that I saw a hint of Kirk's outline behind the facade of earth and stone, and that there was a sort of grim satisfaction in his posture. It looked good on him. He had never amounted to much in his father's eyes, but he'd finally brought Reuben a kind of peace in a Byzantine way. Maybe that was another canceled debt, like the one between Reuben and me. I recalled thinking of Reuben in Shakespearean terms, as a kind of colossus. Now, with Kirk, another line from Shakespeare appeared in my mind.

Nothing in his life became him like the leaving it.

I knelt down for a minute—not to pray, exactly, but to tell Kirk that although he'd given me no choice, I was bitterly sorry. Then I got back on the bike and started home.

My imaginings about Kirk were really for my own benefit, not his. I didn't know what to believe about an afterlife—whether the dead knew or cared what happened here on earth, or if anything that the living did could help them rest, or even if they continued to exist in any way we could conceive of.

But I did believe in an immense, mysterious machine of fate that ultimately exacted true final justice, that couldn't be swayed by influence peddling and didn't accept get-out-of-jail-free cards, and that kept track of who owed what right down to the molecule.

I had to think that everybody involved in these events had undergone a serious shake-up of their bank balances, for better or worse.

SIXTY-SEVEN

I'd called Madbird earlier to tell him I was temporarily off the hook, and he'd said he'd swing by. When I rode back into my place toward dusk, he was sitting on my steps drinking a Pabst. There were a couple of empties beside him along with a bag of store-bought ice. He fished in that, pulled out a fresh one, and tossed it to me. If he guessed where I'd been, he didn't say so.

I sat down beside him, opened the beer, and took a long, long drink.

Before we had a chance to say a word, the black tomcat came stalking into view and started yelling at me for being gone so long and letting strangers come on his turf. He'd probably heard the popping sound of the can's top and was running a guilt trip on me to score some brew for himself. Madbird crumpled an empty can in his fist, folding up the edges to make a crude saucer. He set it on the steps and poured a little beer in. The cat sniffed it, tasted it, sneezed, then started lapping it up. Bits of hay and leaves clung to his fur, and a raw red patch was scabbing over behind his left ear.

Madbird leaned back against the wall. He looked relaxed, like this was Friday afternoon after work and we were talking about maybe going fishing tomorrow.

"Hey," he said, and gave my boot a kick. "When that John Doe fuckwad had the gun on you back there at the camp—you didn't really think I'd sold you out, did you?" His teeth showed just slightly, in the beginnings of that grin.

My face got warm and my gaze shifted away. I reached down to scratch the base of the cat's bent tail. He arched his rump against my hand, but kept slurping busily.

"I guess I did," I admitted.

Madbird nodded approvingly. "You're picking up them Indian lessons pretty good."

That was about as pleasing a compliment as I'd ever gotten.

Overall, I had the sense that this was the culmination of a long series of events—that when I'd gotten my eye busted that night at Rocky Boy years ago, it had rung the death knell of the self that had lived in the familiar world of my youth, and lit the spark of another self, approaching a different world—the one where Madbird had been my guide. I'd never be at home there like he was. But I knew already that he was right about nothing ever being the same again. The immersion of the past few days had been a baptism, and the alchemy would keep working in hidden ways toward whatever came next.

I didn't have a clue as to what it might be. But if it managed to announce itself a little more sedately, that would suit me just fine.

Acknowledgments

These were a tough call—it would be impossible to list the many people who have contributed, in ways that go back many years. I decided to err to the side of brevity. To those not specifically mentioned, my appreciation is nonetheless heartfelt.

Carl Lennertz, who allowed himself to be prevailed upon to edit this book, and—in addition to his already astonishing repertoire—demonstrated clearly that he's a natural at that, too. Jonathan Burnham, Kathy Schneider, Christine Boyd, and Jill Schwartzman, who provided critical help. Many others at HarperCollins, including (then) Dan Conaway, whose initial support got the project off the ground.

Jennifer Rudolph Walsh, who represents me wondrously (and patiently), and her colleagues at the William Morris Agency.

Early readers, including Susan Wasson, Barbara Theroux, John Zeck, David Johnson, Jock Doggett, and a contingent of old outlaws, hippies, and below-the-radar comrades, who gave much-needed encouragement.

Tom Melton, longtime SEC trial lawyer, and Dr. Sid Gustafson, Montana horse vet extraordinaire (and novelist in his own right), for their professional expertise.

The late and truly great Jim Welch, Hank Burgess, and Gus Gardner. This involves decades-old friendships, the Montana Board of Pardons and Parole, and a naive white boy's education in a boxing ring.

The writing communities in Montana and other places (with special thanks to those who provided quotes).

The many fine men (and a few women) I've worked with in construction since I figured out that I wasn't going to medical school after all, and signed on as a union apprentice with Local 153 of the International Brotherhood of Carpenters and Joiners, Helena, Montana, in 1973. In particular, Kim Zupan, ex-bucking horse rider and my work partner of many years.

My, and my wife's, families and the friends we've been blessed with.

And some non-friends and even enemies, from whom I've learned a hell of a lot.

*Turn the page for
a preview of*

DEAD
SILVER

ONE

Friday after work, Madbird and I were drinking shots and beers at the Split Rock Lodge when his niece, Darcy, came prancing through the door. Everybody in the barroom stopped what they were doing and watched her. Darcy knew how to steal a scene.

Like Madbird, she was Blackfeet, and she was some smoke—just turned twenty-one, full-bodied, and vibrant, with hair that fell almost to her waist and gleamed like a raven's wing in sunlight. She'd grown up on the tribal reservation in northern Montana, then spent her late teens moving from place to place, looking for the things you looked for at that age. Now she was trying her luck in our city of Helena.

She was as wild as she was pretty, and Madbird did his best to keep tabs on her—he'd gotten her a job waiting tables here at the Split Rock Lodge because he and I were working nearby these days, remodeling some motel units—but Darcy walked her own walk.

She waitressed the lunch shift on Fridays, then stayed through the afternoon to help clean and set up for dinner. She was a good worker, we'd heard—cheerful, energetic, and possessing that all-important quality of doing what needed to be done, without waiting to be told.

But now she was finished for the day and dressed to party, wearing tight jeans, spike-heeled boots, a turquoise-colored spaghetti strap top, and a black leather biker chick jacket studded with silver.

"Hi, Hugh," she said to me.

"Darcy, you're scorching my eyeballs."

She gave me a big smile and pulled up a barstool next to

Madbird.

"Buy me a drink," she commanded him teasingly.

His mouth twitched in amusement, but the rest of his face remained unmoving. It looked like it had been carved out of a cliffside by a lightning storm, and his own rumbling voice sounded like a diesel engine with a handful of gravel thrown in.

"Well, I guess, since you ask so nice," he said. "But I ain't sure they got Shirley Temples here."

"I'll kick your Shirley Temple ass," Darcy said scornfully. "Gin and tonic."

"Gin?" He frowned. "You got a note from your mother?"

She snapped a quick punch to his forearm, smacking his Marine Corps skull and crossbones tattoo.

"Whoa! Okay, goddammit." He backed away, rubbing the spot dramatically.

"See? He's not so tough," she announced to the room at large.

"You ain't got to say it so loud," Madbird muttered. He signalled the bartender and pushed forward a five from the pile of bills in front of him.

He wasn't much for vocalizing his feelings, but I knew that he had a special affection for Darcy. Even as an infant, she'd been uncowed by his fierce appearance, and she'd soon grasped his quirky brand of humor and learned to throw it back at him. This had developed into ritual sparring that both of them loved.

Over the years, he'd worried about her a lot, with reason. Now he was concerned in a different way, and it showed in his next words.

"I suppose regular bar gin ain't going to be good enough for you, seeing as how you been hanging around with the rich and famous," he said.

Darcy's eyes narrowed just slightly, just for an instant. But she bounced back in a heartbeat with her mischievous smile.

"You got that right," she said, and called to the bartender, "Bombay Sapphire, please."

Madbird whistled softly. "Bombay fucking Sapphire," he repeated, to nobody in particular. He pushed forward another five dollar bill.

"It's a pretty blue bottle. Almost this color." She plucked at her blouse.

"That what your boyfriend drinks?"

"Sometimes."

"He coming by here to pick you up?" Madbird said.

"Sure, why not?"

"I didn't say nothing about why not. I just wonder why he don't ever come inside."

"What, to meet you? You kidding?"

He slumped dolefully against the bar. "Well, ain't that the way it goes. Ashamed of your poor old uncle."

"I'm not ashamed of you! I'm sitting right here beside you."

"Yeah, long as I buy you fancy liquor."

"Hah. Play me a game of eight-ball." She grabbed his hand and tugged him away from the bar.

"I ain't played pool in a hundred years," he objected, but he didn't resist.

"Come on, Hugh," she said to me. "My poor old uncle needs help. You two against me."

I wasn't going to provide much help; I couldn't remember the last time I'd touched a cue, myself. But I gathered our drinks and followed the two of them to the barroom's pool table, a sturdy old veteran scarred by countless cigarettes and drunken gouges, stained by blood from fights and, according to rumor, occasional dousings of more amatory body fluids as well. Darcy punched in some quarters and expertly arranged the rack into a tight triangle, alternating stripes and solids with the eight-ball in the center.

Her newest boyfriend—the source of Madbird's concern—was a Montana state representative named Seth Fraker, from the resort area of Flathead Lake. The legislature had been in session in Helena, the capitol city, for the last couple of months; Fraker and Darcy had met one evening when she was waitressing here and he'd come in with some colleagues to have dinner. He came from a well-established business family, and he had all the trappings that went along with that—money, connections, and sophistication. Except for the inconvenient fact that he was married with kids, he seemed a vast improvement over the aimless, troubled guys and sometimes outright criminals she'd run around with in the past.

But the Cinderella aspect was the problem, and there was no glass slipper. It seemed obvious that this was a variation on an old story—an upper-crust white guy having a fling with a hot young Native girl. But there were hints that Darcy was taking it more seriously. She'd suddenly decided to move to an apartment more expensive than she could afford, with money from a mysterious source. She gave off a new sense of excitement, like she had an important secret. She had let it slip that he described his marriage as being "in name only," without her seeming to realize what a stale ploy that was. While she was far from naïve in many ways, this situation was outside her experience, and maybe she was subconsciously blinding herself besides. That probably happened to just about everybody, in some way, at some point.

For sure, Fraker had no intentions of leaving his family and marrying Darcy. At best, he was setting her up as a mistress; he'd have plenty of pretexts to travel to Helena. If that was the case and Darcy could accept it, it might be a cynical but convenient arrangement for her until something better came along.

But far more likely, when the legislative session ended a couple of months from now, Fraker would head back to his glossy home life and realize that maintaining the affair was too costly in a number of ways.

Madbird feared that besides the hurt that would bring Darcy, it might knock her into a tailspin just when she thought her life was turning the corner, and the consequences could be serious.

And, while this might have been unfair to Fraker, the situation reeked with the sense of a powerful white man figuring that since he was dealing with Indians, he was untouchable. Very few things in the world pissed Madbird off like that did.

I knew that he was torn about whether to intervene. He hadn't, yet.

Darcy started the pool game, lining up on the cueball and breaking with a crack I could feel in my teeth. The balls seethed around and careened off the rails; when they settled, the six had dropped into a corner pocket and three other solids were easy picks. She tapped in two of those and left the third blocking another corner, with the cueball buried in a cluster.

Madbird and I managed to sink a couple of stripes, but mostly we duffed around while she continued to clear the table. At the end of the work week, concentrated effort was very low on our priority list, and this spacious old lodge with its huge stone fireplace was a good place to kick back. Split Rock was a kind of setup that had once been fairly common in the West—a main building that housed a restaurant-bar, and several smaller cabins that served as motel units. Like a lot of the others, it had been hand-built of logs soon after World War Two, when tourism by automobile was becoming an industry. It was located in the foothills of the Elkhorn Range several miles south of Helena, facing the landmark for which it was named—a chunk of granite the size of a two story house, cleft from the top almost to the bottom by a vertical V that looked hewn by a giant ax. Big plate glass windows gave expansive views of the still-pristine surrounding country; often, you could see elk foraging on the mountainsides.

A sudden sound, like a spray of elevator music on acid, made my head jerk. It was the ring of Darcy's cell phone. She dropped her pool cue on the table and flew to dig the phone out of her purse, then pressed it to her ear and walked a few steps away from Madbird and me, talking in a tone too low for us to hear, while her other hand smoothed her hair.

This was the situation that Madbird had tweaked her about. Seth Fraker would drive here to pick her up, but instead of coming inside, he'd call as he was arriving and have her go out to meet him—the modern equivalent of honking the horn. Sure enough, headlights were turning from the highway into the Split Rock parking lot. There was enough daylight left for me to see the vehicle when it got close—Fraker's huge new pickup truck with all the bells and whistles, including smoked windows.

Darcy closed her phone, slipped it back into her purse, and turned to face us. The next couple of seconds were a strange, tense freeze where nothing happened, but it seemed like a lot of things could.

Madbird and Darcy both moved in the same instant. He started walking around the table toward the parking lot. She scooped up the dice-cube-sized chunk of blue cuetip chalk and intercepted him. Her hand moved quick as a snake to smear a touch of it on his forehead. While I stared, she spun around and did the same to me. Just as abruptly, she broke into a brisk skipping dance, circling the pool table and both of us, chanting or singing under her breath.

Then she was gone out the door, leaving him and me standing there, looking like refugees from Ash Wednesday.

"What was that?" I said.

Madbird gazed stonily after her as she hurried across the parking lot and disappeared behind the darkened windows of Seth Fraker's big pickup.

"She threw something at us, to get us off her case," he said.

TWO

The next afternoon, Saturday, I spent banging around my cabin doing the chores that I let slide during the week. I was forever losing ground; it was like fighting a Hydra that grew back two heads for every one you chopped off, except this thing was a combination of giant slug and dustball. Besides the routine business of cleaning and laundry and such, new problems cropped up endlessly—a plumbing leak, a vehicle repair, a three-foot snowstorm that was one too many for the old garage roof. Most often, I'd discover further wrinkles once I started trying to fix the original one; I'd end up driving to town for materials two or three times; and so on. By the time I got the situation under control, I'd have lost a couple more weekends, and the list kept on growing.

But that was far outweighed by the payoff. I could never have imagined a greater gift than this property, left to me by my father: twenty acres of conifers bordered to the north and east by National Forest, which continued in an arc roughly sixty miles long and ten miles wide, encompassing most of the Big Belt Mountains. That area was virtually all wilderness—steep, rugged, and thickly wooded, with a few gravel roads that were dicey at the best of times—and humans were rare.

If I hadn't had this place to come back to during a bad time in my life, I wasn't sure I'd have gotten through. Keeping it cobbled together was sort of like living with somebody who drove you nuts, but who you loved and couldn't stand to be without. You did whatever it took to make things work.

I'd been thinking about the incident with Madbird and Darcy

yesterday at Split Rock. He hadn't been headed outside to brace Seth Fraker—just to get a look at him, invite him in for a drink, size him up. But I understood Darcy's concern, too. Madbird already didn't like what he knew about Fraker; in all probability, he'd like him even less if they met, and that would be clear. Darcy was well aware of it, and in her view, she had nothing to gain and a lot to lose if it happened.

As for the "something" she'd thrown at us, paying any attention to it was silly. But I had come to suspect that there were cracks in the rational fabric of the universe, and such a "something" might just slip through once in a while and rattle cages. In other words, I'd gotten more superstitious instead of more level-headed—no doubt a comment on my general backslide from maturity. That wasn't to say I'd bought into Darcy's gesture in any serious way. It just made me a trifle uneasy.

The supply of stove wood that I kept in the cabin was low, so I walked outside through the wet spring snow to stock up. When I got to the woodshed, my half-feral black tomcat—I'd never named him; I just thought of him as the other guy, which was probably how he thought of me—was crouched on a stack of split fir rounds, staring intently toward the tree line, twenty yards away. I spotted the shape of an animal just inside there. A mule deer, was my first thought; it was roughly that size and of that same deep brown color. There hadn't been any of them around for a while, and I was vaguely interested that they were coming back.

But more impressions clicked in fast. It was sitting upright, which deer didn't do. It was built like a Rottweiler, only more so—powerful shoulders and haunches, and a heavy round head with bone-crushing jaws.

This wasn't any deer. This was a big cat—the reason the deer had taken off.

I'd been seeing its tracks for the past couple of weeks, and assumed it was a cougar; this area had always been on their rambling path. At a guess, he was a young male who'd been driven off adult turf and hadn't yet staked out his own. But there were some factors that didn't fit. Cougars usually kept moving around a large area, and they usually stayed well away from humans. I'd only find signs of them when I went farther into the woods, and I'd only ever glimpsed them a couple of times.

But this guy had been hanging around for quite a while, and he wasn't at all shy. He'd been coming within the boundaries of my property, and right now he was no more than forty yards from my cabin, staring straight back at me. He'd seen me before I saw him, and he hadn't budged an inch. No doubt he was hungry, too. Deer were the main staple of a cougar's diet. He must have been eking out a meager living on small critters.

While I'd never had any trouble with cougars, attacks on people were becoming more common. They'd taken down several joggers around the west, and here in Montana not long ago, a pair of them had stalked a group of schoolchildren on an outing. Courageous teachers had gotten the kids to safety, but the cats hadn't backed off or even made any attempt at stealth.

I wasn't *too* worried, but I admit I suddenly found myself thinking about what I'd do if he came my way. The woodshed was just an open-fronted leanto; the closest place that offered protection was the cabin, and I wasn't at all sure I could make it there ahead of him. My pulse rate started edging upward. But while I was trying to decide whether to stand my ground, or slowly work my way toward safety, or just flat out run for it, he rose up unhurriedly off his hanuches and stalked away.

That was when I saw his short black-striped tail, and realized that he wasn't a mountain lion—he was a bobcat. That explained his taking up residence. They tended to find a home territory and stay there, and they didn't necessarily shun human habitations; like a lot of other wild creatures, they seemed to be learning that we had our uses, such as providing livestock and pets for meals.

"You better watch it," I told the black tom. "You'd be a nacho to him."

He kept staring with his wide green eyes, claws dug into a chunk of fir and tail switching in agitation as his mega-cousin leisurely moved out of sight, pausing every several yards to sniff the air and look around.

When the bobcat was gone, I completed my mission of carrying a few armloads of wood to the cabin. The tom jumped off his perch and followed me back and forth, butting against my ankles—wanting a drink of beer. I was ready for one, myself. I dug into the forty-year old Kelvinator and found a bottle of Moretti left over from a sixpack I'd splurged on a couple of weekends ago. I poured some into a saucer for the cat and drank the rest myself, thinking about how to handle this.

On the one hand, I was relieved. I'd never heard of a bobcat attacking anyone. On the other hand, he was a really *big* bobcat. While I knew that wild animals and fish always grew with the telling, I also knew what I'd seen. I even wondered if a cross with a mountain lion was genetically possible. Besides his size, his coloration, brown and mostly solid, was more cougar-like; bobcats tended to be tawnier, with leopard-like black spots. And yet, there was no mistaking that tail.

I didn't want to shoot him—on the contrary, I wanted to protect him. I'd have been glad to have him around except for worry that he'd eat my pet—the tom was extremely canny, but everybody made mistakes—and maybe even me. When the snow melted and the ground dried, he might head into the back country in search of more satisfying game, but that wouldn't happen for several weeks. And then again, he might not. I considered contacting the Fish and Wildlife Department, but I didn't think they'd do anything unless he was killing livestock or otherwise being a tangible menace, and if word about him leaked out, poachers or trappers would come after him.

I started leaning toward the notion that the best thing for everybody concerned would be to give him a good scare—let him know that he'd better stay away from human beings. But that was easier thought than done.

I decided to give the situation a little more time. I'd start carrying a pistol when I went outside, one that threw big slugs and made a lot of noise. If I met the bobcat with a burst of explosions and chunks showering out of the trees around him, that might get the message across. The weapon would also be a comfort when I came home after dark and walked from my truck to the cabin, just in case he was bold and hungry enough to take on something bigger than a bunny.

I finished the beer and went back to puttering, while the tom curled up on the bed to sleep it off.

Not long after that, the phone rang, bring me a routine touch of angst. I wasn't crazy about telephones—another of my regressive traits. I used mine mainly for work and other necessities, rarely for chatting, and it seemed to me that unexpected calls usually meant either hassles or outright bad news. But the news would come anyway, and answering was the only way to get rid of asshole solicitors who'd otherwise keep tormenting you forever, so I picked up and grumbled hello.

At first I was sure I'd guessed right—it was some kind of a pitch. The caller was a woman whose voice I didn't recognize, asking for Hugh Davoren. But she sounded pleasant, slightly uncertain, and she even pronounced my last name right, to just about rhyme with "tavern." I tried to sound a little less brusque.

"Speaking," I said.

"This is Renee Callister. Do you remember me?"

That caught me by surprise. I hadn't seen Renee or heard anything about her since she was a kid. She'd be in her early thirties now, several years younger than me. Ordinarily, I'd have stumbled over a name from that long ago. But I'd been thinking about her family because her father, Professor John Callister, had passed away a few days earlier.

It seemed unlikely that she was just calling me out of the blue, after all this time. I guessed that her reason had something to do with her father's death, which added a touchy element.

Professor Callister had once been a prominent figure in Montana, a highly respected wildlife biologist and defender of wilderness. But his life was ruined when his young second wife was murdered, along with the lover she was in bed with at the time. Uglier still, Callister was the chief suspect. He was never formally charged, but he was never cleared, either. He'd spent his last several years in a nursing home, after a series of strokes left him incapacitated and, eventually, comatose.

That was the legacy his daughter, Renee, had inherited.